RECKLESS STORM

Cover design by © Books and Moods

Editing by Happily Editing Anns

CONTENTS

AUTHOR'S NOTE

This book contains subject matter that some people may find triggering. A list of the main potential triggers can be found on Katherine's website:

http://www.katherinejayauthor.com

Please note, triggers are not listed here to avoid spoilers for the book.

RECKLESS STORM'S SOUNDTRACK

Beautiful Things - Benson Boon
Here With Me - Marshmello, CHVRCHES
Leave Her Wild - Tyler Rich
RECKLESS - Clayton Shay
Cheerleader - OMI, Felix Jaehn
Dress - Taylor Swift
Shut Up and Dance - WALK THE MOON
Carry You Home - Alex Warren
End Game - Taylor Swift, Ed Sheeran, Future
Don't Give Up On Me - Andy Grammer
Shape of You - Ed Sheeran
Lose Control - Teddy Swims
You and Me - Lifehouse
Sweet but Psycho - Ava Max
Like She Wanted To - Alexander Ludwig
Human - Christina Perri
Arcade - Duncan Laurence
Nobody - Dylan Scott
Friends Don't - Maddie & Tae
Never Been In Love - Haley Mae Campbell
I Would, Would You - Kelsea Ballerini

AVAILABLE NOW ON SPOTIFY

This book is for anyone who's been told they're too loud or too much... don't ever change.

And to the people like Reed who love us exactly as we are... We think you're bloody awesome!

SPECIAL NOTE

While Reckless Storm is set in the USA, the female main character (Hayley) is Australian, therefore her chapters and her dialogue in the MMC's chapters have been written in Australian English.

The remainder of the book is in American English as per the rest of the series.

PROLOGUE

REED

Hayley nibbles the flesh of her gloss-covered lips, silently reading her group chat messages. She angles the phone my way, her gaze briefly flitting to mine as she lets me read along.

> PAIGE: A FAKE RELATIONSHIP?! Yes!

> AMELIA: That could work. Side note: Luke's trying to look over my shoulder but I won't let him see what we're discussing

> PAIGE: Whoops. Are we not supposed to tell the guys? Easton says hi. He loves the idea. But mainly because it takes the spotlight away from him

> KEELEY: Paige, tell that brother of mine to grow up. He's a damn football player. He'll always be in the spotlight

> PAIGE: 😄 Well, grumpy Easton is back. Thanks, Keeley. He wants the discussion to revert to Reed

I shake my head as a smile tugs at my lips. But it's fleeting. They want me to fake a relationship? *As if.* I'm not going along with an idea taken straight out of a Hallmark Christmas movie. What do they think is going to happen? That my best friend will see me dating someone else and fall to her knees, begging me to break it off because she's always loved me?

I'm ninety-nine percent sure she already knows how I feel, and it's fucking with my head. *She's* fucking with my head. So yes, it's about time I did something to change that. But that something isn't this.

"You need to shut it down. *Now*," I tell Hayley, running my hands down my face, forcing a laugh. "I wish I'd never said anything to Luke. He's taken my words *way* out of context."

Unfortunately, it's no secret that I have a thing for my best friend, Bria. I wouldn't say I'm in love with her—like my friends so happily like to point out—but there are definitely feelings there beyond that of a traditional friendship.

And it's been that way for *years*.

Bria and I go way back. We attended the University of California together in Los Angeles, and when I was drafted to San Francisco after college, she followed me here, chasing her dream while I chased mine. Now, she's working her way up the ranks at a big accounting firm with a goal to be the youngest partner by the time she turns thirty. And I couldn't be prouder.

But, in order to attain that type of goal, she's always put her career first. As have I. And because of that, I never told her how I felt. It was never the right time.

Not that she's oblivious. She knows. We've just never discussed it. Or let ourselves cross that line.

Except once.

And it didn't end well.

Cut to last week when I decided to get drunk and open my big mouth to the one guy who has trouble keeping his shut—my teammate Luke Bennett, star tight end for the San Francisco Storm, reformed playboy, and one of my closest friends on the team.

Also known as a loudmouth.

I may as well have shouted it from the center of the field during the Super Bowl halftime show. Because that man can gossip.

Now, his wife, Amelia—as much as I love her—has started a group chat about it with some of the girlfriends...wives...sisters...and even goddamn friends of the players on my team, and there's no way back.

Hayley—one of the previously mentioned *friends*—smirks as she undoubtedly prepares to set me straight, something she loves doing.

"According to Amelia, you told Luke your 'love life was fucked' and that you 'needed to fix it.'"

Jesus, I'm a dick. While I have no recollection of that happening, it definitely sounds like me. Not that I'm going to admit that right now. I'm already in too deep. "So what you're saying is that everyone's taking Luke's word for it, because I was too drunk to remember?"

"Yep."

"Meaning...you're not shutting it down?"

"Nope." Hayley's radiant smile lights up her face as she brushes a few wayward hairs away from her eyes, pinning me with her stare.

I met Hayley last year at a joint Thanksgiving and Christmas get-together with my team, hosted by our reluctant coach. We'd been there to fake it for a film crew—for a TV series about our football team—and Hayley happens to be the director's best friend. The director who's now married to the infamous Luke and the two ex-enemies have a baby together. The beautiful Juliet. The reason for my crazy "my love life sucks" rant.

I want that.

Not the accidental pregnancy and subsequent heartache my friends went through, but the endgame. I want a wife; I want kids.

I want Bria.

But I'm beginning to realize that's not likely to happen.

When I don't respond, Hayley raises an eyebrow in challenge and an idea hits me. After Hayley and I first met, we ran into each other a few times, but in the last couple of months, our relationship has morphed from being a friend's friend, to a friend, to close friends, to now speaking daily. Much to Bria's annoyance.

Hayley could be exactly what I need to show Bria what she's missing. But not in the way they're all thinking.

I try to hide my responding smile, but this is too good to suppress and Hayley notices instantly. "What's that look about?"

"I've come up with a plan."

"Oh, yeah?" Her nose scrunches at the thought. While I wouldn't say my plans are as daring as Hayley's usually are, I have been known to have good ideas *occasionally*.

"Instead of this fake dating nonsense, I'm going to tell Bria I have a thing for you and we'll see how she reacts."

Hayley bursts out laughing. "Oh, Reed." She pats my leg condescendingly, her smile innocent as she teases. "If only it was that easy. It won't work unless she *believes* she's going to lose you."

"It's worth a shot though, right?" I comically cringe and Hayley shakes her head, biting back her sympathetic grin.

"Wrong." She waves off my thoughts. "Lucky for you, now *I* have an idea."

Uh, shit. Hayley and her ideas. While I generally love the way her mind works and all the wild adventures she takes me on, I have a feeling I'm not going to like this. Especially when she adds, "You're going to love it."

I force a smile in anticipation, and she snorts, sitting tall and proud.

"I'm going to be your fake girlfriend."

"You're what now?" My eyes bulge as I do a double take. *I did not see that coming.*

"I'm volunteering," she continues as though I was genuinely confused. "I'm an actress; it makes sense for your new girlfriend to be me."

"Ahh, no. That's insane and you know it. Plus—"

"I disagree," she cuts me off, excitement in her tone. "It makes perfect sense. I'm single. You're single. I'm hot. You're insanely gorgeous and you can't deny we'd make a stunning couple." She winks while I roll my eyes jokingly. "It's a no-brainer, Reed. We get along. We have fun. Give me one good reason why it shouldn't be me?"

"Maybe because I don't think it's a good idea to begin with. Fake dating is crazy. Come on, Hayls. Think about it."

"Reed." She hits me with her arresting gaze, her look telling me she thinks *I'm* crazy, not the idea. But she's wrong. I'm being sensible.

"Hayley." I stare back at her, mimicking her stance when she crosses her arms over her chest and pouts.

"Are you saying I couldn't pull it off?"

What? *Dammit.* She's good. Now I feel bad.

"Hayley Jackman from down under. You know I think you're brilliant. And while I'm sure this could be the acting role of your life, you're forgetting one major plot hole." Hayley's smile returns but it won't last long. I'm about to prove why this is a terrible idea. "I can't act."

"But—"

"Or lie," I add, though she already knows this.

"There are ways around that, Reed. Trust me. I've worked on some pretty amateur productions and people still loved them."

I fall quiet, acutely aware that she is unlikely to give up on this. Once Hayley has an idea in her head, it's not easy to get her past it. And I'm usually the one going along for the ride.

"For someone that thought I was insane, you're sure taking a long time to say no."

"I didn't say you were insane, Hayls. The idea is just..." *God, I don't even know.* I release an overexaggerated sigh, knowing she's about to sass me, and beat her to the punch. "It's not the craziest idea I've heard come out of your mouth. But I'm going to need to think about it. I'm still not convinced."

Her eyes light up in victory, reinforcing the fact that I can't say no to her.

"I'll take it," she says, squeezing my leg as she bounces around on the couch. "For now, anyway. I have no doubt I'll change your mind."

CHAPTER ONE

HAYLEY

THREE MONTHS EARLIER

"And... Action."

Tears streak my face as I run forward, my gaze never leaving the man in front of me, watching as he falls to the rugged terrain, the life leaving his eyes before his body hits the dirt.

I'd scream but it's no use. I'm too late. And it's all my fault.

My heart shatters as I reach him, a million shards cutting me from the inside, destroying me like I destroyed him. A broken cry pierces the silence, and it's only when I fall to my knees and wrap my arms around him that I realize it was mine.

Someone touches my back but I shake them off. I don't deserve their sympathy.

Before we met, this man was an angel. Now he's been reduced to nothing more than the skin and bones tucked beneath my grasp. The frail human that risked everything to protect me.

A man willing to die for someone born to be a killer.

I cry again, but this time my wail isn't so foreign to my ears. This time I recognize it for what it is—the sound of a woman scorned. The sound of a woman losing the last shred of innocence she'd been trying so hard to hold on to. The sound of a woman realizing she's just lost the love of her life, when he was the only good thing left in her world.

Leaving me as a shadow of my former self.

And shadows can easily be taken to the dark side.

"Cut. That was perfect."

"Oh. Thank God." I release a long, obnoxious sigh and slowly lift to my feet, wiping the tears from my eyes as my co-star Evan stares up at me, awe in his expression.

"Holy shit, Hayley. You nailed that. I think I might actually be in love with you."

"Shut up." I happily wave him off, appreciating his humor after one of the most intense days of filming that I've ever experienced.

Evan's eyes widen as his gaze drifts to someone behind me, and I don't need to look to know it's our director. We've been working on this scene for days and that last moment was the final piece to the puzzle and, in my opinion, the most crucial. The turning point for my character. One I had to get right. There was no other option.

The movie we're making is based on a book. An extremely popular cult-like book. And if I hadn't *nailed it,* as Evan said, I'd be crucified at the stake. There'd be no coming back from this.

Yet... I feel freaking amazing because I just gave the performance of my life and I couldn't be prouder of myself.

"Hayley *fucking* Jackman." Our director, Steve, pulls me into a hug, suffocating me in his grip, confirming that he's just as relieved as I am. "There are tears in my fucking eyes and I'm three times divorced after all my exes left me for my lack of emotion. Turns out, I've just been waiting for you to bring it out of me. Maybe my next marriage will work out fine."

I laugh awkwardly while Evan rolls his eyes. Steve's known for his eccentric happy-go-lucky manner, but he's also known as a director who never gives compliments unless they are well and truly earned. We usually find out we've done something right when the assistant director, otherwise known as the AD, announces we're moving on to a new scene while Steve casually walks off set, waving cheerfully as he goes.

It's been a ride, but one I wouldn't get off, even if you had a gun to my head.

"Honestly, Steve, I'm not sure I've ever felt that connected to a scene. Any chance we can go back and re-record a few other scenes now that I'm in the zone?" I elbow him in the chest and comically wince until he smiles.

"Not on your life, Jackman. But..." He pauses, and I find myself leaning in with anticipation, as does Evan. *God knows why.* "I will admit that you have nothing to worry about. You were born to play Riley. Audiences are going to love it."

He walks away without waiting for my response while Evan and I stare at him in shock.

"Did that really just happen?" Evan's the first to speak, his eyes on Steve's back as he heads over to our AD.

"I think it did," I whisper, my voice trapped as I process. "And I hate to say it, but that means hell just froze over."

"I hate to say you're right. Basically, we're fucked."

"Yep."

I'm called into makeup to fix the blood plastered on my face, ready for the next shot, and it's only then that I finally relax. While we're still filming the same scene, this time the camera will be set up mostly behind me, giving me a rest from the tears. I've always been able to cry on cue, and it's gotten me out of many situations, but when it's this tense and emotional, the fake becomes a little too real, and it's hard to pull myself out of it.

I wouldn't say I avoid emotion as such. In fact, I thrive on it. But it tends to skew toward emotions that are positive or protective in nature, not so much the deep, depressing kind.

Those, I keep to myself.

Like discovering the love of your life just died trying to save you—in the case of my character—or that your boyfriend of five years was cheating on you for three of them, and you found out but chose to pretend you were oblivious so that you could follow him to the US to pursue your dream of acting. That one is all me.

Those are not the emotions I let linger.

But hurt a friend of mine, or try to get in my pants when I'm not interested, and I'll hold a grudge for years. I'm not even opposed to violence.

"Hayley, Hayley, Hayley," our head makeup artist, Lucian, gushes with his hands clenched near his heart. "Word travels fast, and I hear you just perfected that performance. Apparently our darling Steve actually praised you."

"He did, and honestly, it's gone to my head. How dare you talk to me like we're friends. Don't you know I'm a huge star?" I deliver my line with no emotion while Lucian's assistant touches up my eyeliner, and he barks out a laugh, forcing his assistant to move away from my face in case I follow suit.

"Oh, Hayley, I could listen to your accent all day. Tell me. What would you say in Australia after an epic performance like that?"

I think on it for a second and grin, gesturing for the makeup artist to continue her work. "If it was me, I'd be saying much the same as I am now. I'm not fake, remember?" *And I try to maintain an American accent while I'm on set.*

Lucian rolls his eyes and I laugh, careful not to let it reach my eyes. We've spent many hours discussing all the actors and actresses that have sat in this very chair, or at least, a chair similar to this one, and it's safe to say he's had a run of bad luck lately. Until me, so he claims. He pouts now, because of my boring answer, but I'm not done. "I *do, however,* know a director who would have said something along the lines of 'you bloody ripper,' if that's what you're after?" My lips pull into a grin, knowing full well that's exactly what he wants to hear.

"That's it. You've done me in. I'm moving to Australia. I need to be able to say 'bloody ripper' and get away with it."

"Let me know if you do. I have a few contacts."

"Mmm." His smile turns mischievous. "If those contacts are as fine as your ex, then hand over your address book, my love, because I'm taking them all."

He's so over-the-top that I can't help but belly laugh, moving my head in the process, eliciting an exasperated sigh from Lucian's assistant.

Schooling my features, I apologize softly, while Lucian waves off her concern.

"Let her live a little, Cher," Lucian says, taking the eyeliner from her hands to finish the job himself. "Our dear Hayley just performed the scene that's going to propel her to stardom. We're in no rush. I have a feeling they'll wait."

My heart jolts, and for the first time, my confidence makes way for something new, something I hadn't anticipated...gratitude. Because while I've always dreamed I'd be a star, always assumed I'd find a way to get there, I never once stopped to think about how I'd feel if I did. Almost like my false bravado was guiding the way, paving a path for me. But now that it's a reality, the relief I feel is boundless.

This could be it. I might be close to becoming the person I always wanted to be.

And the thought of that is humbling.

Who knew?

"And that's a wrap. Well done, everyone."

A collective cheer fills the air as I deflate, grabbing the wall to stop myself from crashing in a heap. Instead of the elation I expected to feel after finishing my first starring role, an emptiness starts low in my belly and works its way through my chest, branching out until my entire body is numb.

I've done all I can do for this movie, and now I'm left to wait for the vultures to suck the life out of me. For the masses to judge me. To put me on a pedestal for their own enjoyment and leave me there until they've decided whether to praise me or throw stones.

My thoughts are a little dark and twisted, I know, but I guess I never considered the aftermath before now. In Australia, I was known as the sweetheart of the silver screen. Audiences loved me because I played characters they couldn't hate. They had no idea that behind the scenes, I wanted to play the dark, gritty characters. I wanted parts that had depth and unexpected layers. Because I felt more connected to that part of myself.

At the core...I wanted *this* role.

And only now that I've finished it, it's hitting me that I'll no longer be seen as a sweetheart anymore. Far from it.

But I have never loved a role more.

I'm engulfed in a million hugs before I make it back to my trailer, and the second I'm inside, I'm stripping off my shirt, in desperate need of a shower before we all head out to celebrate.

With a long sigh, I reach around to unhook my bra and—

"Did you forget I was here?"

"Jesus Christ, Amelia." Abandoning my task, I lower myself to the couch and clutch at my chest while my heart runs rampant. "You bet your ass, I forgot."

I stare at my best friend while she grins at my expense, and I can't help getting caught up in her happiness. "You're lucky I didn't hurt you with something," I joke as I finally smile, shaking my head at my stupidity. I put her name down at security, I was texting her throughout the day, and I still forgot.

Smirking at my dramatics, Amelia arches her brows as her eyes lock on my hands. "Were you going to flick me with your bra?"

I hit her with all the side-eye I can muster, but smile. "You know I could do a lot of damage with this thing. It's not the weapon, but how you use it."

"That's what she said."

"Touché. And there are too many men that have *no idea* how to use it."

Amelia smiles before the glint in her eyes sparkles. "On that note..." she trails off while I bounce in anticipation.

"I'm listening."

"I have a congratulatory present for you, since I can't come out to party tonight."

Ignoring the pang I get from knowing that time with my best friend is about to be cut short, I smile to ease her mind. "Oh, yeah? What's that?"

In the past, I would have argued about Amelia not coming out, but since she's now the mother of a beautiful little girl, I've given her some grace. How could I not? The past year hasn't been easy for her, and I witnessed it all from the sidelines, helping where I could but hating that I wasn't always there when she needed me. Because of this movie.

Amelia smiles sadly and my heart aches. "Amelia, I'm—"

"Nope. Do not get sappy on me because your emotions are in shambles. I've told you time and time again. I'm fine. I was fine. And I had Luke there when you couldn't be."

"Which was more often than I'd like."

"But look how well it worked out."

Ah yes, Luke... Her childhood enemy turned baby daddy turned love of her life. Amelia constantly tells me that if I'd been around more often she may have come to rely on me and she and Luke would never have connected like they did. But even if that were true, I still feel an element of guilt, and always will.

"I'm happy, Hayley. And I've never had a negative thought toward you. You know I love you."

"I do. So what's this surprise then? Please get me out of my emotional funk." I glance around the room and find a box of chocolates on the table, secured with a red bow.

"Aww, you got me chocolates?"

"What?" Amelia's gaze follows mine. "No. My surprise is better than that."

"I happen to love chocolates, and those are my favorites."

"Trust me." She chuffs out a laugh as she shakes her head. "This is better."

"Go on."

Amelia smirks while her eyes light up with excited mischief. "Luke's going out with you. Instead of me."

Huh. "Luke? Ahh...how do I say this? I love your hubby, I do, but—"

"He's bringing a few guys from the team." *And there it is.* The perfect gift. Way better than chocolate. A gift that keeps on giving. I've hung out with the guys a few times now and they're always a ball of fun. It's exactly what I need to forget about the pressure I've put on myself and to enjoy the fact that I just finished filming a goddamn Hollywood movie.

And I was freaking amazing.

No matter what people think about the movie or me when it's released, they can't take that away.

This has been a dream of mine for as long as I can remember.

And I'm going to enjoy it.

CHAPTER TWO

REED

"Are you sure you don't want to come?" I glance over at my best friend, Bria, trying hard not to focus on the sliver of skin peeking out from beneath her tight top as she sprawls out on my bed, her hands behind her head, playing with the strands of her long caramel hair. She frowns but doesn't look my way, not bothering to hide the fact that she's upset over me ditching her.

And I *almost* change my mind.

Truth be known, I'd much rather be here, lying next to her, replacing her fingers with mine, brushing them through her hair, seeing a lot more than a sliver of her skin. But...that's not to be and it's time I got the fuck over it. Or I could man up and have a conversation about it. Only I'm still undecided on the direction I want to take my life.

Tonight, however, I'm going out. Luke asked and I said yes. I'm nothing if not a man of my word. Something Bria has always known.

"I don't understand why you're going," she says, her tone somewhat whiny. "You don't even know her."

The "her" she's referring to is Hayley. Luke's wife's best friend. While Bria's not entirely wrong—I don't know her that well—I have met her a few times and I'm aware that tonight is a big deal. Hayley just completed filming on her first big-budget Hollywood production, and since she's originally from Australia, she doesn't have a circle of friends to help her celebrate—and she deserves to celebrate. I shouldn't have to justify my decision, but of course, I do.

"I know her well enough and she's best friends with Amelia. So..." I trail off because what else am I supposed to say? "I better get ready. I'll see you on Monday though, right?"

Bria nods as she gets up and grabs her purse off the counter, her vibe salty now that I'm practically kicking her out of my house. It's safe to assume she's noticed the shift between us. As she should. I'm not exactly hiding it.

But neither is she.

For the last few years, give or take ten, I've had a thing for my best friend. I'm not going to call it a crush because I'm a goddamn grown man, but it's not *not* a crush. Plain and simple, I want her. And not just in a physical sense. Sure, she's fucking gorgeous, but it's more than that. It's always been easy between us, and I imagine our relationship would be the same. The only minor hiccup in that vision of my future is that I'm ninety percent sure the feelings are *not* mutual, and until now, I haven't been prepared to find out.

But if I'm being honest with myself, our friendship is already so fragile because of my feelings that I can't go on like this. I need to make a decision one way or another. It's just taking longer than I thought.

After Bria's gathered her phone too, I walk her to the door, opening it before she has the chance. And that tiny gesture, something I do all the time, grants me a smile.

"I'm only annoyed because I wanted to hang out tonight," she says, wrapping an arm around my waist, giving me a side hug. "We barely see each other anymore."

That may be true, but other than tonight, I make sure to see her any chance I get. "Why don't we spend the weekend together when I have a bye in a few weeks? You're already coming to our fundraiser. We could hang out before it, maybe even spend the night in a fancy hotel."

At that, Bria's eyes light up, and it's for that very reason I haven't been able to let my feelings go. She has her own wealth—her parents are both big in the financial world—and she frequents fancy hotels. So why does the idea of a night in one excite her? I can't help but think it's because I've added myself to the equation. And yet...here we are, still friends after countless getaways together.

"That sounds like heaven, Reed. And exactly what we need. Do you want to find somewhere or should I?"

"I'll leave it to you, but make sure you charge it to my credit card this time. My treat."

Bria presses a kiss to my cheek, and like always, it sends a warmth right through me. She's my comfort, my home. I don't know what the fuck I'm going to do if that ever changes. But judging by the pit forming deep in my stomach, I'd say I have about three weeks to find out. A fancy hotel seems like the perfect place to finally tell her how I feel, if that's the way I decide to go.

With another smile, Bria heads off and I'm left to once again analyze every part of our goddamn interaction. I'm a goner, sure, but at least I'm self-aware enough to acknowledge it. Although, even if I didn't, I've got my *amazing* friends to remind me.

My phone buzzes with a text, and as I check the screen, I note the time. I'm already running behind.

LUKE: Is Bria coming?

And here's Luke, right on cue. His way of saying he knows we're always together.

REED: Not today. It's just the boys. Unless your sister's coming

Much to Luke's initial annoyance, his sister, Lainey, married our team captain and quarterback, Thomas Kelly, after a secret relationship that spanned a few years. Luke and Thomas were friends and teammates in high school and college too, and couldn't be more different. Luke's cocky and loud, while Thomas tends to keep to himself, choosing to stay away from the spotlight. It's amazing they've stayed close all this time.

LUKE: Nah, she's out. But it's not just the boys. We're there for Hayley, remember?

Shit. I don't even know why I said that when I've never been all that interested in boys' nights. I blame Bria. She's got me so messed up at the moment that I can't decide if I'm coming or going, and it's starting to affect my headspace.

REED: Jesus, what a dick thing to say. I know we're going for Hayley. That's not what I meant

LUKE: I know, I know. You're too easy to tease. See you there in thirty

REED: Yup. I'll be there

Since I'm in sweats and a tee, I rush to get changed, throwing on jeans and a white shirt, then roll up the sleeves. A splash of cologne and I'm done. Ready for my night out. Ready to move on.

The pit in my stomach deepens and I curse myself out loud. This isn't going to be easy. No matter what I choose, my friendship with Bria will be affected, and I'm not sure I'm ready for that. In fact, I'm not sure I'll ever be.

My Uber arrives seconds before I exit my front door, and I find Bria's car still parked in my driveway, making me pause. But as I head over, she waves me off, reversing onto my quiet street with a smile, never once looking back as she drives away. Meanwhile, I'm so entranced watching her taillights as she disappears into the distance that my Uber driver blares the horn to get my attention.

No wonder everyone thinks I'm lovesick.

And what the hell is going on with Bria?

I'm lost in thought on the way to the bar until my driver changes his playlist, switching over to country music instead of the pop he was previously listening to, his eyes meeting mine in the rearview mirror. "Hope you don't mind."

I smile, relieved. "Not at all. This is my kind of jam."

"No shit. Really? I thought you were a city boy."

And I thought he didn't recognize me. Guess we were both wrong.

"I attended college in the city, but I'm a country boy at heart."

My driver gives me an appreciative nod. "I think you just got promoted to my favorite player," he says with a toothy grin, his southern accent suddenly more prominent. "My home team is Houston, but since moving here ten years back, I've got a soft spot for the Storm."

"Oh, yeah? Thanks, man. It's nice to meet a fan. But I have to ask, who *was* your favorite player before now?"

"Bennett." He's quick to answer, making me snort. "Does his confidence ever waver?"

Luke Bennett? No. "That man has confidence in doing things he's never tried before. It's a gift." One of the cockiest players on the team but not without warrant. He's a hell of a player.

My driver laughs. "I thought as much. I watched that show. Fitzpatrick's giving him a run for his money."

God, he's not wrong. Our newest starter, Zane, is making waves and not always the good kind. But like Luke, he can play. And he knows it. If only he was a little more of a team player. I have no doubt he'll get there, but he's young and carefree. One day he'll need his teammates and it will undoubtedly help him grow up a little. For now, he's got some work to do.

We pull up in front of Chasers Bar in downtown San Francisco and I thank my driver, giving him a Storm cheer before I get out. When I turn to face the bar, my jaw drops. There's a goddamn line longer than a football field.

I plaster a smile on my face and move toward the end until Luke calls out.

"Coombs, you considerate motherfucker. We're on the guest list. Get your ass up here."

I breathe a sigh of relief and push through the crowd, reaching Luke and a few of my teammates just as a bouncer opens the door, directing us to a beautiful woman standing near the entry. "Leni will show you the way. Len, they're with the Hobarton party."

"Hobarton?" I ask Luke, confused while he smiles in anticipation, excitement in his eyes.

"It's a code name. This party is going to blow your mind."

I roll my eyes but keep my mouth shut. I haven't had the sheltered life he thinks I have. My life hasn't revolved solely around football and Bria. I've seen things. Done things. I'm not that boring.

We follow Leni as she escorts us through the main bar to a private section at the back, and when I step through the door, I have to admit, my eyes widen a little. But not because I'm shocked by what I see... because I can't believe how many people are here.

For a relatively small space, there must be hundreds moving around.

"Keep an eye out for Hayley," Luke requests as we enter, and despite most of us barely knowing her, he doesn't have to offer a description. There wouldn't be a man on our team that hadn't checked her out—me included —except maybe the committed ones. Though I'd still bet my life savings they know who she is. She's not shy by any means and she makes her presence known. The first time most of us met her, she joined in on a friendly game of football, and she was good. The guys loved her. Even if she does call us pussies because Australian Rules players don't wear any gear.

I have no doubt the guys are already on the lookout. But having said that, I can't imagine it's going to be easy to find her in this crowd, let alone—

She steps into my line of sight, cutting me off mid-thought as a grin tugs at my lips, a response to the proud expression she's currently sporting.

Chatting animatedly with a group of well-dressed men in business suits, she's every bit the confident woman I remember, her beaming smile sucking them in, her self-assured nature and warmth making them all putty in her hands.

The world doesn't know what's going to hit it when Hayley Jackman becomes Hollywood's next big star.

I turn to let Luke know I've found her when someone bumps into me from behind, spilling a drink down my leg. "Hey, what the fuck?" my teammate Rhett snaps as though he's the one currently smelling like beer. But while I appreciate the defense, I shake him off.

"It's okay, Rhett." I smile, turning to the red-faced guy spewing apologies. "No harm done. I'm sure these guys will be spilling drinks before the night's out."

His eyes widen before his red face turns ashen. "Fuck, you're Reed Coombs. I'm so sorry, man."

"Chill. I'm fine. You go and enjoy your night. Forget this ever happened."

The guy nods as he steps around me, and Rhett mumbles under his breath, "You're lucky it was Coombs."

Overhearing the exchange, Thomas steps forward, lightly slapping him across the back of the head, pinning him with a scolding glare. "What the hell, Rhett? It was an accident. Let's not make headlines again."

I cringe at the thought; we definitely don't want that. The headlines Thomas is referring to stem from our time in the spotlight last season when a San Francisco production company decided to make a TV show about our team. The very show my driver mentioned watching. A show that, to everyone's surprise, was a huge fucking hit. But not necessarily in a good way.

"There have been enough headlines already," Thomas continues. "Don't you think?"

We all nod, while Wyatt calls out "Hear! Hear!" and shakes his head, his eyes flashing to Luke since his wife was involved in the production of the show. I'm about to tell Wyatt he needs to stop making that connection, when Rhett wolf whistles under his breath. "I was having a rough day," he says, making excuses for his asshole behavior. "But," he continues, his eyes locked on something, or likely *someone* behind me, "it's about to get a hell of a lot better."

I turn to see Hayley approaching, her expression now full of excitement as she rushes to reach Luke. And while I hate what Rhett's insinuating, it's hard to miss the appeal.

There's no denying that she's beautiful.

As though she's a beacon for all that surrounds her, eyes follow her every move as she swiftly drifts past them, her long, blonde hair bouncing behind her, her tight dress leaving nothing to the imagination, showing off her incredible curves.

She has the room transfixed. She's breathtaking, and on top of all that, she's a hell of a lotta fun. And God knows we could use some fun.

Wyatt groans beside me and I burst out laughing, knowing that like fifty percent of the guys in this room, he's fangirling. Hard.

And when Luke shakes his head before rolling his eyes, I have no doubt it's going to be a night to remember...

Exactly what I need right now.

Chapter Three

HAYLEY

Being the center of attention has its perks, and thanks to the never-ending array of drinks flowing my way, I'm a little buzzed by the time Luke and his teammates arrive, and I'm blaming *that* for my reaction.

"Lukey Pukey, you came." I throw my arms around his neck, rocking him back and forth, squealing with excitement. I made a lot of crew members—namely Lucian—big promises about a hot football team and I always deliver.

Luke laughs at my corny nickname and spins me out of his arms, angling me in the direction of his friends. "Hayley, here are my boys."

He waves a hand across the collection of fine looking men in front of me, smiling as if I could possibly forget anyone from my new favorite team. "First you've got Wyatt," he begins, pointing to his teammate—who Amelia mentioned is the fun-loving man of the group—and I offer a wave. "Here you have Mr. Self-assured ladies' man, Rhett." He grins at his own joke, and I grin back at him, recognizing Rhett from when he introduced himself the first time I met the guys. "The big man here is Carter," Luke continues and I follow his gaze, smiling up at Carter, the man who could easily be compared to The Rock.

With those boys alone, I'm giddy—*there's so much hotness surrounding me*—but before Luke's moved on, my eyes drift over to Reed, sneaking a peek at the tattoos creeping out from the collar of his shirt, and...*jackpot.* That man is a god.

"Last..." Luke slaps Reed on the back, and while he doesn't need an introduction—we've spoken before—Luke gives him one anyway. "Say hello to everyone's golden boy, Reed." I smile at Reed and his lips quirk into a genuine grin. Very golden boy-esque. "Now, boys." Luke spins my way. "This is the one and only Hayley Jackman."

As if trained to do so, they all wave in unison while I bounce on my toes just as Thomas joins us. "Oh, and you know Thomas. No intro needed."

I do know Thomas and it's nice to see another friendly face.

Since Amelia and Luke got together, I've been spending a lot of time with the two of them, getting to know Luke properly, and in turn, I've spent time with Lainey—Luke's sister—and Thomas, her new husband. I've also been attending games and getting to know some of the wives and girlfriends in the suite. Tagging along as though I belong there.

It's been fun.

"Hello, boys." I smile, unabashedly checking them all out. "Thanks for helping me celebrate. I bet you're all *huge* fans of fantasy romance." I wink.

"I've been known to read fantasy every now and then," Wyatt offers and I nod, impressed until Luke scoffs.

"She's not referring to *The Hobbit*, Langham," Luke tells him. "But nice try."

"There's nothing wrong with *The Hobbit*." I smile and the laughter continues at Wyatt's expense, especially when I add, "This isn't really that, though. But I do appreciate you all coming. There's a tab on the bar, a rockin' dance floor behind me, and a few makeup artists dying to meet you. Who's ready for a big night?"

I don't wait for them to answer, spinning on the tip of my stilettos and beelining for said bar, ordering another vodka and soda with a round of shots for the guys, except Thomas—giving him a water, his go-to choice.

After handing out the drinks, the guys make their way over to a table, and I watch them leave as Luke wraps an arm around my shoulder. "Congratulations, Jack Rabbit," he says with a genuine warmth. "You did it. You proved us *all* wrong." He stares at me deadpan and I giggle.

It didn't take long for Luke and me to form a brother/sister type relationship and I kind of love it. I never had siblings growing up, but I get the feeling he'd take on that protective role if I needed him to. "I'm hearing big things, J bird," he continues as we walk toward the guys. "The Jackman name is going to be *huge* in Hollywood." He winks and though it's not *that* funny, a laugh bursts out of me. Maybe I'm more tipsy than I thought.

"In all seriousness"—his cocky expression softens—"I'm excited to say that I know you." He pulls me into a brotherly hug and I wait for his inevitable link back to Amelia. He's obsessed with her and I love it. "So tell me, when are you and my talented wife going to make magic together? It won't be long before she's directing again." His expression morphs to reflect his awe, and a proud smile lights his face.

"You know I'd work with Ames any day. She just has to ask."

Amelia first introduced me to the San Francisco Storm players when she was directing a TV show about the team. The directing gig didn't end well, but her life wouldn't be the same without it. After all, it brought her and Luke closer together when they were forced to work with each other.

"I've been telling her that. Trust me, I'm not at all subtle about it."

"Oh, I know." He grins, his expression mischievous. "She complains about it all the time."

"Shut up." I shove him back as I step out of his hold. "She does not. She loves me and my crazy."

Luke rolls his eyes as though that itself is crazy. "That she does. God knows why."

Shaking my head, I glance away and spot Lucian already watching us. He winks before not so subtly dancing over, immediately insisting I introduce him around.

When I'm finally done, it's not just the makeup team that I've introduced, but a few of my new friends too. The guys met Cameron, who played one of the angels in *Jaded Beginnings*, Araya and Olivia from our wardrobe department, and Evan, my leading man, who I quickly discovered is a huge football fan...but a die-hard Miami supporter. Something he had no qualms about mentioning to the guys.

"You know they sucked last year, right?" Carter reminds Evan, making the group crack up laughing. Evan's a good guy, if not a little full of himself. But I guess a lot of us are in the world of movies. We have to be. How else could we put ourselves out there, time and time again, allowing ourselves to be judged playing pretend?

Evan feigns shock at Carter's revelation and my amusement thickens. "You know you're talking to a Super Bowl winner, right?" I add, attempting Carter's accent, anticipating that to be the next words coming out of his mouth. And when he laughs, I know I'm right.

"Think you'll get there again?" Evan asks and I lean in with intrigue, wanting the answer myself. Luke always says yes, but I've never met a cockier man in my life, so I'd love a second opinion.

"We fucking better," Carter says, his tone deep and serious, leaving no room for argument. "I'm retiring this year and I want another win."

"What about you, Reed?" I turn his way, locking eyes with the gentle giant from across the table where I'm perched between Carter and Wyatt. "You've been a little quiet," I add, though that's not entirely true. He's been in conversations with the guys; I just haven't been able to hear him. And I do love the smooth, deep quality of his voice. There's something a little country about it. A far cry from the accents we have back home.

Reed raises an eyebrow and I grin. "Of course we're going to win. No doubt about it." The guys cheer and Reed winks, making me giggle uncontrollably.

It's safe to say I have a crush on that man. A crush in the sense that I want him to throw me over his shoulder, caveman style, toss me on a bed, and fuck me like nobody has before him.

A pipe dream. One I'd say is less achievable than winning an Oscar.

Not only is he head over heels for his best friend—something I learned within hours of first meeting him—but he's also too nice for that. True that he's built like a freight truck with muscle on top of muscle, and tattoos that tell a million tales while making a girl's panties wet, but there's still something innocent about him. Something pure.

He doesn't need me or anyone else corrupting him.

He deserves to be preserved.

Kept for the woman that wins his heart. A woman worthy of that kind of decency.

And while I have no issues with self-worth, I'm not that girl. I'm here for a good time, not a long one.

A girl can dream. And dream I have. Or perhaps fantasize is a better word.

Reed's pulled into another conversation, but I don't miss the small smile he flashes me before he turns away.

And it has me swooning.

I love a cocky man, always have, but there's something about Reed's genuine smile that makes me melt. And from the looks aimed his way, I'm not the only one.

For the next couple of hours, the conversation is easy, the drinks flow, and my world feels a little lighter, telling me it's time to hit the dance floor.

Only, I'm in need of a partner. My eyes flash to Reed as I consider my options, but as if reading my mind and deciding he's not interested, he jumps up and motions to the group that he's going to the restroom, heading that way without a backward glance.

Shrugging my shoulders, I stand up and rearrange my dress, double-checking that it's covering all the right places, namely the intimate bits that it should be covering, before motioning to the dance floor.

Ever the gentlemen that they are, the guys stand when I do, and in my current state, I can't help the giddy laugh that escapes me. "Anyone up for a dance?" I ask, grabbing the back of the chair in front of me, leaning forward. "We've reached that time of the night, and I'm ready to move."

I don't wait for a response before waving goodbye and heading to the dance floor, knowing without a doubt that at least one of the guys is following me.

And once there, I'm in my element.

On the dance floor I can be who I want to be. I'm surrounded by strangers and I don't have to talk. I don't have to justify my actions or explain myself. I can just be. And more to the point, I can just be *crazy*. I can flirt. I can sing. I can act like I don't have a care in the world because at that very moment, I don't. There's nowhere else for me to be. I'm not Hayley Jackman, the actress, the foreigner, the wild child. I'm a dancer, surrounded by other dancers, all likely experiencing the same high.

I find it relaxing. It can get a little busy in my head sometimes. Being the easygoing, carefree, unapologetic one in a friendship can be extremely taxing.

Sometimes I want to be weak and frail, but I can't be. I have to be there for my friends. I have to be the strong one.

And I always will.

That's my life.

Closing my eyes, I let the music take over and I sway to the beat until my mind clears. And when I open my eyes, I smile to myself, finding Carter and Wyatt have joined me.

I dance around the boys, cheering at their moves, drinking in the attention until Evan sidles up to me, rubbing his junk against my leg under the guise of dancing.

I'd be pissed if I didn't know he was joking. He's harmless enough, and I'm ninety percent sure he'd prefer to go home with one of the guys.

"We did it, little Jackman," he says, wrapping his arm around my shoulder as our castmate, Cam, joins us. "We starred in a *fucking* masterpiece."

"And we killed it," Cam adds, the excitement in his tone infectious.

"Yeah we did, and now all that's left to do is dance." Evan cheers, spinning away from me as he drops down into a half squat, half booty shake and I snort as my gaze flashes to Cam, finding him jokingly rolling his eyes. This is us. To a T. And I'm going to miss it. I smile wide, but the earlier feeling of emptiness takes over me. In such a small amount of time, the *Jaded Beginnings* cast and crew have become my happy place, and now we're about to go our separate ways, off to new projects to make new friends. And that freaking sucks. Sure, that's how this business works, but I'm not ready to let them go. I'm not ready to start over again.

When he's back on his feet, Evan grabs my hand, and I push my worries from my mind. Tonight, they're still here. I'll have plenty of time for self-pity tomorrow when I wake up hungover, undoubtedly in some random guy's bed.

Tomorrow's another day, but now...

"Let's party," I yell above the music, throwing my hands in the air as I toss my head back and cheer. My mood is what I make it, and for the rest of tonight, I'm euphoric.

Time passes, but I couldn't say how much, as I work up a sweat, letting the music consume me.

Closing my eyes once more, I rock my body as the hypnotic beat flows through my blood, transporting me to another world.

A smile tugs at my lips, and when I open my eyes, my gaze instantly locks on Reed, my heart pounding while I catch my breath, holding his stare as he watches me from the sidelines.

I wink, seductively swaying my hips, taking him in as he leans against a bar table, his arms folded, his tattooed forearms peeking out beneath his fitted white shirt, the object of many lustful gazes. Including mine.

And he has no freaking idea.

His eyes drop to his phone, and it doesn't take a genius to guess who's texting him based on the way a smitten grin instantly reaches his eyes.

I barely know him and I can see it.

A thought occurs to me and I smile to myself, picturing his perfectly sculpted body going to waste. Imagining myself putting it to use.

And I can't hold back. It's not in my nature. A blessing and a curse.

Brushing off the guys around me, I'm like a moth to a flame, my eyes never leaving Reed as I walk his way.

I have questions. Actually, I have one *quite personal* one. And I'm not leaving without an answer.

Chapter Four

REED

I can't take my eyes off Hayley as she dances with my teammates. *Hell*, no one can. Everywhere you look, she's the center of the room, keeping everyone on their toes while they worship the ground she walks on.

As they should.

I'm not blind. I can see she's a goddess and one that demands attention everywhere she goes.

She has a presence that makes you want to be close to her, and yet, from what Luke says, no one but Amelia is close to her at all. And I feel like we have that in common. I'm friends with a lot of people, but it's only Bria that knows the real me.

A new song comes on and Hayley relaxes into it, throwing her head back with her eyes closed, swaying her hips, the music taking her over. She smiles to herself, eyes drifting open to meet mine across the room, her gaze questioning until she winks.

My phone buzzes in my hand as I smile, and I don't have to look to know who it is. *Bria.*

I've been expecting this message.

> BRIA: Are you still out? I have a question for you

I check the time and laugh. It's almost midnight. I'd usually be home by now and would have likely texted her on my way. She's checking in. Making sure I'm safe without actually asking me. Refusing to let me know how much she cares.

> REED: I'm currently deciding whether this crowd is ready for my moves

> BRIA: 😅 No one will ever be ready for that. They're not worthy

> REED: Ha. You're too good to me. But I appreciate it. What did you want to ask?

> BRIA: The square root of 12,457,590

An obnoxious snort escapes me and the woman beside me huffs before walking away, seemingly offended by my sudden outburst. *My bad.* But her message deserved that reaction.

> REED: That's too easy. Switch off the light and close your eyes. It works wonders

Bria and I have a running joke when one of us can't sleep—to talk about math. When we first met, she told me she'd get insomnia sometimes, and I had the brilliant idea to think of something boring, like a math equation. Turns out, she was studying finance and loved numbers, launching our friendship off to a great start.

Ever since, when she can't sleep, she lets me know by asking a math-related question, and if I'm free, I call her and we talk until she's sleepy. But if I'm not, she gets the short and sweet response. Like tonight. I call it tough love.

Bria's typing a reply when a presence invades my personal space. Someone pinches my ass, and my gaze snaps around in time to see Hayley push past a young redhead who I assume is the culprit. Unless it was Hayley.

"Did you..."

"Nope." She shakes her head. "Miss Forward over there did it seconds before I got to you. Didn't you see her hovering?"

"No, I—"

"Of course you didn't," she cuts me off. "You're oblivious. The hottest guy in the room has no idea how attractive he is."

A laugh sticks in the back of my throat. "That's a pretty big compliment."

"It's the truth." She lifts a shoulder in a half shrug. "Why would I lie?"

"I have *no* idea." Taking a sip of my drink, I subtly glance around the room, checking out my competition. Being the hottest in the room is only as good as the people I share it with. Wyatt waves from the dance floor and I smirk to myself, taking another sip. I've been nursing the same whiskey for the better part of an hour, but I'm suddenly really thirsty.

Feeling Hayley's eyes boring into the side of my face, I turn to catch her wicked grin before she blurts, "Are you a virgin, Reed?"

I choke on my drink, covering my mouth as the dark liquid attempts to burst free. "What?" I manage to respond, my voice croaky as I swallow.

"Simple question. Are. You. A. Virgin?"

"Okay." I clear my throat when it's still a little hoarse. "The simple answer is no. But where the hell did that come from?"

"Curiosity." She shrugs like it's no big deal. *Just a conversation between friends, right?*

"Are *you* a virgin?" I counter, but the second the words leave my mouth, guilt settles in my stomach. "Sorry, don't answer that. It's none of my business."

Hayley laughs overtly before her palm lands on my chest and she sighs. "Why are you here, Reed? Are you looking to hook up?"

Am I what? I frown, confused. "I'm here for *you*. To help celebrate *your* success."

"Despite barely knowing me."

"Apparently." My brows furrow because she's right, and yet, here I am, out celebrating someone I barely know.

"If it helps,"—she pats my chest—"I'm also *not* a virgin." She bounces on her toes. "Now we can say we know each other a little more intimately."

"That we do." I slowly nod in agreement. "And I feel *so* much closer to you because of it." I stare at her deadpan and she gasps.

"Reed Coombs, are you *sassing* me?"

"Sassing? No. Joking, yes."

"Either way, I like it." She smiles and I'm instantly sucked in, watching as the smile reaches her eyes, her happiness making it impossible not to grin back.

"So, you're not a virgin," she muses, snapping me out of my thoughts. "But you're not here for women."

She's not asking. She's just confirming what she's already figured out.

"Correct. I'm not here for *women*. Just one. *You*."

"God, if only that were true." Her eyes flit closed and she's seemingly lost in thought until she bites her lip and smirks.

"Uh, why wouldn't it be?" I ask, a little taken aback. "I've actually been told numerous times that I suck at lying."

Hayley's eyes flutter open. "Is that so?"

"Apparently."

"Try me. Two truths and a lie. Let's see if I can guess." She steps closer, staring up at me, her gaze alight with anticipation.

"Oh-kay." I humor her. "Let me think." *Two truths and a lie. Two truths and a lie.*

"Want me to go first?" She pops her hip as she leans against the table, her patience wearing thin.

"Nope, I've got this." I think. Although it's harder than I would have thought, and... actually... "One, I grew up in a small town. Two, I have three cats. And three, I'm an incredible dancer but this isn't my style."

Hayley lets out an adorable giggle. "We're gonna circle back to the dancing tidbit." She waves a finger around in a circular motion as she continues. "There's no way that's the lie, and now you've got me picturing it. I'm wondering if it's hip-hop or jazz." She purses her lips before continuing. "But first, you..." She trails off, squinting as though trying to read my mind. "Do *not* have three cats. In fact, I'll bet my next drink that you don't even have *one*. You're a dog person. And I'm in the mood for an espresso martini. With good vodka. Top shelf."

I'd laugh if I wasn't shocked. I delivered my truths and a lie evenly; I made sure of that. How the... Doesn't matter. She proved my point.

"Your nose scrunched," Hayley answers my unspoken question. "The thought of owning cats didn't sit well with you."

"Damn." I shake my head with a groan. "Fine. I owe you an espresso martini. Unless I guess yours."

"You're on."

I smile, expecting her to take a moment to think about it, but she throws out her response so quickly I startle. "One, my hair is naturally wavy. Two, I know how to surf. And three, I'd love to screw your brains out."

"Jesus Christ." My balls tighten but I ignore it. This isn't the first time someone's said something similar to me, and despite what Hayley insinuated earlier, I'm not oblivious to the attention I receive. But something about the words coming from Hayley's mouth has my cock hardening in my pants. And that's not a good thing for either of us. Especially when I'm certain it's her lie.

"The third one," I state plainly, unable to repeat her words back to her in case my voice wavers.

"Dammit. I was sure you wouldn't guess."

"Why?"

"Because *everyone* wants that."

"Except you apparently." I huff out a laugh and relax until she speaks.

"Kind of." She leans in, her lips pressed together, almost coyly, as she lifts to her toes. "If we were fucking," she whispers against my ear, her voice full of want, "I'd much rather *I* was the one losing my mind."

Holy hell. I grip the back of my neck awkwardly. *What do I even say to that?* "I...er...ah—"

"Relax." She grins, stepping back while I fight to hide my frown. "I have no plans to jump you, Reed. But I'm only human. A girl can fantasize."

I pause, finding her honesty refreshing, my mind clearing enough to hold my own in this bizarre conversation.

"What if I were to say yes?" I ask, turning to give her my full attention. "Are you prepared to hand over control? Would you allow me to *blow your mind*?"

Hayley giggles this time, and it's both adorable and a little insulting.

"Something tells me you won't." She points at my chest, her eyes falling to where her finger pokes at my abs. "So I'm willing to say yes."

She glances up again, raising a single brow, and the meaning behind her words hits me. "Fucking Luke," I grumble, getting the impression he told Hayley about my feelings for Bria. And when she bites back a grin, she confirms it.

"The one and only. But there's nothing wrong with knowing what or who you want. I think it's sweet."

"I—"

"You're sweet. Don't try and fight it. I happen to like sweet. Come on, you owe me a drink."

She spins on her toes so fast I have to reach out to stop her from walking away. "I thought you owed me one?"

"To-may-to, to-mah-to." She shrugs. "Let's go."

"Actually, it's nothing like that." I scrunch my nose, making her smile. "But lucky for you, I'm a gentleman. One espresso martini coming right up."

ayley downs more than a few more martinis before the venue calls for last drinks, and I find myself watching her every move, worried about some asshole taking advantage of her inebriated state.

Barely a minute passes before the dim mood lighting brightens and I curse myself for staying out so late. My teammates are long gone and yet, I couldn't bring myself to leave any earlier.

Hayley's right. I barely know her, but Luke asked us to come because Hayley doesn't have many friends here in the US, and I felt it my duty to stay.

Several guys flock to her side now that the night is over, hoping to shoot their shot. But to my surprise, she pushes past them all, making her way over to me, her confident smile locked in place.

"You stayed." She sits down beside me and leans back in the chair, crossing her leg over her knee, the hem of her dress lifting dangerously high on her thigh. "I'm impressed." She closes her eyes and lets out a slow, drawn-out breath, drawing attention to her chest as it rises and falls.

"What can I say." I lift my eyes to hers, smiling when she catches me checking her out. "I was having a blast." I shrug, owning it.

"Yeah, I'm sure that's it." Straightening up, she glances back to the dance floor, her eyes briefly stopping on the men that still hover there.

"Do you think they're waiting for me?" she asks, and I cough to hide my snicker.

"I *know* they are. Without a doubt."

"Should I go home with one?"

My gaze shoots to hers, but I can't tell if she's serious or not. "That's not a question I can answer."

"Would it bother you if I did?"

"Yes," I say honestly because we've already established I can't lie. "But it's not for the reason you're thinking." *It would bother me because I'd fucking worry.*

"Trust me, I know." She shakes her head, her lips pulled in a soft smile. "I see you, Reed. And I appreciate it. I love sex as much as the next person, but I don't need it every night."

"Good to know." I stand and offer her my hand, pulling her up next to me when she takes it. "Come on. Let's get you home."

I turn to walk but she fakes a gasp, drawing my attention before she giggles. "I take back what I said. I'm always up for sex. Your place or mine?"

Suppressing a grin, I shake my head until she laughs out loud and my smile breaks through.

"I don't mind getting an Uber," she adds with a quick glance toward the exit. "It's probably out of your way."

"Do you know where I live?"

"Nope. But I can guarantee it's a better area than mine."

"All the more reason for me to go with you. Come on. We can share a taxi."

She stares at me for a beat, undoubtedly thinking up another excuse. Because despite telling me she doesn't need sex every night, the wanton look in her eyes says otherwise. Too bad I don't mind being a cockblock to her in her drunken stupor. She can fuck whoever she wants when she's of sound mind.

Raising an eyebrow in challenge, I gesture to the bar that leads to the exit, and Hayley releases an exaggerated sigh. "Fine, I'll come." She surprises me, linking her arm through mine, guiding us toward the door, using me as a support more than I think she realizes.

There's a taxi waiting when we step into the fresh night air, and I open the door to let her inside before sliding in beside her, letting the driver know there will be two stops.

After giving the driver her address, Hayley lays her head against the backrest, closing her eyes, and it occurs to me that she may not be feeling so good now that she's stopped dancing.

"Shit. I never asked if you were okay. We should stop for water."

She smiles without opening her eyes. "You really are the trifecta, aren't you," she whispers, her brows furrowing as though her words confuse her.

God knows, they confuse me. "The trifecta?"

"Yeah." She straightens up to face me. "Hot body, pretty face, and one of the most genuine guys I think I've ever met."

"You barely know me." I chuckle, giving her shoulder a nudge.

"That may be so, but you wear your heart on your sleeve. The whole world can see it."

Her words sting as they bite into me but I don't let her see it. "Maybe that's the Reed I want the world to see," I say honestly, keeping my voice light and a smile on my face. "Maybe if you got to know me better, you'd see a different side of me."

Hayley frowns as she stares into my eyes, seemingly looking for the truth to my words, and after a beat, she must find something because a bright smile lights up her features. "I guess that's what I'll have to do."

"Yeah."

"Yeah." She yawns and a smile tugs at my lips. "In fact," she continues, sliding her ass closer to mine, "I think we'll be seeing a lot more of each other moving forward. I'm too intrigued to walk away." She rests her head on my shoulder and grabs my hand, giving it a squeeze. Then, in a moment of vulnerability, she sighs. "You'll make sure I get home safe, right?" she asks, her voice barely above a whisper. "I wasn't wrong... You're one of the good ones?"

"Yeah, I'll get you home." My heart jolts and I squeeze her hand back. "Always."

She whispers, "Thank you," but it's so soft it's possible I imagined it. Either way, I respond. "Anytime."

There's something about her that's drawn me in, and now, I'm too invested to walk away.

CHAPTER FIVE

HAYLEY

I wake seconds before my alarm early the next morning and I instantly regret not changing it. It's my first day off in over a month. I should be taking advantage.

After switching off the incessant beeping, I roll over and pull the covers up, tucking the doona—or as Amelia so often points out, the *comforter*—under my chin. I've been living here for well over a year now and I still struggle with some of the word differences, while others I've easily embraced. Like garbage instead of rubbish—unless I'm using the term rubbish as a replacement for cursing—and a parking lot instead of a car park. I've even embraced the term "mall." But comforter over doona—nope. And a bathing suit over bathers—no way. Some things just can't be changed.

I toss and turn for God knows how long until it's apparent my mind and body are not in sync. And when I check the time, I groan. Six a.m.

What. The. Fudge.

I've slept later than this on filming days.

Don't tell me this is my life now, with my body clock set to the ass crack of dawn. That's not cool.

Reluctantly getting up, I make myself a coffee and sink into the comfy chair on my balcony. I may not live in the most amazing area, but this balcony is my sanctuary, and if I listen carefully, I can hear the sound of the waves crashing against the shoreline, reminding me of home.

A place I've been neglecting lately—not that my parents have mentioned it.

They're not the type to worry—or communicate, for that matter.

They're caring parents but they've never been the hands-on type. I think me being here is actually easier on them, as they don't feel guilty if time passes and they haven't called. In their mind, they know I love Australia but that I want to establish myself here before visiting home, so they're doing me a favor by giving me space.

But what they don't know is that *I* can sometimes be the worrying type, at least when it comes to my future, and I'm scared that if I leave, I won't have the same luck I've had when I get back. Because make no mistake, my life is one snake-eye dice roll away from falling apart. I've been rolling sixes for the past few months, and I have a feeling my luck is about to run out.

And I've never been a big gambler.

When I've finished my coffee, I push my concerns aside and jump in the shower, standing under the water for way longer than I should, exactly like I always do when I'm hungover. But today, I'm surprisingly good.

My memory is a little patchy but I'm fresh. God, maybe it's not alcohol that gives me a foggy head the next morning. Maybe it's the fact that I usually continue to party in other ways until the early hours of the morning.

More often than not, after a party, I'd only just be going to sleep now. But thanks to my knight in shining armour, I was home at a reasonable time last night. Which reminds me. I should thank him.

Grabbing my phone, I shoot off a text to Amelia asking if she has Reed's number and raid the fridge as I wait for a response, discovering I'm in desperate need of more food.

Being on set every day has its bonuses—namely with craft service providing my main meals. It sucks to think I now have to fend for myself until the next one.

The next one.

My stomach knots as I think about auditioning again. Auditioning here is a lot different from auditioning in Australia where the industry is a hell of a lot smaller and everyone knows everyone else's business. Over here, I could go for hundreds of auditions and never meet the same casting director twice. It's exciting to think about the opportunities available for me, but equally nerve-racking to think I have to prove myself time and time again.

At least until *Jaded Beginnings* releases. I'm told the first official teaser is almost ready for release and they're planning to launch it next week. My life is about to change, and God, I'm hoping that's a good thing.

No...screw that. It *is* a good thing. I'm going to be a star. A household name. The next big thing. And I can't freaking wait.

I'm halfway through a sandwich for breakfast when Amelia texts me back.

> AMELIA: Gotta love him. And yeah, I do. I'll share it with you

She sends me Reed's number, no questions asked—for now, though I have no doubt they'll come later—and I don't waste any time texting him.

> HAYLEY: It's Hayley. Your new bestie. Thanks for looking after me last night

The message turns to read almost immediately and a smile lights up my face.

> REED: Happy to be of service. Anytime

> REED: But I have a question... What does being Hayley Jackman's bestie entail? And is Amelia going to come at me? I don't want to get on her bad side

I snort out a laugh and head over to the couch, falling back into the cushions, kicking my feet up and making myself comfortable.

> HAYLEY: Amelia will be fine. She needs to be able to share me with someone else. I'm a lot for one person to take on

> REED: Nah... I don't believe that. You're you

I smile, but the memories of being told I'm "full-on" or "out of control" are never too far from my mind. I own it. And I don't plan on ever changing. But it still stings a little. Reed's just too decent of a guy to point it out.

> HAYLEY: Have you ever said a bad word about anyone?

I'm sure he'll say yes, but I have no doubt he'll be lying.

> REED: Plenty

> HAYLEY: Care to enlighten me?

> REED: Nope. I'm too nice for that (wink emoji)

I laugh again and take another bite of my peanut butter goodness, a giddy feeling running through me. Other than Amelia, I don't have many close friends, and I crave them. Back home, I was one of the guys until I got my first acting role and was forced into a life of solitude. Not because my friends ditched me, but because of the hours I had to work and travel. I moved to Sydney on my own the day I turned eighteen and life changed. I loved it, but it was a huge shock to the system. And I didn't realize I was missing that close bond until I found Amelia, and now, I'm excited by the prospect of another close friend. If it works out that way.

Reed and I text back and forth for the next couple of hours, until I remember I'm due at Amelia and Luke's in thirty minutes, and I technically don't have a legal licence since I'm no longer on a holiday visa.

After quickly booking an Uber, I throw my *bathers* into my bag and smile. I'm a water baby, and it's been too long since I had time in a pool.

Reed texts me again on my way down the stairs, and I'm still laughing when my building concierge waves to get my attention. "You've got mail today, Miss Jackman," Bill says, excitement in his tone. "A little boy hand delivered it. I think you have a fan."

"Ooh, that's cute. Does he live in the building?" I glance around, but when my eyes meet his again, he shakes his head.

"I haven't seen him before. But maybe he saw you come in here."

"It's a shame I missed him. I could have said hi."

With a lopsided grin, Bill hands me the envelope and a single red rose, and I slide the note into my bag, asking him to hold on to the rose until I get back, since I'm already running late.

"You're a gem, Bill. Have a lovely afternoon."

He nods shyly. "You too, Miss Jackman. See you later."

Smiling, I fight not to cringe. Every time he calls me Miss Jackman a shiver runs through me, but I have to get used to it because I'm getting it a lot more often these days. In Australia, I was Hayley or Hayls, Jacko or Little J, but I was never Miss Jackman. It sounds formal, and that's not me.

My Uber's waiting when I step outside, and I continue to text Reed during the short fifteen-minute drive, only pocketing my phone when I get to Amelia's front door, entering without knocking.

"Ames. I'm here," I call out, announcing my arrival like I normally do.

I hear a shush before Luke pops his head out of the nursery. "I just got Juliet to sleep. If you wake her, she's *your* responsibility."

"That's not the negative you think it is," I say with a grin, taking a step toward her room. "I love Juliet's cuddles."

"Please don't wake her," he pleads and I can't help but giggle...quietly.

Raising my hands in the air, I give him a nod and gesture toward the kitchen. "Yes," Luke mouths. "Amelia's that way."

"Thank you," I mouth back and he rolls his eyes. He loves me. We both know it. But he also loves to act like he doesn't. And the feeling is mutual. He was on my shit list for a while but he managed to prove his worth.

When I enter the kitchen, I find Amelia by the fridge, pulling out a bottle of cider as I lean in for an air kiss. "Hey, babe."

"Hey, you. Here." She passes me the bottle and I lick my lips.

"Thank you. This is *exactly* what I need."

"It's Australian."

"All the best things are."

Luke scoffs from behind me, but when I turn around he's grinning.

"Don't even pretend you don't love the slang I've been teaching you." I roll my eyes. "Amelia told me you've used some of my words."

"*One* good thing then. I don't know about '*all*.'" He uses quote fingers.

"Okay... What about Margot Robbie, AC/DC, Tim Tams, Heath Ledger, The Hemsworth Brothers, Pavlova—"

"Isn't that from New Zealand?"

"Blasphemy." I gasp audibly, shocked at his response. "You did not just say that."

"Why? It's true. Next thing you'll be trying to add Nicole Kidman and Russell Crowe to the list."

"Nicole *is* an Aussie. She may not have been born in Australia, but she's an Aussie. Just ask her."

"Sure, okay. I'll give her a call now."

"Do it. I bet—"

"You two are like siblings," Amelia cuts in, shaking her head. "Do I have to separate you?"

"Honestly, I think that's for the best," I say with a shrug. "Let's retreat to the gazebo."

"Hang on." Luke grabs Amelia's arm and hits me with a fake scowl. "Why do you get Amelia? She's my wife."

"That's why. She needs a break."

Luke laughs and I throw a wink his way before reaching for Amelia's hand, dragging her through the house and out to the pool. They recently had their yard remodeled and I love it here, though it's been a while since I've come.

Given the chance, I could spend hours by the water, listening to the waves crash behind their fence. Much louder than it is from my balcony.

My phone vibrates when I sit down, and when I see Reed's name, I smile preemptively, anticipating his message.

"Who's that?" Amelia asks.

"Nobody."

"Nobody?" she deadpans, her arms crossed over her chest, her expression calling bullshit. "Not a certain football player that looked after you last night?"

"Definitely not." The lie slips easily from my lips, knowing that Amelia will see right through it.

"Well, 'nobody' has my approval for making you smile like that."

I throw my phone in my bag without reading the message and give Amelia my full attention. Since I started working on *Jaded Beginnings*, I've been busier than ever, and while Amelia has never once complained, I feel like I've been neglecting our relationship a little. Though I will say I feel better about doing that now that she has Luke by her side.

"So..." Amelia gets comfortable, tucking her knees up under herself and turning to face me, her expression beaming. "What are you and *not* Reed talking about?"

"Everything and nothing. I think we might be friends."

"Ooh, I can definitely see that. You're different but I think you'd get along well. He has a cheeky side that he hides away under all that seriousness. Not to mention his protective nature. *Plus*, I think the world of both of you so it makes sense."

"Wow." I pause for a beat as though lost for words. "It sure seems like you've given this thought."

"Maybe." She shrugs, ignoring my teasing. "I just worry about his friendship with Bria. I don't know her at all so I can't judge. But if all of us can see that he likes her, how could she possibly miss it?"

"Sometimes when you're that close to something it's not so clear."

Amelia frowns, a deep furrow appearing on her brow. "I hope you're right. Because the alternative is that she's stringing him along."

I internally wince. I'll admit my mind has gone there a few times, but I also want to believe that Reed wouldn't let that happen. Though again, sometimes when you're close to something it's *not so clear*. That sentiment works on both sides.

"What does Luke think?" I ask curiously.

"Luke thinks I should stop wasting so much energy on things that don't concern me."

"Oh, okay." I bite back a smirk. "And yet, he still has that group chat for Easton." *One of his teammates.*

"Shhhh," Amelia shushes me as she laughs. "You're not supposed to know about that."

"Oh, but I do. And I wish I could read the messages. I bet Easton hates it." I haven't had much to do with Easton since he's not all that talkative and I love a chat, but I don't have to talk to him to know that I like him. He protected Amelia from her asshole colleague when he barely knew her, so he's all right in my books.

"Easton *is* hating it." Amelia briefly smiles until her concern takes over. "But I hope they help him. I can't even imagine going through what he is." She frowns and I know it's because she empathises with Easton, comparing their situations.

Easton's going through a bad breakup with his ex, and they have a son together. Amelia and Luke weren't even friends when they initially found out she was pregnant with his baby, so things had the potential to get messy. Amelia would love to do more to help Easton, but she's smart enough to know that her help wouldn't be welcome.

He can be an asshole at times. At least on the surface. I'm sure he's a different guy when you get to know him.

"Have I ever told you that I'm glad you and Luke worked things out?" I say, moving the conversation on. "Custody battles suck."

"Me too, Hayls. I'm not sure I would have had the strength to get through that."

"Bullshit." I shake my head. "You're one of the strongest women I know." Not a lie. She's been through so much and I truly admire her for it.

Amelia smiles before reaching out to pat my arm. "Right back at you, Hayls. Don't ever change."

CHAPTER SIX

HAYLEY

I'm bouncing Juliet on my lap as Amelia regales me with stories of the things I've missed over the past few weeks, mostly about Juliet, telling me about the first time she crawled and how she's trying to say her first word—Mama, much to Luke's annoyance.

"Oh, and there's a Storm charity event coming up in a few weeks," she adds when she's done. "Or maybe it's a month away. Either way, you have to come. It's being organized by Storm's new owner and his daughter."

"Paige D'Angelo?" I ask, shocked. "She's here? In San Francisco?"

"Yes." Amelia's lips twist in confusion. "Do you know her?"

"I thought everyone knew Paige. She's a model and a New York socialite. And she's *gorgeous*. I want to be her when I grow up."

"Isn't she younger than we are? I thought Luke said that her dad wasn't that old."

"That's beside the point." I wave her off. "Plus, I'm younger than you."

"But oh so wise."

"Beyond my years." We both laugh since I am definitely *not* wise, and the conversation moves on to the many unwise things I've done.

"Remember that guy you thought was a cowboy but later found out couldn't ride a horse?"

"Oh my God. Yes! And to think I actually considered dating him."

"Lucky you didn't. Could you imagine going on a date in the country and finding out he's terrified of horses when you're already on horseback?"

"How he thought he was going to star as a cowboy in that TV series is beyond me."

Amelia bites back a grin and I wait for what's coming. "Like you saying you could ice skate?"

Dammit. She got me. "I didn't think it would be that hard. I can surf and rollerblade. I have great balance."

"And a great ass for landing on."

"Oh, she copped a bruising, that's for sure. Just the sight of an ice rink gives me the shivers now. I love water...but frozen water repels me."

"Speaking of...should we take Juliet for a swim?"

My eyes light up as I tickle Juliet, loving the way she giggles. "Can we?"

"Of course. She loves the water."

"That's because she was born in the summer."

"Nope. It was definitely winter."

"Not in Australia." I bounce her again before standing up, watching Amelia's happy expression morph into a fake frown.

"I'm not sure that counts."

"Sure it does, doesn't it, Jules?"

"Jules. I like that."

Now it's my turn to frown. "You haven't called her that?"

"No. Luke calls her Angel. But otherwise, she's Juliet."

"Well, she's Jules to me. Like you're Ames and Luke is Lukey Boy."

"Which he loves."

She thinks she's joking, but deep down I know he really does love it because... "He's the king of nicknames."

"He sure is."

"Jackmeister, you're famous," Luke calls out from the back door, giving me a nickname right on cue, making us both burst out laughing.

"Babe, please tell me you aren't *just* realizing that?" Amelia scoffs and my obnoxious laughter increases.

"*No.* But I just saw the trailer and I have to admit. You don't suck, Hayls."

The trailer? Already? No, he must mean the teaser. My nerves kick in as my heart clenches. This is it. The moment the world starts judging me. Case in point, Luke just did it himself.

"Gee, thanks." I pause, pushing my freakout from my mind. "That means so much coming from the star of the Storm TV show."

"You're welcome." Luke winks and Amelia rolls her eyes before she reaches for my hand.

"Did you know it was going live today?" she asks, her eyes alight with intrigue.

"I knew it was soon, but I didn't think they'd do it a day after we wrapped."

"It was short," Luke cuts in. "About thirty seconds. It didn't give much away."

"It doesn't need to." I internally cringe just thinking about it. "All the die-hard fans know the story. They're just waiting to see if I do Riley justice."

"Did you?" Luke quirks his brow and Amelia gasps.

"Luke!" she responds before I can. "Don't ask her that. Of course she did."

"Hayley?" he questions me again, tilting his head as he waits for an answer.

Amelia groans but it's all good because "I nailed it," I say confidently. I did all I can do.

"Then you have nothing to worry about."

Easier said than done.

"Can we watch it?" Amelia asks with pride. "I've been dying to see how it all turned out."

She came to a few of my shoot days to watch, but seeing us run through a scene over and over versus seeing the finished product is completely different. And I'm just as excited as she is.

"Let's do it. *After* our swim."

Luke brings his tablet out when we've finished in the pool, and I wrap the towel around myself as he finds the clip, my emotions a mix of excitement and intrigue.

"Are you ready?" he asks when Amelia's finished changing Juliet, and they both sit down beside me.

"So ready," Amelia says, but when Luke laughs, we realize he was talking to me.

"I was born for this."

I hold my breath as the clip begins, starting with a close-up of me and

Evan—Riley and Patrick—our eyes locked as the camera pans out to reveal his hand clenched around my neck, a knife by his side.

A stick snaps from behind him and he spins around, giving me the chance to disappear.

The second clip opens with an angel on top of a mountain, wings flapping in the wind. It's hard to tell if it's male or female until the camera zooms in and around to reveal Evan—Patrick—with his hands clenched in his hair, his expression pained.

A montage of ten or so moments comes next, all various stages of Riley and Patrick's relationship before it cuts back to me, racing through the streets as night falls. Turning the corner, I'm met with a flash of something evil before the screen goes blank and the words "coming soon" take over the darkness.

The clip ends and I finally breathe.

"Wow." Amelia's eyes flash to mine, but for the first time, I have nothing to say.

All I can do is repeat her word back to her. "Wow."

"That's some chemistry."

"Maybe on the screen, but in real life...not so much."

"Oh. You went there?"

"Of course she did," Luke cuts in. "It's Evan Rider. Even *I'd* go there."

"Actually, I didn't go there. And you're in luck; I think he'd prefer you." Luke's right though. If the opportunity had presented itself, I definitely would have slept with him. That man is *fine* with a capital F. But it wasn't meant to be and that's probably for the best. We would have had a few awkward scenes to film after the fact.

"I should probably avoid actors I'm working with. The last thing I want is to find myself in a situation where the producers overhear we've hooked up and decide it would be good publicity if we faked a relationship. I've heard of that happening before."

"A fake relationship? Surely that's a myth?" Luke scrunches his nose as though the idea disgusts him.

"Didn't you fake a marriage?" I bite my tongue in amusement.

"It was *never* fake, thank you. Despite what Amelia wanted to believe."

"And it may surprise you," Amelia adds, ignoring his comment, "but fake dating happens *all* the time."

"Where?"

"I don't know. But it does."

"Okay. Sure." Luke jumps up and grabs Juliet from Amelia's arms, giving her a kiss. "I think my daughter has heard enough about dating. Since she won't be doing it until she's thirty, I'm taking her inside."

He walks away and I laugh after him. "Good luck with that, Lukey Boy. I can't wait to see that *not* happen."

Amelia insists on watching the *Jaded Beginnings* teaser three more times before I call it a day.

"I can't get over how amazing this is, Hayley," she says, pulling me into a hug. "The lighting, the cinematography, the sets. It's perfect."

"What about the acting?" Trust Amelia to look at all the behind-the-scenes work. She's going to be an amazing director when she finally gets her time to shine.

"You know you're incredible, Hayley. But if you need me to say it... You're incredible."

"Why, thank you. Let's hope the critics feel the same."

"They will. I have no doubt."

Luke offers to drive me home, and it's not until I get inside that I remember Reed's message, and I scrounge around in my bag to find my phone, locating the fan mail Bill gave me instead.

My lips pull into a smile as I slip my nail beneath the seal, ripping it open to find neat, non-childlike handwriting.

Hayley,

Congratulations on what I know is about to become a life-changing part for you. I can't wait for the movie to finally be released. You were born to play Riley and you're going to be a star.

Not long now until we all get to see your beautiful face on the big screen.

Your biggest supporter

X

As sweet as that is, it *wasn't* written by a child. And if it was, and a parent helped, I'd have to question what kind of person is letting them watch my movie? It's *not* PG13. Or even close to that.

Either way, I can't deny it's a nice positive note, so I fold it back up and slip it into my top drawer. With the negativity that's bound to come my way now that the teaser's been released, I might need it one day.

With a smile on my face, I perch on the edge of my bed and grab my phone, ready to check Reed's message.

But before I can, it buzzes in my hand, with my agent asking if I've seen the teaser. We rapidly message back and forth, and it's only after we're done that I finally get to Reed's text.

> REED: Tell Amelia I said hi. But not Luke. I see that guy enough

I giggle to myself and instantly regret not reading this while I was there. I would have taken great joy in passing that message along. Turns out Reed wasn't lying about being nice all the time. There's more to Mr. Coombs than meets the eye.

> HAYLEY: Oh we are definitely meant to be friends

I click send and throw my phone on my bed, not expecting him to reply right away considering it's been hours since we last texted. But I'm wrong. My phone buzzes before I've had a chance to step away.

> REED: Lucky for you, I'm holding auditions on Friday. I'll book you in for ten

A laugh bursts out of me and I fall back onto the mattress, a giddy smile on my lips. *So much more to him than meets the eye.* And I can't wait to discover it.

Chapter Seven

REED

For the next few weeks, Hayley and I text regularly, making promises to catch up in person without it ever actually happening. Apart from watching my first game—without telling me she was there—Hayley's been busy with pickups for her movie and gearing up for the promotional tour. As for me, I'm at the beginning of the season, pushing myself to my limits as we fight for our second Super Bowl win, desperate to prove we're not the one-hit wonders people think we are.

We've both barely had the chance to breathe, let alone see each other.

But that's all about to change because tonight's the Storm charity event, where we'll both be in attendance, and I'm looking forward to spending time with her again.

"Does this look okay?" Bria cuts into my thoughts, holding a dress up in front of her. I open my mouth to respond until I notice she's practically naked behind it, ridding me of all logical thought. My jaw twitches but I fight not to let it drop. *What the fuck is she doing?*

"It's perfect." My goddamn voice cracks and I internally curse myself before subtly clearing it. "It matches my shirt."

"I know." She grins proudly. "Why do you think I chose it?"

I smile but I'm once again thrown by her actions. *Isn't that what couples do?*

With her own sweet little grin, Bria turns on her heels, flashing me her ass in panties that ride halfway up her cheeks, and I groan to myself. If I didn't know better, I'd stalk after her and throw her onto the bed, but I'm well aware that won't bode well for me. She's not that kind of girl.

And I'm yet to talk to her about my feelings.

I was planning to bring it up this weekend since we're spending the night in a shared hotel suite—with two bedrooms of course. I even had an entire speech prepared. But something has shifted in our relationship, and now I'm almost certain that it would be the end of us.

She's confusing the hell out of me with the way she contradicts herself, telling me how much she values our friendship, then doing things like showing me her ass hours later.

And for the first time, she's started talking to me about other guys. Or more specifically, one other guy. It's driving me crazy. She says they're "just friends" but it's obvious she wants more, convincing me that my feelings are probably just as clear.

Once again, I'm in limbo.

"What time do we have to leave?" she calls out from the bathroom, seconds before the water switches on.

"We've got an hour."

"Perfect. I'll be ready."

"Great."

I fall onto the bed and close my eyes, throwing a pillow over my face so I can audibly groan.

Tonight is going to be torture. I can already feel it.

I'm not sure how long I'm lying there, but at five, my alarm goes off, reminding me that a car is picking us up in thirty minutes, prompting me to finally get my ass up to begin getting ready.

Since I showered earlier, all I have to do is get dressed and fix my hair, so I'm still ready well before Bria is. And when she finally steps out of the bathroom, I freeze.

My god, she looks beautiful.

Correction—tonight is going to be hell. I need to know where I stand.

After a torturous drive to the venue—with me trying hard not to look at Bria's breasts in her low-cut dress—we've barely been inside for ten minutes when she pulls me aside and smiles coyly. "You've had a bit of time to check out the guests. What do you think? Am I going home solo tonight?" She waggles her eyebrows and— What. The. Fuck?

I huff out a laugh to hide my shock and work hard to keep the attitude out of my voice. "What does that mean?"

"I'm just curious if there are any girls that pique your interest for later." She bites her lip. "You know what I mean."

Again...what?

This is new. And I have no fucking clue how to take it. Is she fishing for a compliment? Or hoping I'll say yes?

"Since when have I *ever* ditched you for a random hookup?"

"Never," she confirms. "But you don't have to babysit me. I know some of the guys tonight and this is your team's event. You should mingle and have fun."

I am so fucking confused.

"Do you want the room to yourself, Bria?" *Is that what she's alluding too?* "All you have to do is as—"

"No," she cuts me off. "That's not... Never mind. I just wanted you to know I'd be okay."

"Okay." I nod, but since I'm not really sure what I'm nodding about, I change the subject. "I'm going to the bar. Do you want something?" I definitely *need* something and I think it's best I step away from this conversation for a second.

"I'll come." Bria smiles, grabbing my arm and... God, I'm getting whiplash. What does she want?

After knocking back a shot each, we chat with a few of my teammates before checking out the auction items. Together. Bria doesn't leave my side. But when the lights dim and the music gets louder, she's the first one on the dance floor, immediately grabbing my teammate Wyatt as she passes him, not even bothering to ask me.

I let out an exasperated sigh, catching Luke's inquisitive gaze before he mouths something that looks a lot like "are you okay?"

I'm not.

But I'm not about to tell him that, so instead, I give him a thumbs-up and grin.

While Bria dances the night away, I seek out Hayley, meeting her eyes a few times as I chat with various people, making sure I do my bit to keep potential donors happy, hoping they give to the cause.

I'm finishing up a conversation with Thomas and his wife, Lainey, when Hayley walks outside, and I immediately decide to follow her. We've been sneaking glances all night, but haven't had the chance to talk.

And I really want to talk to her.

I manage a single step before a hand wraps around my bicep and I stumble to a halt.

"Where are you going?" Bria asks innocently, but I don't miss the way her eyes flash to the door Hayley disappeared through.

"I'm catching up with a friend. I thought you were dancing."

"I was but I've had enough for the moment. Want to find somewhere quiet to sit?"

Fuck. I internally wince, torn between my options. On one hand, Bria's been flirting with my teammates for most of the night so I should walk away, but on the other, she's here now and...nope. *Dammit.*

"I'll come and find you in a little bit, okay?"

"What?" Her eyes practically bulge out of her head.

"I told you, I'm going to chat with a friend. There's a lounge area through that door. I think Amelia went that way."

"I barely know her."

"Since when has that bothered you?" I snap before reeling it in. "What I mean is that you've been chatting with random people all night."

"Is that a problem?"

"No. I'm just stating a fact. I'll come and find you when I'm done."

Bria pouts and when I ignore it, she huffs as I turn to walk away, glancing back to find her pissed-off expression.

I can't win tonight. She tells me she's fine on her own but then gets angry when I leave her.

Talk about mixed signals.

Taking a deep breath, I continue on my way and head for the balcony, finally relaxing when I make it outside, my eyes immediately locking with Hayley's.

We share a smile and I take her in, noting her arms wrapped tightly around herself as she leans back against the railing, watching me.

A gust of wind blows her hair across her face when she steps forward to meet me and I frown.

"Where's your coat?" I ask, shrugging out of my jacket, securing it around her when she joins me, grateful when she takes it without argument.

"I didn't bring one." She thanks me with a smile. "I don't have anything that matches this dress, and I wasn't wearing another one."

"I don't blame you." I openly ogle her outfit. "That dress is stunning."

"The dress?"

"And the actress wearing it." I wink.

"Why, thank you, Reed." She giggles. "That's so lovely of you to say. Are you having a good night?"

"Do you want the truth or..."

"What about I guess?"

"Two truths and a lie?"

"You know it."

"Okay. I've had two drinks spilled on me, I got stuck talking to a random businessman for over forty-five minutes, and I've been looking forward to this moment since I arrived."

"Okay." Hayley's eyes widen at my immediate response. "You're getting better at this. But...since I can see a splash of red on the bottom of your shirt, I can safely say you've had at least *one* drink spilled on you."

"Unless I did it myself."

"Ohhh, true. *Dammit*. I'm going to say...this *isn't* the moment you've been looking forward to since you arrived. Because Bria is absolutely beautiful in that—"

"Wrong."

"Wrong?" Hayley fakes a gasp, her hand flying to her mouth in true actress style, if maybe a little bit over-the-top. "This moment. Here. Now?"

"Yep." I pop the *p*. "What can I say? You've grown on me."

"Likewise. Would you believe I came out here hoping you'd follow me?"

"You couldn't just come over and talk to me?"

"I wasn't sure you'd want me to. With Bria around." She shrugs and I sigh audibly.

"You make it sound like she's my guard dog or something."

"No, that's not it. I don't know, it's just—"

"You stayed away *for* me." Because like everyone else, she could see how fucked up my situation was.

"I did." She smiles, though a wince would certainly be more fitting. "And now I'm here."

"You are. How about we celebrate with a drink?" She bends down gracefully and stands up again with a full bottle of Jack Daniels in her hand, a cheeky smile on her lips.

I huff out a laugh as my eyes widen. "Something tells me you're not supposed to have that."

"Tell that to the bartender that gave it to me."

"What did he get in return?" The question flows out of me before I realize what I'm asking. But when Hayley says, "My number," I shake my head as another laugh bursts out of me.

"Did he happen to give you any glasses?"

"Just the one. I couldn't exactly tell him I wanted to share it with another man."

"Very true. You're not just a pretty face."

"Oh, there's so much to learn about me, Reed. So much."

"I don't doubt that at all. You take the glass; I'll take the bottle."

Hayley grins, handing over said bottle as she lifts her glass for me to fill. "Such a gentleman."

"Always."

"And you don't think you should have told him that?" Hayley struggles to speak between laughter as I tell her about the time Luke was flirting with our teammate's *very* off-limits sister, after spending the better part of a month complaining about Thomas and Lainey.

"What happened? Please tell me that your teammate saw it."

"He sure did. But it turns out, he'd sent his sister over so that Luke would quit whining about Thomas. We all knew Luke didn't care that Thomas and Lainey were together. In fact, I think he secretly loved it. But that guy craves being the center of attention and he was using that to keep him there."

"Oh, I am loving this. I need more Luke stories. Amelia will die for these. She loves to tease him."

"Still? Even though they're married with a kid?"

"Hell, yeah. People shouldn't change when they get married."

"Very true. I guess I just assumed they were different behind the scenes."

"Nope. But something tells me you are."

I take another swig of Jack and smile, bopping Hayley on the nose. "Wouldn't you love to know?"

"Yes!" she squeals, making me chuckle as I top off her glass.

A fresh gust of wind blows through the space and Hayley shivers, tightening my jacket around her.

"I think it's time we went inside. You're shaking."

"I'm fine. It's just a breeze and I have your jacket."

"True, but you're practically naked beneath it. I'm well aware of how thin the material is on those dresses."

Hayley has her glass pressed to her lips as I respond but lowers it with wide eyes. "And how would you know that?"

"I've taken a few off in my time."

Doing a double take, Hayley puts her glass down and grins. "Now this I've got to hear. But first...have you ever slept with Bria?"

"I haven't." I snort. "We kissed in college, but she freaked out and begged me to pretend it never happened. She valued our friendship too much."

"Ouch."

"Yep."

"So it wasn't Bria's dresses you were removing?"

"It was random hookups after events like these."

"So we're not as different as some might think. I was right. We're going to be great friends. But I kind of like it being our little secret. It's been fun alone out here. Like we're sneaking around."

A soft chuckle rumbles from my belly. "Fine by me. I'm ninety-nine percent sure that if the guys knew, they'd start joking about me falling in love with another one of my friends."

Hayley grabs my arm as she laughs much louder than I did. "Your teammates are assholes."

"Nah, they're good guys. They just love to give each other shit. And this is the only thing they've got on me."

"Because you're squeaky clean."

"You know it." I pretend to shoot her with a finger gun and she giggles until her expression turns curious.

"You do love her though, right?"

"I don't know about love." I sigh, my expression tight as I grip the back of my neck. "But I like her. A lot. I'm playing the long game. It's a talent I possess."

Hayley snorts out a laugh before covering her mouth with her hands. "Shit. Sorry. I wasn't laughing at your feelings. I was laughing at..." She trails off when I raise an eyebrow. "Actually, never mind. It's awful no matter how I say it. But I didn't mean it to be."

"I get it. I do. It's a little pathetic. I'm a twenty-eight-year-old hopelessly falling for a woman that doesn't feel the same."

"You forgot to add that you're a twenty-eight-year-old *football star* that could have any woman he wanted."

I smirk and she laughs again.

"Anyone I wanted, you say?"

"Obviously not *anyone* or you'd have *Bria*." She mouths Bria's name as the back door opens and a few guys walk out. I pause for a second until my gaze passes over their faces with no recognition, and relief fills me.

"I'm just a huge source of entertainment for you, aren't I?" I deadpan, making her smile. "Is that why you want to be friends?"

"Among other reasons." Hayley shrugs and I can't help giving her a friendly shove. "What?" She throws her hands in the air. "I can't help it if your messy love life brings me joy. It's nice to know there are others out there in a similar boat."

"Oh, so you're also fighting unrequited love?"

"Hell, no." She mocks horror. "That's never been an issue for me. But the messy love life...that's something I can relate to."

"Mine's less of the messy and more of the nonexistent variety."

"Actually, I'm the same. Though mine's by choice." She frowns and I mimic her expression as my stomach knots.

"Is there a story there?"

"Not one I'm interested in sharing right now. I think I might be a little tipsy."

"A little? I passed 'a little' a while back. You're a bad influence, Hayley Jackman."

"And you're a good one. I think we're going to be perfect for each other."

I stare at her for a moment as Bria's angry expression flits across my mind. "You know, I think you're right. To new friendships." I hold up the almost empty bottle, and Hayley holds up her glass.

"To new friendships." She cheers the bottle a little awkwardly before adding, "in secret," and I burst out laughing when she winks.

This could be fun.

Chapter Eight

HAYLEY

I knock back another shot of whiskey and shake as the liquid warms my soul. "Do you think we should sneak out to the garden?" I ask, my eyes flashing to Reed's.

The balcony we're on overlooks a beautiful rose garden that's marked as a look-don't-touch situation. But really, what damage could we do?

When I grin, Reed's head drops back as he laughs. "It's the signs, right? You don't like being told you can't do something."

Yes. Ugh. This man gets me. "Why have a garden if people can't explore it? That's just crazy."

"And how do you suppose we get down there?"

Ooh, he's not saying no. I knew I liked him. "Easy. We jump the railing." I shrug and Reed laughs even louder.

"Easy for me, maybe. But in that dress." He motions to my outfit. "I can't see it happening."

I glance down at my skintight number. *Oh, Reed, you have no idea.* Hitching the silk up to my waist, I spin before he can look down, knowing his long jacket will hide my ass, then I climb. I'm two rails up when strong palms wrap around my waist, pulling me down before I'm pressed into the woodwork.

"Whatcha—"

"Act like you're watching the stars," Reed's deep voice rasps in my ear and I shiver at the sound.

"Why?" I ask, swallowing a lump in my throat, distracting myself so I don't picture him whispering sweet nothings instead.

"If you don't, you're about to get busted."

I giggle but do as he asked, pointing to a random constellation. "And there you have the flying running back next to the wildcat."

Reed chuckles, giving my waist a squeeze. "That's a new one but I can totally see it."

"Right? I'm impressed with the way the stars highlight his generous muscles. He's hot."

"Are you sure you're not looking in a mirror? That's definitely me."

Leaning back against his chest, I stare up at him with fake confusion. "You're a running back? I had no idea."

"Sure you didn't." He smirks. "I'm the running back and you're the wildcat," he muses. "You can't fool me."

"What?" My confusion turns real. I hadn't actually meant for that to be me, but it's not far off base. "You're—"

"We're closing the balcony in ten minutes," a voice echoes through the night, halting the comeback that was about to fly out of my mouth. "If you need fresh air, there's a porch at the front of the building."

"What?" I whisper. "No fair."

"To think, if we'd jumped the railing we may have been locked out here."

Spinning around, my eyes widen at the prospect. "That would have made it so much more exciting. She's going back inside. Let's—" I reach for the railing but Reed grabs me again, securing me tightly in his arms.

"I think it's time we went inside."

My lips form a pout of their own accord even though he's right. "Okay, fine." I move around him to walk toward the door, but he grabs my wrist and spins me to face him, making my heart jolt in excitement. I never pictured Reed as the wrist-grabbing type.

"Lower the dress, Hayls." His voice strains as he closes his eyes, and I don't miss the demand in his tone.

"Oops." My skin heats. I'd definitely forgotten my panties were on show. Reed releases his grip, and I fix my dress before removing his jacket from my shoulders.

"You can look now. I'm decent."

"Thank you."

"Here's your jacket."

"Keep it. It's—"

"Secret friends, remember?" Tossing it over his shoulder, I push him back slightly, grinning when his brows rise, ignoring the sharp pang I get from his protectiveness. "Wait five minutes before you come inside. I'm heading back to the dance floor."

"Yes, ma'am." He nods with a smirk and a giggle bursts out of me.

"Thank you. Have a good night."

"You too." He glances away as I turn, but not before flashing me the most genuine smile I think I've ever experienced, and my chest tightens. I've never met a guy like Reed, and something tells me I'm lucky I did.

As soon as I walk inside, I find Amelia and my new friend, Paige D'Angelo, busting moves on the dance floor, and that's where I'm meant to be. Shaking my hips, I sidle up to them and grin.

"What have I missed?"

"Nothing much." Paige shrugs. "I think Dad's going to do his grand speech soon, but otherwise this is it."

"Well, I happen to love this."

Paige and I became fast friends when we met at the guys' game a few weeks back. I wasn't ashamed to admit I've been stalking her for a few years on social media, and lucky for me, she didn't mind. She often posts about her charity work, and tonight, she's proven it's not just for show, putting on an amazing event for the team.

Amelia glances around, her eyes narrowed, and I have no doubt she's trying to work out where I came from. "Where have you been?" she asks, right on cue. "What did *I* miss?" She raises her eyebrows.

"Just talking to a friend."

"A friend?" She sucks her lips into her mouth, but it's impossible to miss her knowing smile. Busted. I'm going to have to add Amelia to my Reed bubble.

Shaking my head, I change the subject, moving the attention back to Paige. "Any guys take your fancy, Paige?"

"Huh?" She frowns as though in a few short seconds her mind had drifted elsewhere.

"Never mind." I think she just answered my question, but who has she found?

"Where's that man of yours, Amelia? He owes me a—"

"Jack-O'-Lantern. You're back." Enter the man of the hour, Luke. Never too far from his wife's side.

"I'm back. And *you* owe me a shot."

"That I do. A bet is a bet. But..." He trails off and I roll my eyes. I bet Luke that he couldn't walk past a mirror without checking himself out, and it took him all of three minutes to fail. "In fairness, I didn't realize the mirror was there."

"It was in our hallway, Luke," Amelia points out, taking my side.

"Yes, but it's the one you put up last week. Sue me for forgetting."

"Either way." I raise my empty hands and signal toward the bar, making Amelia laugh.

Luke huffs in fake amusement before he reluctantly darts off to the bar, looking as grumpy as Easton—like the drinks aren't all free—and when he returns, he has shots for everyone, and he's brought friends. "Ladies, this is our newest rookie, Landon. And you know the other guys." He gestures to Rhett and Carter, who I spent a lot of time with at my wrap party. "And East—" Before he's even finished his name, Easton wanders away, adding to the proof that he's not a social guy.

With a shrug of his shoulders, Luke moves his attention back to the rookie. "Landon, this is my beautiful wife, Amelia," he introduces her. "And these are her friends." He shrugs and Amelia lightly punches his arm, beating me to it.

"It's lovely to meet you, Landon," Amelia says sweetly. "This is Hayley, and this is your owner's daughter, Paige. She's responsible for this amazing event."

"Nice to meet you all. And Paige, you've done a great job. For my first big fundraiser, it's a memorable one."

"Thank you, Landon."

His eyes flash to mine and he smiles shyly, prompting me to wink before I turn to Rhett. "Want to dance?" I ask, already holding out my hand.

"You betcha." He spins me into his hold and I let out a squeal as my gaze finds Reed walking toward the group. He shakes his head with a grin and I smile back, our eyes locked until Bria rushes to catch up with him, dragging his attention away.

"How many dances do I get?" Rhett asks, drawing my gaze back to his. "Because if it's just one, let me request something."

"You can have as many dances as you want, Rhett. I'm not going anywhere."

Rhett and I dance until Paige's dad calls us to attention, giving his grand speech, and when he's done, the masses head toward the exit.

But I'm not ready to call it a night.

And I know I'm not the only one.

"Think we can keep this party going?" I ask Paige when she returns from outside. "There are still quite a few people milling around."

"I'm game. I've got the venue until two a.m. and we're paying the DJ by the hour."

"Perfect. I think these guests still have heavy pockets. It's time we lightened them."

Paige's eyes widen before she laughs. "Do your worst, Hayley. Or should I say best?"

I wink before spinning around to face the DJ, giving him the thumbs-up. "Get ready for a record night of donations, Paige. Keep the drinks flowing."

"I'm on it."

She walks away as the dance music starts up again, prompting a few guests to pause at the threshold and come back inside. I hit the dance floor as I search for Reed, curious if he's staying. But when I find him, he's walking away with Bria, her hands flapping rapidly while his shoulders tense. I cringe on his behalf. I would hate to be him right now. She does *not* look happy. Talk about high maintenance.

"I'm here." Carter cuts into my thoughts, his hand out for me to take. "Are you ready for that dance?"

I spin on my heel and smile. "I sure am. And I appreciate you staying. We need these people to keep drinking and spending. The night's still young."

Carter nods and his next words break my heart. "My aunt had Parkinson's too. I'll do anything for this cause."

"I'm sorry to hear that, Carter, but I'm happy you can help. Paige needs us."

"Let's get this party started. I mean...let's kick it off again and dance the night away."

My head throbs when I wake up and my throat aches like I've been traipsing through the desert. I groan as I pat the bedside table in search of some water. But all I can feel is the night mask that I forgot to put on and my phone. Both useless in my current condition.

My eyes stick like they're glued shut when I try to open them, but that's not such a bad thing, I'm not ready for it to be morning. Just the sliver of light peeking through my lids has me cringing.

What a night.

I didn't think I had that much to drink, but I forgot about the bottle I shared with Reed. It was going down so easily and...*I'm an idiot.*

Thinking back on the night, I remember everything up until Paige's dad left and then things got out of hand. At least they did for me. Having said that, my memory's sketchy from that point on.

Though I do remember someone walking me to my door.

Or did they come in?

Patting the bed next to me, I expect to find it occupied and sigh in relief when I come up empty. Only that means I'll have to get up and get myself a drink.

Blowing out a breath, I force my eyes open and find the room bathed in a bright yellow glow and my dress from last night pulled up around my waist. *Again.* Who would have thought I'd be in this position twice, flashing my panties, and still not get any action? I've lost my touch.

Rolling to the edge of the bed, I grab my phone and find a glass of water and a Tylenol on the other side, just past the point of where my fingers could reach. And I know I didn't put them there. I'm not that prepared.

"Ames?" I call out. "Are you here?"

I'm met with silence and giggle to myself. She left hours before me and she has a daughter. Gone are the days of our sleepovers.

Checking the time, I find a message from Reed and smile.

REED: If you're looking for your shoes, I left
them on the other side of your bed so you
wouldn't trip over them. And I want to state for
the record that I did not pull your dress up. That
was all you

I snort so loud that I cover my mouth until a thought hits me... Reed
was here? He came back to the event? For me?

The idea of that warms my heart.

I'm a lucky girl. My knight in shining armour strikes again.

CHAPTER NINE

REED

My back aches when I wake up and as I try to roll over, I realize I fell asleep on my belt. Groaning, I open my eyes and startle, coming face-to-face with Bria staring down at me.

"What are you doing?" I rasp, clearing my throat as I sit up.

"You came back?" Her lips pull into a smile.

"I did."

Despite telling me she'd be fine on her own, Bria wasn't all that thrilled with me ditching her for the hour I spent with Hayley last night. But she was at least nice enough to wait until the speeches were over before causing a scene.

Before that, she'd been her usual self, and I don't know if it's because I'm not equipped to handle the whiplash, or it's something else entirely, but for the first time...I didn't apologize. And I'm still not sure if I should, though I'm certain she'll expect it.

"Bria, I have no idea—"

"I'm sorry."

"What?" *I didn't see that coming.*

She sighs as she shoves my legs over and sits down. "I was a brat last night." I nod subtly in the hope that it will cause less trouble than agreeing with her. But I do agree... she was. Holding my breath, I wait for her response, but when she laughs, I relax.

"What happened?"

"The guy I've been seeing kind of screwed me over," she admits. "And I didn't handle it as well as I should have. Instead of talking to you about it, I reacted poorly. I'm not making excuses, but I was stuck between feeling vulnerable and wanting to say a big fuck you to love. I shouldn't have taken it out on you."

Love? Jesus Christ. She barely knew that guy.

"And by love," she continues as though answering my unspoken question, "I don't mean that I loved *him* so you can wipe the disgust from your face." She raises a brow and I force a grin.

"Sorry, I was worried for a second. I thought you were smarter than that."

"I am. I don't fall in love that easily. What I mean is that I wanted to flirt and have fun, but I also selfishly wanted my friend."

For fuck's sake. I smile through my heartache and reach for her hand. "I'm good, but I'm not a mind reader. Next time, just tell me what you want and I'll be there for you. Like always."

"I will. And I know. So... Hayley Jackman, huh?" Bria waggles her eyebrows and the ache in my chest deepens. *What the fuck am I doing?* Bria and I are friends. And that's all we'll ever be. I wanted answers this weekend and I got them.

It's time to move the fuck on.

"I still don't know her that well, but we had a good chat last night."

"And..." She smiles in anticipation.

"And that's it." I shrug because I'm not lying. We chatted and nothing more. Unless you consider the fact that I went back to the venue to check on her and found her blind drunk as she danced with one of my teammates. Thankfully, she picked a good one. Or at least, she picked one that was too young and naive to ever believe he had a shot with her. He even moved aside graciously when he saw me coming.

I doubt she'll even remember I was there or that I took her home, until she reads my text. Did I cockblock her for a second time? Possibly. But again, I couldn't leave. And it didn't take much convincing on my part when I offered.

"I think she's pretty," Bria adds, her wide smile stabbing me in the chest.

"She's definitely something. But if anything, we're just friends."

"For now." She winks before her face turns serious again. "Am I forgiven?"

"Of course. But next time—"

"I'll talk to you about my problems instead of being a bitch."

"Not what I was going to say, but close enough." I shrug and Bria shoves me away before standing up and bouncing on her toes.

"Breakfast? I'm paying."

"You're on. I think I deserve lobster."

"Hmm. How about bacon and eggs?"

An hour later, we're sitting down to breakfast—bacon and eggs, not lobster—when Bria's phone rings and she steps away to take the call.

Following her lead, I grab my phone and check my messages since it's been buzzing in my pocket from the moment I sat down. Among the sea of messages from the group chat I share with a few of the guys on my team—Luke, Easton and our retired teammate, Dylan— there's a message from Hayley.

Smiling, I open hers first.

> HAYLEY: Did you at least look? You deserve a panty peek after getting me home safely. Again

My body quakes as I laugh silently. Only Hayley. She's so different from anyone I've ever met. It's refreshing.

> REED: Damn. I didn't. Next time I will. Now that I have your permission

I'm joking. I'd never do that. And despite us barely knowing each other, I trust that she gets that about me.

> HAYLEY: As if. I doubt you'd peek even if I begged

> REED: Look how well you know me already

> HAYLEY: You're too good for this world. Thank you for taking me home

> REED: Anytime

I'm smiling when Bria sits down, and when I look up, she's staring at me with a mix of excitement and uncertainty. "Is that her?"

"Who?"

"Hayley."

"It was."

It should be strange that Bria knows who I was with without me actually telling her, but I have no doubt Hayley's on her way to being a household name. They've only released a teaser of her movie and people are already raving about it.

"I bet she wanted you to take her home."

With her expression unreadable, Bria takes a sip of her coffee and I hit her with the truth.

"I did."

"What?" She chokes on her drink. "After you left? And then you came back?"

She fakes a smile to appear calm, but the panic in her voice says otherwise.

"I went back to the event to see if I could help with anything, and when Hayley was still there, I made sure she got home safely. I walked her inside, got her settled, and then I went straight back to the hotel to make sure you got home today."

The tension leaves Bria's body and her shoulders drop. "You really are a gentleman."

"Yep. That's me." *But I'm starting to wish I wasn't.*

"Do you think you'll see her again?"

My phone buzzes and when I note that it's Hayley, I open the message before answering.

> HAYLEY: Are you free to catch up this week?
> We should go somewhere

I stifle a smile as I type out my response.

> REED: I might be. 😉 Day somewhere or night somewhere?

Glancing up as Hayley types her response, I curse audibly when I find Bria staring back at me. "Fuck. I'm sorry. That was rude." Pocketing my phone, I grab my fork and shove a mouthful of eggs into my mouth, smiling awkwardly.

"You like her?" She grins and my eyes widen.

"What?" I shake my head as I laugh out loud. Is it actually possible that she's oblivious to my feelings? To think, she claims to know me better than I know myself.

"As a friend, sure." I shrug and shovel bacon into my mouth next, suddenly needing this breakfast to be over.

"Like me?" Bria asks, her voice soft and uncertain.

"Nah, not like you," I say honestly because my feelings are vastly different. "Not yet."

Bria's eyes widen and it confuses me until I realize what I said. *Not yet.* Does she think I mean that I'm going to replace her as my best friend, or is that look because she knows how I feel and now thinks I'm falling for Hayley?

More to the point... why do I always overanalyze everything?

Fuck, my life is a mess.

Why the hell can't it be easy?

"It will never be the same, Bria. You don't have to worry about that." She breathes a sigh of relief and I laugh, though I'm not at all sure it's funny. All I know is that I'm fucked.

After texting back and forth with Hayley over the next few days, we finally arrange to meet up the following Tuesday, since we both have the day off.

But like last time, we don't set anything in stone, and I don't hear from her until I'm on my way into the stadium Sunday, getting in the zone for our game against Detroit.

> Hayley: I know the perfect place to go

I smile to myself and respond before entering the building, surprised we're actually making plans.

> Reed: Great! Where are we going?

Hayley: It's a surprise. Pick me up at ten

Hayley: And pack your bathers, but if you're
good you won't get wet

I reply with a single question mark, but of course she leaves me hanging, and... *What the fuck does that even mean?*

One of my teammates walks past and holds the door for me, but I wave him off, quickly typing "bathers" into the search engine to make sure that term includes board shorts. And thankfully it does.

But what the hell are we doing? It's October. And while temperatures would usually be mild at this time of year, we're in the middle of an unusual cold snap, so it's not exactly swimming weather. Or beach weather in general. We can't be swimming because then I'd be getting wet. *Or does she want me to stand-up paddleboard?*

I'm still racking my brain when I get to my locker, so I'm lost in thought when Thomas appears beside me. "I need a favor."

"Huh?" I say, distracted.

"A favor?"

"Oh, sure, man. Sorry. I was in another world. Hit me with it." While the guys assume I say yes to everything asked of me, I don't. But there are some people I'll help without hesitation, and Thomas is one of them.

"I think Landon could use an unofficial mentor on the team, and I'd love for you to be that guy."

A mentor? "Really? Me?" I've been playing for a few years, but I'm not as seasoned as some of the other guys here. I would have thought there would be better options.

"Yes, you." He chuckles. "He needs someone who's going to take it seriously and someone killing it in the game. You fit both. What do you think?"

"I think that sounds good. I'd be happy to help. Just let me know what I have to do." I'm not sure why, but the thought of mentoring feels like a huge responsibility to me, and while I'm far from perfect, I think I'm up for the challenge.

"Thanks, man." Thomas smiles genuinely, and maybe a little relieved. "Sorry I interrupted your thoughts."

Said thoughts immediately drift back to the forefront of my mind and I huff out a laugh. "All good, man. Actually, maybe you could help. Do you know something that requires trunks, but doesn't mean you'll get wet?"

"What?" He hits me with a puzzled expression and my laughter increases.

"My thoughts exactly."

"Are you doing a crossword or something? Wait, what about a yacht or a boat? Wouldn't someone wear a bathing suit even if they're not going swimming?"

A yacht? Nice thought. I can handle that. "Here's hoping. Thanks, Thomas."

"No problem." His brows furrow as he walks away and I chuckle to myself. Only two days until I find out. For now...it's time to get my head in the game.

E aston catches the ball in his grasp and I race forward to block Detroit's cornerback, getting in his way before he has the chance to tackle.

With seconds to spare in the first half, Easton rushes forward, beating the whistle to the end zone, scoring a touchdown to finally put us ahead.

And it couldn't have come soon enough, especially considering we'd all assumed this one would be easy.

Never assume.

That's been my motto as a player for years, but after winning the Super Bowl, I got cocky. As did the rest of the team.

After a quick but tame celebration, I run off the field beside Luke, mentally preparing for Coach's "get your heads out of your asses" spiel. But when Luke waves to one of the private suites, I follow his gaze, smiling when I spot a blonde staring back at us. She waves subtly and I glance away, grinning to myself. Once again, Hayley failed to mention she'd be coming to my game. But somehow that doesn't surprise me. I have a feeling being friends with Hayley is going to be a wild ride, full of surprises.

And it might be exactly what I need.

Even if she does keep me on my toes.

CHAPTER TEN

HAYLEY

Reed stares at the wakeboard park in front of us and shakes his head. "This is what we drove two hours for?" He laughs to himself. "You're on your own, Hayls. I'm happy to watch. But—"

"Come on, it will be fun." Not knowing what I had planned has been eating away at him, and I almost gave in a few times. But holding off and seeing the look on his face just now was totally worth it. "I don't expect you to wakeboard. We can do the aqua course instead. If you don't fall off, you won't get wet." I shrug and Reed's laughter increases.

"I understand your cryptic message now, but it's still a no. I can't afford to break anything."

I pout, but I get it. I probably should have thought of that. "Okay, fine. I have a plan B."

"No way." Reed raises a hand and steps forward, spinning me around until we're facing the inflatable aqua course. "We are *not* leaving until you show me what you've got." He points to the course as a young kid slips off the top of the slide, plunging into the cold water. "I'm going to rent that floating cabana over there." He points to the cabana. "Then I'm going to kick back and enjoy the view."

I stifle a snort and shove him away. "Is that so?"

"Yep. I'll even buy you lunch when you're done."

"How very kind of you."

"I thought so." He bites back a grin.

"You're really not going to participate?" I ask, my brows raised in anticipation.

"I'm really not."

"Your loss." I shrug and walk over to the cabana, stripping my hoodie over my head and throwing it his way, doing the same with my pants, standing before him in my string bikini. "Mind my stuff. I'm going to kick some teenage kid's ass."

I jog away to the sound of his chuckle, and it doesn't take long for a group of young guys to welcome me into their pack. Especially when one of them recognizes me.

"Fuck, you're that chick, from that thing." He waves his arm in front of me, the chains on his wrist jingling.

His cute friend smacks him over the head.

"Do you mean the actress from that movie?" I ask, unable to hold back my grin.

"Exactly." He clicks his fingers and his mates groan.

"That's me. Who's up for a challenge? First to complete the course wins."

"What do we win?" The taller of the three guys steps forward, and I eye him as my competition, keeping a straight face until he's next to get a slap across the head.

"Does it matter, Hunter?" the cute one asks. "We're hanging out with a movie star."

I laugh out loud and turn back toward the cabanas, finding Reed settled into the one he pointed to, closest to us, his arms tucked behind his head as he watches. He's some distance away, but I don't miss the way his lips twist into a smirk, and I can only imagine what he's thinking.

I'm glad I amuse him.

Two of the guys' girlfriends join us before we start, so we settle on a girls versus boys game, with the boys quickly assuming they'll be better than we are.

But the joke's on them. I'm out to prove them wrong. I grew up on the water and I plan to give it my all. I owe Reed a show, and I'm nothing if not a performer.

"Are you ready, ladies?" I ask, smiling at my new friends.

"Hell, yeah," the smallest of the two calls out with the other giving me a high five.

And then it's on.

We line up. First team to have all three people over the finish line wins. And it's going to be the girls.

We call over a dad who's waiting for his kids, asking him to count us in, and the second he says go, I take off running.

But holy shit, this is hard.

I slip on the first corner, thankfully landing on the course while my opponent—the guy who asked about the prize, Hunter—rushes ahead.

I'm cursing myself as I climb the ladder to the slide, but when we hit the balance beam, Hunter makes the mistake of keeping up his speed and falls flat on his face before flipping into the water.

I'm ahead for the next few obstacles and a little cocky rounding the last bend, certain I've got this until I have to leap from one platform to the next and slip on my ass, tumbling straight into the man-made lake.

I'm in the water for no more than a minute, dragging myself out before Hunter has the chance to reach me, racing over the finish line seconds before he does, cheering as I turn to watch my teammates.

Anna, my second, crosses the line at the same time her boyfriend does, leaving us neck and neck. I cup my mouth to call out some encouragement when a deep voice makes me shiver.

"That was impressive," Reed whispers from behind me. "Though I can't help but notice you're wet."

His gruff tone has my body heating up, and I almost tell him that if he keeps whispering like that, I'll be wet in other places, but he's not ready for that joke. Although, who's joking?

"I only fell once," I state for the record, turning quickly so my hair flicks him in the shoulder. "*And* I still won." My final teammate crosses the line ahead of her boyfriend, and I scream out before Reed gets a chance to respond, running over to give the girls a hug. "We killed it. Suck on that, boys. Girls rule."

"Tell the world how you really feel." Reed chuckles, drawing my attention.

"If you'd participated, maybe you would have proven me wrong, but since you didn't..." I lift my hands in a "what are you gonna do" motion and put on a cheesy grin, hoping he'll change his mind on the next round, but of course, he doesn't.

"My loss." He shrugs, repeating my words back to me.

And it really is his loss. "I'm gonna go again. I want to beat my time."

I walk past Reed but he catches me around the waist, spinning me until I'm facing the opposite direction. "Nope," he says, moving to my side. "You're coming with me. It's beach time."

"Beach time?" My eyes flash to his as he nods toward the makeshift beach. "You're willing to go in?"

"I am. Would you believe, I'm not originally from San Francisco. I've felt cold like you couldn't comprehend. This is nothing." Of course it's nothing—we're in California—but I let that one slide.

"Let's—"

"Holy shit," the cute guy calls out, cutting me off. "The movie star knows Reed Coombs."

Damn. I should have seen that coming. "I think we just got busted." I cringe but Reed laughs.

"Do you care?"

"Honestly? Nope. It's beach time."

"Then let's go. What are you waiting for?" He playfully rolls his eyes and I slap his chest, pushing him backward so I can run ahead, beating him to the sand. "Last one under the water buys the first round."

"Is everything a competition to you?" Reed calls out, stripping his sweatshirt over his head, drawing attention from all directions.

"Only if I know I'm going to win."

I dive in before he's even made it to the shoreline and when I surface again, he's there beside me.

"Jesus Christ." He shivers, making me laugh. "I thought it was going to be heated."

"It's a beach." I shake my head, the smile never leaving my face as he complains.

"It's fake."

"Stop complaining; it's fine."

It's not fine. At all. I'm freezing my tits off but I refuse to admit it. I dragged Reed here, and told him it would be fun, so that's what I'm doing—having fun. Waiting for Reed to give in. Which I'm praying isn't much longer since we've already been jumping the fake waves for thirty minutes.

"Have you ever broken a bone?" Reed asks, eyeing me curiously. We're playing get to know you games, and while I assumed it would be fun, it's actually been quite informative.

"Two. I broke my arm falling off a horse when I was in primary school."

"In what?"

"Elementary school." I roll my eyes exaggeratedly. "I'm going to get you an Aussie dictionary."

"Please do." Reed's lips pull into a lopsided grin. "I need it. What else did you break?"

"My big toe. I dropped a ceramic pot on it when I was around twenty."

Reed's face contorts and I burst out laughing. "You reacted more to that than my arm, and trust me, the broken arm hurt more."

"Yes, but I visualized the pot incident and it felt all too real."

"It was real. I still can't move it properly."

"Ouch."

"Yep. What about you?"

"Never." He shakes his head before smiling proudly.

"You've never broken anything?"

"Nope. Never even been to the hospital. I'm like Superman. The man of steel."

My gaze falls to his hard, tattooed chest and I smile appreciatively. "Yeah, you are." I bite my lip and nod, ogling Reed's sculpted abs until he covers them with his arms.

"Stop objectifying me," he chastises, but can't keep a straight face as he sinks lower into the water.

"I can't stop. Won't stop. You brought attention to it. What was I supposed to do?"

"Point taken. Next question."

I think on it for a moment before a question comes to mind. "Are you ready for something a little more personal?"

Reed scoffs as he stares at me deadpan. "You asked me if I was a virgin when you barely knew me. I think we're past that, Hayls, don't you?"

"You're right. So...I didn't want to ask this through messages, but..." I wince in hesitation. "I noticed that Bria wasn't happy when you left the charity event the other week. Care to share?" I raise an eyebrow and Reed laughs awkwardly, running his hand through his now wet hair.

"Not—"

"You don't have to tell me," I cut in. "Forget—"

"Actually, I was going to say...not usually, but in this case I will."

"Oooh. I feel special."

"You should. I'm the guy that helps other people with their problems. I don't talk about my own."

"Yeah, I got that about you. Soo..." I trail off and bounce on my toes, waiting in anticipation—not that he can see my feet.

He's silent for a beat before he breathes out a sigh and I instantly regret it. "Sor—"

With a wave of his hand, he cuts off my apology. "The short of it is that Bria was having a bad day and she took it out on me."

"Damn. Does that happen often?"

"Not really. We've always had an easygoing relationship."

"What changed?"

"The guy she liked ghosted her."

"What?" I cough, choking on nothing. I wasn't expecting him to say that. "Does she seriously have no idea that you want her?"

"Apparently not." He lifts his shoulders in a shrug, a defeated look in his eyes.

"Jesus. That sucks." I cringe, suddenly wanting to slap some sense into Bria. "You have to tell her."

"Actually, on the flip side, I decided it's about time I moved on."

"Oh, yeah? And how's that going for you?"

Reed drops his face into the water and I bite back a laugh when he pops back up. "It's not," he admits.

"You need to get laid."

"It doesn't work. I've tried."

"Does she have a magic—"

"No." Reed chuckles, cutting me off before I've finished my sentence. "It's nothing like that. She's just..."

He trails off but he doesn't have to explain. "Sometimes we just want what the heart wants," I say for him. "No reason behind it."

"Exactly. Because fuck if I know why I still want her after all these years."

"I like your honesty, Coombs."

"Well, Jackman, I value your lack of judgement."

"Who says I'm not—" He cuts me off with his fiery stare and I smile. "Trust me, I am the last person who should be judging anyone about their love life."

"Or lack of it."

"Or lack of it. I'm here to commiserate."

Reed smiles and it's one of those "melt your panties" smiles that has the girls next to us practically drooling. "I appreciate it," he says, once again oblivious to the attention. Something he and Bria have in common.

We fall silent for a beat, people watching until Reed shivers. "Okay, Hayls. This has been fun, but my balls are officially numb."

"I knew it! What happened to 'I've felt cold like you couldn't comprehend'?" I put on my best Reed accent and while he laughs, it's clearly pained. He's struggling.

"I've obviously become accustomed to the warmer weather since I've lived here."

"How long have you lived in Cali?"

"Since I was seventeen."

"Eleven years? Of course you're used to warmer weather now."

"How come you're not cold?"

"I'm freaking freezing." I stand up and point to my nipples standing at attention, visible through the thin material of my bikini. "This would never happen if I was warm."

Being the gentleman that he is, Reed looks away as soon as he realizes what I'm showing him and shakes his head. "Why didn't you say anything?"

"I'm no quitter. But since you said it first, I'm getting out." With that, I run toward our cabana, instantly grabbing my towel, wrapping it around myself as Reed arrives.

"Here." I pass him the extra one I brought with me since he assumed he wouldn't get wet, and he shivers again, curling it around his shoulders, using the end to dry his hair.

"Fuck. It's colder out here than in there."

"It usually is."

"Why couldn't you have chosen this activity in August?"

"Because I only thought of it this week."

"And you always do things as soon as you think of them?"

"Absolutely. I'm impulsive like that. Consider yourself lucky I waited until today. I've been thinking about this since Saturday."

Reed hits me with that genuine smile of his and it brings out one of my own as my chest heats. "What's that for?" I ask curiously.

"What's what for?"

"That smile. The one you half hide away."

He shrugs before locking me with his gaze, his eyes boring into mine. "I had fun today, Hayley. Thanks for inviting me."

"You're welcome. I had fun too. Same time next week?"

Reed barks out an incredulous laugh as his eyes widen. "Here?"

"God, no. I've checked this off my list. I'll think of something else. Unless you want to decide?"

"Nah. I'm good." He shakes his head and a spray of water hits me in the face. "Sorry about that." He chuckles, wiping his thumb over the drops on my cheeks, forcing me to bite my lip as a warmth runs through me. "I'll let you decide," he continues. "Just tell me what time to pick you up."

"Works for me." I smile. "Oh, the possibilities."

"Can't wait." Reed's chuckle turns into a belly laugh, and for the first time in a while, I feel completely at ease. Like I can be my true self around him. And I've only really felt that with Amelia.

"Me either."

CHAPTER ELEVEN

REED

I've just stepped out of the shower, naked as the day I was born, when Hayley's distinct knock permeates the air. Two slow raps of her knuckles followed by three fast ones. Every single time. And every time I hear it, I smile.

"Coming," I call out, drying my hair before wrapping the towel around my waist, jogging to meet her.

"You're early," I state the obvious as I open the door, catching her grin before her eyes drop to my bare chest.

"And you're an asshole. I haven't had sex in *months* and you hit me with that." She tilts her head to the side, releasing a longing sigh as her words sink in.

"You what?" I blurt, following it with a groan. "Fuck. Don't worry. I didn't mean to ask that."

"Why? We're friends. Does it shock you to hear that I'm going through a dry spell?"

"No. *No.* I just wasn't expecting you to say that."

"So..." Hayley raises an eyebrow as she bites back a smirk, clearly enjoying this conversation. "It *doesn't* shock you then?"

"No... *Wait...* I... Goddammit, Hayley."

She grins comically and I reach for her hand, dragging her inside. "Wait here. I'll put some clothes on."

I turn to walk away but she calls out. "Don't do it on my account. I'm good with the towel."

"I bet you are. But please go and find someone else to perv on."

"You're no fun."

Laughing to myself, I throw on a tee and hoodie, dumping the towel in the hamper before pulling on a pair of briefs and jeans, my mind on my awkward reaction.

It's been months since the Storm charity event, when we first started hanging out, and I'm still not used to Hayley's openness.

After our wakeboard park adventure, we started catching up regularly, getting to know each other better, and from day one Hayley made it clear that she's an open book—happy to answer any questions I might have.

That she trusts me.

But when it comes to her sex life... I don't ask.

Not for any reason, except that it's not my place.

Does she ask me? Hell, yeah, she does. On a daily basis.

"Have you been laid yet? Do we need to find you a new girl to fixate on? Why don't you throw Bria on the bed and show her the man you truly are."

She's not one to hold back, and I'm always happy to respond, even if I do answer with wide eyes and an incredulous laugh.

But I don't ask.

If she wants to volunteer information, I'll listen and react—sometimes weirdly, like now—but I don't ask.

Bria and I never really spoke about that part of our lives until our argument at the event. Before that, we kept our love lives out of our friendship, and I never questioned it since it worked to my advantage.

But something shifted a few months back and now Bria's taken to filling me in on every part of her personal life—the dating apps she's joined, the men she's seeing. And yet, when I bring up Hayley, she falls silent, changing the subject in a heartbeat.

I'm not overly thrilled by Bria's newfound openness. It's always been easier to avoid that level of conversation. But I'll admit, I'm curious about Hayley.

Without me asking, she's confided in me about a lot of her past experience, and I assumed she had a healthy sex life.

But she's abstaining? *Mind blown.*

"You look like you have questions," Hayley teases when I walk back in, fully clothed. And she's not wrong. But again, I'm not about to ask. Instead, I shrug my shoulders and smile.

"And *you* look like you have a plan for today," I change the subject. "Where are we going? Swimming with sharks? Rock climbing? What big adventure do you have running through your mind?"

It didn't take long for me to learn that asking Hayley how she wants to spend our time together is a dangerous question, and yet, I can't seem to stop myself asking it. I like the excitement it ignites in her eyes—the happiness it elicits—whenever she tries to talk me into her crazy ideas. Like surfing in fall with ten-foot waves, when I've never set foot on a surfboard, or sneaking me into the San Francisco movie studios because they forgot to take her pass back, signing us up as extras on a well-known TV series.

As though we won't be recognized.

Neither of which I actually agreed to.

I raise my brows in question and Hayley pauses, her eyes full of the zest I love to see.

"I want to go dress shopping."

"Say what?" I frown as she laughs.

"I need your help." She grimaces with clenched teeth. "I have my movie premiere coming up, and the publicity tour. I need a stylist."

A stylist? "Okay." I'm not sure I like where this is going but I wait for her to continue.

"I want you to come with me," she confirms and... *that's what I was worried about.*

"Are you sure?" My nose scrunches and she bursts out laughing again.

"It's not hard. All you have to do is sit there and tell me what you think."

Fuck. That sounds dangerous.

"Isn't that a job better suited to Amelia or Paige, or anyone else on the planet?" I'm not sure she really needs help. I still remember the dress she chose for the Storm charity event *and* the event she went to with Paige, but she's asking, so...

"They're busy and I don't want *anyone* else on the planet. I want *you*. I trust *your* judgment."

"For dresses? So this is what our friendship has come to? Me being your replacement girlfriend when the others aren't available."

"Sure. Like with Bria."

"Ouch, Hayls. Did I hurt you in a past life?"

Hayley shoves me back as she giggles uncontrollably before walking into the kitchen and helping herself to a cider. "I'm just messing with you."

"Thank God." I don't bother hiding my relief as I relax, my shoulders dropping. "So what are we really doing?"

"Huh?"

"If you're messing with me."

"Oh no. We're going shopping. I was messing with you about Bria. I don't really think you're one of her girlfriends."

"But I am one of yours?"

"No. You're my best *guy* friend, and I trust you. I could really use your help. I love fashion, but I'm not great at choosing it. Basically, I need you to tell me if I look hot or not."

I release a breath through my nose and grin. "Okay, Hayls. Let's do this. But you owe me."

Hayley's bright smile lights up her face, and when she rushes over to hug me, it's enough to convince me I'm doing the right thing. And after squeezing the life out of me, she rests her chin on my chest and glances up with an appreciative look in her eyes, further cementing my decision. "Deal."

"Good." I bop her nose before stepping back, ready to get this over with. *How hard could it be?*

Well, fuck me. I am out of my depth. On the drive over alone, she loses me, filling me in on the styles she wants to try on, while I nod along, pretending to know what the hell she's talking about.

She's just finished telling me how badly she'd love to find a silver dress, when she changes the subject so fast I get whiplash.

"Since I know you're wondering... The character I'm auditioning for next week is a virgin," she states matter-of-factly, making me jolt.

"What?" I choke back a laugh. "When was I wondering that?"

"You weren't but you were curious about my dry spell, right?"

Dammit. I shake my head and comically sigh. "You caught me. I'm not going to lie. It did intrigue me."

"Well, now you have your answer."

"Hold up. So you're staying celibate because the character you're auditioning for is a virgin?"

"At first I wasn't. I just wasn't feeling it. But when I heard about this role, it made sense to continue."

Huh. "Well, there you go. I never knew you were a method actor."

"I'm not, usually. But in this instance, I wanted to understand her desperation and intensity. I wanted to feel the restraint she endured before she gave in and made the worst mistake of her life, sleeping with the man that killed her brother."

"Whoa. Did you just spoil the plot for me? Hayley, come on," I scold, jokingly. "Now I can't watch it."

"Shut up. You don't even know what movie it is." She shoves my arm gently so as to not cause a car accident and I chuckle. "Plus, that's not the big twist. You're fine."

"Phew. Thank God. So...since you brought it up. How's the sex ban going for you?"

"I'm done. I get it. It's frustrating as hell. I'm *that* desperate—I'd fuck one of my exes. Even the one that couldn't find my clit."

Jesus Christ. I tap the brake and we both rock forward, making Hayley laugh.

There's a whole lot to unpack in that sentence. First, Hayley doesn't swear all that often, unless she's talking about sex, or she's drunk, but also... she *must* be desperate, because she does not speak favorably about her exes.

"Good to know," I try to joke. As someone who feels the same level of frustration, it's impossible not to react.

"TMI?" Hayley asks, her expression pinched.

"Nope." I shake my head. "I'm good. I asked." I shrug and focus on the road until I sense her gaze boring a hole in the side of my face.

"You feel my pain, don't you?" she asks, squeezing my arm.

"Little bit. Yup." My voice comes out strained and I don't bother hiding it. There's no point in denying it anyway. She knows when I'm lying.

Hayley pats my shoulder as I pull into the parking lot, and I can't help but chuckle.

"I guess that means we both need to get laid."

"Can't argue with that."

When I come to a stop, Hayley grabs my arm before I can get out, clenching her teeth. "We have to sneak in."

Huh? I raise a brow in question and she nods. "The stylist doesn't want me to be seen."

"What?" I may be famous in my own right, but this is a whole new level for me.

The closer we get to the release of Hayley's movie, the harder it is for her to live a normal life. People are recognizing her everywhere she goes and yet, it blows my mind to think we've been out numerous times since the day at the waterpark and have yet to read about it in the media. Hell, when I half drunkenly agreed to be secret friends, I never actually believed we'd succeed. Now it's been two months and the only people that know, other than us, are Amelia and Bria. And a select number of fans that have seemingly kept it to themselves.

"What about you wear my hoodie and go in disguise? I'll happily wait in the truck until you're done."

I comically grin but it does me no favors. "You're coming. And it's not for me. It's for the stylist," she confirms and my confusion deepens.

"Okay? What about I drive you around back and I walk in the front?"

"That defeats the purpose. The stylist doesn't want to draw attention to herself in case I don't choose to work with her. If you waltz in there all 'look at me, I'm Reed Coombs,' it's going to raise questions."

I stare at her deadpan. "Look at me, I'm Reed Coombs?"

"You know what I mean."

"Does that really happen?"

"I don't know. I guess she's been burned in the past and it's affected her sales?" She shrugs as I try to understand.

"If that happens, I'll hire her. She can dress me for the charity event D'Angelo wants to host in late February."

I'm joking but Hayley ponders that for a moment. "That could work." She nods to herself. "*Yes.* Perfect. Drop me off in the back."

"I'm kidding."

"I know. But hooray." She waves her hands in the air as though celebrating. "Congratulations, you've found yourself a stylist."

"Goddammit," I groan, banging my head against the steering wheel. "Remind me why I agreed to come with you again?"

"Because you love hanging out with me?"

That wasn't *exactly* the reason, but...I can't argue with that either.

Chapter Twelve

REED

H_oly fuck_. Who knew this would be torture?
      Me. _I_ did.

That's why I didn't want to come. Despite having a female best friend, I am not a dress shopping guy. I'm not a shopping guy in general.

"How about you try these next?" The stylist passes Hayley another selection of dresses, and Hayley smiles politely before flashing me a pained expression, begging me to save her.

But all I can do is shrug. This is on her.

I'm not about to tell this woman, this _stylist_, that her ideas for Hayley suck. Even though they do. The dresses are nice enough, but there's something about them that just doesn't work.

And if I can see it, you know you have a problem.

I now understand why she didn't want anyone knowing Hayley was coming in. We've been here for an hour, and if she hasn't found something for Hayley by now, I doubt she's going to.

As I wait, my phone buzzes in my pocket, earning me a death stare from the stylist, and I freeze, my hand hovering over my jeans until she disappears into the back room, giving me a chance to relax. She's a little scary.

Though, apparently she's one of the best.

What do I know?

I open my messages, expecting it to be from my mom, and my shoulders tense. If it is her, she'll be asking again when I'm next coming home, and it kills me not to have an answer for her. With practice and games, it's not easy to get home and back in time. And even if it was, I can't handle the bullshit that comes along with it, the inevitable hell I'll get from my brother.

Guilt gnaws at my chest but I shake it off, holding my breath as I check my phone, sighing when it's not her.

> LUKE: Beers at my place next Tuesday. 4pm.
> Think of it as a late Thanksgiving/early
> Christmas celebration

Taking the distraction from my thoughts, I laugh to myself before any responses come through. It's not a question. If I know Luke, he *expects* us to be there, and yet, I have no doubt that Easton's about to say...

> EASTON: I'm busy

Right on cue. This chat may be labeled as Easton's Support Group, but he is *not* a willing participant, and has tried to leave the chat on multiple occasions. Some might say we're holding him hostage, but deep down, he loves it and he knows we're there for him. Especially now.

> LUKE: Paige can come too

Paige D'Angelo... Our team owner's daughter. Who would have thought she was sneaking around with Easton? Or more to the point, that he was sneaking around with her. Either way, I'm glad they have each other because they both went through a lot recently and he doesn't open up easily. It's good to know he has someone.

> EASTON: I have a son. Remember him?

> LUKE: Bring him. We have plenty of spare
> rooms he can sleep in

> EASTON: ...

> REED: Easton, don't leave the group. Luke's
> joking. And Luke, if he can't come, he
> can't come

I'd usually enjoy their banter, but East doesn't need this right now, even though I know Luke's coming from a good place. He was worried when everything went down with Easton last weekend and he's trying to show that we're there for him. I wouldn't be surprised if he came up with this entire idea for Easton alone.

> LUKE: You're no fun. You better be there in his place

I begin to respond but pause. Somehow, without us even discussing it, Tuesday became the day Hayley and I catch up. And if it was Bria, I know she'd be pissed if I ditched her for the guys. I need to at least mention it to Hayls.

> REED: I'll let you know in five

> LUKE: Bria got your balls?

> REED: Nope. Not Bria

Dammit. Fuck. I delete my last message but when I see Luke typing, I know I'm too late.

> LUKE: Where are your balls, Reed? If Bria doesn't have them, who does?

A throat clears, drawing my attention to find Hayley's potential stylist tapping her toes as she gives me that death stare she loves.

There is no way I'm hiring her. And at this point, I'm praying Hayley feels the same.

"Miss Jackman will be out soon." She folds her arms over her chest. "I need you to pay attention. I'm certain she's about to find the one."

And I'm certain she's wrong, but I smile anyway.

She said that about the last lot of outfits and yet here we are. "I'm ready," I lie.

Hayley walks out in a ruffled off-the-shoulder *thing*. That's the best way to describe it. And before I've had time to form an opinion in my head, she's shaking hers.

"I don't think this is me." She frowns, much to the stylist's annoyance. "I need something more..." She trails off but I answer for her.

"Classic but daring," I muse as all eyes flash my way. "Am I wrong?" I challenge them. We may only be a couple of months into our friendship but I already know those two words pretty much sum Hayley up. She's classically beautiful in every sense of the word and incredibly daring. So why not dress the part?

Jesus. Who the fuck am I?

Hayley pauses for a beat before laughing out loud. "You're right. That's it. Evelyn, do you have anything classic but daring?"

Evelyn smiles at Hayley, but when her eyes flash my way I can tell that she's pissed. And after a nod and forced agreement, she spins on her heels and disappears into another room.

Hayley bites her bottom lip, and when I open my mouth to speak, she shushes me. "She's coming," she mouths as the devil woman walks back in.

"Try these two. They're perfect."

I want to say "we'll be the judge of that" but zip my lips. I need to be positive. One of these is going to be it.

With a wave, Hayley heads back to the changing room and I jump back into the group text, having forgotten about Luke's teasing until I reread the message. *That's right.* He's looking for my balls. Which I'm pretty certain are currently in Hayley's handbag. Why else would I agree to go dress shopping?

> REED: 😬 I just remembered I'm busy.
> Sorry Luke

> EASTON: You sound like me. I'm waiting for the notification to say Reed has left the group

> LUKE: Easton!! My man. I was going to say the same thing. Also... that reply took a while, Reed. Does that someone have your balls now?

> REED: My balls are none of your concern. But they're accounted for

Sort of.

LUKE: Good. I'll see you Tuesday. And all the days in between since I can't get away from you

LUKE: Did I mention I've got beer? Just bring your annoying selves. Dylan, I'm including you. I know Summer will be out with the girls. Thomas mentioned it

DYLAN: I'm there

LUKE: Good. East, there's still time to change your mind. You know you want to hear Reed's gossip

EASTON: I really don't. And on that note. It's about time we changed the name of the group, right?

I look at the group name—Easton's support group—and chuckle before glancing up to make sure I haven't been busted. And thankfully, I'm good.

Easton may be with Paige now, but knowing Luke, he'll have some reason to keep the name the same. And instead of hating Luke for it, Easton will turn on me. After all, I'm the one that started the group when Luke needed us.

LUKE: Not yet

I knew it.

LUKE: I'll change it if you come over for beers

EASTON LEFT THE GROUP

LUKE ADDED EASTON TO THE GROUP

I bark out a laugh and freeze when Evelyn scowls. Oops. Cringing, I pocket my phone and glance up with a smile, my timing perfect as the door to the changing room opens.

As I wait, Hayley appears slowly, her eyes watery, her gaze locked on mine.

And I do a double take.

"Christ, Hayls." I swallow a lump in my throat as my eyes drop to her legs, my gaze roaming as I take her all in. And she steals my fucking breath. I'm not sure I've ever seen anyone look more beautiful.

A giddy smile graces her lips as relief overwhelms me. She found something. No, she didn't just find something. She found the one. It couldn't be more perfect.

Giving me a spin, she shows off the gleaming silver dress with plunging neckline and open back, gently holding the flowing skirt. I smile until a flash of skin highlights the split reaching her upper thigh, making me my throat dry.

"It's... You... I don't have the words," I rasp.

She releases the skirt and the material pools at her feet while I can't take my fucking eyes off her. "No words," I repeat like a fool.

"But you like it?" she questions, her expression confident while I fight to form a proper sentence.

"I was here to say hot or not, right?" I ask, ignoring the cracking in my voice.

"Right." Hayley giggles before trapping her lip between her teeth.

"You're a fucking knockout," I whisper in awe, unable to hide how I feel.

"That's what I was after."

Evelyn finally smiles and I laugh because of it. "I'll leave you two alone for a minute to decide, but it's perfect, Hayley. And you look beautiful."

"Don't I?"

Hayley turns again until I'm looking at her back and glances over her shoulder, gathering her hair up to show off her neck. "With my hair up, you'll see the detail on the back, and I'm thinking a drop necklace." She turns to face me again and clutches her neck before letting her hand drop to where the necklace would fall between her cleavage. "Maybe even a simple white gold bracelet?"

I grumble low in the back of my throat and shift my gaze back to her eyes, forcing a smile when she doesn't notice how affected I am. "It all sounds perfect to me."

"Thank you."

"Seriously, you look incredible, Hayls. I wish I had the right words."

"You don't need them. Your expression says it all."

"Fuck." My nose scrunches as I run a hand through my hair. "I'm guessing that means you know my thoughts on all the other dresses?"

"I sure do." She laughs when I wince.

"Don't worry about my opinion. She's great." I fake another smile, but my tone gives me away.

"You don't have to be nice *all* the time, Reed. She's a *bitch*." She mouths bitch and I have to agree with her.

"So...you're not going to hire her," I whisper back and Hayley shakes her head.

"I'm not. But I am definitely wearing this dress."

I nod, my eyes raking over her again, imagining the reaction of the crowds as tension fills my chest. "I'd be disappointed if you didn't."

CHAPTER THIRTEEN

HAYLEY

I smile as the Storm players run off the field at halftime, revved up with their eight-point lead.

When they disappear through the tunnel, the girls—otherwise known as the wives and girlfriends of the players—immediately turn my way. "Show me the dress. *Now*." Amelia stamps her foot with demand and it's so adorable it makes me laugh.

"The photos do *not* do it justice," I explain with an awe to my voice that I completely own. I love that dress. "I wasn't even supposed to take photos."

Before her mouth even opens, my eyes flash to Amelia, ready for her to sass me and she does, right on cue. "Who took the photo, Hayls?" she asks, knowing full well it was Reed, trying to get me to spill.

"Another guest," I lie.

"Mm-hmm. That was lucky. Now show me."

"Jesus. You're keen." With a giggle, I jokingly shake my head until her entire demeanor changes.

"I'm still disappointed I couldn't be there. I hate letting you down."

"Me too," Paige adds with a bummed expression. "I'm sorry you had to go alone." A layer of guilt settles around my middle but I smile through it. I should tell Paige about Reed. After all, she told me about Easton before anyone else. But now is not the time.

Lainey wanders over and I move on, grabbing my phone.

"I don't want any of you to feel bad. I'm all good, and you have *lives*. *Important* lives."

"You're—"

"I know, I'm important too. Trust me. I don't feel neglected. I'm good. I promise."

"Okay. Good." Amelia smiles but it doesn't quite reach her eyes until the moment I show them my new favorite dress.

"Holy shit." Paige is the first to speak while Amelia gasps.

"It's stunning, Hayley," Lainey smiles, taking my phone from Amelia. "Right?"

"So right." Paige stares in awe. "You look delicious. Are you taking a date?"

"Nope." I pop the *p* as all eyes flash my way.

"Why the hell not?" Paige's jaw drops, making me smile. "We need to find you a date."

"Or…" I hesitate for dramatic effect. "I could find one on the night?"

Paige laughs as the girls nod. "I have no doubt about that. Guys will go wild with you in this dress. And it's giving me Riley vibes."

My eyes widen as that realization hits me. "I hadn't even thought of that." Though I do know about the guys going wild. I still have Reed's *restrained* hunger at the forefront of my mind from when he saw me in the dress. "It just gets better and better."

As the girls run through possible scenarios for my night, Paige pulls me aside, her expression serious. "Sorry to interrupt the gushing, but I wanted to run something past you."

"Of course. Shoot."

"I was brainstorming ideas for the next Storm charity event, needing to get my mind off everything else going on in my life, and *you* popped into mind."

"Me?" My brows rise high on my forehead as I grin.

"Yes," Paige giggles. "Keeley was telling me about the Thanksgiving party last year and mentioned that you were playing football with the guys."

"God, that was fun," I reminisce, my eyes glazing over as the memories come rushing back to me, until Paige continues, cutting them off.

"What do you think about the team hosting an Aussie Rules charity game during the offseason?"

"For real?"

"Yes, for real." Her head drops back and she laughs while my mind goes wild with possibilities.

"I love that. I actually know a guy that could show them the ropes. He used to play in Australia but moved here when his son was accepted into an Ivy League college as a kicker."

"No way? I was hoping you'd know a few things or at least point me in the right direction, but a contact, here in the US? Amazing."

We chat through ideas until the teams are back on the field and then I'm in the moment again, staring intently, pretending I have a man in the action, just like the rest of them.

Although, I suppose I do. I have Reed to watch.

And watch, I do.

He's hard to look away from.

The team's amazing. They gel. They're a force to be reckoned with.

But Reed. He has a presence that demands your gaze. And it's not just his muscles that draw the attention. He's strong but incredibly fast, he's—

"Yes! Go. Go." I lose my train of thought as Reed secures the ball from Zane and rushes forward, dodging the opposition to make it to the end zone.

"Yeah, baby," I call out and no one pays me any mind except Amelia, giving me a sideways glance.

But whatever, I'm allowed to cheer on the team.

Subtly rolling my eyes, I continue my support through the second half and we finish the game with another win.

Hands in the air, I cheer out loud, drawing attention from the crowd below, but I don't care about their annoyed expressions. I'm too excited. "Another win!" I cheer louder to be obnoxious. "The guys are on fire. Are we heading out to celebrate, ladies?" I smile wide until one by one they hit me with excuses. Excuses I understand, but ones that still leave me without a much-needed wingwoman.

At least until Storm's media liaison, Keeley, walks in, tucking her auburn hair behind her ears as her eyes scour the space. When her gaze finds mine, I shoot her a bright smile and rush over, sidling up to her when she's filled in on my predicament.

"What about you, Keeley? You're single. Can I convince you?"

A brief moment of uncertainty mars her otherwise poised expression before she schools her features, replacing it with a determined grin. "I'm in." Her smile finally reaches her eyes. "Just let me grab my purse."

My eyes follow her as she disappears back through the door, and the second she's gone, I spin around, ready to ask if anyone else caught her strange reaction. And sure enough, Paige's knowing—or perhaps unknowing—smile meets mine.

"What was that?" she questions, her eyes flashing to the door where Keeley just exited. "I think Keeley and I need to have a chat."

"I can't believe you don't know already. She *is* your sister-in-law."

"Easton and I aren't married."

"Not yet." I wink and she laughs. "Either way, it's your job to get the gossip. Is Keeley keeping a secret? Is it a new guy?"

"Leave her alone," Amelia scolds, her voice lacking conviction. "Everyone keeps secrets, Hayls. Including *you*."

Whoops. *Touché.* "You're right." And for now, I'm keeping it that way. It's been nice having Reed to myself.

When the suite clears out, I follow the girls to where they're meeting their men and wait for Keeley, my gaze searching through the sea of bodies, admiring the goods until I find Reed.

I have to say, the Storm men are fine, but Reed is something else entirely.

With his attention elsewhere, I let my gaze linger longer than it should, taking in the way his stylish dress suit molds perfectly to his body and his collared shirt brings out the brightness of his blue eyes.

I can't say how long I've been perving when he catches me, but as if being busted himself, he glances away, a small smile tugging at his lips before he disappears into the crowd.

"Where's the party tonight?" I ask when Luke greets us, always the first out so he can see his girl, his signature cocky grin perfectly in place. As it should be. He played a hell of a game.

"We're heading to the Westerly Hotel," he's quick to respond. "Are you in?"

The Westerly? "Again? You always go there now." Not that it's a bad place, but I was in the mood for something new, something different.

"What's the matter, Jack Jack?" Luke smirks at his next nickname for me while I mockingly roll my eyes. "Have you already been through the men there?"

"Luke," Amelia scolds, but I brush her off. This is how we roll.

"Actually, Lukey Boy, I *haven't*. So I'm in. I just didn't realize you were predictable and boring."

"I'm not." He pouts until Amelia laughs.

"Seriously, you two." She blows out a raspberry but her lips twitch as she holds back her smile.

"You love it, Ace." Luke kisses her cheek just as the noise level increases and the last of the guys file out, celebrating as they make their way through the halls.

"Are we going to the Westerly?" Keeley asks, wrapping her arm around my shoulder while I search for Reed again.

"I guess we are. You ready?"

"I sure am. Let's go."

Keeley laughs when I'm dipped back, my dance partner's grip on me tightening as he pulls me up into his broad chest. "Smooth." I giggle, letting the dark-eyed stranger spin me away before he reels me back in, his intense gaze never once leaving mine.

We've been dancing for the better part of an hour, and I'm having a blast. *Maybe the Westerly isn't so bad.*

"So, you know the team?" he asks, his gaze bouncing around the various players littering the dance floor.

"I know some." I shrug.

"Is one of them your man?"

An image of Reed comes to mind as I nibble my bottom lip, drawing my dance partner's gaze. "Not tonight," I tell him. "But I never say never."

The guy, whose name I never bothered to catch, laughs, letting his head drop back before he shakes it to and fro. "Something tells me you keep men on their toes."

"I've heard that a bit. But you're doing okay."

Another laugh rumbles from his lips and I smile at the sound, moving out of the way as someone walks past with a tray of drinks. On the dance floor. "Are you thirsty?" my dance partner asks, his eyes on the tray as it moves through the masses.

"I'm good for now. But you should get one."

He nods as he takes off toward the bar, leaving me alone with hundreds of people surrounding me.

And it's nice to have a break.

"Keeley," I call out, waving my arms to get her attention over the loud music. "I'm going to the bathroom." I motion toward the restrooms and she nods, making her way over.

"Want to get some air when you're done?" she asks, her freckled hand fanning her face.

"*God*, yes." *It's like she read my mind.* "The garden?"

"Perfect. I'm dying here." She shakes out her shirt next before tossing her long, auburn hair over her shoulder and releasing a sigh. "I bet they're over capacity. There must be a couple of hundred people here tonight."

"No doubt. The guys bring the crowds, that's for sure. I'll be back." I point in the direction of the bathrooms again and Keeley nods, turning to dance with one of the Storm's cornerbacks, Miller, completely comfortable in his presence.

Though she's always comfortable around the team, and not afraid to flirt. Acting the queen that she is, she made it clear from day one that she doesn't mix business with pleasure, and for the most part, the players listened. Though these days, if any of them *didn't* play by the rules, they'd have her brother to deal with, and Easton's not one to mess around. Not that they all know they're related, since they still keep it mostly to themselves.

Squeezing my way through the sweaty masses on the dance floor, I stop short when I almost cut through a couple about to kiss, and duck in time, only to be pulled back in the opposite direction.

"Where are you going?" My dance partner fakes a pout, his strong grip curled around my wrist. "I thought we were having fun."

"We were. But I desperately need a break. Go and enjoy yourself. I'll be back on the dance floor before you know it."

"What if I want to come?"

"To the bathroom?" I giggle and shake him off, keeping my voice light when his nose flares. "I'll see you back on the dance floor." Without waiting for a response, I walk around the amorous couple this time, taking in the fresh air when I finally break away from the crowd. Turns out it's not as hot as I thought. There's just too many people in the one spot.

As I move through the space, I pass a few of the younger Storm players, smiling when they wave. While I don't yet know all of them, I recognize a couple from the charity event, and wink before continuing on my way.

The farther I get, the cooler the air, and as it seeps into my lungs, I take a deep breath, ignoring the dizziness from drinking a little more than I should have.

With the bathroom in sight, I pick up my speed and stumble over an empty bottle, laughing when I catch myself.

I'm still smiling when I pull open the door until the bottle rolls across the floor behind me as though someone else kicked it out of the way. My heart jolts, but before I can turn, a hand grips my waist and a breath warms my neck. "You left without me," my dance partner's voice filters through the air, and I spin around, my heart racing at the malice in his expression.

"I—"

He covers my mouth with his hand, cutting me off as he shoves me through the door, shutting it behind us. His midnight eyes locked on mine, he grips my shoulder, pushing me into the wall opposite, following closely behind.

My ankle rolls, but just like in the hall, I catch myself seconds before I fall. "What the hell are you doing?" I snap, trying to shove him away.

The guy chuckles, clearly ignoring the disgust in my tone. "Re-laax." He draws out the word, shoving me back. "We're alone."

"That's—"

"You're so fucking gorgeous," he cuts me off. "But you know that, don't you?"

"Get off me." I wriggle in his grasp, but it only works to make him tighten his hold.

"Come on, Hayley. Relax."

Hayley? Ugh. I never told him my name. Sometimes it sucks to be known.

"Don't pretend you don't want this," he continues and my stomach knots. "You've been flirting with me all night."

I stand tall, looking him in the eye, and scowl. "Since when did flirting give you permission to follow me into the women's bathroom?"

"Since now."

"Fuck off."

"Ooh, she has bite."

"I'll show you bite."

Slamming my knee into his junk, I shove him off me and dig my stiletto into his foot, listening to his groans as I readjust my dress. Without a backward glance, I rush to the door, reaching it as it flies open.

"Are you okay?" one of the rookie football players asks, his eyes ablaze as his gaze snaps to the guy in the corner.

"Bitch," the guy spits out, cursing me in his hunched position, his hands clenching his balls.

Without responding, I grab the rookie's arm, pulling him away while his eyes stay locked on the dickhead behind me, watching him cower.

"I'm fine," I say honestly, giving his arm another tug. "But thank you. Can you walk with me?"

His eyes flash to mine before they drift back to the guy, clearly torn on what to do and geared up to fight. "Of course. But—"

"Don't worry about him. If he knows what's good for him, he'll stay away."

"Are you sure?"

"Yep. Come on."

Dragging him by the hand, I slam open the door and beeline for the bar, releasing my hold on the rookie when we're no longer alone. "Thank you again." I pause, wishing I could remember his name. Something starting with L? "I appreciate you checking in on me."

"No problem. Are you sure you're okay?"

"Never better. Enjoy your night."

I wave with a smile before releasing a held breath as soon as I turn away. *What the hell just happened?*

He followed me into the bathroom? *Jesus.*

Making my way back to Keeley, I bump shoulders with a few dancers as my mind whirs, apologizing when it snaps me back to reality.

It doesn't take long for me to find Keeley, but she's talking to Thomas, so I motion to the garden when I get her attention, letting her know I'll meet her out there.

With the smile still locked on my face, I sashay toward the exit, only stopping when the cool night air slaps me in the face, and a breath fills my lungs.

Throwing my head back, I stare at the stars, taking it all in until the door slams behind me and I stiffen before slowly turning around.

"What happened?" Reed asks, his expression ashen.

"What?" My pounding heart jolts at the sound of his voice and I instantly relax.

"Don't mess with me, Hayley. I know something's wrong."

My shoulders drop, a sigh rushing from my chest. "I'm fine, I promise. A guy got a little handsy and it pissed me off. But it's nothing I can't handle, and he won't do it again."

"Who?" Reed's fists clench as he stands tall. And it might be the adrenaline coursing through me, but I burst out laughing.

"It doesn't matter." I survey the garden and when I don't recognise anyone, I grab Reed's hand, pulling him into a hug. "Thank you for coming to my rescue. *Again.* I can always count on you."

"I haven't done anything. Tell me who it was." His teeth clench and my smile widens.

"You've done plenty. But will you stay with me for a bit?" My voice softens and I almost curse myself when the deep furrow between Reed's brows doubles in size. "I'm *fine*," I reassure him. "I just want to hang out."

"Okay." He blows out a breath, clearly still torn but not wanting to leave me alone. "I'm allowed to worry."

"You're allowed to do what you want, Reed. But I'll repeat, I'm fine."

Reed's eyes widen before he grins suddenly, his expression morphing into one of intrigue. "I can do what I want?"

"Yep."

"Thanks. That *will* put my mind at ease."

"Huh?" I frown, a part of me wondering if I just set myself up. "How so?"

"Because now, you're coming home with me."

"I'm what?" *My* eyes widen now as my jaw drops and I'm sure it'd be comical if roles were reversed.

"You heard me." He laughs victoriously.

"Are you pussy blocking me again, Reed? After I told you how desperate I was?"

"Yep." He pops the *p*, folding his arms across his hard chest.

"Harsh."

"Quite the opposite, in fact. I'm looking after you."

"You know this isn't my first rodeo. I've had one-night stands before. I'm more than capable—"

"I don't doubt that, but now you know what type of assholes are out there."

"Oh, Reed." I squeeze his arm and lean in close, breathing him in as he stiffens. "I learned that a *long* time ago. But thanks anyway."

He knows about my past full of assholes, so when his nose scrunches, I laugh.

"I wasn't there back then." He shrugs, his face tense until he stands tall. "But I'm here now, and I'm taking you home. Deal with it."

He hits me with a no bullshit stare and my body heats. *Damn, Reed.* Biting my lip, I match his intensity as I contemplate how to respond, my mind replaying his demanding tone over and over. *Deal with it.*

I need to get laid. By someone who is *not* Reed. And I need to do it fast.

CHAPTER FOURTEEN

REED

Hayley texts while I'm brushing my teeth the next morning, and I know before reading it that it's a thank you text.

Despite her pussy-blocking arguments—and there were many—when she was ready to leave last night, she found me.

And just like I said I would, I took her home, to her apartment, walking her to her door. Exactly like I would have done if it had been Bria.

In fact, it's safe to say, my friendship with Hayley has become just as important as the friendship I share with Bria. And God knows we speak more often. Bria and I have barely spoken since Thanksgiving, and that was almost two weeks ago.

Unlocking my phone as I finish in the bathroom, I chuckle when I read Hayley's text.

> HAYLEY: Thanks for last night. Even though my drought continues

I wasn't wrong, but I forgot to predict the sass.

> REED: You should thank me for that too. You were too good for those guys

> HAYLEY: Even your teammates?

> REED: Especially them. You're welcome

> HAYLEY: If you say so. Are you free Friday night? You owe me for ditching me tomorrow

I chuckle as I throw my towel into my bag and grab my hat and keys. I don't have to think about my week to know that I'm free. I'd usually see Bria Friday or Saturday but after our most recent argument—one that included her accusing me of neglect when she's the one that's been busy—we haven't made plans. Despite the fact that I've tried calling her. Truth is, I'm not neglecting her. I just happen to have been busy on the few instances she made time for me.

REED: I can spare an hour or two

HAYLEY: Good. I'll come to you. Movie night

REED: Only if I choose

I pocket my phone as I lock my door, but I only make it down the front two steps before it rings, making me smile.

"Okay, fine," I whine as I answer. "You can choose the movie." I laugh until Bria sucks in a breath. Yes, I know the way her breathing sounds. *I'm that obsessed.*

"I'm going to guess you thought I was someone else." Her hurt whisper breaks me.

"I did." I cringe as my fists clench. "Sorry. How are you?"

"Oh...ah...I'm good. Great. But I missed you. I know that's on me but—"

"It's not, I—"

"You don't have to defend me, Reed," she cuts me off, her voice significantly lighter. "I was a bitch because I was jealous."

"Jealous?" *The fuck?*

"Yes. Is that so crazy?"

"Bria, you—"

"I don't mean football by the way. In case you were wondering."

Dammit... I'd just convinced myself that the less time we spent together, the easier it was to move on. I'd convinced myself that I *was* moving on. But all it takes is a little hint of something more and I'm pulled back in again. I'm kidding myself if I think I can say I'm done and actually be done. I've felt this way for years. It's not something I can turn off.

Despite all that, I've made the decision to place Bria firmly in the friendship box and I don't want to move her. I can't.

"Bria, you know I don't—"

"Have you seen *her*?"

Fuck. This is exactly what we argued about, but she's never mentioned jealousy before. A pit forms in my stomach even though I shouldn't be feeling guilty. I'm allowed to have friends. "Bria. Come on. This isn't you. I have plenty of friends."

"But this is different. It's like you've replaced me."

"Replaced you? Are you— Actually, no, I'm not having this conversation again. There is room in my life for more than one close friendship."

"So you're *just* friends."

"Yes!" How many times...

"Okay." She cuts into my thoughts, her voice breathy. "Okay," she repeats and I sigh.

"Would it matter if we were *more*?" As I ask the question a small spark ignites inside me, hoping she'll say yes. Praying that it bothers her. But before she answers, I internally curse myself. This is my problem. I tell myself I'm moving on and then I think about shit like this.

Move the fuck on, Reed.

"It wouldn't matter," Bria responds and I ignore the disappointment swirling inside me. "Although, I'd probably cut you more slack. I prepared myself long ago for you to date, but I never imagined being replaced as your best friend."

And with that she dumps a bucket of water on any spark I might have now or in the future, stopping it from relighting.

God, I'm a fucking idiot. I should have moved on years ago.

Bria giggles as though her own thoughts are crazy and then easily moves the conversation toward general chitchat, determined for us to get back to the way we were. *Her words, not mine.*

But what the hell is that? Is that me pining over her while she lives her life in blissful ignorance? Or is that me pining over her and her knowing, secretly loving the fact that I'm always there when she needs me?

Either way, I can't go back. Not this time.

When she's finished telling me about her plans for the weekend with no mention of the fact that it's a huge game for us, I hang up in a slump.

What am I doing? And more to the point...how the hell do I change it?

🏈 🏈 🏈

The day of Luke's early Christmas drinks arrives and I find myself more pumped than I thought I'd be.

Is he going to give me shit about my balls? Yes. But I don't really care. It's almost Christmas, we're on track to make the playoffs again—and win —and I'm seeing my parents in two weeks. Away from my hometown and away from my brother.

So what if my love life sucks. The rest is good. And that's nothing new.

When four o'clock arrives, I knock on Luke's door and he opens it with a smirk, motioning me inside. "Good decision, Reed. I'm glad you came."

"Did you ever think that I wouldn't?"

"Not even for a second."

I laugh as we enter the living room, finding Dylan and Thomas already waiting, along with a poker table and three beers set out on coasters.

"I saved you a seat, Coombs," Thomas jokes, gesturing toward the empty seat with a beer. "And we nominated you as the dealer."

I smile wide as I sink down into my chair. Poker I can do, even if I suck. "Sounds good to me. What are we playing for?"

Mischief alights in Luke's expression and I regret my question even before he responds.

"Secrets." He points to me, bouncing his eyebrow while I flip him off.

There may be no real reason for me to keep my friendship with Hayley to myself, but if I know Luke, he'll never believe that it's not more than friends.

And because he won't accept me simply saying no to the secrets idea, I opt for a better one. "Okay, I've got a secret. I heard that when Luke was a rookie, he—"

Luke reaches across the table and covers my mouth with his hand, his eyes wide with horror. "Fuck. Okay, man. No secrets."

"You don't even know what it was."

"It doesn't matter. I did a lot of stupid shit as a rookie and I'm not willing to risk it."

I actually had nothing in mind, but I took a chance and it paid off.

"My guess is I already know." Thomas's eyes crease as he laughs.

"Same." Dylan nods beside him. "But even if I didn't, you've done so many things in your life, Luke, I don't think anything would surprise me."

"Thanks, *friends*." He rolls his eyes.

"So we're playing for cash then?" I ask, biting back a grin.

"Works for me."

"I'm in."

"Let's go."

Luke takes a large gulp of his beer as I shuffle the deck, and I'm about to deal the cards when Thomas casually cuts in.

"I got Lainey a puppy."

"Wow."

Luke spits out his drink while Dylan and I crack up laughing. "You what?" Luke asks, astonishment in his gaze.

"Man, that was satisfying." Thomas sinks back in his chair, his amused smirk lighting up his features. "Lainey told me to find the *perfect* moment to mention it to you and that was it."

"What have I missed?" I ask, curious about Luke's reaction.

"Lainey's been dognapping Shadow"—his black Labrador—"because she wants a dog of her own. Her finally getting one is a big deal."

"Dognapping?"

"Yeah, she takes Shadow for walks when I'm out and I'm forever coming home to find her missing."

"So she's helping you when you're busy?"

"What? No." His brows furrow as he shoots me a glare, and I wouldn't be surprised if he was silently calling me a traitor. "She's dognapping," he continues. "Do you always find the good in everything?"

"Not everything." My mind drifts back to Sunday night and a pit forms in my stomach. Hayley said she's fine, but when our rookie, my unofficial mentee, Landon, saw me talking to her later that night, he asked if she was okay and filled me in on what had happened. There is no way to spin that situation. The asshole followed her into a goddamn bathroom, and he deserves whatever he gets. I wish I'd been the one to give it to him.

Luke's interest piques. "Who do you need us to hurt, Reed?"

"No one. It's not about me."

"Of course it's not." Luke huffs out an incredulous laugh. "It's never about you. You're always worried about others."

My back stiffens as I sit up, staring him down. "You say that like it's a bad thing." I get defensive.

"It's not. But at some point you need to take care of yourself."

"I'm fine."

"Oh, yeah?" He folds his arms over his chest, leaning back in his chair smugly. "How's Bria?"

"*Luke*," Thomas warns, while Dylan sits taller, ready to step in.

"We're not talking about Bria."

"Why not?"

"Because this has *nothing* to do with her."

"All I asked was how she is."

"She's fine. Now are we playing poker or not?" I toss Luke his cards, cursing when one of them lands face up. Grabbing another, I slam it down on the table in front of him.

"We're playing." He eyes me curiously. "I'm ready to kick your ass."

"Try it."

"Oooh," Thomas cuts in. "Them's fighting words, but unlucky for you, I'm going to cream you both."

We play for the next hour, with Dylan the one kicking all our asses, ending the game with a lot more cash than he started with.

"Thanks for the payday, guys. I need this now that I've retired. And on that note, I'm out of here."

"What?" Luke jumps up, his gaze flashing to his watch. "It's still early. You're not giving us a chance to win it back?"

"Hell, no." Dylan chuckles to himself when Luke jokingly rolls his eyes.

"I'm done too, boys." Thomas gets up and pats both Luke and me on the head. "I've got a wife to get home to."

"Right. It all makes sense now. I'm guessing they just got home from the girls' night."

"You know it."

With Thomas and Dylan leaving, I collect my sunglasses from the table and move to follow them, only stopping when Luke calls out. "Where do you think you're going?" He flashes me an amused expression when I turn. "You don't have a wife."

"Doesn't mean I want to stay." I shrug and the guys laugh.

"One more drink?"

I eye him curiously, trying to read through his facade, wondering if I'm missing something. Does he want to talk? Or is he not ready to call it a night?

Noting my hesitation, he bounces his eyebrows and grins.

"Okay, fine. *One* drink."

"Done. Catch ya later, pussies." He waves to the guys, and Thomas rolls his eyes. Not that he notices, as he's already turned my way. "Should we head out back?"

"Sure. As long as there's beer. One drink, remember."

"Of course."

"**A**nd then she tells me she's all butt-hurt because I'm replacing her as my best friend. She wouldn't give a shit if I had a *girlfriend*, but a friend... that's taking things too far."

Luke curses, shaking his head in sympathetic disgust. "Women. They don't know what they want. Except Amelia. She's a godsend."

"You know she can't hear us, right?"

"Wouldn't change my view." He smiles with heart eyes.

"Good to know. I like her."

"Amelia?"

"Yeah, she's a good one. And she's good for you. You were a dick and now you're a little less dickish."

"Thanks, man." He pats his heart and grins humbly. "I appreciate that. Another?" He holds up his empty glass and I nod enthusiastically.

I gave up looking at the time when we moved on to whiskey, but I'm pretty certain I'm going to regret this tomorrow. Am I going to do anything about it? No.

"So..." Luke slams down my now full glass in front of me and laughs when it splashes onto the counter.

"Jesus, Luke. Gentle."

"My bad." He fakes a wince. "But look, it's all good."

"Good." I knock back half the liquid before turning to face him, trying to remember what we were talking about.

"I can't—"

"I think you need to fuck Bria," Luke deadpans and I choke on thin air. Thank God he waited until I finished my drink.

"Why would I do that?"

"Because... Imagine you discover you don't actually like her."

What? "I'm not a fucking idiot. I know what I feel."

"Do you? Really? To me it looks like you're settling for comfort because you're too scared to get your dainty heart broken."

My brows furrow and I stare at him for a moment, trying to process what he means. "Did you call me dainty, asshole? I have more muscle in my big toe than—"

"I didn't call *you* dainty. Just your heart."

"Same thing."

"Nope. It's not. This is why I wanted you to stay, man. You need to talk it out." He's slurring slightly but I'm hooked on his every word. "You helped me, I'm helping you. When was the last time you did something without thinking of the consequences?"

"I think I'm doing that now." I frown, trying to work out if that's what he meant.

"Other than now."

"*Fuck*. I don't know."

"Exactly."

"What do you expect from me, Luke? My love life sucks. But fuck if I know how to fix it. I don't want to lose Bria, but at the same time, I'm losing her anyway because I can't be her friend anymore."

"Sheesh." Luke winces before getting up and walking over, dropping onto the couch beside me. "That's rough." He pats my back and we both frown.

"It is."

"So what do we do?"

"I wish I knew. But I'll tell you one thing."

"Yeah?"

"This whiskey tastes *gooood*."

"Of course it does." Luke scoffs as though I offended him. "It's top shelf. Nothing but the best for you, my friend."

"Thanks, man. I appreciate it."

"And I appreciate *you*. So much so that I'm going to fix things for you." He jumps up and I stare at him, confused.

"Fix what?"

"You. Your love life. It's happening."

"Yes." I jump up with him but my head spins and I fall back down. "Fuck, I think I've hit my limit."

Luke laughs obnoxiously as he rocks back and forth. Or am I rocking? "Reed, you hit your limit a long time ago. But it's all good. Your life is about to change."

CHAPTER FIFTEEN

HAYLEY

The bubbly casting assistant calls my name and I jump up, not even bothering to hide my excitement. I'm ready to throw myself into a new project. I'm ready for my next big role.

She smiles awkwardly, her painted red lips thinning as we walk, but the second we turn the corner, she spins on her designer heel and grabs my wrist to still me. "You'll be meeting with the casting director, Lily, today, as well as the director, Steve." I nod politely though this isn't new information to me. "Have you worked with Steve before?" She pauses and... *Uh-oh.* Why did her tone make my stomach sink?

"I *haven't.*"

"I was afraid you'd say that. God, please don't tell anyone I told you this, but I'm already a big fan of yours from the teasers alone, so...just be careful."

What?!

"And don't take his criticisms to heart."

My chest fills with warmth and I bite back a smile. "Are you trying to tell me he's an asshole?"

"I didn't say anything of the sort." She cringes and I can't help but laugh. Assholes I can handle. I've been around enough to learn a lesson or two on ignoring their judgement. It's the sweet, innocent ones that catch me off guard. The ones that give you those sandwich compliments and criticisms. The ones that build you up only to tear you down seconds later.

We keep walking until we've rounded another corner and the assistant stops again, this time pointing to a door. "It's just through here. Best of luck. I think you'd be perfect for the part."

"Thank you."

I stand tall, square my shoulders, and lift my perfectly glossed lips into a confident smile. Opening the door, I come face-to-face with Mr. and Mrs. Judgey, both with unimpressed scowls on their faces. Expressions I'm choosing to believe are left over from the previous audition.

Striding forward with poise, I hold out my hand for Steve and then Lily to shake, smiling when they do. "It's lovely to meet you both," I suck up. "Thank you for the opportunity."

Lily's the first to smile back and the warmth of it surprises me. "It's a pleasure to meet you, Hayley. I'm Lily and this is Steve. Who I'm sure you've heard of. As we've heard of you. You're a hot topic around Hollywood at the moment."

"Before the film has even been released." Steve slouches back in his chair and crosses his ankles casually. "You better hope it's good."

"No hope needed." I smile wider. "I know it's good."

"I love your confidence." Lily leans forward and pats the script in front of her. "Are you ready to read?"

"I am, but..." I glance around the room until my eyes settle on the door. "I thought this was a chemistry reading, since you've already cast the part of Rhys."

"Harry is running late. So lucky for you, I'll be stepping in." Steve stands and a moment of uncertainty flashes across Lily's face. "I want to feel the passion," he tells me as he moves around the table. "I'm sure you're aware that this is an emotional role. It's crucial that the audience connects with your vulnerability and fear."

"Of course." I soften my smile as I nod. This is a little unconventional but... "I'm ready."

"Good. We're going to dive right into the scene where she loses her virginity."

"Oh?" My eyes flash to the casting director as she averts her gaze. "I wasn't prepared for that scene. Can I have a moment to read over it?"

"Don't worry about the words; it's about the emotion. I'll talk, you respond."

Jesus. "Okay. Perfect. Thank you."

Steve steps closer and my heart races as a nervous energy runs through me. But rather than processing it, I use it. I embrace my feelings and pour everything I can into this moment.

"Are you sure you've done this before?" the director asks, and it takes me a second to realise he's delivering his line.

"Yes," I reply softly, the word leaving my mouth on a breath.

We run through a few lines and my confidence never wavers. I'd even go so far as to say I'm more confident now than I was when I walked in. I'm nailing these lines, despite not practising this scene.

"Wait," the director calls out, in character, as I turn away. "I don't care that you lied. But..."

He trails off and I turn back, my gaze full of uncertainty. "But what?"

"Do you know what you've done?" He stares at me intently while I swallow a lump in my throat, channeling my party trick as I bring tears to my eyes.

"I never meant to hurt him."

"And cut." The director breaks character and immediately walks back to his seat, crossing his arms as he sits.

"The tears were a nice touch but I wouldn't fuck you. And I don't believe Rhys would either. What did you think, Lil?"

"I thought it was raw and I could see the vuln—"

"You're right." He cuts her off. "Maybe I missed something. We have another audition booked straight after you, a more seasoned actress. It will take a bit of convincing, but why don't you come by my hotel later and we can revisit the scene."

What? My chest tightens as my eyes flash to Lily's. "Will Harry be there for that?"

"No." He waves off my obvious concern. "He has a dinner meeting. It'll just be the two of us. But I can make this decision on my own. I can tell from Lily's expression that she loves you, but I'm not so sure. I don't tend to buy into the hype, and I haven't seen that star quality yet. There was something but it wasn't *IT*. If you know what I mean." He rubs his chin with his thumb and forefinger while bile rises in my throat. "Some of that could be my fault. I threw a new scene at you and I could feel your hesitancy. Given the time, I'm sure you'd nail the part."

My insides squirm as I force a smile. "Thank you for the offer, Steve.

But I'm going to pass. I gave it my all just now. I don't think another audition would make a difference."

The veneered smile drops from his face as he stands. "Excuse me?"

"Thank you for the opportunity. I hope you'll consider me based on my audition, but if not, I appreciate your time."

I nod to Lily even though it disgusts me that she allows this behavior then turn to leave, only to be stopped in my tracks.

"You're not the star you think you are, Miss Jackman. You've had *one* role and it was based on a book. *A book.* You're about to be eaten alive and you don't even know it. You're gorgeous, sure. You've got that going for you. But you lack experience and it shows." I turn to face him, a smile in place while my chest burns. "I saw the emotion on your face, but your body was stiff and awkward. And you've got this Australian boldness that makes you think you're invincible when you're not." *Australian what?*

"I'm not—"

"In my opinion, you've got a long way to go before you've made it. You need this part. Don't fuck it up."

I nod while my stomach sinks. "I gave it my all." I fake a confident stance. "Thank you again for your time."

I keep the smile plastered on my face as I walk through the lobby and wave to the assistant. I keep smiling as I pass by the other women sitting in the waiting area, reaching the door. But before I can bring myself to leave, I pause. *Dammit.*

"I know we're all meant to be in competition, but please be careful in there. He's a sleaze and incredibly unprofessional. Don't do anything you don't feel comfortable doing. If it doesn't feel right, walk away."

One of the girls gasps while the other glares my way, but no matter their responses, I've done my part. I tried.

And now I feel nauseous.

I'm angry as I walk down the street, but by the time I get in an Uber, I'm second-guessing the entire interaction. I'm second-guessing *myself.*

Jesus. Was I stiff or was he just saying that to make me feel bad? Was I too confident? He said he wouldn't fuck me...and in that moment, I was supposed to be fuckable.

What if he's right? What if... Oh, God.

What if I don't get another part?

I force a smile as I walk up the steps to Reed's door. I haven't seen him since he got me home safely on Sunday night, but Amelia filled me in on his drinking session with Luke, and you bet your ass I'm going to tease him about it. I need the distraction.

I've seen tipsy Reed before, but passed-out-at-a-friend's drunk? That's new—and I wish I'd been there.

Oh, to have been a fly on the wall.

Taking a deep breath, I knock on the door, and as though waiting for my arrival, Reed calls out from somewhere inside. "One sec, Hayls."

"How'd you know it was me?" I call back. "I'm earl—"

The door flies open and he hits me with an "are you kidding me" look, making me finally smile for real. Like he always does.

"What?" I ask as I giggle.

"How many people do you know that knock the way you do?" He raises an eyebrow and I stifle a snort.

"No one. But I do it so often I kind of forgot it wasn't normal."

"Nothing you do is normal, Hayls. It's what we all love about you." He opens the door wide and gestures for me to walk in. "Did you pick a movie?" he asks, fake annoyance in his tone. I negotiated choosing the movie since he abandoned me Tuesday and he expects me to choose something bad, but I have the perfect idea and it all comes back to his drunken night.

"I did." I nod.

"And..." He trails off, waiting for me to elaborate.

"*The Hangover*," I suggest, keeping my tone even.

"With Bradley Cooper?"

"Yep."

"Sure. I'm up for a comedy. The first one? Or a sequel?"

"The first one." I suppress my smile as excitement wells in my chest for the first time since my audition this morning. This is going to be fun. *How else can I allude to knowing about his night?*

"Would you like a drink?" Reed asks, making it easy for me as I follow him into the kitchen.

"I'd love a whiskey."

"A whiskey?" His frowns and I nod again.

"Please."

Pausing for a beat, he eyes me curiously before walking toward the fridge, flashing me another glance as he opens the cabinet above.

And I lose it.

A laugh bursts out of me at the same moment he grabs the bottle.

"The fuck?" Reed huffs out a chuckle, spinning around to face me. "What's so funny?"

"Nothing." I try to calm myself but it's no use.

"Hayley?"

"Okay, fine." I laugh again. "Amelia—"

"Goddammit." Reed cuts me off, his expression pained. "Luke and his big mouth. How much do you know?"

"Only that you got drunk and passed out on their outdoor couch. Both of you. By ten p.m." I can't control my giggles and Reed rolls his eyes.

I'm about to apologize when his words hit me. "Wait. Is there more to know?"

"Nope. That's it."

"Are you sure?" Now it's my turn to give him a look. One that says, "I'm on to you."

"As sure as I can be."

"Are you being cryptic?"

"I don't think so."

"Reed!"

"Come on. It's movie time. Do you really want whiskey and *The Hangover*?"

"Yes, I really want the whiskey." *I need it.* "And *The Hangover* still works. It saves me from having to think of something else."

"Done. Make yourself comfortable. I'll set up."

He grabs the remote from the coffee table and pauses midair before spinning around, his wide eyes flashing my way. "Fuck."

"What? Is it broken?"

"No, I didn't ask about your audition." *Dammit.* I was hoping he'd forget—wishful thinking on my part. "How did it go? I was going to text you but wanted to talk to you in person and then you distracted me."

"It was fine. They still had others to see, so I won't know for a few days."

"Fine?"

"Yes."

His shoulders drop. "What happened?"

I mimic his stance before falling to the couch and covering my face with my hands. "It wasn't great. But I didn't get a good vibe from the director anyway so it's for the best."

"Oh, Hayls—"

"Nope. It's one audition. There will be plenty of others."

"But you—"

"Please, Reed." I hit him with a pleading stare and he reluctantly nods before sitting down beside me.

"I'm here if you want to talk."

"I know. And I appreciate that. But I'll be fine. My agent already has another script for me to read."

"Okay, good. That's great."

"Exactly, so let's go. This movie won't watch itself."

Reed's quiet for the first ten minutes until I start laughing out loud, clearly enjoying myself, and his mood lightens. It's hard to be down when you're watching easy comedy gold. And I thank the universe that I made this choice.

We're about halfway through when Reed's phone buzzes across the coffee table, drawing our attention. He leans forward to check the screen and groans as a sarcastic laugh escapes him.

"What happened?"

"Nothing." He shoves the phone face down next to him and turns back to the TV, faking amusement at something that's clearly not that funny.

"Reed?"

"Shhh," he snaps jokingly before grinning. "I'm trying to watch."

I'm about to argue when *my* phone buzzes, and I snort when I read the message.

AMELIA CHANGED THE GROUP TO "REED'S SUPPORT GROUP."

I found out a few months back that Reed, Luke, Dylan, and

surprisingly, Easton have a group chat together. I thought nothing of it, only using it to tease the guys without them knowing, until Paige needed us. Then I created one for the girls. It was previously named Paige's Support Group.

If Amelia's changing it then—

> AMELIA: So... Luke tells me Reed needs our help. He's fed up with the friend zone

Amelia's message cuts off my speculation and a laugh bursts out of me. "Nothing happened, huh?"

"What?" Reed's eyes flash to mine before he glances down at my phone. "Dammit. Luke, right?"

"Nope. Why would you say that?" I fake innocence and he rolls his eyes just as more messages come through, telling us all that Reed needs our help with his love life.

What did he say when he was drunk?

This is exactly the type of distraction I need.

I read my messages privately as Reed gets bombarded with his own, but when Keeley suggests fake dating as an option, I finally show him my screen.

"You need to shut it down. Now." Reed forces a laugh, running his hands down his face. "I wish I'd never said anything to Luke. He's taken my words *way* out of context."

I don't bother hiding my smirk as I think about his drunkenness. It just gets better and better. "According to Amelia, you told Luke your 'love life was fucked' and that you 'needed to fix it.'"

Reed closes his eyes as his head falls back, the annoyance clear in his expression. "So what you're saying is that everyone's taking Luke's word for it, because I was too drunk to remember?"

"Yep."

"Meaning...you're not shutting it down?"

"Nope." We lock eyes again and I hold my stare, brushing a loose strand of hair away from my face.

He matches my intensity but doesn't respond until I raise an eyebrow in challenge, instantly regretting it when something new crosses his features.

As though an amusing thought hit him, he bites back his smile, but the corners of his lips are bursting at the seams. "What's that look about?" I ask, almost afraid of the answer.

"I've come up with a plan."

"Oh, yeah?" My nose scrunches and he smirks. He went from a pained expression to beaming with excitement, and it doesn't take a genius to know that plan includes me.

"Instead of this fake dating nonsense, I'm going to tell Bria I have a thing for you and we'll see how she reacts."

What? I burst out laughing. "Oh, Reed." I pat his leg with a smile. "If only it was that easy. It won't work unless she *believes* she's going to lose you."

"It's worth a shot though, right?" He comically cringes while I shake my head with a smile.

I feel bad but he's... "Wrong." Although, there might be something in that. I wave him off as my smile widens. "Lucky for you, now *I* have an idea. You're going to love it."

Reed forces a smile and I snort before proudly sitting up straighter. This is brilliant.

"I'm going to be your fake girlfriend."

"You're what now?" His eyes widen and he almost does a double take.

"I'm volunteering." Obviously. "I'm an actress; it makes sense for your new girlfriend to be me."

"Ahh, no. That's insane and you know it. Plus—"

"I disagree," I cut him off, excitement coursing through me. "It makes perfect sense. I'm single. You're single. I'm hot. You're insanely gorgeous and you can't deny we'd make a stunning couple." I pause just long enough to wink and he rolls his eyes. "It's a no-brainer, Reed. We get along. We have fun. Give me one good reason why it shouldn't be me?"

"Maybe because I don't think it's a good idea to begin with. Fake dating is crazy. Come on, Hayls. Think about it."

"Reed." I stare at him deadpan. He's the one acting crazy here.

"Hayley." He stares back at me, copying my moves as I cross my arms over my chest and fake a pout.

"Are you saying I couldn't pull it off?" I'm teasing and it's not exactly fair, but now that the idea's in my head, I'm not going to be able to shake it.

"Hayley Jackman from down under," Reed begins and I smile. "You know I think you're brilliant. And while I'm sure this could be the acting role of your life, you're forgetting one major plot hole." He pauses as I wait patiently, knowing he won't convince me. "I can't act."

"But—"

"Or lie," he adds as though I don't already know that. But luckily...

"There are ways around that, Reed. Trust me, I've worked on some pretty amateur productions and people still loved them." And I've worked on some pretty huge productions that people didn't love. *Dammit*. This is supposed to be taking my mind off that.

Reed's silence draws my attention and I rid myself of my thoughts.

"For someone that thought I was insane, you're sure taking a long time to say no."

"I didn't say you were insane, Hayls. The idea is just..." He releases an overexaggerated sigh, but before I can argue he continues on. "It's not the craziest idea I've heard come out of your mouth. But I'm going to need to think about it. I'm still not convinced."

Yes, I almost have him. "I'll take it." I squeeze his leg and bounce around in excitement. "For now, anyway. I have no doubt I'll change your mind."

His expression turns serious and for the briefest of moments, I consider letting him off the hook. But it's a good idea. And with the way Bria's already been responding to our friendship, I'm sure it will give him the answers he needs.

Chapter Sixteen

REED

"I'm sorry..." I trail off because Hayley's staring at me with a glint in her eyes and it's hard to say no to her. But I have to be strong. "I don't think this is a good idea." Hayley frowns and I can't tell if it's real or fake, but either way, I feel the need to clarify. "I'll rephrase. *Us* fake dating is a bad idea. It's crazy." Unable to meet her stare, I look away, catching a glimpse of her smile.

"I thought you loved my brand of crazy?"

Her question draws my gaze, and I glance back to find her grinning my way, her brows raised in challenge. And she's not wrong.

"I do. But if you'll recall, I don't usually get involved."

"Sure you do. You've never missed one. Just because you don't participate... Admit it, you still have a great time."

She's got me there. "I do. There's nothing better than watching you unapologetically live life to the fullest."

Hayley's expression turns serious for a beat before she schools her features and smiles. "Exactly. So..."

"Give me *three* good reasons."

"What?"

"It's like two truths and a lie but they're all truths. I'm sure you can handle that."

"I know what it is, Reed, but I want three reasons from *you* as to why you don't want to do it. I think that's a better angle."

"I thought you were supposed to be convincing me."

"This is part of that. I don't believe you have three reasons." She stares at me confidently until I nod.

"Okay, fine. Three reasons."

"Good. I'm waiting."

She makes herself comfortable, leaning back into the cushions, locking her hands behind her head. I mimic her moves, the movement making my muscles bulge, drawing Hayley's gaze, just like I knew it would.

"Hey!" She fakes a gasp. "You did that on purpose," she accuses, biting back her smile.

"Did what?" I lie unconvincingly, subtly shaking my head as I trap my smile between my teeth, laughing when she squeezes her eyes shut.

"That's not going to work, Reed. I still want your three reasons."

Damn. Well, I tried.

Taking a deep breath, I rack my brain for three good reasons and find it harder than I thought. In reality, I don't actually have to do this. If I looked Hayley in the eyes and straight up told her my answer was no, she'd instantly back off. I think. But she knows me well enough to see that there's something about the idea that intrigues me a little. If anything, it could be fun.

But, it's Hayley. We have a friendship I never saw coming, and I'm not prepared to risk that. She means too much to me.

I take another deep breath and when I don't speak, Hayley raises an eyebrow, making me laugh. But on closer inspection, there's uncertainty in her expression, almost like she's about to take it all back and agree with me now that it appears as though I'm struggling.

"I'm ready." I cut in before she can speak. "For one... I've got a few away games coming up and then I'll be busy with the playoffs. It will make it hard for us to play pretend enough for Bria to notice. Two—and I mentioned this before—I can't act, but more than that, what do I know about being a boyfriend, fake or otherwise?"

Hayley reserves her reactions and nods blankly instead, holding her judgment until I'm finished, and I'm grateful for that because my reasons are weak. At least they are until I remember one vital piece of information.

"Three... I don't want to."

Her face drops, and I hate that I'm the reason. I offer a sad smile, hoping it softens the blow. "Well, *damn*." She cringes. "I can't argue with that."

Shit. "You're taking it the wrong way." I smile, grabbing her hand. "I don't mean it to sound harsh. I like our relationship as is and don't want it to change."

"But...since it's all fake, it wouldn't have to change. Right? At least not behind the scenes."

My stomach knots and I internally grimace. If I'm not careful, this conversation alone might change things between us and I can't afford that. Adding another layer to the friendship is bound to mess it up.

"Of course it would change," I say, trying not to be too expressive when I want to shake some sense into her. "We'd have to make it real. Believable. And that would mean affection and kissing. One kiss and you're bound to fall in love with me," I joke to hide my concern and Hayley laughs, momentarily easing my mind. "I've seen the way you ogle my body when you think I'm not looking."

"Oh, Reed. If you think there's anyone out there that can resist your body, you are not paying attention."

I huff out a laugh as my cheeks heat. But embarrassment aside, I love that we've settled back into our easy banter. "I—"

Hayley's phone buzzes, cutting me off, and when she checks the screen, she giggles. "Gotta love Amelia." She smirks.

"Why does it feel like I'm not going to like this?"

Hayley angles the phone my way and I groan.

> AMELIA: You should put your hand up to date Reed. It's perfect. You get along so well and no one knows that you're friends

Hayley laughs again but I refuse to look at her. "She's got a point," she says with a new happiness in her tone. And we can't have that.

Grabbing the phone out of her hand, I hold it above my head as I stand up and move to the other side of the couch, typing out a message.

> HAYLEY: I don't think that's a good idea. We'll have to come up with another plan

"Hey." She rushes around to catch me, trying to get to her phone, but I'm too tall for her to reach it.

"You are not making me out to be the bad guy. I'm not ruining their fun."

Another idea comes to mind and I duck around her, running off to type another message.

> HAYLEY: Actually Reed thinks it's a great idea but he's way out of my league. No one would believe it

I show Hayley the message and a snort escapes her as she shakes her head. "Speaking of not believing... Amelia is never going to believe *that*."

"Why not?"

"Because I do *not* think you're out of my league."

"Sure you do. You always tell me I'm too nice for the likes of you."

Her expression wavers before she hides it with another smile. Fuck. I open my mouth to tell her I'm joking but her phone buzzes in my hand.

> AMELIA: Ha. You're hilarious. What's the real reason?

Hayley's eyes flash to mine, waiting with anticipation. "I'm sorry, Hayls. But I'm only saying no because I don't want to ruin our friendship over a lost cause like Bria. I honestly don't think it will work."

Hayley's face falls again, but this time, I know it's for me. She feels sorry for me and I hate that. I want to get back to us. The happy-go-lucky friends.

"How about we watch the rest of the movie?" Hayley asks, beating me to it.

"Works for me." We settle back onto the couch, but before I press play, I turn to Hayley with a smile. "Thank you. You mean the world to me."

Her lips pull into a grin and she squeezes my arm. "Anytime."

I understand she just wants to help. I do. But what if it changes everything? I have to hold strong. *Don't I?*

Hayley's sound asleep when my alarm goes off the next morning. So after tiptoeing around the house, trying not to wake her—not an easy feat when you're my size—I write her a quick note and sneak out just after six. It takes everything in my power not to wake her to ask if she's okay. She drank herself into an alcohol coma after our fake dating fiasco, and while she claims she was just enjoying herself, I'm certain the drinking had nothing to do with our dating conversation and everything to do with her audition.

I'd love for her to talk to me about it, but I'm smart enough to know that waking her up at five thirty in the morning to ask is *not* the way to make that happen. For anyone. But especially Hayley. She'll tell me when she's ready.

After a short drive, I pull up in the Storm parking lot to find Landon on the phone near the entrance, making me smile as I think about how much he's changed since I first started mentoring him not too long ago.

He's not a cocky rookie like we've seen in the past, namely with Zane, but he's also not the shy guy he once was, and that's progress.

I wave as I approach and he hangs up from his call, grinning my way. "Morning." He holds his hand out for a fist bump—like I often do—and I smile as I return it.

"How are you, Landon? Ready for a big game tomorrow?"

"I'm ready to watch." He laughs and it brings about my own.

"You'll be game ready before you know it. Coach has been watching you more and more. Don't pretend you haven't noticed."

"Oh, I've definitely noticed. He's always the first to let me know when I fuck something up."

"That's better than the alternative. At least he knows you exist." I pat him on the back as he opens the door for us both. "I bet you'll be a starter in no time."

I walk in ahead of him and he jogs to catch up with me. "I know what you're doing, Reed. And I appreciate it."

"I have no idea what you're talking about," I lie, biting back my smile. "I'm just being honest."

"Well, thanks anyway. For *not* mentoring me or whatever. I'll take all the help I can get."

"Anytime, man. I'm happy to help. You just have to ask."

Chapter Seventeen

HAYLEY

A ringing wakes me the next morning and I groan as I reach out to stop it. "It's too early. Go away." Waving my hand where my bedside table should be, I come up empty, opening my eyes to find I'm not in my room.

My heart seizes until a foggy memory works its way into my mind, instantly relaxing me.

I'm still at Reed's.

After we decided not to fake date, we watched the rest of the movie while drinking ourselves stupid. Actually no, I drank myself stupid—since I no longer had something to distract me from my nightmare audition—while Reed supplied the goods, complaining that his head still hurt from his drinking session with Luke. Three days earlier.

My phone rings again and I find it on the floor beside the bed—where a side table *should* be. *Who doesn't have side tables?* Where does he put his water? Or lamp.

Dangling over the edge of the mattress, I stretch out to grab my phone, securing it seconds before it stops ringing.

"Hello. Sorry."

"Thank God. Hayley, it's Mel." *My agent.* "I've called twice already."

What? "Sorry. I was asleep. What time is it?" I must have slept in. God, Reed's probably on his way back from practice already, and—

"It's seven."

"*Seven?*" I sit up quickly. "In the morning?" *Did they ring her about the audition?*

"Yes, Hayley." She laughs but it holds an edge to it that's not usually there. "I know it's early. But I had to call you right away."

"Oh God. They called you. What did they say?" I fall back onto the bed and grab the pillow, ready to cover my eyes. I was vague on the phone to her on my way to Reed's yesterday. I should have been honest.

"No, I haven't heard anything and I want to... Actually, let's talk about that later. I called for a different reason."

"Okay." The urgency in her tone has me sitting up again and running a hand through my hair.

"I had a late dinner with the head of Whitaker Productions last night, and they want you for the part of Cynthia Rose in *Reckless Desire*."

"Bullshit." I sit up straighter, biting back a squeal. *Reckless Desire*. Holy shit. Maybe it's good I didn't get the other role. I would die for the part of Cynthia. Sure, it's more pressure because it's another movie based on a book. But this one's a romance, not a fantasy, so I'd be hitting a whole new audience. "Please tell me you're not joking."

"Do you think I'd be calling this early if I was?"

"That would be harsh."

"It would be, and that's not me. They *want* you."

"Oh my God." I allow myself to squeal this time but move the phone away from my mouth until Mel's muffled voice permeates the air.

"Sorry, I missed that."

"I said, there's a but."

"A but?"

"Yep. They're worried you're too promiscuous for the part."

"They what?" My jaw drops and I stare into space. "Why?" My shoulders hunch but the second the question is out of my mouth, I know the answer. "The photos."

"Yep."

The goddamn photos. It turns out someone was keeping an eye on me after the Storm game the other night and took photos of that dickhead following me into the bathroom. And another of me walking out with a different guy—the Storm rookie who came to my aid. Thankfully, you couldn't really see the rookie's face, but I'm the first to admit it doesn't look good.

"This is bullshit. I haven't slept with anyone for months." She doesn't need to know any details, but *I* feel the need to put it out into the universe, to remind myself more than anything else. I am *not* promiscuous. But even if I was, it's *nothing* to be ashamed of and it shouldn't rob me of a part.

"Unfortunately, the truth doesn't matter. The photos make it look like you had sex in a public bathroom. Twice. With different people. Or maybe two at once."

Jesus Christ. "What it doesn't show is that the first guy dragged me in there and the second guy saved me. Too bad they didn't get a photo of me kneeing him in the balls."

"I'm sorry. I wish I had better news."

"It's not your fault. But why are you calling? To tell me I *almost* got an amazing part?" I'm shitty and taking it out on her, but tough.

"I'm on your side, remember?" Her voice softens. "I'm calling because they're giving you a chance to change your image and read for the role."

"What?" I fall back onto the bed, sighing in frustration. "What does that even mean?"

"It means we need to bring back Australia's sweetheart but with an American twist."

"Oh-kay. And what does that entail?"

"I'm not sure yet. But for now, fewer bars and less drinking."

My head chooses that moment to throb as though reminding me about the copious amount of alcohol currently in my system, and on top of that, I'm taking this phone call in someone else's bed.

This image change is not going to be easy.

Closing my eyes, I force a smile so she won't hear the annoyance in my voice and reluctantly agree. "No bars. Less drinking. Gotcha."

"And no bad boys."

"Bad boys? God, this is ridiculous." I haven't been with *any* boys, let alone bad ones, and now I have to avoid them completely. *Is this real life?*

"Do you want the part or not?" Mel asks, her voice serious.

"I do."

"Then no bad boys."

Dropping the phone to the bed, I throw my arms out and sigh, feeling a piece of paper beneath my hand.

Rolling over, I find a note on Reed's pillow and smile as I read it.

I'm off to practice. There's food in the fridge and a bottle of water on the floor next to you. Help yourself to anything. I'll be home around lunchtime, but if you need to leave before then, the door locks by itself.
Reed
P.S. I slept on the couch

My heart races as I smile to myself. Of course, he slept on the couch. Taking a deep breath, I laugh as a memory from last night springs to mind. "What about good guys?" Since I'm now in the spotlight for the wrong reason, paparazzi are likely to start following me around, and I have no doubt that someone will get evidence of my friendship with Reed. I refuse to stop spending time with him for a damn role.

I need him too much.

I need one constant in my life. Amelia's amazing, and Paige and I have become great friends lately. But they both have a lot going on, and I don't want to get in the way. Reed has a life outside of our friendship, and yet, when I call or text, he always makes me feel like I'm his number one priority, even when he's teasing me, and I've never had that.

Not even with my parents.

The last few months have really opened my eyes up to the way I've allowed myself to be treated in the past. Yes, I've always held my own and stood up for myself and my friends, but there was a lot I accepted as normal that was anything but. Friends that got pissy when I didn't have time for them. Boyfriends that showed me off and paraded me around like a trophy.

I was well-known in Australia. Hell, I *am* well-known in Australia. But because of that, the high-profile boyfriends I had back home weren't in the relationship for me. They wanted the recognition it gave them. And I let it happen. Mostly because I was subconsciously doing that same thing to them.

God, I even allowed my last boyfriend to cheat on me, pretending it never happened so that he'd invite me to the US when he was cast in a series over here.

I hold myself in high regard. But I never held anyone else to that same standard. When I'm with Reed, it feels like he sees me the same way. No, screw that, it doesn't just *feel* like it. *He does.* And he treats me as such.

I can't lose that. And on that note, I get why he didn't want us to fake a relationship. God, why didn't I think of this yesterday?

"Hayley?" Mel questions me, bringing me back to the present.

"Sorry, I missed that."

"I said... What did you mean when you asked, 'what about good guys'?"

"Oh. What if I'm seen with a good guy? I have a close friend and—"

Mel gasps. "Yes. That's perfect, Hayley. If you can find someone that's squeaky clean then I say go for it. It might win you some bonus points in the sweetheart department."

"Go for what?" I hesitate, not liking where this is going.

"You should pretend to date your friend. The good guy."

Dammit. "I was worried you'd say that."

"Why?"

"Never mind. I'll figure something out. I promise." What? I have no idea. But fake dating is off the table. I know now that it was a bad idea. I was too busy trying to distract myself yesterday, and I didn't truly listen to what Reed was saying.

"Great." Mel's tone lifts and I can hear the smile in her voice. "I'll leave it to you then. This is a huge role, Hayley. If you think *Jaded Beginnings* was big, wait until you see the fanfare around this one."

"I know. I've already been hearing about it." Tension works its way into my chest, but I smile through it. I was a fool to think it was going to be easier after the success of my last movie. My star may be rising with the general public, but with the people that matter, I'm just another actress looking for her next role. And the joke's on me.

"Good," Mel responds, oblivious to my spiral. "Then you know what's at stake."

"Yeah. A huge commission."

Mel laughs out loud and I can almost picture her giving me a slow clap. "I love Australian humor. Let's talk soon."

"Okay. Bye."

She hangs up and I burst out laughing. But it's not one of those "this is a funny situation" laughs; it's more of a "what the fuck just happened" laugh and it's not at all humorous.

My head spins when I try to get up, so I let my eyes glide closed, giving myself another hour since it's still way too early for my liking.

I swear I've just drifted off to sleep when the front door bangs open and I jolt, grabbing my phone to check the time. *Midday?! What the hell?*

Jumping out of bed, I run my fingers through my messy blonde hair and make my way down the hall, my eyes locking on Reed as he dumps his bag on the floor.

With a sigh, he kicks the door closed and runs a hand down his face.

I'm silent as he checks his phone, but when he turns my way, I finally speak. "Hey."

"Jesus Christ." He startles, his fist clenching until he sees that it's me. "You stayed?" he questions, his face marred with confusion.

"I did."

He frowns as his eyes bounce around the room. "Is everything okay?"

"Is everything okay with *you*?"

"Of course." He scratches the back of his neck. "Why?"

"Because you were clenching your fist and I didn't think you had it in you to punch someone."

That perks him up. "Are you calling me weak?" He raises an eyebrow as some of the stress evaporates from his features, his shoulders dropping.

"With those muscles? *Never.* But you weren't your happy self when you walked in."

"Just more Bria bull...stuff"

"I'm sorry. I really wish that would all work out for you. Want to talk about it?"

"Nah." He shakes his head. "I want to eat. Do you want to stay for lunch?"

"You're my ride home, so... I'm at your mercy."

"Is that why you're still here?" he questions, hitting me with a smirk that could melt steel.

"No, it's not actually." I stand tall, folding my arms across my chest. "If you must know, I was woken up early by a phone call and fell back to sleep after. Your arrival woke me."

"At twelve?"

"Yes, at twelve. Put that judgy expression away."

Reed chuckles. "Sorry, it's been a while since I slept that late. Actually, no, I've never slept that late. But you do you, Hayls." He bites back a smirk and I snort.

"You said something about lunch? Put yourself to use, would ya."

"Anything for you."

Anything for me? I grin but my mind drifts back to my conversation with my agent. *Would you fake date me for me, Reed?* I bet you would. Lucky for you, I'm not going to ask.

CHAPTER EIGHTEEN

HAYLEY

I groan as the cheesy goodness coats my taste buds, the heat warming my soul. "I don't know how toasties taste different over here, but they're sooo good."

"Toasties?" Reed cocks a brow as his lips pull into a grin.

"Sorry." I roll my eyes. "Grilled cheese. You and your American words."

"Funny that. You know, with me being American."

"It's still annoying," I huff. "It's safe to say I have at least one person a day staring at me like I have two heads. And a director at the audition last month asked me to say, 'put another shrimp on the barbie.' We don't even call them shrimp, you jackass."

"You don't?" Reed questions and I'm about to have a go at him when he cracks up laughing. "I'm kidding. I knew that. It's prawns, right?"

My eyes narrow and I fake a pout. "Lucky. You're right."

"Hayls." Reed bites back a smile as he schools his features. "Would you like me to teach you how to be American?"

"What?" I bark out a laugh. "No, thanks. I'm good. Did you not see the trailer for *Jaded Beginnings*? I nailed it. I can be American. It's the Australian me that I'm struggling with."

Reed frowns and I realize I've said too much, rushing to change the topic. "How did—"

"Whoa. Whoa. Back up... What does that mean?"

"Nothing. It was a throwaway comment."

"*Hayls*," he lightly scolds and despite knowing he'd never push me, I've never been good at holding back, especially with Reed.

"The last twenty-four hours have been a bit of a wake-up call. And I'm having a moment."

"Again. What does that mean?"

"The director said something about my Australian boldness yesterday and then my agent called this morning. I don't think my acting skills are an issue, but my personality might be."

"Okay..." Reed's brow creases and I can tell he's holding back some anger. "I'm not following, but I feel like I should be pissed off on your behalf."

I rush out a laugh and reach forward to squeeze his forearm, giving him a less complicated version of what Mel said. And one that won't make him any angrier than he already is. "My agent told me about a part I'm up for but that the producers want someone a little less wild?" I question myself, not even sure that's the right word.

Burying my face in my hands, I groan at how ridiculous that sounds until silence falls around me. I cringe, guessing what's coming, and when I glance up, sure enough, I haven't succeeded in reducing Reed's rage.

"What the fuck does that mean?" he snaps.

Shit. "They want a relationship type, I guess, and that's not me." *Wait. Double shit.* "I don't—"

"They want you to have a boyfriend?"

"No. Ignore that. I just need—"

"A boyfriend," Reed repeats and I grimace, turning away from him. He's silent for a moment before his palm lands on my shoulder, making me jump until his breath warms my skin. "Well, Baby." His deep, raspy voice penetrates my soul, momentarily stunning me. "I may not agree with them, but I can be your man."

I stare at him for a beat, swallowing a lump in my throat. *Damn*, that man's voice could set ice on fire. He raises an eyebrow and I shake off my thoughts. "Baby?" I question him, pretending the term of endearment doesn't sound delicious rolling from his lips.

"Yep. And there's more where that came from. But you owe me. Big time."

"No, I don't. Because I don't need—"

"You need a boyfriend, Hayls, and apparently, I need a girl. So it's a win-win."

"Reed, I—"

"Nope." He steps even closer, cutting me off as he wraps his arms around me, rocking me back and forth. "You know I'm always going to be there for you. I hate that they expect you to be someone you're not, but if it helps, I'll do anything."

"But yesterday—"

"It doesn't matter what I said yesterday. Today's a new day."

"Okay, that may be true, but now *I've* changed my mind."

"Why? Because you realized I was right?" He raises a brow and I shake my head.

"No, because I realised *I was wrong*. I shouldn't have tried to convince you."

"Good thing you're not convincing me then." He steps back and folds his arms over his chest, leaning back on his heels. "I came to this decision all on my own."

"This is crazy." I let my eyes drift shut, running a hand through my hair as I consider my options. "I—"

Reed chuckles softly, but when I look his way, he zips up his lips. "Sorry. But you sound like me."

"God, I'm sorry. I shouldn't have said anything. You don't have to do this. We don't have to do this." I cover my face with my hands again and shake my head. He doesn't want this. He's only doing it for me.

The energy around me shifts, and when I uncover my eyes, I find him standing closer than I expected, his gaze soft as he watches me.

"I'm joking, Hayls. I promise I want to do this. For you."

Tension swarms my chest as I smile up at him. But this, right here, is precisely why we shouldn't be doing it. He always puts others ahead of himself. It was okay when I was doing it for him, but now... "I don't think it's a good idea."

"Why?"

"Because my reputation needs saving, but what if I bring yours down in the process?"

"Not possible. Haven't you heard? I'm the golden boy of the NFL." He winks and my heart jolts.

"Exactly." I turn away, groaning. I should never have suggested the idea.

"Hayley, stop. I don't know why they'd ever want you to be someone you're not. But if you think being in a relationship could help and that we could pull it off, it could benefit us both."

I almost laugh, seeing through his attempt to make this about him when it's never about him. "What do you get out of it again?" I ask, subtly calling him out. "Bria?"

Reed lets out a long sigh, his fingers curling around the back of his neck, clearly uncomfortable with the change of topic. "I don't even know," he admits. "Maybe it would show her that she missed out. That I was standing right in front of her and she fucked up."

"Really? So if Bria knocked on your door at 4 a.m. the day after we go public, with a tear-soaked face, begging you for forgiveness, asking you to choose her, you'd say 'suck on that, Bria. Now you know how I felt for all those years. Booyah.'" I fist pump the air and Reed's jaw falls to the floor.

"Wow." His eyes light up before he laughs. "I have no words."

"So... no?"

"Never change, Hayls. You're perfect exactly as you are. As for me, I have no fucking idea what I'm doing, but if I can help you and help myself in the process, what have I got to lose? Just tell me what I need to do."

The tightness in my chest dissipates a little, and a sense of calm takes over me. Reed's a good guy, and I know how to keep things professional, to play a part. Maybe we can do this without it ruining his reputation. But he has to get something out of it too. I have to help with Bria. Somehow.

"Okay, *boyfriend*." I smile, ignoring the nervous energy running through me. "Let's do this."

Reed smirks at my new name for him, and when my smile widens, he nods. "I'm in. Where do we start?"

"God, I have no idea. I'm going to have to think about it."

"That's probably wise. For both of us. But...ah..." Reed glances at the clock on his wall and cringes. "I'm supposed to be meeting Bria in an hour and—"

"Maybe don't tell her. Not yet. She already knows we're friends, so you won't need any buildup. Let's chat again Tuesday and work it all out."

"Tuesday sounds perfect."

"Good. If that's settled, I'll head off and let you get ready. I need chocolate and a bath. Stat."

"Ahh, the little luxuries. Do you do that often?"

"When I'm stressed," I rush out and instantly regret it. "Wait. This isn't—"

"I get it."

"Good. Thanks." I think about my muscles relaxing and bite back a groan. A bath is definitely needed. If only I had a hot tub. "I'll see you Tuesday?"

"You will."

With a smile, I leave Reed to prepare for his time with Bria, but only make it to the bottom step before he jogs out the front door, chasing after me. "You don't have a car, Hayls. I'm your ride, remember?" he calls out and his panic makes me laugh.

"I booked an Uber. I'm resourceful like that."

"Let me drive you. *Please*." A spark of pain flickers in his expression as though not helping me physically hurts him, but my Uber's almost here.

"Next week. As soon as we're official, I give you permission to be the world's best boyfriend. Deal?"

His expression turns mischievous. "What have I gotten myself into?"

"You're going to love it. Just you wait." I smile and he winks before heading back inside.

Are we crazy? Maybe. But if this has to happen, I've definitely found the best person for the job. And if it helps Reed move on, one way or another, even better.

Bill is back at the concierge desk when I walk through my lobby thirty minutes later, and he waves me over when I walk past. "Miss Jackman, I have another letter for you."

"Another letter?"

"Yes, more fan mail. A little girl dropped it off."

"A little girl? The same as last time?"

"No, ma'am. That was a little boy."

"Oh, of course. I remember." I smile but confusion takes over me. "Thank you."

Bill hands me the note and my gaze drifts to the entryway, expecting to see someone waiting for me.

"It was a few hours ago," Bill cuts in, seemingly answering my thoughts. "Right. Yes. Thank you. Hope you have a lovely afternoon."

"Thank you." He nods and I smile again, clasping the letter in my hand as I head toward the elevator. My curious expression greets me as I stare at my reflection in the mirrored doors, the letter heavy in my hand. *One letter is cute, but two?*

I don't wait until I'm in my apartment this time, opening the envelope as soon as I'm alone.

Dear Hayley,

I wanted to wish you a Merry Christmas and let you know that while you may be lonely this holiday season, with your family back in Australia, you're not alone. You have a huge fan base and we're all counting down the days until the world sees what we see.

Don't worry about what the gossip says. Your real supporters know who you are. Don't ever change.

Take care

Your biggest fan

My real supporters know who I am. Don't ever change? That's close to what Reed said.

Maybe it's time I believed it.

And for those that can't see that, I'm going to change their views. I'm going to rewrite the narrative and get that role.

Cynthia Rose is mine.

And apparently, so is Reed now.

Oh, God.

CHAPTER NINETEEN

REED

I jog across the road, running late to meet Bria at our go-to park, Hayley's confession still on my mind. She says she's fine, but I couldn't help noticing her spark had dimmed ever so slightly. She was starting to doubt herself and that's not her. Her self-confidence has never been an issue.

If it was Bria, I'd say she was hiding her feelings, but she's not Bria, and Hayley's always been an open book. I'm not sure she realizes how much it's affecting her.

But now that we're *dating*, I can make sure she knows her worth while helping her get the role she deserves. It's a win-win. It's nerve-racking as fuck, but I'm committed now.

Here's to being a boyfriend.

I'm lost in thought as the lush greenery comes into view, but when I arrive at the park entrance, Bria's MIA and she's always early. I grab my phone to text her, making sure she's still coming after her ridiculous text this morning—a text that had me reeling until Hayley distracted me—when my phone rings in my hand.

"Hey." My answer is curt, nothing like it usually is.

"Gah, I'm sorry. I'm almost there." Unlike me, Bria is her usual upbeat self, and though it shouldn't, it makes me feel bad. "Parking is a nightmare."

She laughs while my gaze drifts across the five different birthday parties spread out across the lawn. "Everybody who's anybody is here today."

"Want to go somewhere else? Somewhere less crowded?"

"Nah, I'm good if you are. They're all occupied and no one's taken our tree."

"How thoughtful of them."

"I thought so." Throwing my head back, I let out a sigh and prepare to question her about the text. I need to get it off my chest. "Bria—"

"Yes. Got one," she cuts me off. "Give me two minutes."

"Okay. Yup. See you soon."

Since there are no parking spaces within *five* minutes of the park, I take my time dodging the crowd, strolling the walking track instead of passing through the masses. I've just reached our favorite spot, our tree, when Bria rushes over.

And like always...my heart stops.

Things have been off between us for weeks now, but when she hits me with her carefree smile, it's like all is right in the world.

Only it isn't. It's a whole lot of fucked up.

"Sorry again," she rushes out, rearranging her dress as she sits down on the blanket I laid out, curling her feet underneath herself. "I have a surprise for you. I stopped off at Johan's to get your favorite *fake* treat."

Her nose scrunches as she hands me a colorful veggie bowl with slices of tender steak, and I surprisingly burst out laughing. "Don't knock it until you've tried it."

"I have. And I'm not saying it doesn't taste good. I'll just never understand how you can call it a treat. *This* is a treat." She pulls a chocolate-coated pretzel out of a paper bag followed by a cup of dipping sauce, and a genuine smile tugs at my lips.

I bet Hayley's eating something similar right now.

"Want a bite?" Bria asks and I shake my head, screwing my nose up just like she did. "I'll stick to my veggies, thanks."

"I thought you'd say that. Otherwise I would have brought two. This one's all mine."

She takes a bite and my gaze drops to her mouth, still remembering how she tastes after all these years. After our one and only kiss. The intrigue, the excitement.

The feelings come back to me until I remember her message from this morning, and my stomach sinks.

> BRIA: Did she stay over like I used to? Am I still getting my turn?

She used those actual words. *Her turn? What the hell?* I was so pissed off I couldn't reply, and after a shitty morning of walkthroughs and meetings, I returned to the locker room to find another message.

> BRIA: I'm sorry. That was uncalled for. I miss you. Please don't cancel

Because that makes it all right.

Hell, no. I'd probably still be pissed if I hadn't gone home to find Hayley in my apartment, lifting my mood. Like she always does. Even when we're having a serious conversation.

But even so, Bria and I need to talk it through. "About—"

"I'm sorry again," she cuts in, anticipating the topic change. "Can things go back to the way they were *before* it got weird between us? Go back to this." She gestures between us and I force a grin. "The two of us, hanging out, no behind-the-scenes bullshit causing tension."

While I'd love that more than anything, I don't think it's possible. Even now it feels awkward. "I think we need to find a new normal," I say instead, trying to focus on my words rather than the sad expression she's giving me. "You're dating more and I've—"

"Got Hayley?"

Fuck. Now would be the perfect time to segue into my new relationship, but we said we'd wait.

"Having other people in our lives doesn't mean our friendship is any less meaningful. It means we have to make more of an effort to keep in touch. It won't be as easy, and—"

"You're right." She cuts me off, though I knew it was coming. She's never been great at handling conflict, and I'm usually the one that helps her through it, not the one she's conflicting with. "I shouldn't have sent that text," she adds and I nod in agreement.

"No, you shouldn't have. But I get it." Sort of. A little bit.

"Do you forgive me?" She smiles. She knows my answer. I *always* forgive her. But I'm starting to question why. She's been a constant comfort for me since we met, and it's hard to shake that. She was the first person I connected with after moving thousands of miles away for college. She supported me when my brother took off with his girlfriend, going MIA for three fucking months while I traveled home to be with my parents. She gave me sound advice when my college roommate got addicted to performance enhancing drugs and I spent sleepless nights helping him through the detox. She came to the funeral when my last surviving grandparent died.

She was there for me. Always.

And now our friendship is turning to shit.

"Reed?" Bria interrupts my thoughts, her voice hesitant. She knows she fucked up. Just like she knew last time. But how many fuckups do I have to endure before I stop letting her off the hook?

It was never like this between us, and other than me deciding I wanted to get over my feelings for her, I don't know what's changed.

I sigh but force a grin. "You know my answer, Bria. I wouldn't be here if I didn't want to be. But how about you make it up to me and come to my game tomorrow?" I'm not sure why I continue to ask, but I do. You never know. One day she might surprise me.

"Ugh. I wish I could. I do."

But that day isn't today.

"All good. Maybe next time."

"Yes. Definitely. Thank you for forgiving me, Reed. I don't know what I'd do without you."

"Anytime." I smile and for the first time, it feels like a lie.

With seconds to go in our game against Miami, Thomas launches the ball eighty yards toward the end zone and my heart stops. If we don't score now, we lose. This is our last shot. Zane sprints forward, his eyes locked on the ball as he dives across the line, securing it in his grasp seconds before he hits the ground.

And the crowd roars.

We did it. We fucking did it. Again. And I didn't suck. In fact, I was on fire.

After my abysmal practice yesterday, I wasn't so sure of myself, but catching up with Bria in the afternoon helped—a little—though it was Hayley's texts that really pulled me out of my head.

> Hayley: Kick some ass today, boyfriend. I only accept the best from my man

It was such a typical Hayley message, and yet, it was like a punch to the chest. I'll put my money on her knowing I needed it. Her little moments of comedic gold are always well timed. And in this case, it couldn't have been more perfect.

While I'm lost in thought, Luke jumps onto my back, cheering in my ear.

"We fucking did it," he yells and he's right. We're all so in sync, some would say it's sickening.

"The Super Bowl is in our sights." He slaps my abs before waving to the crowd and jumping off me, landing not so gently on the ground. "If I was a betting man, I'd be placing my bets now."

"The cocky Luke is back, I see."

"Did he ever really leave?" He winks and I burst out laughing.

Celebrations are loud as we head back to the locker rooms and I glance toward the suite, a smile on my face as I seek out Hayley, not even knowing if she's there but almost certain that she is.

It's been a little over twenty-four hours since we committed to fake dating, and while we're yet to decide how to go public or tell our friends, if she's here, I'm making the first move. It's about time we at least acknowledge each other.

When my gaze finds the partners' suite, sure enough, Hayley's watching me, her painted lips pulled into a thin-lipped grin, her eyes full of sass.

I lift my hand in a soft wave and wink, dropping a breadcrumb for whoever may be watching, smirking when she shakes her head.

In the locker room, Coach delivers his normal subdued celebratory speech—refusing to give us too much praise in case our heads grow larger than they already are—and then our owner, Salvatore D'Angelo, steps up to the mic. A rare occurrence unless he has news.

"Congratulations on another amazing win." He pauses for the cheers and when we get too loud, Keeley brings us back to attention. "Thank you, Keeley. Men, I appreciate the hard work you're all putting in to impress the new boss, and trust me when I say, it doesn't go unnoticed." He pauses again, and this time he's met with forced smiles and a few awkward claps. "Wow. You really are trying, aren't you? And here I was joking around. I bought this team because I saw something in you all. And you've proven through all the wins *and* the losses, that no matter what, you're a *team*. The support you have for each other is commendable. You've been through a lot this past year and come out of it shining. We have another Super Bowl in our sights, and I have no doubt you're going to raise hell to get there. Remember who you are when the tough times hit, and we'll always come out on top. Thank you all."

That was weird.

He steps down from our makeshift stage, otherwise known as a bench seat, and locks eyes with Keeley, his expression wan while she offers a reassuring smile. With the controversy surrounding our team lately, my first instinct is that something else is coming. Something we're not going to like.

My gaze bounces around the room to check if anyone else caught that little interaction, but I'm interrupted before I can process it.

"I hear you're dating the Jackonator." Luke waggles his eyebrows, laughing at himself, or me, while I stare at him confused.

"I'm what?"

"You're dating Hayley, right?"

Jesus. Luke knows? I guess that means Hayley's told Amelia. "It's, ahh..." *Fuck.* What do I say to that? We haven't decided what we're doing and—

Luke's laughter turns obnoxious. "You should see your face. *Relax.* I know the truth. But I'm the only one, so let's hope you're a damn good actor, because Hayley sure is. If anyone fucks up, it's going to be you."

"Wow. Thanks for the vote of confidence." I play along, but on the inside, my stomach churns. It's highly likely that he's right. It *will* be me that fucks this up, and I don't want to let her down. Especially now that it isn't about me.

"There's more on the line than getting over your little crush," Luke adds, digging a knife into my already sensitive wound. "You're doing it for Hayls now."

Fuck fuck fuck. "I know that, asshole. I wouldn't have agreed to it if I didn't think I could do it."

Well, at least, Hayley thinks I can.

"I know." Luke's expression turns serious as he steps closer. "And I'm here if you need me. I said I'd help you move on, and I meant it. The fake dating may not have been my doing, but I set the wheels in motion, and I plan to see it through." He cups my shoulder and grins like a Cheshire cat. "Now get changed. It's time to find our girls."

CHAPTER TWENTY

HAYLEY

Amelia smiles as Reed disappears off the field, and I count down in my head, ready for her questions in three, two, one...

"I need *all* the details. Your text gave me nothing."

"That's not true. I told you the most important part."

"You said... 'Reed and I are fake dating' and when I texted back with a million question marks, I got nothing in return."

"I knew I'd be seeing you today. And honestly, I don't know any more than that."

"How do you feel about it?" She offers me a sympathetic smile.

"At first I loved the idea, but then I felt bad when Reed was hesitant, and now I'm good again. You know me. When I commit to something, I'm all in."

"I *do* know that. And I'm a little scared for Reed."

"Don't be." I laugh through my words. "He knows what he's getting himself into. I've always been real with him."

Amelia's nose scrunches and my smile widens. "I don't doubt that," she confirms. "But...what made him change his mind?"

With a hushed tone, I fill Amelia in on my conversation with my agent and her jaw drops. "Are you kidding me? Hayls, that's ridiculous. Do you really want the role if they're going to expect you to change?" Her reaction is exactly why I held off telling Reed the whole truth. He deserves to know, but if I'd told him yesterday, he would have wanted to kill someone. My heart races just thinking about it.

"People change for movies all the time. Actors lose weight, gain weight, change hair color. Hell, some shave their heads. Technically, I'm not changing. I'm just making people believe I'm the person they want me to be."

"When you should be showing them the amazing person you are."

I smile when she squeezes my hand. "Thanks, Ames, but I don't think the public is ready for my awesomeness."

"You're probably right." She laughs out loud. "But that's their loss, not your issue."

"Damn straight."

"So Reed agreed after you told him what your agent said?"

"No, I never actually told him everything. He suggested it before I had the chance to explain. Told me he wanted to help."

"That sounds like Reed."

"Am I wrong to have agreed with it? Am I taking advantage?"

"No, I don't think so, because while he thinks he's doing it for you, it's also helping him, even if he refuses to see it."

"That's true." I smile, though a little doubt seeps back into my mind. I'm committed now, but I can still worry about him.

My phone buzzes in the back pocket of my jeans at the same time Amelia's rings, and when she lifts her Bennett jersey to reach for it, I smile. She's offered me a no-name jersey many times before and I've always said no. Something tells me that's going to be on the horizon soon. After all, I'm dating a football player.

I'll repeat... I'm dating a football player. What is my life now?

Since Amelia, Lainey, and Paige are all waiting for their football-star husbands or boyfriends to finish with their post-game duties, I wait around with them—getting myself accustomed to the life that's about to become mine—and when they're ready to go, I follow.

Reed's chatting animatedly to Luke when he walks out of the locker room, and when Amelia whispers 'go time,' my mind hears it as 'action' and I run forward, throwing myself into Reed's hold, wrapping my arms around his neck.

"What a game!" I cheer as Reed's huge palms settle on my waist, squeezing me as a deep chuckle rumbles from his chest. He lowers me to the ground, but keeps his hands in place, leaning forward to whisper in my ear.

"We're doing this?"

I nod, ignoring the way his breath tickles my skin. Pulling back, our eyes lock and his crystal-blue orbs sparkle. "Yeah. We're doing this." I nod.

Smiling, he lifts me again, spinning me around before placing me back down, curling an arm around my shoulder.

"Friends first?" he questions as we walk back to the group, and I immediately agree.

"I think that's wise. We can show them we know each other and let the rest come naturally."

"Naturally?" Reed huffs out a questioning laugh and I poke him in the stomach, almost breaking my finger in the process.

"You know what I mean. Now act like you like me."

"Ugh. I'm not *that* good of an actor." He playfully rolls his eyes.

I'm laughing when we catch up with Amelia, Luke, and the girls, and when Thomas joins us, he doesn't even bat an eyelid. In fact, none of them do. In the past year they've all become quite accustomed to my overtly friendly behaviour, and what do they care if we're friends. It's not the big deal I made it to be.

After the wives and girlfriends congratulate their men, Luke turns to the group, a cocky grin lighting up his features.

"Only three rounds to go, and we are killing it. I'm ready to party. Who's heading out? Hayley, I can count on you, right?"

I open my mouth to say yes, but pause, remembering my conversation with my agent. "Actually, no. I'm having a night in. I have a big week coming up and need my beauty sleep."

Luke groans and it doesn't take a genius to know this is more about Amelia than me. "Come on," he whines. "If you're not coming, I'll have no chance of convincing Amelia."

And there it is. Always.

"He's right." Amelia laughs. "But I'd only be able to come for an hour anyway. I need to pick up Juliet soon."

"Okay, fine." Luke pouts. "It pains me to do this, but Lainey?"

Lainey and Luke argue in their true sibling fashion while Reed eyes me curiously. We have a lot to talk about before we officially become a couple. Namely, the details surrounding my need for a fake boyfriend—or rather my need to have *Reed* specifically as my fake boyfriend—and I will tell him. Just not tonight.

Flashing him a smile, I shake my head when he opens his mouth to speak. Now is not that time. Tonight is about celebrating his win.

"Looks like it's a boys' night," Luke says reluctantly and I laugh at his sour expression.

"Stop whining," Amelia jokingly chastises him. "You love the guys. Go and have fun."

After chatting for a few more minutes, the guys head off while the rest of us make our way to the parking lot, and the second we're out of earshot, all eyes are on me.

"Is there something you're not telling us, Hayley?" Paige asks, her expression shrouded in suspicion. *Maybe they do care who I'm friends with?*

"I was thinking the same thing," Lainey adds just as Keeley runs out to catch up with us.

Saved by the media liaison.

"Paige, I'm glad I caught you. Do you have a minute to talk about the spring fundraiser? I have to sign off on the food."

Paige's eyes flash to mine and I shrug innocently. "You better go. Food is important. I'll wait here." I'm getting a ride home with her and her driver anyway, so I can't escape her for too long. Who knows, maybe she'll forget.

"I want answers when I get back." She points at me before following Keeley inside. *Or she might remember.*

I sigh as I turn back to Amelia and Lainey. Since Amelia already knows what's going on, it's only Lainey I have to catch up, but instead of questioning me, she surprises me, holding a hand up in front of my face, stopping me from talking. "Is it better if I don't know?"

I doubt it would matter because she doesn't know Bria and likely doesn't know the producers of the feature film I'm striving for, but before I can respond, Amelia does it for me.

"Let's just say we're going to be seeing a lot more of Hayley and Reed. And I, for one, can't wait to see it unfold."

I roll my eyes and she pokes her tongue out.

"Good to know." Lainey laughs before her expression turns thoughtful. "I can see it," she muses.

"See what?"

"You and Reed. It's perfect."

I rush out a laugh of my own, while inside, a tension overwhelms me.

Does she mean fake dating, or us? Because if it's the latter, I'm not sure how I feel about that.

The topic changes to Amelia's beautiful daughter, as she fills us in on her latest milestones, and when we've been standing in the parking lot for forty-five minutes, Amelia and Lainey rush off, leaving me alone, wishing I'd gone out with the guys.

Wishing things were different.

My face drops as I draw in a breath. Am I really about to change who I am? For a role. Yes, I can be a handful at times. I'm loud and in your face. And yes, since moving to the US, I've had my fair share of sexual partners, but I'm not the type to shove that in people's faces or brag about it to anyone that will listen. Not to mention... *I haven't been with anyone in months.*

I should be standing up to them... Shouting from the rooftops that if they don't *want* me as I am, they don't *get* me. But like I told Amelia, the reality is, this happens all the time. And after my last awful audition, what if I don't get another opportunity like this one?

That part is *my* Super Bowl. The part you get when you've truly made it. I want it. I *need* it.

And I think I just answered my own question.

I *am* going to change. But I'm going to do it *my* way.

Standing tall, I head back toward the stadium entry to wait for Paige, and I've just sunk back against the wall when my phone buzzes and I remember the message I got earlier.

Checking the screen, I have three texts, two from my mum and one from Reed. Mum asks how I'm feeling, and I'm surprised until I read the second text.

MUM: Sorry, wrong person. Talk soon, sweetie

My stomach knots but I ignore it. Of course she wasn't checking in. We only speak if I'm the one that calls them. And I don't call that often.

Shaking off my melancholy, I open Reed's text.

REED: What's the role? And is it worth that sad look on your face?

What? My gaze lifts to search the parking lot. *Is he still here?* Can he see me? Is this what it would feel like to have a stalker?

I laugh to myself and shake off my insane thoughts.

> HAYLEY: I don't have a sad look

At least not anymore.

> REED: Are you sure about that?

Jesus freaking Christ. He *is* here. I smile intensely, really forcing the creases in my cheeks as I scan the parking lot again, coming up empty. *Of course he's not here.* I'm still smiling hysterically as I reply, lost in my own world when Paige laughs from beside me.

"Hell!" I startle. "When did you get back?"

"Just long enough to question your expression."

"Honestly, I'm questioning it myself."

"Everything okay?"

"It will be. I'm sure."

Paige frowns, her furrowed brows telling me she wants to ask more, but she knows better—I'll talk when I'm ready. Giving me a pass for now, she moves the conversation to the Storm charity event as we walk to her car, greeting her driver as he waits by the door.

It's not that I don't want to tell her what's going on; I just want to wait until I've figured it out for myself. And for that to happen, I have to work it out with Reed.

On the drive, Paige pulls me out of my funk with her bubbly personality, and it's not until I get home that I realize I never responded to Reed. And now, I have a new message waiting for me.

> REED: I'm here if you need to talk

I smile, more genuinely this time, and release a slow breath.

> HAYLEY: Tuesday. Let's talk about everything

I hope you're prepared, Reed. Because I'm not one to hold back.

> REED: Sounds good. Night, Baby. 😴

I smile and shake my head, falling back onto my bed.

Something tells me that not only is Reed prepared for my crazy, but he's looking forward to it. And I've got to admit, that fills me with warmth.

But God, I hope this deal benefits him too. I couldn't stand it if this backfired for him.

CHAPTER TWENTY-ONE

REED

Hayley's waiting in the lobby when I arrive at her apartment building on Tuesday, pulling me into a hug. "I was down here checking the mail," she says a little distractedly. "Are you ready for this?"

"To talk?" I blow out a raspberry, waving off the concern in her tone. "I was born to talk. How hard can it be?" I'm well equipped for deep and meaningful conversations; this isn't my first rodeo.

Staring at me deadpan, Hayley shakes her head, brushing away the hair that falls across her face. "You have no idea."

"Try me."

She rolls her eyes and grabs my hand, intertwining our fingers as she pulls me toward the elevator. "I'm going to need a big, greasy meal after this, so you're taking me out for lunch. I'm craving burgers, but first...let's get this *talk* over and done with."

"God, woman. This was your idea and you're making it sound like a prison sentence. We need to make this fun or we'll never survive it."

"I'm always fun and you know it." She bumps her shoulder to mine and presses the button for her floor, her eyes flashing to the front glass doors before she releases my hand. "So...what should we discuss first?" She turns my way.

"We're diving straight in then? No foreplay. Noted." I bite back a smirk, waiting for her reaction, and right on cue she punches me.

"Foreplay is always needed, Reed. *Always*. Don't ever forget that."

"I could never. But first, is everything okay?"

"Of course." Hayley's nose scrunches as she scoffs. "Why wouldn't it be?"

"You seem uneasy."

"Nope. I'm good. Promise."

"Okay." I allow her off the hook, but I don't feel good about it. "So... what's our foreplay then?" I smirk, bringing back her smile.

The elevator stops at Hayley's level and I hold the doors open as she steps out. "Would you like a drink, Reed?"

"That would be lovely."

"A comfortable chair?"

"Please."

"What about some snacks?"

"Only if they're healthy."

Unlocking her front door, she rolls her eyes again while her expression remains amused. "You are fresh out of luck there."

"Damn. You need to work on your foreplay game."

I hover in her doorway and she shoves me inside. "Shut up and sit on the couch. I'll bring you a carrot stick." She hits me with a tight-lipped smirk before turning away, and I can't restrain the chuckle that bubbles out of me. Maybe this is going to be easy and fun. Why was I doubting it?

Flicking through one of her glossy magazines while I wait, I spend way too long catching up on the latest breakups and pregnancies in Hollywood, so when Hayley returns, my mind is spinning.

"Did you know Rhys Mason and Chelsey Harvey broke up? I'm devastated."

"Who?" Hayley's brows crease in puzzlement.

"*Exactly*. Why do you read these?" I toss the magazine on the couch beside me and release a soft grunt. "It can't be good for your mental health. What if you're featured?"

"Then I'll know I've made it."

"Bullshit. You've made it, Hayls. And when *Jaded Beginnings* comes out next month, you're going to be a star."

"What about—"

"Nope. You are going to be a star," I repeat, my eyes boring into hers, making sure she believes me.

"Thanks, Reed." She smiles and there's a shyness to it that I haven't seen before, saddening me a little. She has every right to be the cockiest B out there, but she's not. And that would be fine if she was still the same

Hayley she's always been. But something has changed since her audition last week, and I'm going to get to the bottom of it.

"Now for my promised snacks." She hands me a platter of fruit and veggies, with avocado and small slices of smoked salmon, and I burst out laughing.

"These carrot sticks look amazing."

"I thought you'd be impressed."

"Did you do all of this for me?"

"Hell, no. I eat healthy."

"Aren't I taking you out for greasy burgers?"

"It's all about balance. I worked out for an hour this morning and I'm planning on going for a run later today. I work hard for this hot body, and it deserves treats."

I ogle said hot body, ignoring my cock when it twitches. "You won't hear me arguing."

"About deserving treats?"

"No, about your body," I admit, waggling my eyebrows.

"Does Bria know you have this playful side of you?"

"Of course she does. She knows *everything*."

"Except the way you feel."

"Apparently." I shrug, releasing a mix between a huff and a laugh. Although...she might know that too. It's the million-dollar question.

"It's time we found out," Hayley confirms. "Let's get down to business." Grabbing a carrot stick, she drags it through the smashed avocado before raising it to her lips and pausing. My gaze follows the journey of the carrot until her mouth lifts into a smirk.

"Did you want this?" she sasses, faking a grimace.

"Well, I mean, you *did* say the carrots were mine."

"Reed Coombs. This is going to be a blast."

"Couldn't agree more, Jackman. Let's do it."

Hayley makes herself comfortable while I relax back into the cushions, resting my ankle over my knee. "Where should we start?"

"First..." She trails off, glancing away, deep in thought until she smiles. "I think *you* should decide what we talk about."

"Okay. I'll take the reins. First, we need to be completely transparent about what we hope to achieve out of this."

"Wow." Hayley's eyes widen and she straightens up. "That was fast. You've thought this through."

"Of course I have, Hayls. It's kind of a big deal."

"You're right. It is. I'm sorry." She bites back a cheesy grin.

"Maybe *you're* right?" I say jokingly. "Maybe I'm not ready for this. For *you*."

"I promise, I'll behave." She moves her hands to her heart and smiles with a wistful sigh, but before I can respond, she's raising a finger between us, hushing me as she smirks.

"I promise," she repeats. "And if you want to know the whys, that brings me to my first reason. Remember when I told you I'm on some bigwigs' radar for a life changing role? Well, it's the part of Cynthia in *Reckless Desire*, the movie I told you about when it was announced last month."

My chest swells with excitement until I remember what she said about said bigwigs. "So they're the ones that want a relationship girl?"

"Sort of."

"Sort of?" My brows furrow and she grimaces.

"I lied a little bit." She lifts her hand and holds her thumb and finger an inch apart, clenching her teeth.

"How *little* are we talking?" My words are slow and full of questions, not just the one I'm asking.

Hayley laughs through another confusing grimace. "They didn't specifically say they needed a relationship type."

"Oh-kay. What did they say?"

"They said they needed me to fix my image. To become a little less *me*. To—"

"What the fuck, Hayley?" I stiffen as alarm bells sound inside my head. They can't be serious. Why would anyone want to extinguish Hayley's light? It all makes sense now.

"This right here"—she waves her hand in front of my face—"is the reason I didn't tell you the other day."

"What reason?"

"I had a feeling you'd get all protective of me, and I didn't need that while I was still processing everything that happened."

Fuck. I get that, to a degree, but I'm still not happy. "Would you prefer I thought that request was perfectly fine?"

"No." Hayley sighs. "I just wanted you to know why I previously kept it from you."

"Gotcha. Okay. I'm guessing there's more."

"Yep." Her nose scrunches as her eyes flicker closed for a beat. "I was specifically told...fewer nights out, less drinking, and no bad boys."

"*Ouch.*" I wince. "Are you suggesting I'm *not* a bad boy? Look at these tats." I roll up my sleeve and tense my bicep, bouncing my eyebrows. Not that she notices. No, Hayley has her eyes locked on my muscles as though they're a beacon she's drawn too. I test the theory, lifting my shirt to reveal my tattooed chest, and her gaze shifts, despite the fact that she's seen it all before. I drag my finger from the rose tattoo positioned near my heart, down to the eagle that spans my waist, disappearing under the waistband of my jeans, chuckling when her eyes follow.

But when she licks her lips, I groan. "Christ, Hayley. Snap out of it."

"I can't help it." She waves her hands around and unabashedly continues her perving. "It's a work of art, Reed. It's no different to me than staring at a painting in the Louvre."

I scoff at her comparison and let go of my shirt, making her pout as it covers my chest. "I appreciate the compliment. I'll pass on your admiration to the artist."

"Oh, Reed, this is way bigger than admiration. I'm obsessed. While we're dating, I'm making it my mission to find out the meaning of every single tattoo. Be prepared. Have your stories ready, 'cause I'm coming for you."

Yeah, that's not happening. "What if they're personal?" Keeping a straight face, I wait for her to panic before I laugh.

"Shit, I'm— *Reed.*" She playfully huffs at my laughter. "I guess the first thing you need to know is that I'm always open with the people I trust, and I sometimes forget others aren't."

"I'm kidding, and I know that about you. I don't mind sharing my stories." *Most of them, anyway.* "We've got to trust each other completely for this to work."

"Agreed. So where were we?"

"You were in denial about me being a bad boy." I wink.

"You are so far in the opposite direction, you're practically an angel."

"An angel? I've seen the trailer for your film; not all angels are good."

"In your case, it's true."

"Yeah, yeah. So what you're saying is that if you date a good boy... me." I wave my hands in front of myself and Hayley laughs. "You think they're going to see you in a better light, and cast you for the role?"

"That's the plan."

"So..." I nod while I process. "That's what you were worried about? You're doing this so that you look good, but what if I suddenly become a bad boy because of your bad girl influence?"

Hayley cringes and I regret hitting a nerve. "Kind of. I was considering what this might do to your reputation, since mine's not great and—"

"Whoa. Hold up. The thing you'll learn about *me* is that I don't care about my reputation. I'm not *this* guy, the golden boy as they call me, because I'm *striving* for it. It's who I am. You need to push that shit from your mind, because, for one, it's not on my radar as being an issue, and two, you are not who they say you are. And that last one's *extremely* important."

Hayley's lips pull into a soft, thankful smile and it breaks my heart. *Does she believe what they're saying?*

"Hayley—"

"No, I'm good."

"Are you sure?"

"One hundred percent. But thank you."

"Anytime."

"You say that a lot," she muses, grabbing another carrot stick with one hand before reaching for salmon with the other.

"Say what?"

"Anytime."

"Because it's true. Maybe it should be my catchphrase."

"Stop." Hayley shakes her head, but this time when she smiles, it's back to the full force I love to see, the Hayley I know well, putting my mind at ease.

"So what's next? Anything else I should know?"

She taps her chin as she thinks, her brows furrowed in question. "Yes. My exes suck, so I'm comparing you to a low base."

"That's always good, but we both know I don't need the help." I wink and she bursts out laughing. "Anything else?"

"Um..." She taps her nails on the arm of the couch this time. "I don't think so."

"Okay, good."

"I guess that means it's your turn." She points my way and I nod.

"It sure is, and I've been thinking about this. A lot."

"Always the sensible one. Hit me with it."

Chapter Twenty-Two

HAYLEY

Reed sits forward, his elbows resting on his knees and his chin balanced on his knuckles. "As you know, I was reluctant to do this." He quirks his lips and I smile. "But since we got here anyway, I've been thinking about the benefits. First, I'm doing this for *you*, Hayls. I wouldn't be doing it at all if this was just about Bria."

"I know." Avoiding his intense gaze, I reach forward and grab a handful of blueberries before sitting back and ferrying them into my mouth. I know he's doing it for me, but the sincerity in his eyes is too much to take right now. *What if I fuck it all up?* "Trust me, I know and I'm grateful for that, but I think this can help with Bria and––"

"I agree, but not in the way you think..." He trails off and I find myself mimicking his position, leaning forward in anticipation. "I need to know, once and for all, whether or not Bria feels *anything* for me. Beyond our friendship. But..."

"But?"

"*But,*" he repeats before pausing, straightening in his chair. "If she does have feelings for me, I'm not sure it'll change my decision. I still want to move on."

"Wow." I rest my chin on my knuckles, exactly as he'd done earlier and nod slowly.

"Yep. Wow." Reed's voice comes out breathy as he huffs out an incredulous laugh, and I imagine it's because he doesn't quite believe it himself. "Anyway, that's my reason. Is it time for lunch?"

"*Wait.*" I straighten quickly, throwing a hand up between us. "You're just going to drop that bomb and move on? Reed, that's a big decision. Why do you want to know so badly if it's not going to make a difference?"

I'm genuinely shocked and not at all hiding my reaction. I don't think he's thought this through.

"That one's easy." He smiles awkwardly, suggesting it's not that easy at all. "Bria's changed in the last few months, and while she has every right to be whoever she wants to be, I don't feel the same about the new version of her. In truth, I'm hoping our little game proves that she *doesn't* want me the way I've always wanted her. Maybe then we'd have a fighting chance of getting our friendship back to the place it was before. I miss the old Bria."

Even when he's hurting, he finds a way to be nice. I don't think she's being "whoever she wants to be." I think she's unhappy about no longer having his undivided attention, but it's not my place to express that. "Again, *wow*."

"Profound, I know." He bites back a smirk but it's easy to see it's a cover. "I'm a deep thinker like that."

Covering my mouth, I try to hide my laughter but it comes through. "I'm sorry, I'm not laughing at your situation."

"Why? You should be. It's ridiculous."

"It's not. At all. You'd be surprised how often friends fall in love. That's why there are so many movies about it."

"True. But they always end happily ever after."

"And so might *yours*. Don't close yourself off for that yet. Let's wait and see." I'm smiling reassuringly but as I say those words, a niggling feeling settles around my middle.

"Okay, wise one," Reed continues, unaware of my inner thoughts. "Let's wait and see."

Smiling again, he moves the conversation back to lunch but I cut him off. "We haven't worked hard enough for lunch. We still have to decide how this is all going to work. Thoughts?"

"Fucked if I know. I don't know the first thing about being in a relationship. I'm guessing there will be public displays of affection."

I nod.

"And kissing?" He looks positively terrified at the prospect of that, and I laugh out loud.

"We can work up to it, if we need it. Not all couples are that openly coupley." Despite welcoming the opportunity to maul him, I could easily make Reed the centre of my world without his lips ever touching mine. It's better to set those boundaries.

"Okay. Yes." Reed nods. "That works for me. Do we need ground rules?"

"Probably. I do prefer winging it, but if I'm looking at this like an acting gig, then yes, that's for the best."

"Cool. Cool. What's number one?"

I blurt out the first thing that pops into my head. "Don't fall in love with me."

Reed snorts as his shoulders bounce. "I bet you got that straight out of a movie, didn't you?"

"Sure did." I nod before thinking about that for a second. "Or maybe a book; I can't remember."

"Well, it makes sense. It can go on the list, but right back at you."

"Deal." I hold out my hand for him to shake and he leans forward, shaking it with a laugh before moving on.

"Two...we need to be upfront and honest with each other. At all times."

"Agreed." I nod vigorously until a sharp pang hits me in the gut. I'm mostly honest, and he doesn't need to know all my insecurities when it doesn't affect us. "That comes back to the trust thing and leads to number three. If one of us wants out, we agree to fake an amicable breakup and end it."

"Of course. That's a given. We're trying to help each other, not make life worse."

"*Exactly*." I click my fingers, excited to be on the same page. "And four... no crossing boundaries."

"Yep. Good one. And five, no sleeping around."

Groaning, I bury my face in my hands. I really should have slept around before this. "I'm trying to *lose* that reputation," I remind myself as well as Reed. "I have no intentions of doing that." As disappointing as that is.

"I know, I know. Just putting it out there."

"Good idea." Maybe this *is* going to work. "Should we have a natural end date?"

"Yes. Definitely."

I glance away to think, but Reed hits me with an answer.

"What about halfway into filming for you? You mentioned there's a significant breakup in the book, and your character falls apart. If we break up, the audience might feel *her* pain as *you supposedly* live it."

"Reed!" I gasp. He remembered that? *"Holy shit."* I gave him a brief rundown of the book when it was first announced, but I never expected him to be paying attention. I only told him because I was too excited to hold it all in. "That's perfect. But that only works if you've already got what *you* need."

"I don't think it will take long for Bria to show me how she truly feels. If it was just on me, we could be done by the weekend."

"You're that confident?" I bite back a grin.

"Yep. She's never been able to hide her emotions. That's why I'm convinced she's not hiding her feelings for me. I would have made a move if I thought she was. But knowing for sure will help."

"How will you know if she *doesn't* have feelings for you? I understand that her jealousy is likely to present quickly if she *does*, but what if she *doesn't*?"

"She'll welcome you into her life." He shrugs like it's that simple. "She's always said she can't wait for the day I have a girlfriend. She'll be happy for me."

Ummm. I cringe, my brows furrowing involuntarily. I highly doubt that. "And what if she has reservations, like she doesn't think I'm good enough?"

"Nah. She's not protective like that."

What? "She should be. *I* would be. Hell, I *will* be."

"When?"

"When this ends and you move on with someone else. When you... oh, God." My eyes widen as I cover my mouth with my hand. *Why the hell hadn't I thought past the relationship ending?*

"What?"

"Your future girlfriend is *never* going to accept me as your friend. This is going to be the end of us."

He snorts comically before his shoulders drop and he pouts sympathetically. For someone that has two female besties, he really doesn't know women. "I thought you weren't worried about this changing our friendship, Hayls."

"I'm impulsive, you know that. I should have thought it through and—-"

"You're worrying over nothing. At least where that's concerned. I don't plan on keeping secrets from my 'future girlfriend.' She's going to know this was fake. We're good."

"But what if we kiss? She's still—"

"Hayley, stop." With his palm on the coffee table between us, he balances his weight on his hand and leans forward, pressing a finger to my lips. And honestly, it shuts me right up because... *Damn.* "What happened to winging it?" he asks, his eyes boring into mine while my heart races. "Stop worrying about hypothetical situations."

"Okay," I whisper against his finger, a soft smile playing on my lips.

"Okay?"

"Yep." I nod and he removes his hand, sitting back. "I'm good."

"Good." He crosses his arms over his broad chest, and I have to stop myself from reacting. That was a little bit hot. "Next question," he continues, completely oblivious to what he's doing to me as my body heats. "When should we make this thing public?"

Chapter Twenty-Three

REED

It turns out, Hayley was right. Fake dating is not all that different from being her friend. Unless you count the fact that we've seen each other three times this week when it's usually only once.

During our talk on Tuesday, we decided to wait until the weekend to go public. With Christmas coming up, it made sense to go shopping together, because that's what couples do. Right? I mean, that's what my parents used to do, so I figured all couples were like that.

As far as ideas go, it seemed like the easiest way to present ourselves to the world. We wouldn't be making a statement or doing anything formal. It would be casual and relaxed. And it was the best idea we had.

Granted, it was the first and *only* idea we'd come up with, but it was a good one. At least, it *was* until we arrived at the mall and I remembered how much I hate shopping, especially around Christmas.

"Goddammit." I take off my cap and run a hand through my hair, messing it up. "What was I thinking?"

"Come on, boyfriend," Hayley grins as she links her arm through mine, giving me an encouraging tug. "Who should we buy for first?"

Someone bumps me from behind, and I rush out a sorry before pulling Hayley to the side of the walkway, waving apologetically when the guy looks back.

Hayley frowns, her eyes bouncing between me and the guy, watching as he walks away. "What just happened?" she asks curiously.

"What do you mean?"

"Some dick bumped into you and *you* apologized." She points at me in case I don't understand who she's referring to.

"We were standing in the middle of the walkway, Hayls. It's our fault."

"So, it's not the people?"

"What's not?" I frown, confused.

"The reason it looks like your life is over."

"Oh. No." I huff out a laugh. "It's the stress. What if I find the perfect gift but someone grabs it a second before I do, or a little kid stares at it longingly, having saved up his entire allowance to buy it for his special someone. Or what if I don't find anything at all?"

"Wow." Hayley bites back a smirk, taking a deep breath before she responds. "That's... I don't even know what that is."

"That's why I shop online."

"Maybe so. But you've got me now, and I'm ruthless. How many people do you have to buy for?"

"Ahh." I quickly do the math before relaying the information to Hayley, realizing happily that it's not that many. "My mom, my dad, my *brother*, his *wife*, and you." I can't help the mild disdain in my tone when I mention my brother and his girl, but thankfully, Hayley doesn't say anything about it. Instead she focuses on herself.

"Me?" she questions, rocking back on her heels with a giddy smile.

"Of course." I roll my eyes and Hayley laughs, giving my arm another tug, prompting me to start walking.

"So five people? That won't be too hard. But...I didn't know you had a brother."

"I do. We don't talk much, but he exists."

Hayley pauses, spinning me to face her when I try to keep walking. "But you like *everyone*."

"I never said I didn't like him." Although that's the truth, he's one of the few people I want nothing to do with. I frown thinking about the distance between us. The distance that's been there since I was a kid.

Hayley's previously happy expression falls and I hate that I did that. "I'm sorry," she whispers, her voice soft.

"What for?"

"There's a story there." She releases my arm but grabs my hand as it falls to my side, giving it a squeeze. "I'm not going to push it, but please know that I'm here for you."

"Thanks." I smile reassuringly, hoping that will help ease her mind. It's not that I don't *want* to talk to her about it, but now is not the time or the place. And it's a long, depressing story. I'd like to keep things happy and fun between us. "How many presents do you have to get?" I change the subject.

"I have a few." Hayley releases my hand, raising hers to her chin in thought. "Amelia, Luke, Juliet, Paige, Isaac, and if I'm getting something for him, I should probably get something for his dad too, so add Easton to the list. Then there's Keeley and Lainey, Thomas. You, of course, I would have done that regardless, and on that note...maybe I should get something for Bria. Right? In case she does 'welcome me into her life.' Ooh, and my agent."

She looks up from counting on her fingers and I stare at her in shock.

"You buy for *all* of those people."

"Yep."

"What about your family?"

"I do that online and send it to them directly."

"Of course." I shake my head. Apparently I forgot that Hayley's Australian. Not sure how that happened with her cute little accent constantly reminding me. "So..." It suddenly hits me that we could be here all day and I groan. *Fuck.* "Do you have any ideas for the hundred people you're buying for?"

"Shut up. It's not a hundred."

"Well, it's not five, like I have."

"I'm curious about that." Hayley's brows rise in question. "You didn't list Bria."

"Good observation. I did not."

"Why? I mean *I* listed her." She frowns, crossing her arms over her chest, and honestly, it comes across as though she's girl-coding me right now. I wouldn't be surprised if the words "typical men" release under her breath.

"You did." I bite back my laugh. "But you don't have to get her anything either. Bria and I decided a few years ago that we wouldn't do Christmas presents. Instead, we'd make a bigger effort for our birthdays."

"Oooh. Okay. Okay." She nods multiple times before shaking her head. "Yeah...that's not happening for us. In this relationship, we make an effort for *all* occasions. Christmas, Easter, Birthday, Valentine's Day. Hell, I'm not opposed to exchanging gifts for Halloween. A cute little pumpkin mug or a candle."

I rush out a low chuckle, grabbing Hayley's hand as her excitement bubbles over. "Don't ever change, Hayls. I love your energy. And rest assured...I'm taking mental notes. Next Halloween, I'm getting you a mug."

She giggles and it lights up her features, confirming that we're doing the right thing. If I can bring even an ounce of her spark back, it will all be worth it.

"This will be well and truly over by then," she adds with a grin.

"Maybe so, but we'll still be friends. That's a promise."

"I can't wait."

Since it's mayhem at the mall, we walk around relatively unnoticed for the first hour or so of shopping. But when we break for lunch, the whispers start, followed by photos—that are not at all subtle—a few people approaching us, and it's then we get the attention of an obvious paparazzo.

He tries to hide it at first, but when he has to move to get a better angle, he throws caution to the wind and stands in our direct line of sight, unapologetically getting his shots, making his money.

"How long do you think we have before that hits the media?" I ask Hayley, subtly motioning to the camera.

She snorts as she pointedly stares his way. "A day, if we're lucky. An hour, if we're not."

"And you're good with that?" There's no going back after that.

"Of course I am." She smiles brightly, tossing her long hair behind her shoulder before posing. "It's all part of the plan. And in case you haven't noticed, I look pretty damn amazing today."

"I was going to mention that." I nod appreciatively.

"Thank you."

After shoving the last French fry into her mouth, Hayley jumps up and grabs my hand, pulling me to stand next to her. "Four presents down. Ninety-six to go," she jokes with a wink. "We better get moving."

"Who's next?" I ask reluctantly, ready for this day to be over.

"Your parents. They should be a priority."

"Uh." I groan. "I have no idea what to get them this year." *Or any year for that matter.*

"What do they want?"

"Grandkids." The word shoots out of my mouth without thought and I burst out laughing. "Fuck, I'm sorry. I hear about it every time we speak, so it's ingrained in my mind. I don't expect *us* to give that to them."

"Well, it's impossible to arrange by Christmas, but we could *definitely* have fun trying."

My airway closes and I choke, an unexpected image of a naked Hayley working its way into my mind. I slam my eyes shut, but that only works to strengthen the visual and *damn*...

"You're thinking about it, aren't you?"

"*Fuck*, Hayley." I groan under my breath. "You sure know how to mess with a guy's head."

"What did I do?"

"You know *exactly* what you did." I shake off my thoughts and wrap an arm around her shoulder, directing her toward the store selling indoor plants. "This way."

She pulls back with a frown, grounding me to a halt. "You are *not* giving your parents an indoor plant. Come on. Let's get them a giant-ass TV."

"They have a giant-ass TV."

"A car?"

"I can't give them a car."

"Why? You can afford it."

"It's—" Fuck. I throw my head back and sigh. "It's easier if I don't. Subtle is best. Things that might cost a lot but aren't in your face."

"Are your parents too proud to accept things? Mine have asked me for a new house. As though I can already afford it."

An incredulous chuckle bursts from within me and I subtly shake my head. "No. It's not my parents. My brother causes trouble anytime I do something he considers 'showy.' It's easier if I don't."

"Asshole."

"Yep."

"You know he's jealous, right?"

"If only. It's a lot more complicated than that." My stomach sinks just thinking about it, but I smile through it, just like I've always done. "Can we take a raincheck on this conversation?" I ask, not wanting to dampen the mood.

"Of course. What about a holiday then? You could hand over a two-hundred-dollar travel gift card as well as an all-expenses-paid trip. They show him the gift card and pretend they booked the holiday themselves."

Her idea pulls me up short and I seriously consider it. If I could make that happen, it's actually kind of perfect. "I'll chat with Mom about that one. A *vacation* might work." I wink, making a point of enunciating "vacation" and Hayley pokes out her tongue. But joking aside, I'm grateful for the idea.

"Thanks, Hayls." It sucks that I still have to be cautious even though he won't even be there, but he'll call on Christmas Day and it will be the first thing he asks. He always does.

"Anytime." Hayley bounces her eyebrows at the use of my catchphrase, pulling me out of my head.

"Seriously, though, I appreciate it."

"I know. You don't have to thank me. In fact, I doubt you'll want to after my next question."

"Oh, yeah? What's that?"

"What should we get for your brother?"

"A car?" I joke and Hayley laughs out loud, curling herself into my shoulder, giving me a side hug.

"Come on. I've got a better idea." She smirks, directing me back to the indoor plants.

Two hours later, Hayley's panicked gaze bounces between a pink, frilly dress and a white one, deciding which to add to the other million things she's already bought for Juliet.

She occasionally glances my way while I smile and nod, essentially no help at all.

We're nowhere near finished with our Christmas shopping, but... I. Am. Done. After she makes this decision and the item is in her bag, I'm taking her home.

It's another couple of minutes before she finally selects the pink dress and scurries off toward the counter. I could let her go—we'd be done faster —but guilt hits me and I call out for her to stop. "Go with the white," I tell her. "You wanted that first and then talked yourself out of it. Go with your gut." I'm not sure her indecisiveness is even about the dress, so the least I can do is help.

She frowns, glancing down at the tiny piece of material in her hands. "But white will be impossible to keep clean. She's crawling."

"True, but it's adorable and nothing you buy is going to stay clean. You said so yourself. She's crawling."

"Okay. Yes." Her eyes blaze with happiness and it makes my chest light. "White it is." She rushes back to get the white, flashing me a wide smile as she passes, and I feel significantly better. I don't usually run out of patience so quickly, but the sheer number of shoppers is doing my head in. It's like people can't be civil anymore. No one's saying thanks or using *any* basic manners. It's time to exit the building.

"Everyone else is getting cash in a card," I tell Hayley as we're walking toward the parking lot. "How do people do this all the time?"

She giggles, and it's obvious from her expression that she's judging me. "Would you believe some people find shopping fun? Therapeutic even."

"Well, they are welcome to their opinions, but it's not for me. Let's go."

"Wait." She grabs my bicep, pulling me to a stop. "We didn't get anything for each other."

"I'm good. I have an idea."

"You have?" Her lips part in a gasp. "What is it?"

"It's...a surprise." I wave my hands around with exaggerated excitement and she pouts.

"I hate surprises." She jokingly crosses her arms over her chest. At least I hope she's joking. "I'm an in-the-moment kind of girl, remember?"

"Too bad. So sad."

Her eyes bulge in disbelief but she can't hide her smile. "Too bad? So sad?"

"Yep."

"Wow. I'm learning a lot about you, Reedy boy. And it ain't all as pretty as advertised." She gestures from my head to my toes with a sweeping motion and I chuckle.

"Too late to back out now. We've already been outed."

"I can deny it. Throw around the 'just friends' tag."

Ouch. *I've heard that before.* "You could. But then you'd have to find yourself another 'golden boy' and let me tell you, we are rare."

Hayley suppresses her smile while I chuckle. "You've been spending *way* too much time with Luke," she tells me. "His cockiness is rubbing off on you."

I glance away, pretending to be lost in thought before faking a gasp. "You're right. What was I thinking? I'm sorry, Baby," I joke. "Please tell me how I can make it up to you?"

"You could tell me your present idea." She hits me with a pleading grin, and a little part of me hates that I'm about to refuse her, until I remember that's the entire point of gift giving.

"Not a chance. Come on. Let's blow this joint."

"Only if you carry my bags." She hands over the *one* bag she's holding and laughs to herself. I've been holding her bags all day. "Thanks." She glances up at me like I'm her hero. "Let's go."

CHAPTER TWENTY-FOUR

HAYLEY

Not one magazine publishes the photos of me and Reed from the mall, and I have to laugh at myself or I just might cry. Does it mean we're not famous enough for a sale? Or is it just me? God knows, Reed's plenty famous.

It's safe to say, I've been analysing it to death.

With only a week left before the publicity tour for *Jaded Beginnings* ramps up, and no family to spend Christmas with, I switch over to hermit mode, disappearing on everyone in my life, including Reed and Amelia, giving me plenty of time to myself.

So, on top of overanalysing every aspect of my life, I spend the week reading or binge-watching TV, relaxing on my balcony, and...I even try meditating a few times. Not that it works for me. The silence has my mind running rampant with plans and worrying about the future, when I'd much rather be a take-each-day-as-it-comes kind of girl.

The week passes relatively quickly. While alone time usually wreaks havoc on my mind, it turns out to be exactly what I needed and I could have gone longer—if I didn't have to come out of hiding to wish everyone a Merry Christmas. All *one hundred* of my friends.

Since Reed flew his family to San Francisco for Christmas, I wait until I know they're gone to call him. But before I get the chance, my phone rings in my hand, with Reed's name lighting up the screen.

"Hey, Baby," he greets me when I answer, bringing about an immediate smile. Is this our thing now? "How was isolation?" he asks, his voice holding a hint of mockery.

"Amazing," I say honestly, ignoring him. "I needed it before the chaos. What have I missed?"

"Christmas," he states matter-of-factly, and I jokingly cringe even though he can't see me. "You missed the biggest holiday of the year, Hayls."

"I did." I giggle, picturing his fake frown. "But there's no rule against celebrating a few days late."

"You're right. And I have your present for you."

"Still keeping it a secret?"

"You bet. Is that why you went into hiding? Couldn't stand facing me, knowing I was holding this back?"

"Yes, Reed. It was *all* about you," I deadpan and he chuckles.

"Damn Luke. You're right. He's rubbing off on me."

"You're forgiven. When are you free? I can come over right now...or you can come here. But it has to be now. Now."

Reed chuckles again, clearly thinking I'm joking. But I'm not. I love spontaneity. I love living life to the fullest. I don't love surprises that I know about ahead of time. If he'd sprung it on me when I next saw him... brilliant. But telling me about it, while *not* telling me about it, is pure torture.

"I won't see you until you get back, will I?" I pout, remembering he has an away game this week and they leave tomorrow.

"No. Sorry. But on that note... What are you doing for New Year's Eve? There's a party at the Westerly Hotel and the guys are—"

"Our first party as a couple?" Holding the phone away from my mouth, I squeal, my mood instantly lifted. "I'm there. It can be our dress rehearsal."

"Our dress rehearsal?"

"Yes. For my premiere. If you can come, that is. It's a Wednesday night so I'm not sure how that works with your practice schedule and—"

"I'll be there," Reed's quick to confirm, making me smile. "When is it? I'll make it work."

"Three weeks?"

"Perfect, the season's over by then and we'll get a week off before the playoffs. The timing couldn't be better." The excitement in his tone has my heart fluttering and my nerves easing a little. I've been stressing about the premiere and following release, but having Reed there will make it a lot easier to get through.

"It's meant to be." I laugh, bouncing on my toes. "Do you have a tux?"

"Do I have a tux?" he scoffs. "What kind of question is that?"

"Sorry, I've only seen you in suits. I didn't—"

"I don't have a tux," he admits before chuckling to himself. "But I'm sure I can get one easy enough, right? Maybe I could ask the stylist you rejected."

I burst out laughing and choke on thin air. "Reed." My voice rasps until I clear it. "People will be dying to dress you. You don't need her. I doubt you'll have any trouble."

"Good. So that's settled. We're locking in a party and a premiere, both great opportunities to show the world how perfect you are for Cynthia."

"*Exactly*. And if we're lucky, Bria will be reaching out one way or another before either has even happened. Have you told her yet?"

"I haven't." His voice croaks before he subtly clears his throat. "She went home for Christmas this year, so we haven't had a chance to talk properly."

The mood changes and even though we're not together, I can sense his unease. "Are you worried about it?"

"I don't know if it's that or something else. But either way, after New Year's Eve, she's going to know."

"Wait. You invited her, didn't you?"

"Surprise." Reed's voice rises and I picture him waving his hands around. "She kind of invited herself. I hope you're ready."

Jesus. Am I? My stomach sinks at the prospect, but I smile through it. "As I'll ever be."

With Reed in another state for his away game and me being busy during the week, we don't see each other until he arrives to pick me up for the New Year's Eve party the following Thursday, and when he walks in, I have to pick my jaw up from the floor.

Holy shit.

Greeting me with a casual it's-just-another-Thursday smile, Reed's wearing a fitted long-sleeve Henley top and *grey* sweatpants. I'll repeat, *grey sweatpants*.

He's obviously trying to kill me.

Slamming my eyes shut, I massage my temples and count to three, repeating my newly created mantra over and over. *I cannot sleep with Reed. I cannot sleep with Reed. I—*

"What's going on, Hayls?" he interrupts. "You look troubled."

"Troubled?" My eyes flash open. "I wouldn't call it troubled so much as *horny.*" I grin nervously, feeling a little joy when Reed's face twists uncomfortably, as though my words cause him physical pain. Now he knows how I feel.

"*Christ, Hayls.*" He shakes his head.

"Sorry, but you're wearing sweatpants and they suit you." I tilt my head as my eyes drop to the natural bulge between his legs, making me sigh dreamingly.

"*Hayls,*" he scolds and it makes the moment even hotter. "I *was* going to give you your present right now, but I think I'll change first." He throws his bag over his shoulder and gestures toward the bathroom.

"This isn't my present?" I pout, my gaze still locked on the bulge.

A strangled groan gets caught in his throat. "I'm going. I'll be back." He stalks away and I shift my focus to his ass, my laughter bursting out of me.

"Sorry," I call out, laughing harder when he tells me it's fine.

While he's getting ready, I try to get the image of him railing me against a wall out of my head for long enough to finish curling my hair. And when I'm done, I step into my tight little black dress, shimmying it up over my body before walking out with the zipper undone.

I've got to stop buying dresses when I can't reach the zipper. It's problematic. But I guess it has led to me getting to know my neighbour well since I often beg her to help. I've even had her six-year-old help me once.

We won't talk about the time I slept in my dress because I couldn't get the zipper back down.

Today, I have Reed. Add that to the pros of having a boyfriend.

Said boyfriend is staring out my window as I walk back into the living room, and when he turns to face me, it's *his* jaw that drops this time.

"Fuck, Hayls. You're breathtaking."

My heart skips as I laugh, jokingly lifting his jaw. "Flattery will get you everywhere, dear boyfriend. Can you zip me up?" Spinning around to flash him my back, I pull my hair aside and draw in a breath, feeling exposed all of a sudden. Reed steps closer and the energy around us changes. It thickens somehow. Try as I might to write it off as the magic of New Year's Eve, it's harder to ignore when his fingers brush my skin and a shiver runs through me.

Geez, Hayls. It's innocent. Get a grip.

When he announces he's done, I snap myself out of my daze and spin around, acknowledging his new attire, wolf whistling as I openly drink him in. "I'm glad you never hired that stylist, Reedy boy, because *damn*, you can dress yourself. Looking good."

"Thanks, Hayls. I try." He shrugs and I grin.

"Soo...now that we've both acknowledged what a hot couple we are, I believe there was talk of gifts?"

Reed's entire demeanor changes and he nods, walking over to his bag with a bounce in his step. But when he stands, his expression turns nervous. "I thought this was a good idea at the time, but now I'm regretting it."

"Why?" My brows crease as I try to see through him to the gift behind his back.

"It's very coupley."

My expression lifts as excitement swells in my chest, and my eyes follow the little bag when he shifts it in front of him. "Good thing we're a couple then." I bite back my smile, only letting it shine when he chuckles.

"You're right. Merry Christmas, Hayls." He pulls a small box out of the bag and places it in my outstretched hand, and after dropping the bag, he steps back, tucking his hands into his pockets.

A nervous yet giddy energy runs through me as I open the box, and when I find what's inside, I gasp.

"Reed!" My hand flies to my mouth. "My God. It's beautiful." *And must have cost a fortune.*

I stare down in awe at the classic diamond and gold tennis bracelet, my eyes wide as my heart beats chaotically in my chest. This man pays attention. I drooled over this very bracelet when I saw it in a store window the day we went shopping. A store I've *never* thought to walk into because until now, I've never been able to afford any of their creations.

"This is—"

"I know. I hope that's okay." He rocks back on his heels, and it's so freaking adorable that my heart jolts. "I could tell you wanted it, but that you were holding back and—"

"It's perfect," I reassure him, though that's not enough. I don't have the right words to say, except maybe... "All I got you was a set of wireless earbuds."

I grimace and Reed chuckles low, pulling me into a hug. "I needed a new pair," he says with a smile in his voice, rocking me from side to side.

"That's why I got them." Pulling away, I reach behind the couch where I hid Reed's present and hand it over. "Here."

He's quick to open the bag and when he sees the little box, he smiles. "They're perfect, Hayls. My favorite brand."

I knew that too but I don't mention it out loud.

Reed disappears to put his earbuds with his belongings while I fight with the clasp of my bracelet, trying to secure it on my wrist before he gets back.

"Wait, let me." His voice comes from behind me, his breath warming my neck before he steps around and reaches for my present. His fingers zap my skin as he fastens the delicate clasp, and when he lingers for a second longer than required, I step back.

"Thank you," I rush out, hoping he doesn't notice the emotion in my voice. "What time is it? Should we get going?"

Reed's eyes snap to mine and he forces a smile as he lightly shakes his head. "Yes..." He nods. "Definitely." He nods again, seemingly just as affected as I am. "Let's get this party started."

Chapter Twenty-Five

HAYLEY

Bria catches Reed's eyes the second we walk in, waving to him from across the bar. I force a smile, waiting for him to excuse himself, but he surprises me, circling an arm around my waist, pulling me tight against him. "I told her this is new," he tilts his head in to whisper, "and that we're seeing how things go."

"Taking each day as it comes? I like it. And she's smiling." I glance up at him, giving him a reassuring smile. "That's a good start, right?"

Reed mentioned that Bria knew about us while we were on the way here, but before he could go into detail, a car cut in front of us, and we got distracted, never finishing the conversation.

"It is good." He squeezes my waist. "And I can already tell it's genuine." He hits me with a soft smile of his own, but when it doesn't reach his eyes, it's difficult to tell if he's happy or upset. Because, does that mean she doesn't have feelings for him? As much as he says that's a good thing, I'm not so sure that he means it.

When we reach Bria, she pulls me into a quick hug before turning her attention to Reed, and I don't want to be judgey...but it felt forced.

"It's about time you found yourself a girl." She smiles up at him. "I'm so happy for you both."

"Thanks, Bria." His returning smile widens. "I'm happy for us too."

"Good. Good." She smiles again and it's all smiles round here.

Feeling like they need a moment, I glance away to find a guy hovering uncomfortably close beside us. I'm just about to not so politely tell him to buzz off when Bria reaches for his hand and pulls him to her side. "I didn't want to be the third wheel all night. So I brought a friend from work. Reed and Hayley, this is Andreas. Andreas, this is my best friend, Reed, and his new girlfriend, Hayley." She introduces me like we're old friends when technically we haven't officially met. But I think that moment has passed.

"Nice to meet you both." Andreas speaks in a thick Greek accent and Bria's eyes light up as he does. "This is a beautiful party. Thank you for having me."

"Thank you for coming," I say like it's my function before adding, "and keeping Bria company." Because that's the most important part.

There are more awkward smiles and it's then that I notice Reed hasn't said a word. Out of the corner of my eye, I can see him smiling, but it's impossible to tell if it's real unless I look his way, and I don't want to draw attention to it.

"We're going to go and dance," Bria says, linking her arm through Andreas's, her gaze bouncing between mine and Reed's. "But Hayley, we should *definitely* chat later. I can give you some tips on *handling* Reed."

I throw my head back and laugh out loud, hitting her with what I'm sure she believes is genuine warmth while her words don't sit well in my chest. Something about the way she said "handled" has a pit forming in my stomach. But I ignore it. My feelings could just as easily stem from my distrust of women in general over Bria's actual motives, and I need to give her the benefit of the doubt.

"I can't wait." I act the part, my smile widening.

Bria and Andreas disappear after that, and it's so crowded, we barely see them for the next couple of hours, spending most of our time mingling with the football team or dancing in the next room—me, not Reed. Like always, he hovers on the edge of the dance floor, chatting with his mates, watching, laughing at my expense.

Bria's barely in our presence, and yet, I haven't been able to shake the feeling of someone watching us. It started not long after they left, but whenever I glance around the room, she's nowhere to be seen.

It's a little unnerving. But I refuse to let it ruin my night.

"I need water," I shout over the music, using Reed as a support structure while I catch my breath. "I'm dying." I fan my face.

"Well, you have been head thumping like nobody's business."

"Honestly, I was not expecting that style of music. Someone must have requested it."

"You were loving it." He shakes his head, calling me out as though I'm denying it, but he's wrong.

"Oh, I absolutely was. But I can't keep that up all night. I need some pop. Music that allows me to shake my ass."

"You were doing that too." He bites back a smirk and I grin.

"I knew you were watching."

"How could I not? You were shaking your ass at *me*."

He's not wrong. I've been having fun flirting, making it known that I have a man to anyone that'll listen.

"Want me to grab you a drink?" Reed asks, ever the gentleman.

"Nah. I want us *both* to go. I need a break."

He nods before curling his arm around my shoulder, careful not to muss my already ruined hair, sweetly pretending he hasn't noticed the matted mess it's become from the "head banging" I was doing.

Paige and her dad are at the bar when we arrive, and the second I see him, I grin excitedly. "Daddy D'Angelo. How are you?"

All eyes flash my way as Paige snorts. "*Jesus*." I press my fingers to my mouth. "I said that out loud, and I'm not even drunk. Apologies, Mr. D'Angelo. I'm a friend of Paige's."

"Dad, this is Hayley," Paige introduces me. "The actress I was telling you about."

"Ah, yes. Hi, Hayley. It's a pleasure to meet you."

"Likewise. And you know—"

"Reed, how are you?" Salvatore smiles. "Don't worry, I'm not here to cramp your party style. I'm just picking up Paige since Easton had to sneak out early."

My gaze bounces to Paige's and I frown. "You're not staying until midnight?" I ask her. "Is everything okay? Isaac?"

"Everything's fine. Easton's just being Easton, but I kind of want to be with him."

Reed's deep chuckle draws my attention while I nod in understanding. Easton being Easton pretty much sums him up. "We could have driven you home."

"Are you ready to leave?" Paige asks, her eyebrows raised, already knowing the answer.

"Nope. I'm here until the end."

"I thought so. Dad doesn't mind, do you?"

"Nope, never. I'll take any time I can get. And on that note, are you ready?"

"Sure am. Have a great night." Paige gives both Reed and me kisses on the cheek as her dad waves goodbye.

"I trust you not to party too hard, Reed," he deadpans. "We've got playoffs in our sights." He winks my way while Paige groans.

"*Dad.*"

"Nah, he's right," Reed cuts in. "I'll behave. I always do."

"I know you will. Have fun." Salvatore pats Reed on the shoulder as he and Paige depart, and the second they're gone, he turns my way.

"Daddy D'Angelo?" he questions, biting back his smile.

"I know." I let my face fall into my hands. "I can't *believe* that came out of my mouth. But even you have to admit, that man is *fine.*"

"I am *not* admitting that." He chuckles incredulously. "He's my boss and your friend's dad."

"I'm not going to go there. But I can look. It's no different than this situation." I motion back and forth between us. "I can look but I can't touch."

"You can touch." His gaze drops to my hand on his arm. "We touch all the time."

"Not what I meant, Reedy boy." I give his bicep a squeeze. "But I love your innocence." I wink and he rolls his eyes, groaning.

"Let's get our waters and go. We need to move on from this conversation."

"Why? Did I get you thinking about what I could touch?"

"Hayls," he warns.

"Sorry." I scrunch my nose and smile before turning to the bartender. "I'll have two waters, please."

"Coming right up."

The night goes on with Reed once again hovering on the edge of the dance floor, swaying his hips with a comical smirk. My chest aches from laughing as I grip his shirt, pulling him closer. I shimmy backward, trying to get him to at least set a foot onto the wooden floor, but he's too strong to budge.

"I am going to get you here one day. Just you wait."

"I'm looking forward to it." He winks and I playfully roll my eyes just as the music stops and the countdown to midnight begins.

"It's midnight already?" I whisper-yell while everyone else shouts out the seconds, filling the room with excitement.

Reed chuckles, his genuine smile bringing about my own, and when I glance up and our eyes lock, the energy between us shifts. Reed blows out a breath, drawing my gaze to his lips as his fingers brush my cheek, tucking a rogue hair behind my ear.

Five...

He steps closer and my breath hitches, fighting the new sensation taking over me.

Four...

My chest flutters as our eyes meet again, the tension so strong I want to look away until he speaks. "I'm going to kiss you, Hayls," he rasps, his voice clear above the noise. "Just so you know."

Three...

His hand falls to my mouth, his fingers curling around my chin, his thumb brushing my bottom lip. It wasn't a question, but even if it was, my answer would be yes.

Two...

Reed tilts my head, bringing my lips closer to his as his eyes flicker between mine, seeking permission, despite never actually asking for it. My pulse spikes and I nod, tightening my hold on his shirt, pulling him closer until our bodies are flush.

One...

Midnight strikes and cheers fill the air, but Reed drowns them out, pressing his lips to mine, stealing my breath as the crowd ceases to exist.

His mouth caresses mine, explorative but sweet, gently consuming me as my heart slams in my chest, the pounding competing with the beat of the music—a techno version of "Auld Lang Syne."

Curling his hand into my hair, Reed leans in, tilting my head farther so he can deepen the kiss. My breasts rub against his chest and another gasp escapes me, eliciting a groan from the back of his throat. With my lips parted, Reed sneaks his tongue into my mouth, swirling it once before it's gone. And I instantly miss the feeling.

I want more. Of everything.

Pulling him impossibly close, I moan against his lips, the fervor increasing between us.

While there's no doubt we're playing this off as a New Year's Eve kiss, we are *way* beyond that and too far gone to stop. At least I am. He's damn good at this. If I'm not careful, this could become an addiction.

Time loses all meaning and I'm consumed by the moment, by the softness of Reed's lips and the tender way he cups my cheeks. I'm in sensory overload of the best kind, so when someone grabs my shoulder, I jolt, snapping out of my trance.

I force a laugh, catching Reed's confused gaze before he spots Luke and chuckles along with me.

"Nice touch." Luke nods, gesturing between the two of us. "I saw quite a few cameras flashing in your direction." He whispers, leaning in close so that no one else hears him, "I have no doubt this will make the news by tomorrow. I can see the headlines now. *Golden Boy Reed Coombs finds love with Hollywood starlet Hayley Jackman, no relation to Hugh.*"

He winks and I burst out laughing again. I can always rely on Luke to bring the jokes.

"Who are you calling a starlet, Bennett?" Reed chips in, wrapping his arm around my shoulder as my gaze flits over the many eyes watching us from around the room. *Maybe we did need to kiss to be taken seriously.* "Hayley's way past that," Reed continues, making me smile. "My girl's a star." He squeezes my shoulder, and I fight the instinct to roll my eyes.

"Where's Amelia?" I ask, moving the conversation on.

"She's on the phone with my mom, letting her know we'll be there in thirty minutes."

"*Thirty minutes?* That means you're leaving now." I pout and Luke bops me on the nose.

"Cheer up. I'm sure you'll be seeing me soon. After all, you're dating my teammate."

"I'm not pouting over *you*, Bennett." I shove him out of the way, making him laugh. "I wanted to party with Amelia. I'll be back. I'm going to catch her before she goes."

Reed chuckles as I leave, so I shake my ass for his pleasure, smiling over my shoulder. He shakes his head and mouths his next words, but something catches my eyes and my attention shifts, watching Bria walking in his direction.

She waited for me to go. Sneaky.

A tightness works its way into my chest as her narrowed gaze locks with mine.

She's not *welcoming* me into her world. It's quite the opposite.

And I hate to think what it's going to do to Reed.

He'll never admit it, but I think this is going to break him.

Chapter Twenty-Six

REED

I'm still reeling from my kiss with Hayley—my mind struggling to process the feelings coursing through me—when she walks away. Luke follows after her and I stare intently, watching them go. My head spins, and I'm so consumed by my thoughts that when someone tugs on my arm, I startle.

"Fuck."

"Sorry." Bria laughs from beside me, drawing my attention. "Happy New Year."

"Of course." I force a smile. "Happy New Year. Are you having a good night? I've barely seen you." My eyes flit to where Hayley's talking to Amelia, before moving back to Bria, confusion swirling inside me.

"I'm surprised you were even looking. That was some kiss."

"Can't ring in the new year without one." I force a chuckle this time, but Bria shakes her head.

"We've spent plenty of New Year's Eve's together and never *once* kissed."

Jesus... this is new and the worst fucking timing. "That's true, but we're friends. Remember? Hayley's my girlfriend."

Bria's eyes bulge and her gaze darts in Hayley's direction. "Your girlfriend now? I thought you were just 'seeing how things went.'"

I cringe because I shouldn't have worded it that way. "We were. We *are*. But she's still my girlfriend. So..." I trail off and Bria turns back to face me, a soft smile in place.

"Yeah. I get it." She pauses, sucking in a breath. "It's strange, you know."

"What is?"

"Seeing you with a girl. I mean, I know you're not a virgin. Or at least I assumed that after catching girls sneaking out of your room in college, but actually *seeing* you with someone...it's different."

I stare at her, my expression void of emotion, and she laughs. "Don't mind me. I don't know what I'm saying."

What. The. Fuck? We have *never* spoken about this before. Ever. *What are you trying to tell me, Bria?*

She glances away shyly and it's like someone has stabbed me in the chest. She's not jealous per se, but she's definitely upset about the change in dynamic between us, and I have a bad feeling our friendship isn't going to survive this.

"Don't worry, I'll still have time for us." I test the waters, watching closely for her reaction. "Hayley's incredibly understanding about our friendship. She knows how close we are and she'd never want that to change."

"Wow. Great." Her tone lacks enthusiasm and I almost call her out. "I'm so happy you found someone like that. She sounds perfect."

"Hayley's great. You're going to love her."

"I'm sure I will."

She smiles again but it's so obviously forced that it pisses me off. Rather than giving me a spark of excitement at the prospect of realizing she might actually have feelings for me, I'm angered. She's supposed to be supportive of this. She's been talking about the men in her life for *months* and I was expected to be happy about it.

"She's on her way back," I say, my smile widening to greet Hayley. "We should all go and get some air."

"Actually,"—Bria grimaces, taking a step back as she points behind her —"Andreas is waiting for me. Have a good night, Reed."

She squeezes my arm as she walks away, letting it linger for a few seconds longer than she normally would, and I stare down at her hand. She's clearly not herself, and in the past I would have gone after her, begging her to tell me what's wrong. But when Hayley smiles hesitantly in front of me, the rest of the room disappears.

"Are you okay?" she asks, her voice full of concern. "How did that go?"

I stare at her for a beat, working her questions around in my mind, and when I answer, I completely surprise myself. "I'm great. It's a new year, we're going to make the playoffs, and we have a shot to win the Super Bowl again. Life is good. And to top it all off, I have the most beautiful woman by my side."

"The *most* beautiful?"

"Don't pretend you don't know that. I mean, just look." I wave a hand around the room as Hayley's eyes follow, a flirty smile in place, until she shivers.

"I'd say I'm in the top three." She forces her grin to return and I want to laugh, but something about her expression has my hackles rising.

"What made you shiver?"

"What?"

"You shivered just now. What's going on?"

"Oh. You caught that." She grimaces before hitting me with another fake grin until I hold my stare and she sighs in resignation. "Okay, fine. All night I've had this feeling like someone is watching me. I can't explain it. I've just felt off."

She shivers again and I stand tall, my muscles stiffening as I search around the space, seeking out anyone looking in our direction, and there are plenty of options. I'd say we're a big talking point right now. But are any of them threats? My fists clench and Hayley laughs.

"What are you doing?"

"I'm looking for someone. Why didn't you tell me?"

"Honestly...because I thought it was Bria. Or that I was imagining it."

"I don't mean to scare you, Hayls. But you're kind of a big name. Please don't ignore your gut. If you're worried, tell me. Tell anyone. And don't go anywhere alone."

"Okay, Dad." She rolls her eyes. "I'll make sure to take a friend with me when I go to the bathroom."

"I'm serious, Hayls. After the conversation I just had with Bria, it could very well be her, but what if it's not?" A nervous energy settles in my chest, but I try to ignore it as my eyes bore into hers.

"All right. I'll be careful." She nods and it's then I relax, thankful that something I said got through to her.

"Thank you." I smile, not bothering to hide my relief in my sigh.

"You know you're kind of hot when you get protective like that?"

"Hayley, you think I'm hot *all the time*."

"It's true, I do. No point in denying it." She hits me with a coy smile and while I'm certain it's fake, it smacks me in the chest. I meant what I said—she's the most beautiful girl in the room, and tonight she's by my side, much to the disappointment of most of the guys in this room.

"So, what happened with Bria?" Hayley interrupts my thoughts and I freeze.

Bria's here.

Bria's in this room, and for the first time, I'm consumed by somebody else.

Wow. Progress. I think.

"Earth to Reed." Hayley waves in my face, trying to get my attention. "You're thinking about her now, aren't you? Do you need me to kiss you again so you'll snap out of it?"

I shake off my thoughts and laugh. "I'm pretty sure *I* kissed *you*."

"Same, same."

"But different."

"Sure, okay. But I need to know. What happened?"

"I'm not really sure to be honest." I frown, still confused by her reaction. "She was happy and then she wasn't. Then she said she was but she was definitely lying."

"So she was jealous?" Hayley's frown rivals my own and my confusion deepens.

"I don't know. Despite having *two* female best friends, as you like to point out, when it comes to this stuff, I'm lost."

Hayley bites back a grin as she grabs my arm, giving me a comforting squeeze. "Oh, Reedy boy, you're just too nice. Want me to find out?"

"What? How?"

"I have my ways." She glances up at me, her eyes peeking through her thick lashes.

"Why does that scare me?"

Her laughter fills the air and I panic. "It should." She tugs her bottom lip between her teeth, releasing it slowly. "One day I might use my powers on you." She points at my chest and my gaze follows before lifting back to her eyes.

"What powers?"

She stares at me for a second before taking a step closer and hitting me with a devastating frown, the sadness in her eyes something I haven't seen before. "I don't know what to do." She sucks her lips into her mouth as her eyes water and my heart breaks. "Reed and I just started dating. And I think...I think he has feelings for someone else. What if he never gets over her? Am I crazy? You know him better than anyone else. What should I do?" A lone tear slides down her cheek and emotion clogs my throat. But when she smirks, I'm snapped out of it.

"*Hell*. That was Oscar worthy."

"Right?" Her proud smile makes me laugh uncomfortably. I knew what she was doing and I still fell for it. But...

"Do you really think that could work? On Bria?"

"Yep. She'll either tell me you're a good guy and that she'll suss it out for me, or she'll admit my concerns are warranted and that you do have feelings for someone else. *And* that she's not sure you'll ever get over them."

"What if she reacts another way entirely?"

"Whatever she says will be telling. I know it."

My nose scrunches as I contemplate her idea. This is the first night Bria's seen us together. She probably needs time to warm up to the idea. After all, we've been best friends for over ten years, and I've never so much as kissed a girl in front of her or even mentioned one. "Let's keep that in our back pocket in case we need it," I say after giving it some thought. "I think she'll reveal her feelings soon enough."

"I'll do whatever you want me to do, Reed. You just have to ask." She smiles and *damn*, why did that make my cock twitch?

"Want to dance?" she asks, changing the subject, completely unaware of my little problem.

I laugh to distract myself, shaking my head. "Nope. I'm going to get a stiff drink. Do you want anything?"

"Less drinking." She pouts. "Remember?"

I cringe. "Sorry."

"That's okay. I don't mind. I can still have fun without it. I'll see you in a bit. After I've worked up a sweat."

She runs her hands down her body as she shimmies, and while it looks innocent enough, my gaze follows, my thoughts anything *but* innocent, imagining her working up a sweat in ways that have nothing to do with dancing. Her body bouncing on top of mine, her hair stuck to her face and... *Holy shit. What the fuck?*

Once again oblivious to my inner madness, Hayley presses her lips to my cheek and sashays away, grabbing Keeley's hand as she moves past, dragging her from where she's talking to Zane.

Shaking off my thoughts, I get my ass out of there and find Thomas at the bar, two waters in his hand as he chats with our new assistant coach, Brad, and I pray to anyone that will listen that one of them is able to distract me.

"And you really think he's pulling the pin?" Thomas asks Brad, immediately drawing my attention.

"Yep. There's something going on, but I haven't been included in the conversations yet."

Brad started with the team at the beginning of this season, around the same time our general manager "resigned"—was forced to leave—and the timing sucked. From day one, Brad's name was thrown around as part of the controversy with our exiting GM, and it was hard to watch. Brad didn't deserve that. He's a great guy and a talented coach. Now it sounds like something else is going on. Which I guessed based on D'Angelo and Keeley's little interaction the other week.

"Fuck." Thomas runs his hand through his hair, finally noticing me. "Reed, my man. How much did you hear?"

"Not enough for you to worry, but if you want to fill me in, you know I'm a vault."

"I do. But I don't want to stress you out. I'm doing enough of that for the both of us."

Yeah, too late for that. "I already had a feeling something was going on. I saw D'Angelo shoot Keeley a strange look after his big speech the other week."

"You caught that too?"

"Yep."

Thomas sighs. "We think our new General Manager's going to resign."

"What?" *Jesus.* I did not see that coming. "He just started."

That's all we need. Another GM controversy. It took them long enough to find this guy. Mind you, he hasn't really proven himself yet.

"Think you can convince Wes this time?" I perk up. I wasn't around when Wes Johnson played for Storm but we all know who he is. He was an incredible player before he had to retire due to injury. He's now married to Lucy, our ex-teammate Dylan's sister, and Thomas knows him well.

Thomas laughs at my comment. "I'm sure as hell going to try. And this time it might involve begging. Or maybe I'll get Lucy on my side. I know Carter's already giving him hell." Carter is our teammate and Wes's close friend. "That aside, the team's got enough going on without another fucking controversy. The media only just stopped talking about that goddamn TV show."

"It doesn't help that Zane keeps bringing it up."

"No, it doesn't, but I'm going to give him a pass." He frowns and my eyes widen.

"Do you know something I don't?"

"I might." He chuckles though it doesn't quite reach his eyes. "I see a little of myself in him. Not myself *now*, but when I was younger. I think he's self-destructing."

While I don't know a lot about Thomas's private life, he's been extremely open about his struggles with alcohol and depression. If he's seeing something in Zane, I trust him completely.

"I'm only telling you this because I know you're a good guy and one of the only guys that hasn't written him off yet. There may come a time when he needs his friends and he's going to realize he doesn't have many."

A feeling of déjà vu hits me. I've thought the same thing many times before. "I'll be there," I say truthfully.

"I know, man. Thanks." He pats me on the back and smiles at Brad. "I better get this to Lainey." He holds up one of the drinks in his hand. "She hasn't left the dance floor all night."

He turns to walk away but his gaze flits back to mine. "Shit, I keep forgetting to ask... How's the mentoring with Landon? He mentioned you've been checking in on him."

"Yeah, I think he's onto me. But I don't think he'd mind having an official mentor. He's eager to learn and responsive to suggestions."

"I thought that might be the case. And he's in the right hands."

"What can I say, I'm trying." I shrug and Thomas laughs, though I'm not really joking. I'm trying because while Landon's eager to learn, I'm conscious of not making him feel like he needs a mentor more than anyone else on the team. We have a mentoring program—that he's a part of—but it focuses purely on the game. What I'm doing with Landon is more than that. I'm trying to build his confidence and integrate him better into the team. And deep down, I know that's what Thomas really meant. Otherwise he wouldn't have asked *me*.

"Thanks, Reed." Thomas nods, his warm knowing smile flashing my way before he disappears and Brad turns his attention to me, changing the topic.

"So...you and Riley, huh?"

"What?" *Riley?* Oh... "You've read *Jaded Beginnings*?"

"No." He shakes his head. "My girlfriend has and she's obsessed. She made me watch the trailer. At least *fifty* times. No exaggeration."

"I bet she's excited for the release."

"She wants to go to the midnight screening." He rolls his eyes jokingly and my heart jumps as a warmth takes over me.

"Hayley will love hearing that. Is your girlfriend here?"

"She just left." He cringes, a sadness in his eyes. "She has to work early tomorrow."

"Oh, shame. Remind me next time we're all together, and I'll introduce her to Hayley."

"Bullshit. Really? That would earn me brownie points for a lifetime. She barely took her eyes off Hayley all night. She was definitely fan-girling."

I laugh until a thought hits me... That explains Hayley's feelings about someone watching her. Her intuition was right. Only it wasn't Bria like she guessed.

"Next time, you should bring her over. Hayley would love to meet a fan."

"Thanks, man. I will."

He walks away smiling and I order my drink, grabbing Hayley a water while I'm there.

Then, like Brad's girlfriend, I'm drawn to Hayley, unable to take my eyes off her as she owns the dance floor, letting herself go, completely in the moment. She says she's the type to do what she wants and never hold back, and it's true—she's exactly like that. But here, now, there's something free about her, something deeper. And it's beautiful to watch.

Her eyes flicker open, and just like the first time I saw her dancing, her gaze locks on mine, and the most breathtaking smile graces her lips. My breath catches and I'm taken back to the moment our lips first touched, the first time we kissed. To the spark that shot through me. To the way her breath hitched as my tongue caressed hers.

I have never felt as close to anyone as I did in that moment. And while at the time, I refused to believe that it meant anything, now, I'm not so sure.

Hayley nibbles at her bottom lip, bringing me back to the present, her eyes lighting up with mischief. With a wink, she pretends to cast a fishing line my way, reeling it in, hoping I'll follow.

When I don't move at first, she gasps, her hand flying to her mouth as she shakes her head, pointing at me sternly. "You," she mouths, motioning to the spot on the floor in front of her. "Here now," she mouths again. At least I think she does. Either way, I let this play out for a little while longer.

She pouts, seemingly giving up with a shrug of her almost bare shoulders. But I know better than that. Once she has her mind on something, there's no going back.

She points again, this time to something behind me, and when I turn to look, confusion mars my features until familiar arms circle around my waist.

"You didn't think I'd give up that easily, did you?" She lifts to her toes, whisper-yelling in my ear as I spin back around. "Are you playing hard to get?"

"Nope." I chuckle, circling my arms around her neck. "I'm just waiting for the right song."

"Austin" by Dasha comes on next and Hayley's eyes light up before she immediately starts dancing, waggling her eyebrows as she moves. She mouths the words to the song, curling her finger, motioning for me to join her.

I have to admit, it's a good song. Not my favorite but I like it, which means, I'm fresh out of excuses.

Nodding a little, I watch her closely, tapping my hand against my leg, pretending that's all I can do.

Melting into the sea of bodies, she shakes her head with a smile and rolls her eyes, turning away from me.

In a move I've memorized, she raises her hands above her head, and her dress lifts higher up her thighs. I try to resist, wanting to tease her a little more, but when the guys around her all dance a little closer, I groan, losing my restraint as I stride forward, shocking us both when I grab her waist, spinning her to face me.

"*Yes.*" She lets out a squeal, stepping back, giving me the space to show off my moves.

But I want her close. Touching me.

So instead, I sway my hips, holding back from giving her everything I've got. We've got time for that later.

Hayley shoots me a knowing smirk but she has *no idea*, and for now, I like it that way.

Grabbing her hands, we dance around, laughing and smiling, full of life. And when the song ends and another comes on—some techno shit I don't understand—I continue to dance. *Because who am I to fuck with Hayley's beaming state of happiness?*

It's infectious.

She's infectious.

And I'm choosing not to process that thought right now. I'm taking a page out of Hayley's book, and living in the moment.

It's time to party with my girl.

CHAPTER TWENTY-SEVEN

REED

Thomas passes the ball back to me and I fake a throw before taking off in a run, heading for my opponent at full force, showing him I mean business. I dodge left and when he strikes, I change direction, rolling past his body, using the impact to propel me forward.

I'm so focused on the play that the crowd around me ceases to exist, but just knowing they're here, knowing they're screaming my name, has me pushing myself to the limits, powering my legs to avoid another strike, diving into the end zone as someone's arms wrap around my legs.

The whistle blows and my teammates cry out, most of them running forward to dive on top of me, flattening me into the turf.

"Hell fucking yes." Rhett's the first to speak. "You are on fire today. Whatever you're doing or *whoever* you're doing, don't ever stop."

I snort as he helps me up. But while I'm waving off his comment like it's ridiculous, my mind wanders to Hayley. Exactly where it shouldn't be going partway through a game.

Fuck if I can get that kiss and the rest of our night out of my head. I've only seen her once since New Year's Eve, but we've spoken daily, and every time my thoughts drift into unsafe waters, I reel them back in.

Like now.

I've always prided myself on my focus, and today is not the day to give up on that.

After we kick the extra point, the first half ends and we run off the field in high spirits. Even if we lose our final game of the season today—which we won't—we're still sitting pretty in the top spot of our conference, guaranteeing us a place in the divisional round of the playoffs.

I hate to get ahead of myself, like some of my teammates do, but I'm feeling good. We're here for back-to-back Super Bowl wins. Our time to shine isn't over yet.

We kick ass again in the second half, securing the win by twenty points, obnoxiously cheering as we enter the locker rooms. But as we each spot Wes Johnson, decked out in a suit—looking very GM-like—silence ensues.

"Fuuuck." Luke's the first to break the tension when he's one of the last guys through the door. "So the rumors are true." He does a slow clap while most of the guys stare in shock.

It's hard to say if it was speculation, or if someone had insider information, but for the past week, whispers have surrounded us about another change in the management team, just as Thomas predicted.

And since Wes is here, it's safe to say we've lost another GM.

"Wes, my man." Luke walks over, offering him a fist bump as Wes shakes his head, giving him nothing in return. I'd laugh if we weren't surrounded by various reporters ready to throw us to the wolves again.

I can see it now... *"What's going on in the Storm camp? It can't be one big happy family if they've lost another GM so quickly."*

Let's hope Wes is here to stay. If that's why he's here. He may just be filling in for the interim.

Keeley gets our attention as D'Angelo steps up onto one of the bench seats, giving us a wave. "We fucking did it," he begins, hitting us with a smile, starting off on a positive note. I grimace internally. If it were me, I'd have started with the bad news, but I'm not in his position, so I smile wide, trying to give him the excitement he's seeking. "We're top of our conference," he continues. "Ahead of the pack. You're all making me look good, and honestly, I don't even have to try. But..." He trails off. "Since we just had another fantastic win after a phenomenal season, and you're all looking at me like I killed your cat, I'm going to get straight to the point.

"I'm not going to pretend you're naive. You know what's going on. I'm sure you've heard the rumors. So, I'm giving it to you straight. Miles Stanford was politely asked to leave after it became apparent he didn't share the same values as the rest of us. At our last charity event, I spoke about wanting us to be true leaders, to be a team our fans could be proud of, and though you may not have seen it, Miles was not on the same page. *But...*I come bearing incredible news because we've secured someone who is. He's a man of great integrity, a man that's proven himself on and off the field, and today, he steps forward as our new general manager. He's coming back to the place he once called home. Everyone, please join me in giving a huge Storm welcome, or welcome back, to former tight end champion, Wes Johnson."

Now the team roars like never before. We should have had Wes from the start.

While some of us, including me, haven't had the pleasure of meeting him, the excitement is still very real. He had an incredible career before his injury and went on to coach the D1 Heartwood University team before most recently becoming their GM. This role makes perfect sense for him.

And God, I hope he sticks around.

Wes joins D'Angelo beside the bench, and they shake hands before Wes steps up, offering a shy smile.

"I'll make this short because you're all in desperate need of a shower. I want you to know that I didn't come to this decision lightly. In fact, I rejected the position the first time around because I wasn't sure it was right for you, myself, or my family. But after long chats with my brother-in-law, Dylan—who I think you may know—and Carter over there, I was *politely* persuaded." He pauses for the laughter before continuing on. "Together, Dylan and Carter sat me down and spoke to me from the view of the team. As *your* voice. They reminded me what it's like to be a player, and how hard you've all had it while being forced to live up to your full potential. All while facing the criticisms and controversy behind the scenes.

"I hadn't allowed myself to think like that before. I'd been a player, sure, but that was so long ago that I'd put that part of myself behind me. Until your teammates, along with my beautiful wife and children, reminded me of the guy I once was. Of the guy who would have done anything for his team. This is my team. And I'm here to tell you, the player is now fresh in my mind. I'm here for each and every one of you. And I'm not going anywhere anytime soon. Not unless you force me out. So...since I said I'd be short and I've been rambling for what feels like a lifetime, I'm going to hand the floor over to somebody else. And if you need me...my door's always open. Thank you."

He jumps down, passing the mic over to Keeley while the media erupt with questions.

"What really happened to Miles Stanford?
"Is this the last of the Storm controversy?"
"Is the Storm in financial trouble?"

Keeley fields the questions while we all peel off to shower and change. Most of the guys pretend they're not paying attention to the media, when it's obvious we're all listening in. The thought of financial trouble never once crossed my mind, but now that I'm thinking it, it's possible. *But what does that mean?*

When we're finally released after our media commitments—which lasted a hell of a lot longer than usual—I'm a mix of emotions as I exit the locker room, but when Hayley runs toward me, launching herself into my arms, all that changes.

"Holy shit, Reed." She wraps her legs around me as I secure her in my hold, and hits me with her infectious smile.

"You were amazing. I mean, you're great in most of your games, but today. My God. I'm not going to lie. It was hot."

I shake my head, a low chuckle rumbling from my chest. "I don't know, Hayls. Something was different about tonight. Something felt right."

"Whatever it was, you killed it out there." She bounces in my arms, the movement rubbing against my cock, and I lift her higher as it pulses, smiling to hide my pain.

Hayley raves about my touchdown leading into halftime while my mind drifts to her chest, noticing her attire for the first time.

"Are you wearing my jersey?" I bite back a groan as an unwanted visual works its way to the forefront of my mind.

Hayley smiles, her eyes sparkling with mischief. "*Technically*, I'm wearing a *team* jersey. I don't have one with your name on the back."

"Well, we have to change that." *This is something I have to see.*

"Yeah?"

"Fuck, yeah. You're mine."

The word "mine" slips easily from my lips and while I follow it with a wink, my chest tightens with a new warmth I haven't felt before. *What the fuck is that about?*

Ignoring my feelings, I smile at Hayley, spinning her around as she laughs, drinking in her happiness, squeezing her ass when she wriggles against me.

Shaking my head, I glance up and find Bria standing a few feet behind us, her eyes locked on my hands, her expression pained until she notices me watching her, her frown morphing into a proud grin.

"Bria's here?" I question, whispering into Hayley's ear, my face in her hair as confusion sets in.

"I know." Hayley pulls back, her eyes full of something I can't quite decipher, while her smile remains in place. "I had the pleasure of running into her on my way up to the suites. There are thousands of people here, and yet, of course I managed to find her."

"You knew she was coming?"

"No, but I knew if she ever came, I didn't want to run into her." Her adorable grimace makes me smile.

"Completely understandable." After our New Year's Eve chat, Bria messaged me to say I should be careful with Hayley. That I should make sure she's serious before falling in love with her. It was the reaction that deep down, I knew was coming. But it didn't fill me with hope like I thought it would; instead it broke my heart. Because while I'd love to believe she was looking out for me as a friend, she didn't bother getting to know Hayley before making that assessment and I always believed she was better than that.

"Did you talk?" I ask, hoping like hell that Bria was nice to her.

"We exchanged pleasantries. She doesn't like me."

I cringe, though I don't think she's wrong. "Everybody likes you." I smile comically until Hayley laughs.

"*Not* your bestie."

"Her loss, not yours."

Hayley wriggles to get out of my hold, rubbing against me again, and I dig my fingers into her ass, locking her in place just above my hardening cock.

"Are you holding me hostage?" she asks, her interest piqued as she smirks.

"Only for another minute."

"And why's that? For Bria?"

I wish. "Nope." I wince, regretting our promise to always be honest with each other.

"When you wriggled just now, my cock decided to rise to attention, assuming your pussy had come out to play."

Hayley's eyes bulge and I can tell she wants to look down, but she holds strong, her gaze locked on mine.

"Lost for words?" I ask, loving the fact that I could elicit a surprised reaction out of her, even if it was at my own expense.

"A little bit. Where did that come from?"

"What?"

"The openness. The dirty talk. Was that a joke or..."

"Wouldn't you like to know." I cock an eyebrow and she pouts.

"Obviously." She shakes her head like I'm crazy, and I smile with a shrug. "Ugh, fine," she relents. "Either way, I like it. Let me know when I can get down."

I glance away, locking eyes with Luke as he gives me a thumbs-up. And seeing his obnoxious face helps calm things down until I'm no longer hard. "I'm good now." I release Hayley. "Thanks for your patience. It won't happen again."

Hayley lets out a squeal as I lower her slowly, dropping her feet to the ground, careful not to wriggle this time. "Only *you* would apologize because a girl turned you on."

"Only me." I wink again, and as she shakes her head, I draw in a quick breath, preparing myself to see Bria, only then thinking about the fact that it's been years since she attended a game. *She's always been too busy.* But now that she's here, I'm not as excited as I thought I would be.

"I'm sorry, Hayley, I should—"

"Go. You need to talk to her. It's going to drive you crazy if you don't find out exactly how she feels."

"Thanks. But you'll be here when I'm done, right?" The thought of her disappearing makes me not want to leave.

"Yep. I'll be here. I owe Juliet a cuddle, and I'm sure Amelia and Luke will welcome the chance to have a moment alone."

Hayley presses a kiss to my cheek before mouthing "good luck" and skipping away to find Amelia. I watch for a minute as Juliet reaches for Hayley, instantly snuggling into her chest, and then I gather my inner strength, heading over to my best friend. The woman who currently feels like a stranger.

CHAPTER TWENTY-EIGHT

HAYLEY

I'm wrecked by the night of the *Jaded Beginnings* premiere, making something that should be a joyous occasion a little bit tainted. The US press tour has been taxing, and the thought of heading off for the international tour is making me anxious. Especially since I still haven't lined up another role for when I get back.

The last two weeks have consisted of junket after junket, interview after interview, audition after audition. And I'm not sure how much more I can take.

We had promotional tours back home, but they were nothing compared to this, and if I'm being honest, I was not prepared.

I was also *not* prepared for how much I'd miss Reed.

After heading out to celebrate his final game—alcohol free and a lot less flirty—he headed straight into playoffs preparation and I entered hell. At least, I'm imagining hell to be like this.

Who knew so many people cared about little things from my past. Or my co-stars' past. Or the director's... You'd think they'd want to talk about the film, the story, the craft. And yet, time and time again, I was asked about my ex, and what I think he feels about my rising stardom. Or my family life back home. Or that supposed *bestie* who decided to speak out about the girl I was in high school, when I barely recognized her face.

I'm exhausted. Both physically and mentally. And now that the premiere is here, I'm terrified for the release.

What if they don't like the film?

What if they don't like me?

Taking a deep breath, I work hard to calm myself down, checking my makeup for the hundredth time. This isn't me. I love life and everything it throws my way. *Mostly*. I'm usually the first to tell someone I'm going to succeed, and this time around I shouldn't feel any differently. I nailed that role. The director did a phenomenal job. This movie is going to break records. It's time I got out of my funk and sorted my shit out.

It's time to be *better*.

My intercom buzzes from our concierge, and I preemptively laugh as I rush over to summon Reed.

"Oh, Henry, you know I was joking... You can send Reed up, even if he's not dressed like a prince."

Henry chuckles. "Your guest, Mr. Coombs, is on his way, and you'll be happy to know he gets my seal of approval."

"Ooh, I can't wait. Thank you. Bye—" I move to hang up but he calls out.

"Miss Jackman. One moment. I have some flowers for you and a card. They arrived seconds after your guest or I would have sent them up with him."

"Flowers? Wow. Okay. I'll grab the card on my way out. But you should keep the flowers. You know I'm hopeless with living things."

"Thank you, Miss Jackman, but they're a little big for our desk."

"A little big?"

"Huge."

"Oh." I giggle, glancing down at my dress as Reed knocks on my door. "I'll send Mr. Coombs back down. He'll be there soon."

"I appreciate it."

"Anytime." I smile, skipping over to the door to greet Reed, thinking about his catchphrase, and as I reach for the handle, my expression turns giddy. I bet he looks gorgeous. I'm smiling wide when I open the door, but the second I see him, the smile is replaced with God knows what, as my brain turns to mush.

Reed swallows and his jaw goes rigid, making it harder for me to focus, especially when no words come out of his mouth.

"Christ." I fill the silence. "I... I... God, you're beautiful."

Reed barks out an awkward laugh before stepping inside and moving me out of the way so he can close the door. "Beautiful isn't *exactly* what I was going for."

He relaxes when we're alone and it snaps me out of my stupor. "What were you going for? I've got options. Hot, dashing, sex on legs, bangable, delicious, drool worthy, panty melting—"

"I get it. I look good."

"Good is not the word I would use." If he wasn't Reed, I'd be dragging him into my bedroom and screwing before our car arrived. But since he is, I'll settle for perving all night. "Anyway, sorry about that. How are you?"

"I'm pissed, if I'm honest. You stole my moment."

"Your moment?" I stare at him confused. "What—"

He steps forward, securing his hands on my waist, the little gesture setting my skin on fire. "You are beyond breathtaking, Hayls. You...this dress... I don't think I've ever seen anyone more striking. But you never gave me a chance to tell you that."

Emotion catches in my throat, and I ignore the way my heart flutters. "Are you trying to make me fall in love with you?" My voice cracks before I subtly clear it. "I told you. This will only work if we're friends."

Reed rolls his eyes before stepping back, hitting me with a genuine grin. "If you're falling in love with me, that's on you. I'm just being honest."

"Thank you." I give a little shrug and gaze over him from head to toe again. "We make an attractive couple, don't we?"

Reed's laughter fills the air before he grabs my hand and pulls me into a hug. "We sure do, Hayls." He kisses my hair. "How long before we have to leave?"

"Oh." I remember the flowers. "We have a few minutes. Any chance you want to take your gorgeous tux-clad body back down to the lobby? Someone sent me flowers."

"Flowers?" His eyes widen and I giggle when he curses under his breath. "Why didn't I think of that?"

"You're already coming as my date. You don't have to do anything else."

"So you don't want the congratulatory gift I got you?"

"What?" My eyes flash to his empty hands, and then his bag on the floor. "Of course I freaking do. Gimme. Gimme. Gimme."

"You'll have to wait until I get back." He turns to walk away but I dart forward, curling my fingers around his wrist.

"*Reed.* You know I hate—"

He turns back with a smirk, simultaneously pulling a small box from his pocket, cutting me off as he holds it out. "Open it now if you must. I'll be back with your flowers." Placing the box in my hand, he winks before he disappears, leaving me staring in shock until the door clicks shut.

"Dammit, Reed," I yell, hoping he'll hear me. "I'll wait."

And wait I do.

He's barely been gone for five minutes but it feels like a lifetime as the box burns a hole in my hand. *Is it jewellery? Or something else? And what does it mean?*

The door opens and Reed steps in with an obnoxiously big bouquet of flowers. Actually, you can't call it a bouquet; it's more like a bucket. With a floral arrangement so big, I can't see his face.

"What in the world?"

"I'm wondering the same thing, Hayls. It weighs a ton."

He brushes past me, placing it on the kitchen counter with a thud before handing me the note. "From your secret admirer?" he questions jokingly and I want to laugh, but a sinking feeling settles in my stomach, making me grip the note tightly.

If he'd asked me that a few weeks back, I wouldn't have flinched. Hell, I'd have been proud of that notion. But lately, things have changed and I constantly feel like someone's watching me—outside my apartment building...at New Year's... I'm probably imagining it, but still.

"I'm sure it's from the studio," I say with a smile before hesitantly dragging a finger through the seal, holding my breath.

Hayley,

Congratulations on the premiere of Jaded Beginnings. *I wish you every bit of happiness and can't wait to see you in your beautiful dress. I know you already have a date, but if you knew who I was, I have no doubt I'd be the one by your side. We'd make the perfect couple. We* will *make the perfect couple. It's only a matter of time.*

I'll be seeing you.

Your secret admirer

x

I work hard to keep a straight face but when I glance up, Reed's creased brow suggests that I failed.

"Who sent them, Hayls?" I cringe at his curt tone.

"Um. A secret admirer." My nose scrunches as his jaw drops.

"I was *joking*. How do they have your address?"

"I don't know. I'm guessing he either lives in the building or nearby. He's probably seen me walking in. The letters are never addressed. They're hand delivered. He doesn't know my apartment number and—"

"He? Letters? This isn't the first?"

Dammit. "This is the first that's made me uncomfortable. The rest were fine. Nice even."

"What does this one say?"

Reed steps forward, beckoning for the letter. There's a fire in his eyes that makes me almost say no. But I can't keep this from him, not now that he knows.

Cringing again, I gently place the letter into his outstretched hand before squeezing my eyes shut, waiting for his reaction.

"The fuck."

"I know."

"And you have no idea who this is?"

"No." I finally open my eyes when Reed falls quiet, his tense gaze locked on the letter, his jaw rigid, his free hand clenched by his side.

It's a beat before he looks up, and when our eyes lock, he sighs. "How many has he sent?"

"This is the third."

"That's it? Nothing else?"

"Like what?"

"Anyone lurking around or following you?"

"*What*? No." *Maybe. I don't know; I could be crazy.* "I don't think there's been anything else."

"You don't think?" Reed shakes his head, tossing the letter onto the counter, his expression pained.

"I *know*. There's been nothing specific. And I promise this is the first letter that's had me concerned."

He nods, pulling me into a hug. "I'm sorry, Hayls. I just worry about you."

"I know."

"And I think you should tell someone."

"It's *harmless*." And I'll bet other celebrities have had way worse than this. The police would laugh me off.

"Harmless?" Reed growls. "He's clearly infatuated with you."

"That's my job. That's how I *want* people to feel."

"Hayley."

"I promise. I'll look after myself."

"You won't have to. I'm not leaving your side tonight." As if proving his point, he settles beside me and fakes a smile, making me pout.

"I'm okay with you gluing yourself to me. But Reed...this is supposed to be a fun night. Can we rewind? I haven't even opened my gift."

Reed's entire demeanor changes as his shoulders fall. "Yes. I'm sorry. I'll put protective Reed away."

"God, no. Don't do that. He's hot. Just keep him on a leash."

Reed's lips quirk into a delicious smirk and my heart races. "You're lucky I don't keep *you* on a leash." His gravelly voice travels straight to my core. "Behave tonight, yeah?" he continues. "Don't stray too far."

Jesus Christ. I balk, my eyes wide, biting my lip as I ignore the ache between my legs. After that comment, *and* visual...how could I walk away?

Reed sighs with a breathy laugh before massaging his temples. "You are going to be the death of me, Hayls."

"What?" I smirk. "I didn't say a word."

"You didn't have to. Now it's present time. Open it up."

I stare down at the box as a nervous energy runs through me. With a tight chest and soft smile, I open it slowly, hesitating until I see what it is and burst out laughing.

"Is this chocolate?"

"It sure is."

He got me a chocolate Academy Award statue. "How?"

"I know a guy."

"That makes chocolate? Why didn't you tell me that sooner? Is he single? Good-looking?"

"He's seventy-six but he's pretty attractive for his age. Some would say he's a silver fox."

I laugh harder, pulling Reed into a hug, squeezing him tightly. "You're freaking awesome. You know that, right?"

"I do now." He winks and all I can do is shake my head. *Who is this man and how is he still single?*

Oh, right... He's in love with his best friend.

Before we leave, Reed suggests tossing the flowers, and while they're incredibly pretty, I wholeheartedly agree, only I can't bear to see them go to waste, asking him to leave them in the hallway instead, in case someone else wants them.

I touch up my lipgloss as I wait, and just as he gets back, Henry buzzes me again, letting me know our car has arrived.

It's go time. The moment we've all been waiting for. The star-studded event of a lifetime. And I'm nauseous. "I should have had a shot," I tell Reed as he helps me into the car and settles in beside me. "What if they hate it? God, what if it's terrible? I'll be there. In the room. With all of them judging me."

As the car starts to move, Reed grabs my hand, intertwining our fingers before rubbing his thumb slowly across my skin. "They're going to love it, Hayls. They're going to love you, and we're going to have an amazing night."

I stare up at him, drinking him in as he smiles. "How do you know?"

"Because it's *you*. You were born for this moment. You're already a star, and have been for a long time. You're just waiting for the rest of the world to catch up."

My heart jolts as his beautiful eyes bore into my soul, begging me to see myself the way he does, and I do. *How could I not?*

"Thank you," I whisper, my voice caught in my throat.

"What for? I was just being honest."

"I know, but you have a way of calming me more than anyone else ever has. I'm grateful you're coming with me tonight. I have no idea what to expect. For all I know they might drag me away for press commitments or whatnot. But whatever happens, I'll be thinking of you and grateful to know that you're there."

"You don't have to thank me for that. I'm here for anything you need. And I'm sure I'll be able to entertain myself. Anyone important that you want me to schmooze?"

"Schmooze?" I question, and a little of the tension leaves my shoulders, allowing me to relax into my seat.

"Yeah. I want to spread the word of your greatness, make sure you're at the forefront of everyone's mind. By the end of the night, Australia's sweetheart will be back, even if you're a badass on the screen. I'm going to have them crazy over you."

I hit him with my sassiest smile, though I'm certain he's not joking. "Don't work too hard. You need to enjoy yourself."

"I know. I will."

Our car comes to a halt in traffic and I jolt forward. Despite wearing a seatbelt, Reed shoots his hand out to protect me and my heart races. "God, you're a good guy." I shake my head with a smile. "Why can't this be real?" I'm messing around as usual, but as I say the words, it doesn't feel like I'm joking.

Reed laughs anyway. "What are you talking about, Baby? This *is* real." He stares at me pointedly before his eyes flash to our driver and I burst out laughing.

"Thank you for being the best boyfriend ever."

"As always, anytime."

We're on the same street as the theatre but it takes us another thirty-five minutes before we come to a stop out front, and in that time, my nerves return tenfold. I'm about to tell the driver to make another lap of the block when Reed pulls a little bottle from his jacket pocket, smiling when my eyes light up. "I had this in case of emergencies. Just to calm the nerves."

"Oh my God, I love you." I throw my arms around his neck, careful to keep my body away from him so I don't mess up the tape stopping my nipples from making an appearance. "Thank you." I press my lips to his in a chaste kiss. "You're a lifesaver."

Reed chuckles as he hands over the single shot of vodka before getting out of the car and walking around to meet me. I down the liquid courage as soon as he's gone, letting the warmth work its way through my body.

It doesn't instantly help me, and I'm still nervous when the door opens on my side, but when Reed reaches for my hand, intertwining our fingers again after helping me out, a calm takes over my mind and it finally hits me... It's not the alcohol I need. It's Reed.

CHAPTER TWENTY-NINE

HAYLEY

Reed squeezes my hand as the audience collectively gasps and then smiles when I glance his way. "They love it," he mouths, his proud expression penetrating my chest, working to ease a little bit of the tightness. I now understand why actors try to avoid this. Watching yourself on the big screen is one thing, but watching yourself with hundreds of people as they judge everything about your performance is another thing entirely.

And if I didn't have Reed, I'm certain I'd crumble.

He's the perfect date, the perfect gentleman, the perfect boyfriend—doting, comforting, playful. He makes me laugh to ease my mind and whispers sweet nothings in my ear, eliciting smiles that I have no doubt will be on the front page of tomorrow's gossip magazines. He plays up to the cameras, steps aside when someone asks, and holds my hand when it's clear that I need it. He's playing a part and he's playing it well. But more than that, he's just being *him*.

The beautiful kind soul that deserves everything in this world. And I couldn't be more grateful for him.

The credits roll to loud applause, and my heart races as I stand, awed by the reaction, stunned into silence.

"You did it, Hayls." Reed stands, leaning in close to press a kiss to my hair, while I fight not to cry, which is goddamn impossible when he says things like, "You were fucking phenomenal."

A proud energy courses through me and I let myself feel it, unsure if I'll ever get this high again.

This moment is everything, and I couldn't have picked a better person to share it with.

Our director says a few words, thanking guests for coming, asking them to shout from the rooftops to spread the word about the masterpiece they've seen tonight, and to have a good evening.

Then it's time for the party.

Or at least, it's time for a tame, elegant, mingling of like-minded individuals that is so far away from my scene we're on opposite sides of the world. But I'm an actress. I've got this.

As we walk, Reed seamlessly slips his hand into mine like we've been doing all night, giving me a comforting squeeze. Then he does exactly what he said he would do—he schmoozes, talking me up to anyone that will listen. And there are a lot of people who now want to listen.

"You two make a gorgeous couple. How did you meet?" someone asks, and I internally cringe until Reed takes the reins.

"We met a while back, but I knew I wanted to get to know her better when she was doing her thing at one of the Storm charity events, shining brightly, convincing everyone they needed to dig deep for the cause." He pauses and my eyes flash to his, a smile on my face while inside, my heart races, threatening to beat out of my chest. "We raised record funds for Parkinson's Disease research that night," he continues, leaning in to press another kiss to my head, smiling at the crowd of people that have joined us. "And honestly, we owe it all to her. She lights up a room wherever she goes, and her heart... Anyway..." He trails off, rolling his eyes playfully as though he's embarrassed. "I'm sure you don't need to know all that. How good was *Jaded Beginnings*?"

The conversation moves back to the movie, and just as Reed reassured me on the way here, they loved it.

"I've read the book and I'm actually surprised by how true you stayed to the story. It blew me away."

"Patrick is my hall pass. And until now, he's only been fictional. But that man..."

"No one else could have played Riley. The way you seamlessly shifted between the lightness and the dark, truly encapsulating all that she believed in, all that she wanted to be. I want to cry again just thinking about it."

The more praise I receive, the more my heart grows—and my head if I'm being honest—but Reed's constant support and awe keep my feet locked on the ground, reminding me to stay in the moment. Because before too long, I'll be on my own again.

Drinks flow and as the night goes on, loose lips take over, prompting Reed to guide me out onto the balcony for a moment of relief. "You're not allowed to listen to anyone that's drunk," he says firmly, his penetrating gaze boring into mine. "Do you understand?"

"Yes, Dad," I snark, questioning why I stayed sober myself. "But, you've got to—"

"No buts. The last woman got your name wrong. I doubt she was even thinking about the same movie. And none of it's been bad. They just have that alcohol confidence that makes them suddenly think that they're experts."

He's right that nothing has been overly bad, but I did have a woman tell me that my hair was the wrong kind of blonde for Riley and that my lips weren't as plump. I initially laughed it off until I was in the bathroom, glossing my thin lips, questioning my life choices. Should I get filler? Is that the direction Hollywood is going right now?

Reed groans out loud before sighing incredulously as he pulls me into a side hug. "What are you fixated on?"

"My lips. That posh woman said they weren't plump enough."

"What?" he scoffs, faking outrage. "What would she know? They're plenty plump."

I stare at him deadpan, folding my arms over my chest. "What would *you* know?"

"I know plenty. But if you need specifics...I'm a man with eyes. And your lips are delectably plump, the exact amount one would want in a woman."

I laugh out loud, shoving him away. "God, you're full of shit."

"Am I? Shall we ask for a second opinion?"

As if his question summoned a response, the sliding door to the balcony opens and a couple walk out. I smile when Reed bounces his eyebrows, but when I turn to face the couple, I internally groan.

"Ugh. That's my ex," I whisper, burying my face in his chest. "Why is he here? And is he with Chelsie Watson?"

Reed spins me around, leaning down to whisper, "I can't answer that." He frowns. "But I am curious... Is this the guy that couldn't find your clit?"

I snort out a laugh before covering my face with my hands. "No." I shake my head, laughing again as I picture the response if he heard that. He'd riot. "Actually, he's the one that cheated on me."

Reed stiffens, but I wave off his concern. I felt shitty about it at the time, but I've come to realize it was the best thing to ever happen to me.

"And...he's coming over. Of course he is. Let's see if you're *really* boyfriend material." I'm joking because he's proven he is multiple times tonight, but he plays along.

"Me?" He raises his brows. "I don't think that's going to be a problem." Shifting closer, he presses his lips to my cheek before whispering in my ear, "Be prepared to swoon, Baby. I've got this."

Oh, God.

"Hayley, hi," my ex Lachy interrupts us before I can respond, and I force an over-the-top grin, thanking him when he congratulates me on the film.

"It's good to see you," I lie. "How have you been?"

"I'm good. I'm really good. I'm here with Chelsie Watson. She's working with your director on *Sheridan Shores*." He points behind him toward Chelsie standing over by the railing, as though we've been living under a rock and don't recognize the star of the biggest TV show in the world right now.

I'm desperate to roll my eyes, but when Reed cocks his head to the side, confusion set in his features, I'm proven wrong. He has no idea who she is.

"I love Chelsie," I say with a smile. "You traded up." I'm joking but I swear Reed growls from beside me.

"Lachy, this is my boyfriend, Reed. Reed, this is Lachy."

"Her ex," Lachy adds with a smirk. "We go *way* back. From Australia." I'm sure he expects Reed to get jealous, but Reed shocks him by smiling wide.

"Nice to meet you, Lachy from Australia. As Hayley said, I'm Reed, *from America*. And we're going *way* forward."

I burst out laughing while Lachy stares at him in confusion before shrugging with a smile.

"Well, it was nice seeing you, Little Jackman. And good to meet you, Reed. I better get back to Chelsie. I just wanted to say hi."

"Good to see you too."

He walks away but glances back, confusion still marring his features, and I laugh again, turning my face into Reed's chest, stifling the sound. "That man can act, but he was never the brightest spark." I wrap my arms around his waist and grin.

"And yet, you dated him." Reed's playful tone draws my gaze as he winks.

"Yeah, well. He could do this thing with his—"

Reed's palm wraps around my mouth and I giggle, raising my hands in question. "Real or fake," he grates, "I don't need to hear about another man's skills."

"Why? I was only going to tell you about his motorcycle." I smile innocently and Reed huffs out a laugh.

"Sure you were."

Feeling significantly better, I agree to head back inside and spend another hour smiling and mingling, posing for photos, answering question after question about what's next. Sometimes they ask about my career, a topic I try to avoid while ignoring the pang in my chest, and sometimes it's my love life––an easier topic with Reed by my side. It's a long night, but when it ends, I'm not at all ready to go home.

How could I? I'm high on life and success, however temporary it may be. I need to embrace this feeling.

Mind made up, when Reed walks over with our coats, I let him know there's a change of plans.

"I want to go dancing." I squeeze his hand as I bounce on my toes.

"Dancing?" His gaze falls to my six-inch stiletto heels before he cringes. "Are you sure? You've been on your feet for hours."

"And I could easily stand for hours more. I'm sure."

"Okay." He laughs to himself. "Come on. Our driver's waiting. Where do you want to go?"

An idea comes to mind and my smile widens. "I'm not sure yet. But I want to go *line* dancing." He eyes me suspiciously, and a laugh bursts out of me before I get the chance to cover my mouth. I'm teasing and he knows it.

"Line dancing?" He keeps a straight face. "Do you know a place?"

"I don't. Do you?" I raise an eyebrow in question and he chuckles, shaking his head.

"Do you have access to a private plane I don't know about?"

"What? No."

"Well then, you won't find anywhere decent here."

I pause as we reach the car, a giddy feeling swelling inside me. "Reed Coombs, are you a secret cowboy?" I suspected as much, but I'm excited to finally get my answer.

Our driver opens my door as Reed jogs to the other side, hiding his expression until he glances at me over the roof. "I—"

"Wait. Don't answer that until we're inside. You can't lie when I'm looking you in the eye."

"Sure I can. I lie all the time. And you never guess."

"Mm-hmm. You're lying right now." I don't think he's ever been able to lie to me, but still I want to look him in the eyes while he tells me this delicious bit of news.

I climb in awkwardly, lifting my dress to above my knees, and when I turn to Reed he cringes. "Shit. Sorry, I should have helped you in."

"I'm good. I problem solved." I point to my dress and Reed's eyes drop to my now visible thighs before he winces and quickly glances up, lifting his gaze to meet mine.

"I'm a football player," he deadpans. "Not a cowboy."

"But you were?" My eyes narrow as I attempt to see the truth in his words.

"I lived near a ranch, if that counts."

"Oh my God. Yes! I knew it. I knew you had a country twang."

"I don't have a twang."

He turns to face the window, but I grab his arm and stop him from moving. "You have to take me dancing. One day. *Please.*"

"One day?"

"Yes, one day. To a real cowboy bar."

Reed stares at me for a moment as if deciding whether or not that's a good idea, until I press my palms together and beg. "Okay. Deal," he finally agrees.

"Good. We can go now."

"Where are we going?" Reed asks warily.

"I'll know it when I see it. Can you please head toward my place for now?" I ask our driver. "But there might be a stop along the way."

CHAPTER THIRTY

REED

We make it all the way to Hayley's apartment without stopping, prompting me to assume she gave up on the dancing idea when our driver drops us off.

But I should have learned by now—*never assume.*

"I'm going down." Hayley motions to the basement as we walk to the elevator, before skipping ahead and pressing both the up and down button. "I'll wait by your truck while you grab your keys. Here..." She hands me the key to her apartment and smiles while I stare at her, confused. "I don't want to wear out my dancing feet." She giggles.

"Are you sure you don't want to sleep?" I ask, though I know it's a lost cause.

"Not yet? Do you?"

A little bit, yep. I have practice at eight a.m. tomorrow and I could use some rest. But that's not what I tell her. Because tonight is her night, and I promised to be there for anything she needed. "Nah, I'm good," I lie.

"Good. Be quick." She pushes me inside the elevator as she walks to the second one, making me laugh out loud. If there's one thing I can rely on when it comes to Hayley, it's that she always keeps me on my toes.

It doesn't take long for me to grab my keys and join her in the parking lot, and when we get in my truck, she sends me in the direction of downtown San Francisco.

We drive in silence as she searches her phone for somewhere to go, and I take in the familiar sights until...

"Stop the car," she yells suddenly, and I slam on the brakes in a panic, my eyes flashing to the rearview mirror. "What happened?"

"I found a place."

"You what?"

"I found a place to go dancing."

"Jesus, Hayls." I run a hand through my hair as my pulse slowly returns to normal. "I thought we hit something."

"Wouldn't you feel that?"

"*Almost* hit something then. Either way." I shrug.

"Oooh. Nope." She shakes her head, completely oblivious to the inner turmoil she's caused, and I sigh to myself before noticing we're in the middle of nowhere.

"Are we dancing in your mind?" I ask, grimacing.

"Always." Hayley snorts with a smile. "But for now, I remembered a secluded beach close to here. It's the perfect spot."

"Oh-kay. Is there a club on this beach?"

"Nope. I've got a better idea. Turn around. It's just down the road."

I follow her directions, pulling up in front of what appears to be an overgrown forest, my face scrunching in concern. "Are you sure about this?"

"Of course. I found it when I was out running. It's a short walk through the trees." She hits me with an excited smile and my hesitation instantly washes away. This is Hayley. Her spontaneity is something I admire about her.

"Okay. Let's do it."

"Yay." She reaches over the dash to hug me before glancing into the back seat. "Do you have any spare clothes in your truck?"

I follow her gaze and spot my spare gym bag. "I probably have a tee and some shorts in that bag."

"Are they clean?"

"Yes, Hayls. They're clean."

"Grab them."

"Okay." After my many adventures with Hayley, I've learned not to ask too many questions once she's on a roll. And tonight is no different. Without another word, I follow her out of the truck, grabbing the bag of clothes before letting Hayley drag me along the narrow path, through the trees, dodging branches as we move through the darkness.

She doesn't stop until we reach the edge of the sand and I take in the moonlight striking the beach in front of us. The fresh night air hits my face, and I quickly shrug out of my jacket, wrapping it around Hayley's shoulders as we both stare out at the ocean. Hayley's thankful gaze flashes to mine as the waves crash, and I can't help but smile. I've always liked the beach. Especially private ones. And I don't think you could get much more private than this.

Or perfect.

"I had no idea this place even existed," I muse, unable to take my eyes off the water.

"Sometimes I think about how much is out there that no one knows exists," Hayley whispers thoughtfully. "The tiny wonders of the planet that go unnoticed, undiscovered. I'd like to believe I'm the only one that knows about this place, and now you, but I doubt that it's true. God, wouldn't it be amazing?"

She stares out at the shoreline while my attention stays on her, in awe of her spark. She brings a brilliant light to the world, and I'm not sure she even realizes it. In fact, I'd bet my life savings on the fact that she doesn't. I was worried that spark had dwindled for a while, but it seems to be back after the premiere and I, for one, am grateful for that.

I'm slow to tell her how perfect this is and she quickly moves on, reminding me why we're here. "This is where we dance."

I grimace.

"Here?" I laugh to myself as I take off my shoes and socks.

"Yep." She nods, throwing my jacket back to me before slipping off her stilettos and hooking the straps over her wrist, her smile wide. "It's perfect. Come on." She runs forward and I follow, curling my toes into the sand as we move closer to the water, the glow of the moon lighting our path.

"How about *you* dance and I watch?" I question. "I wouldn't want to break tradition." I offer her my coat one more time and when she shakes her head no, I spread it out onto the sand, making myself comfortable. "See. *This* is perfect."

Giggling, she drops her heels beside me and gathers her dress into her hands, draping the delicate material over one arm.

And then she dances.

Like the free spirit she is, she sways her hips to an imaginary beat, waving her hand in the air, her eyes closed as she loses herself to the moment.

Grabbing my phone, I scroll through my music and bring up "Shape of You," by Ed Sheeran, remembering she once mentioned that she loved him.

Her eyes widen before she giggles again, changing her moves to match the new tempo.

She's carefree and happy...until she's not. "This isn't working," she huffs, letting her dress fall as she sulks over to me.

"What's not? You looked pretty content to me."

"I was. I am. But this dress." Her gaze falls to my bag and her eyes light up. "I was saving the clothes in case we got wet but...why not." She squats down, rummaging around in my bag, locating the tee I'd mentioned earlier. And before I can speak, she's unzipping her dress, letting the material cascade down her body as she turns to face the water.

My gaze drops to the curve of her thong-covered ass and I slam my eyes shut, working hard to erase the image until Hayley's giggle permeates the air.

"I'm decent. I promise. You can look."

Not sure I can trust her, I open my eyes slowly and internally groan. She's covered. She's not lying about that. But she's anything but decent.

Hayley's not a short woman, but since I'm still much taller, my T-shirt hits the top of her thighs, barely covering her panties.

I force a smile when she laughs, then change the song to distract myself, selecting a random playlist, too fucking flustered to concentrate.

We joke all the time about being attracted to each other, but I've never felt the pull I do now. I've never wanted to throw caution to the wind and risk our friendship like I do at this moment. And I can't for the life of me figure out why.

Everything about her is sucking me in—her joy, her laughter, her body.

Fuck, her legs are begging to be wrapped around my waist while I slam into her, and God-fucking-dammit.

Seemingly unaware of my internal flip-out, Hayley resumes dancing, swaying her hips to whatever song I put on. I can't even tell if I've heard it before.

When her eyes flutter shut, I take the opportunity to really watch her, to drink her in without getting caught, but when the tempo changes, she raises her hands above her head and I do everything I can to shift my focus, praying I have the willpower to avert my gaze.

Staring up at the stars, I count backward from a thousand, willing my thoughts into safer waters, and I've just reached nine hundred and thirty-five when Hayley drops down beside me, nudging her shoulder into mine.

"It's beautiful out here." She squeezes my hand. "I barely saw the stars where I lived in Sydney. Sure, they were there, but it was nothing like this."

"It can get like that here too. But near the ocean, it's a different story."

"Do you watch the stars often?"

"Me? All the time," I lie unconvincingly. "I'm especially fond of the Running Back and the Wildcat constellation."

Throwing her head back, Hayley laughs out loud, biting her lip before she spins to face me. "That just so happens to be my favorite too. What a coincidence."

"Nothing's a coincidence," I blurt out, having heard that many times in my life without really thinking about it.

"I may have heard that once or twice." She smiles. "Does that mean our relationship is meant to be?"

"I think it might."

Hayley's laughter softens as the song changes, drawing our attention.

"Okay, break's over." She shakes off her hands. "It's time for you to join me."

I chuckle, glancing her way until her expression turns serious. "Oh, no." I shake my head wildly. "No, thanks. I'm good right here."

"It wasn't a question, Baby." She winks as she stands, grabbing my hands to pull me to my feet. Or at least to try and pull me to my feet. And when I don't budge, she pouts. "Please," she begs, frowning as if I could ever truly say no to her.

"Ugh. Fine. But I'm choosing the music. What is this crap?"

Hayley shakes her head with an incredulous smile, stepping back as I roll up the cuffs of my pants and stand.

"This crap is the number one song in the US right now."

"Not on my playlist."

"Okay, DJ, take it away. I can't wait to see what you've got." She hits me with a devilish grin, biting her finger as her gaze locks with mine. And despite being cold outside, my body temperature rises.

This could be dangerous, but fuck if I can stop it right now.

Chapter Thirty-One

HAYLEY

Reed chooses one of the few country songs I know, and I suck my lips into my mouth, stifling a smile when he hooks his thumbs into the waistband of his dress pants, shuffling toward me. Like he's boot scooting. At least, I think that's what he's doing. I've only really seen it in the movies.

We playfully dance for a while, making fools of ourselves while nobody's watching, working up a sweat to whatever song comes on. And by the time a slow song begins, I welcome the change. I need it.

Leaning back against Reed's chest, I lift my arms and reach behind me, wrapping them around his neck, letting my eyes drift shut as I sway my body to the rhythm, allowing myself a moment to just be. I'm lost in the sound of the waves when Reed's palms circle around my waist, pulling me into him as my tee—or rather his tee—lifts, exposing my ass in the process.

His light touch caresses my stomach and goose bumps coat my skin, a shiver running through me.

We stay like that for a beat in comfortable silence, moving in sync with my back to his front, gently brushing against each other until Reed curses, letting me go.

"Fuck, Hayley. What are you doing?"

Huh? I spin around, finding Reed's pained expression boring into mine. "What do you mean?"

"I need air." He shakes his head and steps back, running his hands down his face.

"We're outside."

"Space, then. I need space."

He presses a chaste kiss to my temple and forces a smile, turning and walking away, but he only gets a few metres or feet—whatever they say here—and stops.

The moon lights his hands as he clenches them by his side, lifting his fists to his face, digging his knuckles into his temples. He's clearly a mess, but I don't get time to process it because no more than a few seconds pass before he pivots to face me and stalks back, blowing out a breath when he reaches me. "I'm sorry. I'm good."

"What happened?" My heart races as a panic takes over me.

"You're playing dirty and you don't even know it."

"What does that mean?"

"I'm hard as a rock, Hayls." He chuckles to himself. "You're a fucking dream in my tee, and you're rubbing your half-naked ass against me. It's been months and I'm abstaining."

I can't stop the giggle that bursts out of me until Reed's agonised groan fills the air. "Sorry." I cover my mouth with my hand. "Why are you abstaining?"

He stares at me deadpan.

"I mean, what's wrong with your hand?"

"It's on strike."

Laughter escapes me until Reed frowns my way and I stop. Again. "I'm sorry. But wait. Are you telling me, you've been in love with Bria for *years* and—"

"I never said I loved Bria, Hayls," he cuts me off, his face scrunching. "That's all *you*."

"And Luke. And Amelia. And Dylan. And Easton. And Paige."

"Christ, Hayls."

"Oh, and I forgot, Bria. I bet if I asked her, she'd tell me you love her."

"Don't ask her." He raises a hand between us. "That would be weird coming from my *girlfriend*."

"Very true. But back to the abstaining because you've got me intrigued... What other options would you normally have, if not your hand? Do you have a regular call list that I'm blocking you from? Or are you *always* sexually frustrated?"

"The fuck? No," he huffs out. Something tells me he doesn't usually talk about his sex life. "I'm not talking about back then. I'm talking about *now*."

"Two truths and a lie," I throw out, hoping to get answers but also to lighten him up a bit.

"Fine." He glances away, seemingly in thought, before nodding and turning back to face me. "One, I love riding mechanical bulls. Two, I gag on avocados—I can't stand the texture. And three, two of my cousins got married. To each other. But technically one was adopted."

I pout at his response, my arms folded over my chest. "Now who's playing dirty? None of those have anything to do with the information I'm seeking."

"Didn't they?" He raises an eyebrow and stares at me while I frown in confusion. *What?* He loves riding a mech— *Oh my God.* I snort, slapping his chest.

"Shut up. You do *not* get off by riding mechanical bulls."

"Maybe I was referring to avocados." He shrugs and I slap him again, jokingly, of course.

"I'm kidding. But you never said it had to be about that."

"Dammit, Reed."

"Why do you want to know so badly? It's *my* issue." He blows out a breath and I shrug. Because while I have no idea why I need to know, I'm fascinated by the inner workings of my man, fake or otherwise.

"Call it curiosity. We are dating after all."

"Fine. I don't have a call list, but I did sleep with other women while I had *feelings* for Bria. You knew that already. And it's been a while."

"Presumably that would mean you use your hand quite regularly. Why is it only *now* going on strike?"

"Let's just say I've needed it a little more often lately. Some hot blonde keeps *rubbing up against me*." With his teeth clenched, he groans.

"I told you you'd fall in love with me." I smirk when he scoffs.

"That's not love, Sweetheart. It's attraction. And we both know you're equally as attracted to me...if not more so."

"Guilty." I bite my lip as I fake a grimace. "But that was never in question."

"What's the question then?"

I pause, thinking about how I want to play this. Reed shakes his head and stares out at the water, giving me the chance to watch him, and when his throat bobs, I'm done for.

"Do you really want to stop dancing?" I ask, my eyes wide as I draw his attention, my heart beating uncontrollably in my chest.

Reed eyes me curiously, his gaze dropping to my half-naked legs before subtly moving to the bulge in his dress pants.

"Do you?" he counters, his voice deep and rusty.

I let out a rushed breath as my thoughts run rampant. *Do I want to stop dancing?* Yes. But I don't think we're talking about dancing, and the gentle throbbing between my legs answers for me. "I was just getting started."

Reed nods but hesitates, and I don't blame him. This could change everything. But I am not going to be the one that stops it.

Running back to Reed's phone, I change the song to something fun and start dancing around him, smiling while he laughs at my craziness, giving him a chance to warm up again. But just when I think it's not working, he grabs my wrist, pulling me against his firm chest. Wasting no time, he glides one palm to my back, while the other curls into my fingers, lifting my hand in the air.

The music doesn't call for it but we dance slowly, our bodies in perfect rhythm, gliding against each other, silently drifting toward the invisible line we drew in the sand. The one we promised never to cross.

My mind swirls with possibility as a spark ignites inside me, and before I know what I'm doing, I spin around, resting my back against Reed's chest, my head settling against his collarbone, a sigh on my lips.

It's a beat before his fingers curl around my hip, but when he does, I draw in a breath, resting my palm on top of his hand and gliding it slowly down my body until we reach the hem of his tee. His calloused fingers brush against my already sensitive skin, setting me on fire before he seemingly understands what I'm doing, snaking his hand under the loose material and brushing his fingers up the outside of my thigh.

I still as his touch heats me within, sending a wave of excitement to my core. While my eyes flutter closed, I focus on his painstakingly slow movement, my heart beating out of my chest.

Reed passes over the string of my thong, releasing a strangled groan from the back of his throat, pulling me out of my daze.

"Fuck, Hayls." He sucks in a breath as his palm flexes. "What am I doing?" He tries to pull back, but I anticipate his move and stop him, locking my hand on his, holding him in place.

"I need you to touch me, Reed." My voice is soft but desperate. I'm needy and not afraid to admit it.

"We can't."

Somewhere, on some level, I know he's right, that we shouldn't be doing this. But I have never wanted anyone to touch me more than I do right now, and I'm willing to suffer the consequences. "Please."

"No."

"But—"

Reed spins me around, cutting me off as he effortlessly lifts me into his arms, holding me close until I wrap my legs around his hips. I grab his shoulders, and his palms settle on my ass, his fingers biting into the flesh.

At first, he refuses to meet my stare, but when he finally glances up at me, my breath hitches as his name rushes from my lips. "*Reed.*"

His dark eyes bore into mine with an intensity I haven't seen before, a blaze that burns through all my reservations and ignites my soul, setting me alight.

Considering there's a strong fire burning between us, we're both frozen for a second until Reed rocks his hips, squeezing my ass beneath his strong hands, pulling me into him, grinding me against his cock. The move has me moaning without permission, the friction against my pussy shocking the sound right out of me.

It doesn't take long before I feel Reed's hardening cock twitching against me, and I want nothing more than to reach between us and rub my hand over his bulge, working him until he comes. But I know better than that—he'd stop me before he ever let that happen.

My legs start to slip from his waist and I boost myself higher in his arms, changing the angle of our connection, eliciting a guttural groan from Reed as his body jolts.

With his trance broken, I expect him to stop, but he surprises me, closing his eyes as his head falls back, his grip on me tightening.

I'm so worked up that the drenched silk of my thong sinks beneath my folds, working my clit like his fingers would and I cry out as my legs clench. "God, Reed. Yes."

He clears his throat and readjusts our position, grinding harder, faster, his thick erection pressing against my covered pussy, begging for entry. Entry I'd be more than willing to grant him.

His body quivers and the pressure builds low in my belly, the tension pulsing between my legs.

I rock my hips and Reed jolts again, slamming into me as he shudders. "We shouldn't—"

"Don't stop," I cut him off. "Please. You *can't* stop."

"I'm not stopping," he grates, his voice strained. "But...fuck. I'm going to come in my pants."

"Do you want more? Do you—"

"No. Keep going... Ah, fuck." His grip on me tightens before he takes a few steps backward and lowers to the ground, lying down as he settles me on top of him.

My knees dig into the sand, and the second I've got traction, I roll my hips, riding him in this new position, feeling the burn as his hard length grinds against me.

"Oh, God. Oh, God." Arousal pools at my center and my orgasm builds, my release lingering just out of reach. "I'm close. God, I'm close."

Reed grabs my hips, guiding my movements, sending a spark of electricity to my core. We move in sync until he releases his hold, curling his hand around my neck possessively, turning my head so he can whisper in my ear. "Give it to me, Hayls. I want it all. I want to hear you scream my name as you come for me."

"Oh. God." His deep controlling voice catches me off guard and my body spasms. Doing as he asked, I scream his name, his words on repeat as I pulse against him.

"That's it, Baby," he continues, driving me wild. "You're doing good. But I need more and I know you've got it in you." He doesn't stop rocking his hips, grinding into me, his movements erratic as my body shudders against him.

When I cry out again, he moves a couple more times before an unrestrained growl rips from within him, his body jolting as he curses under his breath.

Watching him come apart makes me come so hard my vision blurs and I fall onto his chest, shaking. "God, Reed," I whisper, struggling to catch my breath as we both slow our movements. "What the fuck did you do to me?"

Reeds grunts, but it's something between a laugh and a groan, making me smile against his skin.

"What did *I* do?" he grates. "I came in my goddamn pants, Hayls. I should be asking you the same."

Chapter Thirty-Two

REED

F*uck.* What am I doing?

Why can't I ever just be *friends* with a woman?

CHAPTER THIRTY-THREE

HAYLEY

As though a flip switched inside me the second Reed gave me an orgasm, I can't look at him now without picturing his hands on my body, his eyes boring into mine, his cock between my legs...and it's really *freaking* inconvenient.

Especially when he appears completely unaffected.

"I feel like a burrito bowl." His expression curls into a contemplative look. "Should we order lunch?" he asks nonchalantly, the Saturday after our high school-style romp, while I'm still thinking about what that mouth could do to my pussy. *Three days later.*

He's hinted at having a dirty mouth before, but I always thought he was joking around. He wasn't. That man can—

"Hayls?"

"Huh?"

"Lunch?" He waves his hand in front of my face.

"Oh. Yes. Let's get lunch. I'll grab my coat."

"You don't need a coat to order in." He chuckles for a beat until his expression turns serious. Stepping closer, he palms my shoulder as he stares into my eyes, searching for something. "Is everything okay?" His voice projects the concern he feels, and a wave of guilt washes over me.

"I'm good. I'm just..." I trail off, not really sure if I should make this an "us" problem, when it's definitely *my* issue.

"Just?" Reed questions me, never one to let things go when he thinks my feelings are involved.

The rules of our fake relationship run through my mind, and I curse myself for always wanting to be honest. "You kind of broke me."

"What? How?" A crease forms between his brows as he searches his mind for what he's done. "I—"

"You didn't *do* anything, per se. It's more of a *me* mind fuck."

"A you—" He cuts himself off and smirks. "You want more of what happened the other night, don't you?" He laughs but it's a little bit strained. "I rocked your world."

He thinks he's joking but he's not far off base. Only I shouldn't. We crossed a line the other night, and we definitely shouldn't take it any further. *So why can't I stop myself?*

"Well..." I trail off, cringing as Reed's eyes widen.

"I was kidding, Hayls. I didn't— Wait. Really?"

"Don't you? I can't be the only one that hasn't stopped thinking about it, imagining the benefits we could add to our little arrangement."

Reed's nose scrunches and I gasp. "Oh, Jesus. Am I the only one?" I cringe and he groans.

"You're not *now*." He rakes his hands down his face as he shakes. "Nope. Nope. Definitely not."

"No, what?"

"I'm trying to convince myself that we can't do the things I'm imagining."

Oh, God. I clench my legs so I don't squirm, then torment myself by asking a question I shouldn't. "What are you picturing?"

"*Hayley*," Reed warns but it's too late. My mind is running wild with ideas, and if he doesn't tell me, God only knows what "things" I'll conjure.

"Reed," I say sternly. "I need you to tell me, or I'm going to be picturing more than you could possibly imagine."

"I highly doubt that. It's better if you don't know."

An image of Reed bending me over a counter and dropping to his knees has me shaking my head as I silently curse myself. This is not helping.

"Hayley," he warns again through his clenched teeth. "We're moving into dangerous territory."

"Moving? I thought we already passed that."

"Fuck." He spins around, running a hand through his hair, giving me a chance to marvel at his magnificence without scrutiny.

Is this the longest I've been without sex since I started having it? Yes. But I've also been honest about my feelings for Reed since the very beginning. I'm attracted to him. There's no denying it. But did I ever think I'd go there? No. Because our friendship means more than that.

But what if we could have both?

Dammit.

Reed turns in time to catch my indecisive expression and he groans again, the sound vibrating through me, sending a pulse to my core. "What are you thinking, Hayls? Aren't you worried about our friendship?"

"Of course I am. And I will always put that first. I was just being honest. Like we promised we would be."

"We also promised we'd never cross a line unless it was for show, and the other night was not for public viewing. At least I hope it wasn't."

He cringes and I can't help the hysterical giggle that escapes me. "It was just us. And you're right. Let's chalk it up to another crazy idea of mine and leave it at that."

"It's not—"

"I blame *you*, you know. You're too sexy for your own good. I'm only human." I shrug and he chuckles, shaking his head as he motions toward my body.

"And what about you, Miss Jackman?"

"I thought I was 'Baby'?"

"Okay, Baby. What about you?" His voice lowers and a hint of his country drawl comes out, making my body heat as I mentally melt. If anyone else called me "baby," I'd probably dick punch them, but with Reed... "Hayls, you opened your door this morning wearing a fucking midriff top and tight booty shorts, and you're saying it's *my* fault?"

"I—"

"I think about getting you naked at least once a day. *Baby*. And I'm not going to pretend your moans from the beach aren't running on repeat through my mind, because they are. But I didn't bring it up. *You* did. And now I can't un-think it. So I'll repeat... *What do you want?*"

As though I'll awake from a dream if I don't answer quickly, I rush out my response, my eyes locked on his. "I want you to make me scream, Reed. I want you to release the tension between my legs so I don't have to use my hand. You barely touched me the other night and worked me over more than I *ever* could have imagined. I know I shouldn't want that. I *know*. But—"

"Fuck, Hayls."

"What do *you* want? If we weren't friends. If this was a one-night stand or a real relationship, what would you want?"

He shakes his head, turning away from me, his fists clenched. "I don't want to lose you."

"You won't." That much I can promise him. Because if there's one thing I know for certain in this world, it's that I need Reed in my life.

"But we *are* friends, Hayls. We can't pretend that we're not."

"*Please.* I—"

"I'd want to wrap my hand around your throat while I destroy your pussy with my fingers, three of them pounding into you while my thumb teases your clit, circling the little bud without ever actually touching it."

My legs clench and I bite back a groan. Holy mother of all that is good in this world. That *mouth*.

His eyes bore into mine, waiting for me to respond, but all I can think about is the arousal undoubtedly soaking my panties. "Do you kiss your mother with that mouth?" I rush out, struggling to control my breathing.

"Jesus, Hayls, let's keep my mother out of this."

"I had to go there, because the alternative was me dropping to my knees and worshipping your cock."

"She jokes." Reed shakes his head. "After all that's been said, she jokes."

"Who's joking? Feel my heart." I grab his hand and place it on my chest between my heaving breasts. "I'm going to need you to say something else," I whisper as he stares at our hands. "I need to know more. What would you do next?"

Reed's pained expression finds mine. "Hayley."

"Please."

"We can't."

"Reed." My voice is pleading and I'm consciously aware of the fact that I should let this go, but I'm too far gone to stop it.

"You don't know what you're getting into." He pulls his hand from mine and steps back, putting some much-needed space between us.

But I don't give up.

"I do. I—"

"*Fuuck.*" Releasing a loud, drawn-out groan, Reed stalks forward and pushes me against the wall, his hand sinking into my hair. He tugs on my ponytail, tilting my head to face him, and stares into my soul. "We have to set some ground rules," he demands, the gentle version of Reed making way for this new alpha and I'm totally here for it. "If this is about added benefits then we need boundaries."

"Of course." I nod, my gaze locked on his mouth. "But I can't think and—"

"We both have to *need* it. It can't be a want. Only a need." He leans forward, pressing his lips to my neck before sucking the flesh into his mouth. And I melt against him, no longer able to hold myself up. *Who is this guy?*

"Do you need this, Hayls?"

"Yes," I rush out on a breath, working hard to concentrate. "Yes, we have to *need* it. And no sex. We can't go all the way." I don't think I could come back from that.

"No sex," Reed agrees. "But how far will you let me take it?"

Holy shit. My chest tightens as my heart beats rapidly. "Hands?" I ask, setting the boundaries that I hope will protect us. "No mouth." Reed pulls away from my neck and licks his lips, a guilty expression in place. "I mean, no oral. You can keep doing that."

Grabbing the back of his neck, I guide him toward mine and twist my head, giving him better access. "I wasn't ready for you to stop."

Reed groans against my skin, and my entire body erupts in a shiver.

"We really shouldn't." He fights his urges, trying to preserve the shreds of his good-guy persona. The Golden Boy. But now that I've seen the other side of him, I can't let the good guy win.

Grabbing his free hand, I lower it between us, guiding him toward the waistband of my shorts. He stiffens momentarily, but doesn't stop me as his head drops to my shoulder.

"Last chance to say no," he rushes out between breaths, his palm flexing beneath my touch.

"I need it, Reed. I *need* it."

He growls before shaking himself free of my grasp and shoving his hand down my shorts, his fingers brushing against my panties. Without wasting any time, he cups my pussy and rolls his palm against my clit, cursing when he undoubtedly realizes how soaked I am.

"Is this all for me, Hayls?" he asks as I moan. "Is this wet pussy weeping for my hand?"

Oh, God. "Yes." I'd prefer more but I'll take his hand and that *mouth*. I bet he could make me come with his words alone.

He grinds his palm again, curling his fingers, creating a friction as my panties rub against my entrance. Squeezing my breast with his free hand, he repeats the movement and I cry out, my hips bucking as I fall into him.

"God, Reed."

"Is that good, Baby?" The cockiness to his tone has me gripping his shirt and groaning his name as I rock against his hand. "I'll take that as a yes." He chuckles while my pulse spikes, my pussy throbbing in response.

And he's paying attention.

With a strangled groan, he releases my breast and removes his hand from my pants, grabbing the waistband before dragging my shorts down my legs. My panties follow and he steps back, his wanton gaze locked between my legs.

"Fuck, I knew you'd be pretty but damn..."

I fall back against the wall this time, moaning as my legs clench. "*Reed.*"

"I know, Baby. It's coming."

He moves forward in two easy strides, grabbing my waist and spinning me around. When my back hits the kitchen counter, he lifts me up, perching my ass on top.

"Open," he demands, and my legs part instantly, my pussy dripping as he stares down at me again.

With my eyes locked on his every move, I watch as he steps closer and runs a finger through my soaked folds, groaning as he reaches my clit, teasing me until I'm begging for more.

Ignoring my impatient moans, he repeats his ministrations a few more times before two of his fingers brush against my entrance, making me cry out in relief.

"Yes."

"This?" he questions and I gasp in agreement, pleading for more as he whispers, "I've got you."

My eyes flash to his, finding his bottom lip trapped between his teeth as he stares down at his hand. I follow his gaze, both of us watching as his fingers disappear inside me, the veins in his heavily tattooed forearm bulging as his muscles tense, a low deep growl rumbling in the back of his throat.

"Is this what you want?" He curls a finger against my wall and my pussy constricts as I silently scream his name. And when his thumb brushes against my clit, I lose my mind, begging him for more.

"In this moment, I'm yours, Reed. Do with me what you will."

Chapter Thirty-Four

REED

Jesus Christ. *"Do with me what you will."*

"Fuck, Hayls. You're asking for more than I can give you." It takes everything in my power not to release my cock and fuck her into oblivion. But we had a deal and I'm sticking to it. My plan is to act now and process the consequences later. Although judging by my pounding heart, I think I already know.

"Then give me everything you can." Hayley sits up and lifts her feet to the counter before lying back and opening herself wider for me, giving me a clear view of my fingers working her core.

My cock throbs against my zipper, begging for action.

After twisting my fingers inside her, I take a chance and tease her back hole, letting my finger linger as she moans.

Her hole puckers but she cries out, lifting her ass to get closer to my hand. "Yes, Reed. *God.*"

Resisting the urge to finger her ass—yet—I continue my pursuit on her pussy, pumping inside her as she meets my hand thrust for thrust.

Our ragged breaths fill the air as I work her, my eyes locked on her expression, watching what I do to her, marveling at how beautiful she is when she silently comes apart.

I brush my thumb against her clit and her lips part as she mewls, drawing my eyes to her mouth.

My heart slams to my chest and in that moment, I want to kiss her more than anything else in the goddamn world, which is exactly why I shouldn't. Why I won't.

Focusing on her legs, I tease her clit again and she pivots her hips, seeking more. "Yes. Please," she begs, her voice desperate, sending a spark of electricity straight to my cock. "God, Reed. I'm so close." She bucks against my hand and cries out, her body heaving off the counter.

Spreading her with my fingers, I circle her clit, careful not to touch it, teasing her before I lean forward, blowing on her hole at the same time I finally give her what she wants.

"Oh, God. Oh, God. Yes." Her head drops back and she lets out a high-pitched moan, falling over the edge. "Reed." Her body quakes as she finds her release. "God. Reed."

With her fingers curled into the hard surface of the counter, her body writhes in front of me, her hips jolting against my hand as she gasps for air. And when I finally slow my movements, she sucks in a breath, smiling in relief.

But I'm not ready for this to be done.

"I want more," I rasp, my eyes locked on her swollen pussy as I taste her, licking her arousal from my fingers. "I know you've got another one in you."

"*Jesus.*" Hayley's eyes widen and I palm her inner thighs, dragging my hands along her skin, making her shiver as I lean in, spreading her legs farther.

"This time I want you to coat my fingers as you scream my name. And I want it to be loud."

"Holy shit, Reed. Who are you?"

Ignoring her question, I glide my thumbs toward her ass, teasing her rim as my gaze meets hers, seeking permission. Her eyes roll into her head but she gives me a nod as the word yes rushes from her lips.

Turning my hand, I line up with both entrances before ever so slowly inching inside her, watching my fingers as she takes me in.

"God, Reed. This. I—"

"Do you want me to stop?"

"Hell, no, it's good. Too good."

I move slowly, caught between edging her and making sure she's okay until she rocks her hips, fucking my hand with perfection.

As I pump harder, she meets my fervor, her cries loud, ragged, uncontrollable, and I'm loving every second of it. Watching her fall apart is like ecstasy, and I want more.

Her walls tighten and she clenches her teeth, her body shaking as her second orgasm builds. "God, I—"

"I know, Baby."

I rub her clit with my thumb, playing the little bud as my fingers continue to work her, watching as she's screaming my name, thrashing against me, coating my hand just as I asked. Her body spasms and I crowd her in, trapping my hand between us, only slowing down when she begs me to stop.

She falls back onto the counter and covers her face with her hands, drawing my gaze to the rise and fall of her chest. *And God, I wish she was naked.*

After lying quietly for a beat, she lets out a soft laugh and I chuckle back at her. But when she moves her hands, her eyes locking with mine... I'm fucked.

Hayley's a bombshell, all the fucking time, but in this moment—sated, flushed, vulnerable and *mine*—she's so goddamn beautiful my chest aches.

She bites her lip and smiles shyly with no idea how badly I want her. Sitting up, she runs a hand through her messy blonde hair. "That was..." She trails off, shaking her head with a sigh.

"Lost for words again?"

"Yes. It seems to be a common occurrence with you."

"I like it."

"I bet you do."

I turn away as I chuckle, feeling uncomfortable now that she's half naked and I'm no longer getting her off. I'm about to throw her some clothes when she grabs my wrist to stop me. "Your turn?"

Fuck.

I'm hard as stone but I'm not sure that's a good idea.

"I'm good. Let's—"

Hayley slides to the edge of the counter and drops her feet to the ground, instantly wrapping a hand around the bulge in my pants. "It's happening. But don't worry, Reed. This isn't about you. It's all for me."

She rises to her toes, nibbling on my ear as her hand slips beneath my waistband, whispering... "I've been thinking about this for *months*."

Christ. My cock pulses and Hayley moans, laughing to herself. "Maybe it's a little bit for you too."

She curls her fingers around my girth before rubbing her thumb over my tip, collecting the pre cum that's dripping for her, showing her how desperately I want this. I hold my breath so I don't come the second she starts moving, but she shocks me by releasing her hand and pressing a kiss to my cheek.

"Don't hate me." Her nose scrunches as her shoulder lifts in a shrug. "I have to do this."

"What—"

Dropping my pants, she falls to her knees, wrapping her mouth around my tip, rolling her tongue before her soft lips glide along my length. I curse as she moans, my head falling back until I register what she's doing and growl.

"Fuck, Hayls. We said no mouths."

She shakes her head and grabs my ass, using the leverage to rock my hips as she sucks me deeper, working my cock while I protest.

"Hayls. This... Ah, fuck."

My tip hits the back of her throat, and the sensation has me jerking into her, making her cry out as she gasps for air.

"Fuck, I'm so— Jesus."

She grabs my balls to cut me off and I buck against her, glancing down as she finds her rhythm, staring up at me with a satisfied smirk.

And I lose all restraint.

"You want this?" I snap, running my hands through her hair as she nods up at me. "All of me?"

She pulls back, releasing my cock with a pop as she smiles. "All of you."

That's all I needed to know.

Grabbing the back of her head, I grip my cock and line it up with her mouth, guiding her closer as her lips part. I give her a second to breathe before our eyes lock and a silent conversation takes place.

She wants everything I'm planning to give her and she wants it now.

With my fingers curling around her ponytail, I tilt her head, opening her throat as she grabs my ass and nods in acknowledgment.

I groan at her obedience before pumping into her, fucking her face with abandon.

She cries out as her body jolts and her nails bite into my flesh, pulling me closer, desperate for me like I'm desperate for her.

My balls tingle as my release builds, and when she moans against my cock, the vibrations set me off and I tug her hair, forcing her to look at me so I can tell her what's coming.

"Get ready for me, Baby. I'm about to fill that pretty little mouth."

She moans again, louder this time, and I spill into her, grunting as I watch her drinking me in, my cum spilling down her chin. She continues to suck me, swallowing as much as she can until I'm convulsing against her, my cock jolting uncontrollably.

"Fuck, Hayls. You're perfect." I curse as I pull out of her, reaching for her hands so I can lift her to her feet, both of us falling against the counter, our rapid breathing in sync, my heart pounding in my chest.

And my fingers still intertwined with hers.

We're quiet for a beat, my mind reeling over *what the fuck I'm doing* until Hayley breaks the silence, bursting out laughing. "How the hell did Bria resist you with that mouth?"

What? My eyes flash to hers and I frown. Why would she bring up Bria? And... "Why would I *ever* talk to my best friend like that?" *Fuck, I just spoke to Hayley like that.*

"Why *wouldn't* you? Because if you *did*, she wouldn't be your best friend anymore."

She bounces her eyebrows and I somehow manage a strangled laugh. "Does that mean we're not best friends anymore?" I ask with a smirk.

"No," she giggles lightly. "Our situation is vastly different."

I internally cringe but she's right. Only, I'm glad Bria never knew me that way. Because while I may be confused at the moment, I don't think I want her to like me anymore. *Not like that anyway.*

"So..." Hayley lifts herself up onto the counter, drawing my attention to the naked flesh between her legs. I stifle a groan, glancing away until she crosses her legs, placing her hands in her lap. "What do you think?"

Huh? "About what?"

"About Bria knowing all that."

What the fuck? "Are you suggesting we tell her?"

Hayley nods and my chest aches for all the wrong reasons. "If your goal is for her to melt at your feet and worship the ground you walk on, then I would. Definitely." She grins proudly, and I smile back, though I'm not feeling it.

I haven't spoken to Bria since she turned up at my football game, surprising me for the first time in years, before proceeding to tell me she's worried about me, that I'm changing, and she's not sure if she likes the person I've become.

And instead of arguing back and reminding her how much *she's* changed, what did I do? I questioned myself. I spent the better part of the next day wondering if she was right. Thinking that maybe it was all my fault since I couldn't handle this crush anymore.

And that fucked me up even more.

"How are you *not* married already?" Hayley continues, bringing my mind back to the present. "You're the complete package. I mean, you were already a catch before now with your ripped, tattooed exterior and sweet caring center. Now you're adding a dirty mouth? Honestly, I'm surprised I'm not dead. Because...I don't even have any words."

"You're talking a lot for someone that's speechless." I smirk and she rolls her eyes.

"If I don't talk, I'm likely to use my mouth for something else."

Her eyes drop to my cock again and it twitches right on cue. Fuck. I grunt deep in the back of my throat. "Rule number whatever we're up to. No teasing *after* the fact. This is about a release, and we've both had that already."

I'm not sure I can handle any more today. Hell, I'm not convinced I'm sane for agreeing to this plan in the first place. Or did I initiate it? I don't even know anymore. Only, now that the seed has been planted in my brain, fuck if I can shake it.

"You're really worried I'll fall in love with you, aren't you?" Hayley asks with a mocking smile, clearly having no idea that it's *quite the fucking opposite.*

"I'm worried we'll lose *us* in the process," I lie and pray she doesn't call me out on it.

Hayley frowns and I know she feels the same before she speaks. "Me too." She reaches for my hand, giving it a squeeze. "But we're not going to let that happen."

I didn't think I'd let that happen with Bria either, and yet, here we are.

A moment passes between us before Hayley chirps up and gives me a shove. "No more sappy shit, okay? As you said, we both had a release. A damn good one. We should be over the moon with happiness."

"You're right." I chuckle. "To happiness." I put on a big smile and Hayley joins me.

"Good. Because I have news."

"Oh, yeah?"

"Yeah. I think I'm ready for lunch now. My brain is officially able to function again. We could even go out."

Only Hayley. I grin, grabbing her under the arms and lifting her from the counter.

Positioning her in front of me, I guide her toward the bathroom, tapping her bare ass when she reaches the door. "Let's get you cleaned up, then we'll eat."

Hayley spins my way as her eyes light up. "Eat wh—"

"Don't," I groan, cutting her off. "I know you taste delicious."

CHAPTER THIRTY-FIVE

REED

A flash goes off as Hayley shovels food into her mouth and she groans grumpily. "Why do they always take photos while I'm doing some weird pose, and you look perfect. Every article I see of us makes me cringe."

I lean in close and grab her hands until she glances up at me. "Want me to destroy the camera? Because you know I will. For you."

A beaming smile lights up her face as another flash goes off, and I have no doubt it'll be a better shot this time.

"That was sweet." She squeezes my hand.

"Well, you do keep telling me I'm a sweet guy."

"You are." She nods, scrunching her nose sympathetically. "There's no escaping it. But now I know there's more to you than meets the eyes."

"Got to keep some parts hidden." I wink and she giggles until she stops abruptly and frowns.

"What happened?" I spin around to see what she's looking at but I'm met with an empty street through the window.

"Nothing. I'm probably being silly."

"It's not nothing. You're pale."

Hayley raises an eyebrow and I reluctantly smile. "More pale than usual." Since it's winter here, Hayley's lost part of her tan and she's constantly complaining about it, despite still being beautiful.

"I saw a guy in a red jacket out the front just now. And when I looked up, he ran."

"What was he doing?"

"Nothing. But I saw him outside my apartment yesterday. *And* last Friday. I assumed he must live there, but now he's *here*."

My body tenses though I hide it, needing to keep Hayley calm. "Do you recognize him?"

"That's the thing; I've never seen his face. He always has a scarf pulled up to cover his mouth and his hood pulled low."

I clench my fists beneath the table while my expression remains stoic. "Do you think we should go to the police?" I ask quietly, my eyes locked on her face to catch her reaction.

She's still staring outside, but when I mention the police, her gaze shifts to mine. "No. I don't have to bother them with this. He's just an overexcited fan."

"He's what?" *Fuck*. A fan? I was thinking of an ex that wanted her back, or the paparazzi. My mind did *not* go to a stalker. "You think it's the same guy that sent you the flowers?"

"What?" She shakes her head. "No. *No*."

"Hayley?"

Her shoulders drop and she sighs until a small smile plays on her lips. "Not here."

"Not here?" *Jesus*. Okay. I smile back at her and jump up to pay, not even waiting for her to finish. If she thinks I'm letting this go, she's wrong.

Taking my lead, Hayley gulps down the last of her coffee and gets up, linking her fingers through mine when I reach her. "Shall we walk?" she asks.

"Yep. There's a quiet garden not too far from here."

"A garden? Perfect."

We walk in silence for the few minutes it takes to find the place I was talking about, and the second we're through the gates, alone—just like I expected—I turn to Hayley.

"Do you have a stalker, Hayls?"

"I didn't say that."

"No, but you're thinking it, aren't you?"

She sighs again, glancing down at the bracelet I gave her, spinning it around her wrist.

"I don't know. I didn't until today. He's a fan. Most of his letters have been nice. And even the one with the flowers wasn't *that* bad. But now I—"

"He said that you'd make the *perfect couple*."

"And maybe we would." She smirks, playing it down. "I don't know him."

"Hayls." My voice grates in frustration but when she frowns I regret it. "Sorry, I'm—"

"Worried, I know. But you shouldn't be." She grabs my hand again before dragging me over to a bench and sitting me down.

"This is all part of the job," she begins as she settles beside me, her soothing tone attempting to reassure me while I try not to groan. "It happens. Probably a lot more often than we hear about and—"

"We're going to the police, Hayls. Even if they laugh at us. *Please.* It will put my mind at ease."

"Ugh. I'm sorry I told you."

"And here I was thinking we promised no secrets."

"We did, but I honestly didn't think it was a big deal, until I saw that coat."

"Then I'm glad you saw it. No more holding back. *Okay?* This relationship may be fake, but I still *fucking* care."

"I know. I promise. No more holding back."

After spending two hours at the police station, we walked out no better off than when we walked in. We handed over the letters, but other than the handwriting, they didn't have much to go on. Just like Hayley predicted.

And while I still feel better about it, I'm at a loss for what to do next.

"I promise, I'll be okay," Hayley insists over and over.

She reaches out to squeeze my jaw, trying to force a smile out of me when we arrive back at her apartment. "I'm not even going to be in the country for the next two weeks, and I'll have security on me twenty-four seven."

Yet another reason to frown—Hayley's international tour. I knew this was coming—we spoke about it a couple of weeks back—but that was before things changed between us. At least, before they changed for me. And now...I'm really going to miss her.

"If they'd have waited a month, I could have come with you." I pout jokingly, or maybe not so jokingly, but still it makes Hayley laugh.

"Want me to ask them?" she muses. "I could say... My fake boyfriend is in the playoffs and set to win the Super Bowl, but he'd like to come with me on the tour. Can we delay these little get-togethers—that definitely haven't been planned for months—so he can come?"

"It sounds selfish when you say it like that."

Her expression softens and she smiles. "You're not being selfish; you're being protective. But I promise. You have nothing to worry about."

"Okay. So how do I fill my time while you're away?"

"Practice, practice, practice. I need you to make the Super Bowl because I've never been and I'll be back by then. It's a once-in-a-lifetime opportunity." A smile tugs at my lips, and Hayley's eyes widen in satisfaction. "*Oh, yay.* That worked."

"It did." I reluctantly smile again. "I promise I'll get out of this funk while you're gone. But it would help if you didn't have a stalker."

"You're cute when you're all pouty." She tries to pinch my cheeks but I grab her arms, locking them by her side as I flip her onto the couch.

"Reed," she squeals.

"Take it back."

"Never." She shakes her head as I tickle her waist, right below her rib cage. "*Jesus.* Oh my God. No. I'm not taking it back. You're cute. Adorable. My golden boy. Do your worst."

I continue to tickle her until she plays dirty, reaching between us to rub my cock.

"Christ." I pull back instantly and Hayley cackles triumphantly, her chest heaving as she catches her breath.

"The fuck, Hayls."

"I had to do something to make you stop." She bounces her eyebrows.

"You could have just asked."

"*Oh.* Yeah." She stares up at me puzzled and I can't help but chuckle. "I never thought of that. Sometimes I forget that with you, things really are that simple."

My nose scrunches as I process that notion. "Ah. What—"

Hayley giggles as she cups my cheeks, gently this time. "That's a good thing, Reed. Trust me. Relationships shouldn't be complicated. People should be who they say they're going to be, and with you...I've got that. I just forget sometimes."

"What happened?" I ask, my eyes boring into hers, pleading with her to see that I'm here, to know that I'm always willing to listen.

"What do you mean?" She frowns but she knows—she's just delaying her response.

"What made you so wary of relationships? You've talked about your exes, but it's always in a joking way. You're an incredibly strong woman, Hayls, and nothing will change that. But you don't have to be strong with me."

She sighs and wriggles out from under me, pushing me away before she sits up. Crossing her legs, she spins until she's facing me, pausing before she speaks. "I don't think I ever took myself seriously enough when it came to love. I always picked guys that were good for my image, or the ones I thought would be the most fun and adventurous. I guess, because of that, none of them treated me the way I've come to realize I deserve to be treated. I pity the man that comes after you, Reed. He'll have a hell of a lot to live up to."

She smiles softly and I force one in return, my stomach sinking. I should be happy about that. She deserves to be treated like a queen, and if I helped her to see that, I should be over the moon. But I'm not. And fuck—again... *Why can't I ever just be friends with a woman?* Plenty of people do it.

Hayley changes the subject, and since she's flying out early tomorrow, I head off shortly after, giving her some time to herself.

And the second I'm home, I crumble.

What the fuck is going on?

She's supposed to be my *fake* girlfriend because I have feelings for someone else, and yet, I haven't so much as thought of Bria for the past few days *except* when Hayley's mentioned her.

I'm consumed by Hayley. Intrigued by everything she does. Desperate for more time with her. And that's a bad place to be.

Her being away might be a good thing. It'll give me a chance to sort my shit out. To get myself in a better headspace, ready for when she returns.

My part of the ruse may be over, but Hayley has a role to win, and I promised I'd be there for her. She's going to get it. I have no doubt.

It's time to get over whatever these feelings are.

I have a part to play. I can't fuck it up.

Chapter Thirty-Six

REED

I wave to the Uber driver and stumble up my driveway, still on a high after winning our first playoff game. We celebrated hard tonight, but we deserve it. With only one game left before the Super Bowl, the championship is in our sights. And I don't want to be cocky...but fuck, we are good.

Everything fell into place today and we couldn't be stopped. A force to be reckoned with. I couldn't be more proud of the guys. It was a team effort all around.

The only thing that would have made it better was if Hayley hadn't been MIA—holed up in some exotic country, leaving her mark on the world.

I smile to myself as I think of her—her long, blonde hair blowing in the breeze like she has her own personal fan, cameras flashing, everyone enamored by her talent.

I miss her.

Patting my pockets, I locate my phone and bring up her name. She's only been gone a week but it feels like longer. She's back after our next game. We're almost there. But I can't resist messaging her.

> REED: One down. One to go, Baby

I text her, smiling as I press send, only then noting the time.

> REED: Fuck, it's 2am. Sorry

> REED: Wait, no it's not. What time is it?

Where is she? She was in London yesterday, or was it the day before? I know she's in another time zone right now, but other than that...

The three little dots appear and my throat bobs as excitement builds in my chest. Did I mention I miss her? In such a short span of time, she's cemented herself in my life, and now that she's gone, I'm a little out of sorts without her. And not at all ashamed to admit it.

To myself.

I'm not sure she needs to know just yet.

> HAYLEY: It's seven. I'm in London. But lucky for you, I'm already up to catch an early flight

I was right...London. I knew that because I've been keeping up with her premieres. Not in a stalker way like that guy who better leave her the fuck alone, but in a supportive way—like a boyfriend would. And I can report... *Jaded Beginnings* is killing it. Audiences are eating it up, just like I knew they would. Australia's sweetheart is taking over. Or is she America's sweetheart now?

Either way.

> REED: Paris next, right?

> HAYLEY: Oui

I smile, getting comfortable on the couch, kicking my feet up on the armchair beside me, flexing my toes to stretch out my aching calves, though I can't for the life of me figure out why they ache.

> HAYLEY: Congrats on the win. I saw the end of the game when I got back last night

> REED: You watched?

> HAYLEY: Of course. You're my man. 😉

> REED: Of course 😏

My heart jolts but I ignore it. I'm going to chalk it up to the copious amounts of alcohol I have coursing through my body. Hayley's my *friend*. That's why she watched. That's what friends do. They support each other, even when they're busy.

At least that's what they're supposed to do.

My chest tightens for an entirely new reason now and I ignore that too. Even a simple "best of luck" message would suffice, but no... *fuck*. Now is not the time to process feelings...good, bad, or indifferent. Especially where Hayley and Bria are concerned.

> HAYLEY: Also...Luke told me I had to watch. He said he'd have a pop quiz for me today. On that note, who scored the first touchdown?

A laugh bursts out of me and I straighten up, leaning forward to type. Fucking Luke. That checks out and...

> REED: Luke scored the first touchdown. Lucky you asked

> HAYLEY: Christ, that would have been a bad one to get wrong

> HAYLEY: I never would have lived it down

> REED: Nope. Never. What else do you need to know?

> HAYLEY: What about the score at half time?

Another message comes through before I can respond, and my body tenses when I see that it's Bria. I'm ninety percent sure this is the longest we've gone without speaking, but I'm choosing not to think about that too. I'm still trying to process how the fuck I feel. I miss her. I do. But until I know how to fix *us*, there's not much I can say.

Ignoring her message, I read Hayley's follow-up text and chuckle.

> HAYLEY: Actually wait... he's likely to ask something obscure, like what color shirt was D'Angelo wearing?

REED: You mean Daddy D'Angelo 😌 😂 😭 😎

God, I'm funny.

I'm still chuckling to myself when my phone rings, vibrating in my hand, making me startle and drop it. Watching it slide under the couch, I curse. *Dammit.*

I jump down to get it, stretching my hand as far as it will go, rummaging around until my fingertips finally strike gold.

"Hello," I answer as I straighten up, banging my head into the coffee table. "Motherfucker," I curse, rubbing the ache.

"I've done a lot of things, but never that."

"Shit. Sorry about that. But probably lucky it was you, Hayley Baby." I smile at her nickname and she giggles.

"I knew it! Golden Boy, are you drunk?"

"What? Nuh-uh," I whine, shaking my head even though she can't see me. I'm not drunk, I just drank. There's a difference.

"I'm going to take that as a yes."

"I'm *fine*. You were asking about a shirt?"

"Bonus points for remembering."

"I don't remember. The color, I mean. I should have been paying more attention."

"So disappointing." Hayley giggles again and the sound makes me melt.

"I'll be better next time."

"No need, I'll be watching. It's my last day before I fly home, and I've made no other plans."

I smile, my chest tight with emotion. "Thanks, Hayls. I'll blow you a kiss. It's nice to know you care."

"Of course I care. You're my man." She repeats her earlier sentiment, but hearing it out loud makes it so much sweeter.

"If only you were here so I could show you how *your* man would be rewarding you right now."

"Reed!"

"Yeah."

"That's not fair."

"What's not?"

"Teasing me like that. I want to be rewarded."

"Jesus. H. Christ. I said that out loud? That's not very golden boy of me."

Hayley's infectious laughter lights up the sound waves before a muffled announcement permeates the air and her laughter abruptly cuts off. "Shit. That's me. I have to go."

"Talk soon?"

"Definitely."

"Bye, Baby."

"Bye, Boyfriend."

She hangs up and my head spins. *Maybe I am drunk?* I'm definitely tired.

Lying back, I close my eyes and dream of my bed instead of getting off my ass to walk to my bedroom. I imagine my head sinking into the soft pillows, the warm comforter tucked under my arm, Hayley curled into my side. It's peaceful and—

What the fuck?

Nope. No feelings. Not right now. I need to sleep.

A week later, spirits are high in the locker room ahead of our conference final. We made it this far, and I have no doubt we're going all the way. Up next, the Super Bowl. There's an energy in the air that I haven't felt before. We're not just confident, we're determined, and in this moment, I'm happy to be the cocky asshole Luke is, and say...we *deserve* it.

When I'm changed, I shake out my shoulders and stretch my arms, bouncing on my toes. With a few minutes left before we're due on the field, I run through my pregame ritual, clearing my mind, taking a few deep breaths as I live in the moment. I'm about to make my way out when one of my teammates grabs my arm.

"Is that yours?" He points to my phone on the floor and I frown. *What the fuck?*

"Yes, thank you." That's new. I'm usually so organized. Shrugging to myself, I bend to grab it and find a text from my mom, making my brows furrow.

While I wouldn't normally check my phone this close to game time, something doesn't feel right. She called to wish me luck earlier, and she *never* texts.

Bringing the screen to life, I click on her message and my stomach sinks.

> Mom: Dad and I appreciate your offer for a paid vacation, but we've decided it's not the right time for us. We're going to spend the $200 voucher on a night in a city hotel and return the rest to you. We are looking forward to getting away for the weekend. Thank you.

Thank you? They appreciate my offer? It wasn't an *offer*. It was a *goddamn* Christmas present. It's paid for. Nonrefundable. And they were over the moon about it.

At least, they *were*.

My stomach churns as my muscles tense. This has nothing to do with my parents. My brother figured it out and he's making them feel guilty. Just like he always does. Something I've been fighting my entire life.

As my teammates exit the locker room, a few of them slap me on the back, completely unaware of my building anger, and I force a smile.

Glancing down at the phone again, my hand itches to call Hayley, and it's not lost on me that I'd usually talk to Bria about this stuff. Especially since she knows the back story.

Shaking off my thoughts, I toss my phone into my locker and take another deep breath, drawing it in through my nose, out through my mouth. It calms me for a beat until I remember if I don't leave now, Coach is going to fine my ass. It's time to get my head in the game. I'll have time to tackle this issue when I'm home. *After* we've celebrated.

When we're on our way to the Super Bowl.

For now...we've got a game to win.

Chapter Thirty-Seven

HAYLEY

M outh agape, I stare at the TV, alone in my hotel room, stunned as tears prick my eyes.

They lost.

Storm lost their final playoff game and I'm on the other side of the goddamn world when Reed really needs me. Twenty-four hours before I'm due to fly home.

My phone buzzes on the desk beside the bed, and I dive across the mattress to check it, crying out when my wrist hits the wooden edge.

My heart pounds as I check the screen, desperate to speak to Reed. But of course it's not him. It's Amelia. Reed's barely even walked off the field.

> AMELIA: They lost, Hayls. They lost

My stomach sinks as the reality of the loss sinks in.

> HAYLEY: I'm watching and I feel sick. I'm not there, Amelia. I should be there. What do I do?

I picture Amelia's soft smile as she types her response, and I know before I've even received it that she's going to say it's fine. But it's not. It's far from it.

> AMELIA: Reed understands, if that's what you're worried about. You can't beat yourself up over this. Who knows, maybe Bria will step up and reach out?

Bria? I groan and immediately curse myself for reacting that way. I should *want* Bria to step up. I should be hopeful of that, for Reed's sake. Because deep down, it's what he wants. I have a strong sense that he's in denial about his feelings, hoping it will help him move on.

And if that's the case, I'm terrified she has the power to hurt him even more.

She had her chance.

When Reed told her about us, *that* was her time to step up, to show herself as the true best friend she always claimed to be. But she failed. She pulled back the second their friendship stopped going the way she wanted it to go. She's supposed to support him through *everything*. She should be the one picking up the pieces. We shouldn't be questioning if she's going to reach out. She should be there. On the sidelines. *Ready*.

She should have always been doing that.

> HAYLEY: If she doesn't? Can you give him a hug for me?

> AMELIA: Of course. We're all here. We'll make sure he's okay

The tightness in my chest builds until I bite my cheek to shift the pain, finding it more comfortable to focus on the physical than the emotional. I can't do anything from here. But when I get home, I'm going to make it up to him.

My eyes roll into the back of my head, but I force myself awake. I'm almost at Reed's. So what if I haven't slept in the last eighteen hours. He needs me, and if I'm being honest, I need him too.

The second the Uber pulls up to the curb, I rush out a thanks and grab my bags, power walking up Reed's driveway, knocking with the urgency I feel in my chest.

When I'm met with silence, I bounce on my toes and pray that he's home. "Come on, come on, come on."

A female voice calls out, and I freeze, a chill running through me as I instantly regret not giving him notice. I consider turning around, but in the short space of time before she gets to the door, I conjure up so many scenarios that I'm no longer worried. I'm livid.

We may be in a fake relationship, but we had rules and *not* fucking around was one of them. Just because I was on the other side of the world doesn't—

"Hi. Can I help you?" A striking young woman opens the door, her long, dark hair pulled off her face, highlighting her sharp features and resting bitch face. Her cruel dark eyes appraise me from tits to toes, and when she finally makes it to my face, she smiles coldly, undoubtedly registering my tired expression, marking me as harmless.

No competition.

But she's wrong. I will stake my claim and slap a girl if I have to. Reed is mine, bitch. No one-night stand is going to—

"Hayls?" Reed calls out from the end of the hall, his voice full of wonder. "You're home?"

He takes off in a slow jog, gently brushing past the woman without even glancing in her direction and pulling me into his arms. "Fuck, you're a sight for sore eyes. I can't believe you're here." He leans close and whispers in my ear, "Exactly when I need you."

My brows furrow as he pulls back, but when Miss Thinks-she's-better-than-me frowns, I smile.

"Who's your friend?" I ask Reed and the woman scoffs.

"Hayley, this is my sister-in-law, Megan. Megan, this is my girlfriend, Hayley."

Megan judges me again before her callous eyes widen. "You're that actress."

"I am." I fake a grin, remembering that this woman and her husband are the only two people in the world that Reed can't stand. Which means I can't stand them on principle.

Reed hits me with a tight-lipped apologetic grin and I smile back, turning to the woman whose name I've already forgotten. "No offense, but were you leaving? I want some alone time with my man."

She scoffs again before calling out for "Jace," her voice whiny as another giant of a man steps into view. A guy that looks a hell of a lot like Reed, but also doesn't. He's more like the discount version of the great specimen standing before me.

"You're not ready to go yet, are you, honey?" the bitch asks Reed's brother, folding her arms over her chest as she grins my way.

"I said what I needed to say," Reed cuts in before his brother can answer. "I'm not going to change your mind. Why bother staying?"

"Aww." The woman fakes a pout and a little part of me wants to slap it off her face. "We were just getting started."

Oh, hell no. *Who does she think she is?* "Sweety,"—I put on my most innocent voice, gently squeezing her arm—"you say that like your opinion matters, and yet, you were the one that answered the door, all while the conversation continued without you." I'm making baseless assumptions, but I roll with it, hoping she's insecure enough to believe me. "In fact, judging by your man's bored expression, I'd say he's not happy you called out just now. It's men's business. Am I right?"

"Fuck off," Jace says, moving quickly down the hall to reach us. "Don't talk to her like that. You little—"

"Get the fuck out of my house." Reed's booming voice echoes through the room and all eyes dart his way. Silence ensues as he points to the door, and I smile proudly, watching as Jace and his wife pick their jaws up off the floor. I think it's safe to assume Reed usually keeps the peace. "You are not welcome here anymore," he continues, and this is yet another version of him that impresses me. "I don't give a fuck about your opinions. I will be civil to you in front of our parents, but otherwise you are dead to me, and I wish they felt the same. Get out."

Reed's sister-in-law gasps while his brother scoffs, but before he can respond, Reed grabs his bag and tosses it outside, motioning for them to follow.

"Goodbye. Hope you have a safe trip."

A laugh wants to burst out of me but I bite my lip to stifle it, holding my breath as I wait to see what they do.

And it catches me off guard when they do as he asked, sulking as they leave.

I step farther inside as they pass, and when they're out of the way, Reed slams the door shut before stumbling back into the wall, his face in his hands.

"Fuck. I'm so sorry about that."

"Sorry? That was beautiful."

"What?" He huffs out an incredulous laugh and stands tall, his ashen expression lifting.

"How long have you wanted to stand up to them?"

"Forever."

"How many times have you done it?"

"Just this once." He lets out a grunt as he curses himself. "He gets me so worked up all the time and then... the way he spoke to you and... Fuck. I'm going to regret that."

"Don't. He deserved it."

"I know." He runs a hand through his hair, clearly worried. "Fuck. I know. But he'll take it out on my parents."

Shit. My stomach sinks as guilt consumes me. I didn't think about that. "I'm so sorry. I should have kept my mouth shut. That's never been my strong suit and—"

Reed steps forward, covering my mouth to silence me, pulling me into a hug. "What you said was perfect. I wanted them gone and they're gone. I'll make it up to my parents. They're desperate to meet you, so maybe that will work."

I smile at his reassurance, but can't shake the pit forming in my stomach. I really need to stay out of other people's business.

Starting tomorrow.

I'm already invested now.

"What did they want? Have they visited before?"

"Never. That's not saying they've never been to California—or San Francisco for that matter. But they've never visited me. This one and only visit was *my* doing. I laid down a challenge and my brother accepted it. He's never been one to let anything go."

I raise a brow, impressed. "Call me intrigued."

"My parents politely declined the vacation I gave them."

"They what? Why?"

Reed opens his mouth to speak, but he doesn't have to answer as realisation hits me. "Motherfucker. Your asshole brother."

"*Yep.* That's why I invited him here. To talk to him about it."

"Rightly so. But how did you get him to come?"

"They were in LA for work, so I wired him some money and told him if he used it to visit me, I'd wire him some more, telling him we needed to talk."

"Wow. Okay." My mind processes that and I laugh when a thought hits me. "Wait. He *took* your money?"

"He did." Reed smirks.

"After telling your parents they shouldn't?"

"Yep."

My lips lift and I can't hide my beaming smile as I pull him into another hug. "You're brilliant."

"You're only just figuring that out?"

"Maybe." I wink until I remember the brothers' tension just now. "I'm guessing it backfired?"

"Nope." Reed shakes his head. "They both listened and took the extra money, but they were assholes about it and I doubt they'll change. I'm hoping it doesn't matter though. It was only ten grand, but it should be enough for me to convince my parents they can do the same without feeling guilty."

"How very civil of you." I smile. "Not the way I would have handled it but I understand your approach."

"If I could ensure they never saw a cent of my money, I would. But on the flip side, if I knew they'd fuck off and never see my parents again, and that my parents would accept that and be better off, I'd give my brother everything I've got. Only it's not that easy." He huffs in disbelief and turns away from me, running a hand down his face. "Enough of the bullshit." He spins back around, his light-filled gaze meeting mine. "You're here. My Hollywood star is back. I want to hear all about it."

"And you will." I grin though it doesn't reach my eyes, and when he notices, a bit of his light dims. "First," I continue, my lips now curling into a sympathetic smile, "will you tell me about your family? About your past? I'm here to listen if you want to get it off your chest."

And I kind of need to know.

A strained breath releases from the back of his throat as both his head and shoulders drop in resignation. "It's a long story, Hayls."

Lifting his chin, I stare into his weary eyes and wink. "Good thing there's nowhere I'd rather be."

CHAPTER THIRTY-EIGHT

REED

Hayley smiles and I find myself staring at her in awe. She's here. As though my internal thoughts conjured her to my door. Exactly when I needed her. I'd been fast approaching a breaking point with my brother. Just having him in my home felt like a betrayal to my parents, even though my mom would do anything for us to get along. She doesn't realize what she's asking—that she's expecting me to be happy about the way he treats her, manipulates her, *guilts* her.

I'm ninety percent sure Dad would have beaten the shit out of him if it wasn't for my mom. Like me, he sees through the bullshit, but he's not willing to hurt her like that. No one is.

Except Jace.

I close my eyes, breaking the connection with Hayley, and before I've had the chance to open them again, I feel her soft touch on my hand, the brush of her skin instantly calming me.

"I'm sorry about all that." I sigh as I glance at her again, catching her sad expression before it morphs into anger.

"What are you sorry for? You didn't do anything. That woman, on the other hand...she was not giving off good vibes. I really wanted to slap some decency into her." I smile as Hayley cringes. "Sorry, I can get a little protective over the people I care about."

"Believe it or not, I know this about you. And I'm not sorry. I'm grateful."

"Good." She finally offers me a closed-lipped grin and my heart jumps. She's here. And God, she fucking beautiful. "So...how did the conversation go? With you brother and the b-" She trails off when I smile softly.

"She wasn't always like that, you know. We all thought she was going to be a vet. She worked with my dad for years. Always smiling. Always willing to help. But my brother has a way of sucking people in, making them fall for his charms, and then he drags them down with him. Megan is so far gone, I don't think she'll ever find herself again."

Hayley frowns, highlighting the one major trait my brother is missing —empathy. Actually, he's missing more than that, but this is a big one.

"Don't waste too much energy on her though. She's smart enough to know what she's doing. She may be under my brother's spell, but I've seen her lash out when he's not around. She's not entirely innocent. She loves the attention my brother gives her, and for all his faults, I've never seen him treat her badly. He reserves that for everyone else."

"God, a little part of me feels sorry for her now. But if she's hurting you, I want to hate her."

I huff out a laugh and pull her into me, wrapping her under my arm to walk her to the couch. I've witnessed her fierce protectiveness before, felt the love she has for her friends, but being the one on the receiving end is an entirely new feeling. One I don't want to get used to.

I'm about to continue on about my brother when a thought hits me. "Does that mean you hate Bria too? Since she hurt me?"

Hayley laughs but it holds a nervous edge. "I don't know the right answer to that question. You'll probably deny it, but you still care about her deeply, so I'm going to tread carefully. I don't understand her. I wouldn't say I hate her, but I'm confused by her actions. If she realized she wants you as more than a friend, then why the hell isn't she fighting for you? And if she doesn't feel that way, then why is she pulling away? Why isn't she calling you to find out the details? Sharing in your joy? I don't get it. Mind you, I've never shared a bond as close as yours was. Maybe the rules are different. I've always had friends, but apart from Amelia, it was always surface level. We never shared secrets, nor were they lasting friendships, for that matter. Because of that, my diplomatic response is that no, I don't hate her." She pauses and I subtly close my mouth before she notices it dropped open, laughing when she adds, "Not yet, anyway." And there's my protective girl again.

"I'm not sure I know how to respond to that. But thank you. I think."

Hayley smiles, brushing a stray strand of hair behind her ears. "Thank you works." She shrugs. "Now back to your brother, who I *do* hate."

"I'd much rather talk about Bria." The current situation with Bria may be complicated, but compared to my relationship with my brother, it's much easier to explain.

Hayley snorts in amusement. "I bet you would." She shakes her head and I frown until I realize what I said. *I'd rather talk about Bria.*

"I didn't mean it like that." I smile, leaving out the fact that it would be awkward to talk about my old feelings for Bria with the girl I'm developing *new* feelings for. But... "It's an easier discussion. The stuff with my brother is a whole lot more fucked up."

"Honestly, I didn't think that was possible." She smirks. "Your issues with Bria are pretty f—"

"Thanks." I cut her off with a chuckle. "You should get out now, before you're trapped here in my messed-up world."

"I like your world, Reed. You're one of the best guys I know. If not the best. So hit me with it. Take me down with you. I'm ready to fall."

My pulse spikes, taking her words to mean more than they do, and I curse myself for once again getting caught up in my feelings. She's being a friend. Just like Bria once was.

Letting out a long sigh, I lie back against the cushions and close my eyes. "Where do I even start?"

"The beginning? Or the end. Or somewhere in the middle. Whatever feels right."

I open my eyes to find her silently laughing to herself. "Thanks, Hayls. You're so helpful."

"I know." She winks while I playfully roll my eyes, feeling a little more at ease. And that's what Hayley does for me. All the time. She eases my mind. I'm at peace around her. Even with these insane feelings rolling around in my head, she calms me. And I'm only now realizing how different this friendship is from my friendship with Bria. Bria was always there when I needed her, but her presence often brought about a certain level of stress. I was always worrying about the future, about losing our friendship the moment she figured me out. But with Hayley...I can't even explain it. But I like it. And something tells me that even if I told her about my feelings and she didn't reciprocate, she'd find a way to make it all okay.

"What's going on in that head of yours?" she asks, when it takes me a moment to answer. "Are you trying to hold me in suspense?"

"That's exactly what I'm doing. This is all about *you*."

"Good. It should be. And I'm ready." She straightens before crossing her legs underneath her and twisting her body to face me. "Let's go."

I smile to myself, ready to tease her again, but as always, she's helping. So instead, I launch right into it. "My brother is a narcissist. He wasn't always that way, and I have no idea what happened to trigger it. But it's been a long time since he cared about anyone other than himself. And Megan."

Hayley's eyes widen but she keeps quiet, nodding subtly, encouraging me to continue.

"I wouldn't say we ever had a close bond. He was eight when I was born and didn't love the loss of attention. But he was never awful to me. At least, I don't remember it if he was. But when he was around sixteen, he changed, more than I imagine the average sixteen-year-old changes. He became angry all the time, and he'd stay out all night, knowing my mom was staying up waiting. He'd scream at her for no reason and make her feel guilty if she cried. Tell her she was weak and worthless. My father worked a lot. He was...*is* a horse trainer. His hours were longer back then. Now he's a supervisor and has more time with Mom. But in those days, he'd get home late and my mom wouldn't say anything. She'd smile and tell him about her wonderful day, despite spending most of it sitting on the couch, staring at the wall.

"At first I tried to fight him. When he'd yell, I'd yell back to defend her. But I soon realized that made things worse. So instead of making her life harder, I did the opposite. I did anything I could to make things easier on her. I became the golden boy you see today. And I kept her secret because she asked me to. At least until I was old enough to see her sadness for what it was and I couldn't take it anymore."

I pause and glance up at Hayley, finding her staring back at me with tears in her eyes. "Reed?"

"Wait. Let me get it all out. Please." She nods, but grabs my hand again, giving it a squeeze. "Thank you. When I was about fourteen, I told my dad what was going on and all hell broke loose. He felt guilty for not seeing it, he fought with my brother, and threatened to kick him out.

And my mother got worse. She went on medication for depression, blaming herself for my brother's actions, convincing herself it's because she was depressed that she didn't treat him as well as she should have. But she was a great mom to me. It wasn't her. She just couldn't see it. She threatened to kick my dad out if he didn't stop blaming my brother, and we fell into a pattern—Dad and I—both of us turning a blind eye to my brother's actions, but being there to pick up the pieces every time she broke.

"Jace moved out when he was around twenty-three, and things got better for a while. But they were never perfect. And when I started garnering attention for my football skills, he wasn't happy. He made Mom believe she hadn't dedicated enough time to him growing up. And that he never had the potential because she'd failed him.

"At least once a year, I used to beg her to talk to someone about him and to cut him out of her life. But all it did was result in her blaming herself for making me worry, then she wouldn't speak to me for a while. Because of that, I've let it go for the past few years. And Dad's the same. He wouldn't cope if he lost her, and he's worried if he pushes her too far, he might. And that's it. My whole fucked-up life story."

A tear falls from Hayley's watery eyes and she sniffs as she wipes it, rushing out a soft apology. "I'm so sorry, Reed. That's a lot to deal with as an adult, but a child... I can't even imagine. And to have to sit back and watch as your mom went through all of that. God, my heart is breaking for her. For you. For your dad. Did he ever hurt her...physically?"

"Never. And the only time he ever touched me or Dad was when he was fighting back. If we got in the way of his verbal abuse."

"Have you ever reported him to the police?"

"We have. The first time resulted in him telling my mom that we'd pushed him into drugs. That he wanted to take the pain away. And the second time, he took off. He disappeared for weeks, and Mom was convinced he was dead and that it was her fault. The only way to save her is to make her life as good as it can be when he's not around, and helping her through it when he is."

"So today was about trying something new? A different approach?"

"It was. My brother has to travel for his job. He's a sales rep for a few truck brands. And apparently his bosses love him. Dad told me he'd be in

LA this week, so I set the challenge. Next thing you know, he's at my door, opening his palm for a handout."

"But... I sense a but..."

"When I asked him to give Mom a break, he lost it. Told me I have no idea about his relationship with Mom because I left. He tried to guilt me into believing that her depression was my fault for moving away. That it had all been my fault for being born. But I've heard it all before and I'm kind of immune. When I first moved out, I believed him. But my dad worked hard to convince me that he was wrong. They're good people, Hayls. My mom and my dad. It's just..." I trail off and she squeezes my hand again, drawing my attention.

"I never doubted that, not even for a second. But I wish I knew how to help. I wish I knew what I could do."

"You're doing plenty. Keep being the light that you are. It helps."

"Like what you do for your mom?"

My forehead creases as I consider that. "I guess so, but I never want you to feel like my happiness is your responsibility. I'd never do that to you."

"I know. You're too nice for that." She forces a smile.

"Lucky this is all fake between us, right? You don't want to get caught up in this mess."

"Fake or not, I'm here for you. I want to be. I wish I could do more."

"Feel free to change the topic. Tell me something good. Something about your trip. The fanfare. The people you met. Hell, you could tell me about your outfits—I'll take anything right now. Between this and losing the game, I've had a shitty few days." I pause and Hayley's eyes widen.

"Oh my God," she gasps, her hands flying to her mouth before she jumps up and throws herself into my arms.

"What's—"

"The game. That's why I came. I'm so sorry, Reed. You were so close."

I pull her closer, breathing her in. "Feels like a lifetime ago. I've already got my sights set on next season."

"Don't bullshit me." She pushes against my shoulders, leaning back to look at me, trying to catch me in a lie. "You all played your asses off." Her beautiful blue eyes narrow and I love how serious she is. "You deserve to be there. You—"

"Didn't make it," I cut her off, giving her waist a squeeze. "We didn't make it and that's okay. Boston was incredible. They outplayed us every chance they got. *They* deserve to be there."

"Wow." Her eyebrows shoot up to her hairline. "I'll bet all my money I get a very different response out of Luke. Maybe I should corrupt you. Make you see that you don't have to be nice all the time."

"I like being nice," I say honestly. I like the joy and warmth it brings my friends and family but also... "If I wasn't this nice, maybe we wouldn't be here right now."

A silence settles between us as I let that sink in, wondering if Hayley's thinking the same. Sure, we'd probably still be friends if I was different, but we wouldn't be this close. And she wouldn't be finally seeing her worth, something I know has brought us closer.

"You're right." Hayley glances away thoughtfully before her gaze settles back on me. "I don't want you to change. I want you to be the person you are, at the core of your soul. Not the person you are as a product of the way your brother was while you were growing up."

"I get that, I do. But that person is me. The product. That's me. And I happen to like the man I've become, even if it is because of my circumstances."

"I happen to like him too."

"Good. Because you're kind of stuck with me."

Hayley smiles before shuffling her ass to sit next to me and resting her head on my shoulder, linking her fingers through mine. "I wouldn't want it any other way."

Chapter Thirty-Nine

HAYLEY

The tightness in my chest doesn't subside until Reed begs me not to worry about him. And even then, it only fades to a dull ache. He'd hinted at a bad relationship with his brother and the effects it had on his mom, but I never could have predicted the hell they've all been through. The hell his brother put them through. I almost wish I'd known that before I came face-to-face with him earlier today, but then again, like Reed and his dad, I don't want to do anything that could come back to bite his mom. I've never met her, but I have never wanted to protect someone more in my life. Including Reed.

"Hayls, you're doing it again." Reed shakes his head but smiles softly. "We have to change the subject. There's nothing we can do, so there's no point stressing about it."

"I'm never going to *not* stress about it, Reed. Not now. I need you to know that."

"Me either, Hayls. Me either." He presses a kiss to my temple and I snuggle into him. "Tell me about your parents. Do you talk often?"

"Often enough." I shrug as sadness runs through me. I really should talk to them more. But that's on me. "My parents have always been great. They're supportive enough and they care."

"But..."

"What makes you think there's a but?"

"Call it intuition." He hits me with a cocky grin.

"They have their own life," I rush out, returning his smile, only mine's softer. "They were pretty excited when I moved to Sydney, and I don't think all that excitement was for me. They were decent parents, but never wanted to be parents. We're probably more like friends these days than parents and child. Don't get me wrong. I love them and they love me, but it's not a traditional relationship."

"Fuck, I'm sorry, Hayls."

"Don't be. It made it easier for me to move across the world."

"Maybe so, but I can hear the sadness in your voice. You miss them." His thoughtful, caring eyes bore into mine and my stomach knots. I don't think anyone's ever looked at me like that. With that much concern. For me.

"I do miss them. But at the same time...I don't regret my decision to move. Just like I don't regret my decision to stay with my cheating boyfriend. How could I? It got me here. Which in turn launched my career and brought me to Amelia. And you."

"That last one is especially important." He jokingly bounces his eyebrows but it's true.

"I agree. And I'm here for you, Reed. Here for whatever you need. Just like I know you're here for me."

After our big talk about our pasts, and truly opening up to each other, Reed and I fall into an easy, comfortable rhythm, and before we know it, we've been faking a relationship for nearly two months. But while we've been doing enough to get me the audition for *Reckless Desire*, and my agent is all smiles about me turning my reputation around, I'm worried about Reed. He's got so much going on with his family, and he barely speaks to Bria anymore.

He's constantly brushing off my concern, but I'm not convinced he's as happy as he says he is. Especially when he seems to be overly invested in my life, as though I don't know that's one of his traits.

"Did you call Bria today?" I ask when we're curled up on his couch watching a movie. He promised he'd call her this week, and I'm not letting him off the hook. They need to talk it out or they'll both be stuck in limbo while I carry around the guilt of messing it up for them.

Reed groans and I have my answer. "We're supposed to be celebrating your audition, Hayls. Let's talk about this tomorrow."

"But—"

"No buts. I promise I'm good. Bria and I will work out our shit eventually. For now, I want to focus on you. How long does it usually take before you hear anything?"

"Reed."

"Nope. Not today."

"Okay. Fine. In answer to your question, it depends. It took weeks for me to hear back about *Jaded Beginnings* because the director got sick or something. I can't remember. But with others, mostly rejections, I heard back the next day."

"So the longer the better." Reed bites back a smirk.

"Maybe."

"And in the meantime, we need to show them that you're the right woman for the job."

"We're already doing that. Just look at me." I stand up and spin around, waving my hands down my body. "I'm a new woman. I don't drink. I don't party. I have the sweetest, most attractive football-star boyfriend. I am living the dream."

"Fuck, Hayls. Tell me how you really feel?" He frowns and I laugh, diving on top of him.

"It's all the truth. I feel amazing since I stopped drinking and partying, and I really do have the sweetest, most attractive football-star boyfriend. Where's the lie?"

Reed opens his mouth to speak, but I cover it with both hands and shake my head. "Do not ruin this moment by saying 'our relationship.'"

Reed licks my palm before shaking his head, laughing when I squeal, pulling my hands away. "I wouldn't dream of it, Hayls. The only lie is the title. I've always been real with you."

My chest tightens but I ignore the tension threatening to make me feel things I shouldn't. Reed is real with everyone. And at the end of the day, this relationship, fake or otherwise, has an expiry. One that's creeping up on us.

I glance away, but Reed grabs my chin, dragging me back in. "What happened?" His soulful eyes bore into mine.

I hesitate, but like always, I tell him what I'm thinking. "I'm going to miss this."

"I'll always be here."

His words hit me harder than they should, but before I can respond, my phone buzzes with a text seconds before Reed's goes off.

"Group chat?" I question as I reach for my phone, welcoming the distraction, checking my screen to find three new messages.

> AMELIA: Does anyone else have a moping husband/boyfriend since missing out on the Super Bowl? It's been a few weeks and Luke's still sulking

> KEELEY: Oh yeah, my husband's devastated. He won't get out of bed

I laugh out loud at Keeley's sarcasm, turning away when Reed tries to see my screen.

> PAIGE: Keeley, we need to find you a man. Are you sure you're against dating players?

> KEELEY: Never been surer of anything in my life

> HAYLEY: What about actors? I know a few decent ones

> PAIGE: Ooh yes. Great idea, Hayls

> KEELEY: This isn't supposed to be about my love life. Moving on... I may not have a boyfriend but my brother's all moody over the loss

> HAYLEY: Isn't Easton always moody?

> KEELEY: Yes

> PAIGE: Yes

I laugh again and Reed groans beside me, but when I poke my tongue out, he smiles.

PAIGE: Easton's actually okay about the game, though. It's surprising me

AMELIA: So it's just Luke then?

LAINEY: Nope. Thomas is pretty upset about it

AMELIA: Oh good

AMELIA: Wait. No. I didn't mean that. I just...I don't know

HAYLEY: 😕 Oh Ames

PAIGE: I have an idea. Who's up for a beach day? If I tell Easton it's for the charity event, I might get him there. What do you think, Keeley? I'll have Isaac convince him

KEELEY: Yes! I can arrange that

HAYLEY: I'm in

AMELIA: Us too. Which beach? Do I need to bring a beach tent? Or is there shade?

LAINEY: We're in too. What about the beach near your house Amelia?

PAIGE: I love that beach. It's not too far from us either

AMELIA: Or Reed or Dylan. Sounds good

I look up as the organisation messages come through and find Reed staring at me, his eyes wide in surprise. "That was intense. I feel left out."

"What was?"

"Your messages. They're coming through faster than I can type. It's like how I imagine a conversation would go with all of you out drinking."

"We had plans to coordinate."

"The beach?"

"Yes. How did you—"

He spins his phone around, cutting me off, and I glance at his screen. In all that time there are only five messages.

> LUKE: Anyone else still pissed that we lost?

> REED: Of course. But it just means we'll come back fighting next season

> EASTON: Get over it

> LUKE: Okay. Done. Moving on

> LUKE: Beach tomorrow?

I watch the next couple of messages come through in real time.

> THOMAS: Sounds good

> DYLAN: I'm in

> EASTON: Nope

It's that easy. No questions on where or when or how. It's just done.

"Okay, well, it seems your method of organisation is much faster. But where are you going?"

"I assume that's what you're organizing?" He shrugs and a laugh bursts out of me. This is Reed and me to a T, easily shifting between the heavy and the light. Always comfortable. It's going to be hard to move on in the end. But now is not the time to think about it. Right now, I've got a beach hang to organise and it's exactly what I need.

More messages come through and I smile as I show Reed my screen. "I'll let you know when it's finalised. It could be a while."

🏈 🏈 🏈

I
t's not at all beach weather but the sun is shining, so we're embracing
it. And when Keeley pulls an Aussie Rules football out of her bag, I
squeal.

"You didn't!" I race forward, snatching the ball from her hands,
handballing it to myself.

"I did. But you're going to need to teach us how to play."

"I know how to play." Luke punches the ball out of my grasp and grabs
it off the sand, kicking it to Reed who catches it easily. "I may have watched
a few games when I heard Keeley was planning this."

My jaw drops. "Wow. I'm impressed. And I have to admit, you don't
suck."

"Of course I don't," Luke scoffs. "I'm good at everything."

Easton rolls his eyes as he grabs Isaac's hand. "I'm going to take Isaac
for a walk. We'll—"

"Can we stay, Dad?" Issac tugs on Easton's hand, pulling him back
toward Paige, a pleading smile on his cute little face. "I want to play."

Paige bites back a grin as her eyes flash to Easton's, and she gives him a
shrug. Easton forces a smile and Keeley bursts out laughing. "Easton's in.
Who else wants to play?"

It turns out that Luke isn't the only one who watched an Aussie Rules
game. Or two. Dylan, Thomas, and Reed all admitted they've seen it
before, but when it comes to playing, I wish I had a video camera.

Despite his clear annoyance at having to play, Easton's actually the best
by far. His handballing is on point and that man can mark. Reed's probably
the second best, and a spark of pride runs through me every time he kicks
the ball. But it's when he grabs Isaac and lifts him over his shoulders—
helping him secure a mark over Easton—that I really pay attention. And I
hate to admit, my ovaries tingle.

That man is dad material and it suits him.

I'm beginning to wonder if there's anything he's not good at. He's
definitely proven himself in the boyfriend department. And now this.

Amelia nudges me in the stomach when she notices me staring, and it
brings me back to a time I was doing the same to her about Luke—teasing
her when I caught her watching him. But this is different. She was having
Luke's baby; I think Reed's hot. I can't help it if everything he does reels
me in.

As the game goes on, the guys draw a crowd, and soon enough, we have a cheer squad. A solid mix between teenage boys braving the cold to surf and girls out for a walk, clad in their skimpy exercise gear, laughing and flirting whenever they can. Not that the guys notice. They're all obsessed with their own women. Even Reed doesn't pay them any mind.

When Luke's cockiness gets too much, knocking Dylan over when he attempts what we call a specky—marking the ball with his knees on Dylan's back—Keeley calls time, confiscating the ball to avoid any injuries.

"I think we're going to need a few more practices before the preseason event. But I've got to admit, it's a good start," she says as we all grab a drink, no longer worried about the cold weather, well and truly warmed up. "My award for the best player goes to Isaac for his amazing *screamer*..." She trails off as she says the word hesitantly.

"Screamer is correct. And I agree, Isaac, you were amazing."

Isaac beams up at us, his shoulders bouncing in giddiness, and when I glance up at Easton, I'm surprised to see him smiling.

"That's my man." He lowers his hand in a fist bump and Isaac matches his energy, making it look like his hand explodes after their fists touch.

A strange tension runs through me and when I glance over at Paige, seeing her loving smile back at her boys, my heart jolts.

Do I want that? Jesus. I think I do. A hand wraps around my shoulder, pulling me out of my head and I laugh, having no idea what I'm laughing about. "How'd I do, Hayley Baby?" Reed says, drawing my attention as he winks. "Do you think I've got what it takes?"

"You're a natural." I spin to face him. "I'd be proud to take you home."

"Really?" He raises an eyebrow and smirks. "I'm going to hold you to that. I'd love to visit Australia. Maybe I'll retire there. Get away from the drama over here."

He winks like he's joking, and I smile despite the nagging feeling starting low in my belly. Reed shouldn't have drama in his life, and I'm contributing to some of it. I can't help with his family stuff, but I can help with Bria. He needs to talk to her, and he needs to do it soon.

CHAPTER FORTY

REED

After the Australian football was put away, a group of young kids nearby kindly tossed us a *proper* football—not that I would ever say that out loud to Hayley.

We messed around with our new friends, teaching them some skills, having a friendly game until it was time for them to leave. And while I was more in my element, I've got to admit, watching Hayley shine with her Australian rules skills was something to behold.

When we all get hungry, Dylan and Thomas head off to grab burgers and I settle on the sand, watching Hayley as she chats animatedly with the girls, dancing around as she reenacts one of her football moves. I'm about to join their conversation when Luke calls out, drawing our attention.

"Rookie!" He waves obnoxiously to Landon as he jogs along the beach.

Landon's eyes widen as he slows, scanning our group, shocked to find us all there. But when his eyes settle on me, he smiles.

"Come on over." Luke beckons him to join us, before jogging to his side, leaving him with no room to say no. "I didn't know you lived out this way, Rookie," he continues, bringing Landon over to our group. "You just missed a friendly game, but I'm sure we'll play again soon. Right, Reed?"

"It's highly likely. How are you, Landon?" I make a point of using his name, and Luke grimaces.

"Sorry, *Landon*. It's a habit. I still call Zane Rookie sometimes."

After rolling my eyes at Luke, I jump up and introduce Landon to the girls, minus Keeley and Hayley who he already knows, and when Dylan and Thomas get back, we settle into a more relaxing afternoon, chatting and laughing, catching up on the last couple of weeks.

The time flies and we're all peaceful until Keeley notices a photographer. "All right, guys, up off your asses. It's time for some good publicity. There's been too much negativity surrounding the team."

"It's the offseason, Keels." Easton groans, and that groan intensifies when Paige and Isaac get to their feet.

"We're ready, aren't we, Isaac?" Paige says, giving him a smile.

"Yep. Come on, Dad." Isaac grabs Easton's hands and pulls him up to stand easily—with Easton's help—and I can't help but grin. He's so different around Isaac. It's nice to see them together now that his ex is out of the picture.

"I'm in." I jump up, dusting off my ass before grabbing Hayley's hand. "And so is Hayls." I don't have to consult her to know that I'm right. She's always up for a bit of fun.

"I think we should have another game of Australian Rules," Hayley says, trying to hide the excitement in her tone. "God knows you all need the practice. I'll captain one team and Reed will captain the other." She stands tall, her arms folded over her chest, and Luke scoffs.

"This isn't *Survivor*, Hayls. Why do you look so serious right now?"

"I'm ready to kick some butt."

"Righty oh. I'm on Hayley's team," Luke announces, rushing to join her.

I huff out a laugh and turn to Landon as he subtly backs away. "Landon, you have to stay, at least to watch some of us make fools of ourselves."

"He's referring to himself, Landon." Luke raises an eyebrow, his eyes bouncing between mine and Landon's, making sure I note his use of Landon's name. *Progress.*

Landon laughs and I consider it a win. "I'm in. But I have never played Aussie Rules before."

"The fact that you called it Aussie Rules already makes you a winner." Hayley smiles warmly and Landon visibly relaxes, setting off a chain reaction when Thomas nods my way. He must really be worried about Landon fitting in. *Well, Thomas, I'm trying.* "And because of that, Landon, you're on my team," Hayley continues, subtly winking my way.

I fake annoyance. "How have you had two picks already? I've got

Amelia then. And Dylan." I fold my arms over my chest to mimic Hayley's stance and she giggles.

"Since Summer's not here,"—Keeley steps forward, raising her hand— "I'll be Dylan's stand-in girlfriend. So that means I'm on Hayley and Luke's team. I can see the way you're splitting the group up."

Hayley beams proudly while the others laugh and we split into teams, with Hayley's squad having Luke, Paige, Landon, and Keeley, while I have Easton and Isaac, Dylan, Amelia, and Lainey. Thomas opted to be an umpire to keep the teams even.

Thomas starts the game, and within seconds, Dylan's tackling Luke to the sand—payback for his previous screamer, or specky as Hayley called it —and it lights a fire in us all.

There's laughter, fake tears, screaming, cheering from the sidelines, and a hell of a lot of fun being had. All while Keeley smiles in satisfaction, knowing the photographer is securing gold.

She's right. We need some good publicity.

Although, now that I think about it, he's probably been here for hours, since we haven't exactly been subtle. Who knows—maybe he got all of this before.

Dylan kicks the ball to Easton and he lifts Isaac into the air to catch it. But when he tries to pass it to Lainey, Luke intercepts before kicking our version of a goal. Hayley cheerfully gloats and an idea comes to my mind.

We're here together because of a role she wants in an upcoming movie. Her audition went well, but I need to make sure she gets the part. The producers wanted a relationship type. Well, according to the world, we're in a relationship, so I'm taking advantage. Some would say I'm playing *my* part.

"What's the score again, Cap?" she asks as she turns my way, raising a finger to her lip as though lost in thought.

"I think it's three to one," I reply, my lips curling into a smirk. "But team Jackman has an unfair advantage, and it's time we changed that."

"What?"

"Let's see how well they play without an Australian in the mix."

Hayley's lips quirk before panic takes over—perhaps noticing the mischief in my eyes. She turns to run, but I'm faster, catching her in seconds, throwing her over my shoulder, laughing when she squeals. "What are you doing?"

"Something I should have done weeks ago."

"What? Lose your mind?"

"Maybe."

"Dylan!" I call over my shoulder, patting Hayley's ass. "It's your turn to shine."

Laughter follows us as I run toward the water, fully clothed, with Hayley arguing in protest. "Don't even think about it, Reed. I know where you're headed."

I'm not actually going to throw her in, since the water is likely to be freezing, but a little teasing never hurt anyone.

I squeeze her ass again. "I thought this would be right up your alley. What happened to you being my wildcat?" She wriggles and I grin. "Trust me, it's going to be worth it. It's time we put on a show. Audiences will be eating out of the palm of your hand."

I cringe when my feet hit the water, but it's too late now. I'm committed and I'm not giving in. When I'm knee deep and shivering, I pretend to toss Hayley into the waves but catch her in my arms, lifting her before her feet get wet. Whether instinctively or from panic, she wraps her legs around my waist and frowns adorably as her hair blows across her flushed cheeks. "Reed, what are—"

I'm so struck by how beautiful she is that I can't stop myself from slamming my lips to hers, cutting her off mid-rant, the weight of my feelings crushing my chest as she melts into me.

But it's so fucking worth it.

She plays with my hair as my lips caress hers, her legs tightening around me while I hold her up, the waves crashing against my calves.

I rock involuntarily and her lips part in a gasp, making me desperate to seek out her tongue, but once again knowing that's exactly why I shouldn't.

With one hand secured underneath her, I cup her cheek with the other, working her mouth until she pulls back, gasping for air.

"That was some kiss, Boyfriend."

"Only the best for my girl."

"Then why no tongue?"

"I'm saving that until you beg."

Her eyes widen, but before she gets the chance to respond, the mother of all waves hits us out of nowhere, and nothing I do can shield us from the attack.

"Jesus Christ," I bellow as Hayley squeals, the water soaking us both, the cold instantly seeping through to my bones. "Time to get out." I shake, my voice a little higher than usual.

Hayley's laughter fills the air as I spin around and hightail it out of the water. When we've made it to the sand, she tries to wriggle free, but I shake my head and growl, carrying her in my arms as I jog back to our friends, cursing when the wind hits my wet clothes.

"Jesus." Hayley crosses her arms over her breasts. "My clothes are drenched and I didn't bring any extras."

"I brought a towel."

"Thank you. But I'm going to need your jumper too. It's bigger than mine and I need something to cover my ass."

"You need what?" I smirk and she rolls her eyes, shaking her head.

"Your *sweatshirt*, smartass."

Amelia has a towel ready when we get back, wrapping it around Hayley as I frown at the guys. "Where's my teamwork?"

"You should have thought of that before you tried to drown Hayley," Luke jokes, making me chuckle as my body trembles.

Being the nice guy that I am, I toss Hayley my sweatshirt and grab my towel, getting dry and redressed in record time. Unlike Hayley, I *did* bring a change of clothes—you never know when you might get wet—but I do miss the warmth of my "jumper."

When I'm done, my eyes lock on Hayley as she twists her wet hair on top of her head, my sweatshirt riding up to show off her skimpy black panties, the cheeks of her ass on display.

Glancing over her shoulder, she finds me watching and shakes her booty. "Enough with the distractions," I playfully scold. "You're going to get me in trouble one day." I chuckle at my own joke as someone lets out a strangled cough from behind me.

Landon cringes when I turn his way, apologizing under his breath, clearly embarrassed at getting caught staring at my girl.

I smile before putting him out of his misery. He's not the only one. "No harm done. You can look but don't touch."

His face reddens as he shakes his head. "It's not that. It's...ah...she's really famous, huh?" He whispers the last part and I chuckle again.

"She is, but she's still the same Hayley. Nothing has changed since I first introduced you." And something tells me it never will. She's a genuine soul like that.

Landon nods, his eyes flashing to Hayley as she comes sashaying over, but when his gaze locks on Keeley, his attention drifts, making me laugh. I should warn him he doesn't stand a chance, but like all our newer teammates, he can learn the hard way.

"I like this *sweatshirt*," Hayley teases as she reaches me, pronouncing the word sweatshirt pointedly. "I think I'm going to keep it."

"It looks better on you," I say honestly, letting my eyes linger where it hits her high on the legs. "Consider it yours."

Hayley's talking to her agent on the short drive back to my house, and when we arrive, she's still shivering. The tiniest shred of guilt settles in my chest until I remember her happiness after. Though I don't want her to be cold.

As she finishes her call, I run her a hot bath, laying out a towel and a fresh change of clothes.

I'm turning the tap off when she calls out, her voice getting louder as she approaches, seeking me out. "Reed?"

"In here."

She follows the sound of my voice and gasps when she steps through the door, her eyes on the steamy water. "Please tell me this is for me."

"Of course it is. It's only fair considering it's my fault you're cold."

Her eyes shift my way, her gaze raking over my body as she shivers again. "It's your fault I'm hot too. What are you doing about that?"

My mind runs wild with images I have no business conjuring. "Get in the bath, Hayls."

"Are you coming in?" Her blue eyes darken as a fire ignites, and I swallow a lump in my throat.

"Nope." *Bad idea.* "I'll have a quick shower and get us something to eat." I turn to leave, hoping to get away before she strips out of her clothes, but she grabs my wrist, stopping me in my tracks.

"Get in the bath, Reed. I *need* you. And I *need* it now."

Chapter Forty-One

REED

My eyes flit between the tub and Hayley's challenging gaze. *Why would I run her a bath?* I could have just as easily turned on the shower, although she probably would have invited me there too. *This is a bad idea.* Hayley naked in a small—okay, medium to large, more like a hot tub sized—bath is not something I should be wanting. No matter the size, she'll still be naked and... *Fuck, she's stripping my sweatshirt over her head.*

"Hayls," I groan, my voice strained. Did I mention this was a bad idea? "We—"

She turns to face me, standing in nothing but her panties, her breasts on display and— "Fuck, you're perfect."

What I wouldn't give to wrap my mouth around her tits as I bite down on her nipples, listening to her cries when I slide into her, burying my cock to the hilt. I'd— *Shit.* What am I doing?

I glance away and she giggles. "Gotta get naked for a bath, Reed."

"It's a hot tub," I growl. "Swimwear is fine."

"I don't have any swimwear. And it's a hot tub now? Where are the jets?"

"I'll get in if you keep your panties on."

Hayley curls her fingers around my wrist again, and I squeeze my eyes shut. If I get in that bath, with my heart pounding the way it is, there is no going back for me.

"If you don't want this, Reed, I'm not going to force you." Her concerned voice enters my subconscious and I groan again. "It's just—"

Dammit. Spinning around, I grab her by the shoulders and walk her backward until her knees hit the tub. "I *do* want this, Hayls. *That's* the problem."

"Why is it a problem? We've set the boundaries. And—"

"I want to obliterate them." Turning her toward the mirror, I stand behind her and cup her breasts, brushing her hair to the side before sucking the flesh below her ear. She tastes like salt, sand, and reckless decisions, and as badly as I wish things were different, they're not. "I *want* to obliterate our boundaries, Hayls. But that's why I *need* to keep my cool," I whisper softly in her ear while simultaneously rolling my thumbs over her nipples, my "cool" well and truly gone.

She arches her back and a sigh rushes from her lips. "If you were really my girl,"—I glide a hand down her taut stomach, skating my palm across her skin, stopping when I reach her panties—"make no mistake. I would be tearing these apart, bending you over the edge of the tub, and fucking you from behind, pounding into you while my fingers tease your ass." I sink my hand beneath the thin material barely covering her pussy and run a finger through her heat, groaning as her body turns to jelly.

"Oh God, Reed. I want that. Let's do that."

"Hayls," I growl again, cupping her pussy as I bend her over the counter, my hardening cock pressing against her back, "we can't do that."

"Why? You're already—" I plunge a finger into her soaked pussy and massage her walls, cutting her off as she cries out. "Reed. Jesus. I need you inside me."

"I *am* inside you." I wiggle my finger to prove my point and add a second, making her laugh as she moans.

"This is good, so good. But wouldn't it be better if you were fucking me?"

Jesus. My balls tighten as I picture her pussy taking me in, inch by inch, and I consider her request until my heart pounds and I silently curse. "No," I whisper honestly. "It'd be so much worse."

She rocks into me as she giggles, clearly not taking me seriously, and I wish I could give in. I wish I could throw all my reasoning out the window, but I can't. If I fuck her, I won't be able to hold back anymore.

I pride myself on being able to separate sex and emotion, but with Hayley, I'm already too far gone to do that, and that's fucked me over before. I can't lose her like I lost Bria, because with Hayley, I'm not sure I'll survive it.

Ignoring my throbbing cock, I remove my fingers from her heat and pinch her clit, groaning when she jolts against me.

"I can't give you my cock, Hayls. But I promise I'm going to destroy you. I'm going to ruin you for all future men." I pause, the words tasting sour on my tongue, but for now, that's our reality, and I'm sticking to it.

I open my mouth to say more when Hayley's high-pitched mewl fills the small space and she grabs my hand, stilling me before I can pinch her again. She turns in my arms, pushing me back. "You've already done that, Reed. But by all means, do your worst." She curls her fingers under the hem of my tee and lifts it over my head, dusting her fingers across my skin. Her gaze lingers over my tattoos and when she reaches the waistband of my shorts, she attempts to pull them down until I grab her wrist, forcing her to stop.

"Not yet. This is about *you*."

Gripping under her ass, I lift her up and walk us back to the counter, checking to make sure she doesn't shiver again when she sits on the cold, hard surface. "Are we good?" I ask when she doesn't react. "Are you still cold?"

"No, we're good." She spreads her legs and grabs my waist, dragging me in until I'm settled in front of her. "I'm hot, Reed. And I need whatever it is you're about to do to me."

"Good." *Because I need it too.*

Pushing her panties to the side, I step back and drop to my knees, spreading her with my fingers, my eyes glued to her pussy as it drips for me. All for me. "Tell me this is mine and I'll give you what you want."

"Yes," she rushes out, grabbing my hair, trying to shove my head down. "It's yours. Touch me."

"Uh-uh. Not yet. Patience."

Rubbing my fingers along the side of her folds, I tease her as she bucks the air, seeking more, desperate for my touch. "Reed."

"I know, Baby. Do you want my fingers or my tongue?"

"Oh, God. Is your tongue an option?"

"It is. But only if you beg."

I circle her clit with the tip of my finger, careful not to touch her as she cries out. "Jesus Christ. I want your tongue. *Please.*"

"You *want* it?" I stare at her deadpan, gently caressing her entrance before gliding my fingers over her ass, circling back as her legs clench.

"I need it, Reed. *Now.*"

"Now?"

"*Please.*" Her desperate voice makes my cock pulse and I immediately give in, burying my face between her legs. And the first taste is more delicious than I ever could have imagined. Better than the taste of her on my fingers.

I bite down on her clit, sucking the bud into my mouth, soothing it with my tongue. Hayley's hips jolt as her body flies off the counter, her pussy rolling against my mouth.

With my free hand, I push her back down, holding her still as I lavish her heat with attention, working her into a frenzy. She bucks and shakes, her breaths ragged as I feast, and just when I think she's going to snap, I sink two fingers inside her, sucking her clit while I slowly add a third.

"Reed," she cries out as her body shakes.

"Is that good, Baby? Do you like my fingers filling your hole?"

"Yes. God. Yes."

"Do you need more?"

"More?"

"Another finger."

"Oh, God. I don't think—"

"You can take it, Baby. Breathe." She's so tight, I struggle not to think about what it'll feel like when she takes my cock. How her pussy will strangle me. How—

Dammit. I groan out loud as I insert another finger, stretching her pussy as I pump harder.

With my thumb massaging her clit, I scissor my fingers and kiss a path across her stomach, making my way up to her breasts, sucking her nipples before making my way back down.

"Oh, fuck. That feels... God, Reed." Her body tenses as her walls tighten around me, exactly how I imagine she'd tighten around my cock. My length throbs and I stifle a growl from deep in the back of my throat.

"You're so fucking tight, Baby," I rasp, getting my head back in the moment.

"I told you," she rushes out. "It's been a while. And never like this."

"Never?"

"Never."

"Sounds like you've been with the wrong men."

"Yes."

"Does this feel good?" I stare into her eyes as I thrust my fingers, and her head falls back as she moans.

"So good. God. So fucking good."

The more I work her, the more she squirms beneath me, soaking my fingers, making me want to taste her again. So I do. Replacing my fingers with my mouth, I flatten my tongue against her slick heat, circling her back entrance with my thumb. She bucks her hips again, rolling her pussy against my face and I groan.

"That's it, Hayls. Fuck my face. I need it. Let me feel how much you want me."

"Oh, God."

She does as I ask, moaning and gasping as she rocks against me, giving me everything she's got, her body trembling as her release builds.

"I'm close. I'm—"

"What do you need? Tell me, Hayls, and it's yours."

Lifting to her elbows, she stares at me pointedly and I snicker, knowing what she's thinking. "Not that."

"Fine. I'll have your fingers back. I want them inside me."

"Done."

Opening her wider, I press three fingers inside her and curl them against her wall, massaging gently as I lick her throbbing clit, taking in her moaning cues as her breaths quicken.

"Are you ready for four again?"

"Yes, fill me. God, this is so good."

"Are you imagining my cock?"

"Yes."

"Are you picturing what it would be like for me to take you from behind, pounding into you while my fingers work your clit?"

"God, I am now. Harder, Reed."

"That's it, Baby. You're almost there. Give it to me."

I suck her clit, and she cries out as her orgasm hits, her body convulsing against me. I continue my ministrations, alternating between licking and sucking until she whimpers, begging me to stop.

"Not yet," I demand, holding her still. "I need more. I think you've got another in you." I suck her clit again, curling my fingers inside her as I push my thumb deep into her ass, loving when her body spasms and her voice breaks as she screams out my name. "That's better."

She jolts, struggling to catch her breath as another orgasm consumes her, her body bucking uncontrollably until I pull back, gently holding her waist, keeping her still as I lightly caress her flushed skin. "I've got you, Hayls. I've got you."

Her movements slow as her breathing calms, and when she's finally still, I lift her again, carrying her over to the bath, holding her on the edge as I add more hot water, checking the temperature before I lower her in.

With my shorts still on, I climb in behind her and pull her in close, wrapping my arms around her stomach.

She moans as she shifts back, wriggling against my cock, and I silently groan as it twitches.

Needing a distraction, I grab the body wash—one of those exotic types that smells like coconut and island breezes—pumping the liquid onto my hands. Without thinking of the consequences, I massage the soap into her skin, coating her thighs, her arms, her stomach, careful not to touch her breasts.

She moans again, resting her head on my shoulder, and as she closes her eyes, a soft sigh escapes her.

I hold my breath, staring down at her, acutely aware that this might just be the *worst* idea I've ever had. I should have fucked her, because this is far more intimate than that would have been. And I don't need that right now.

My heart jolts and I hate myself for wanting this more than I should. For wanting *her* more than I should...and fuck...

I shouldn't be touching her. I'm taking advantage and—

"You really are trying to make me fall in love with you, aren't you?" Hayley's tranquil whisper cuts into my thoughts and I chuckle to hide my true feelings.

"I don't have to try." I laugh again. "Is it working?"

She hums under her breath, and I swear she whispers "more than it should" but then again, maybe I'm hearing what I want to hear.

We fall silent for a beat, and I let myself take in the moment, closing my eyes to imagine a different life—a life where this is real—where I finally get the girl. But the water sloshes, snapping me out of it as Hayley spins around.

"I'm ready to return the favor." She bounces her eyebrows, her exaggerated grin eliciting a nervous tremble which I cover with a smile.

"Nah, tonight was about you." I squeeze her hand, my gaze locked firmly on her face. "But don't worry, my turn will come." I hate that I'm lying, but we can't do this again. It's not right when I'm feeling this way.

"Are you sure?" Hayley crinkles her nose, making me smile again as I rub the little crease between her brows.

"I'm sure. So you better be ready for me." I wink, an uncomfortable feeling settling in my chest. *What the fuck am I doing?*

We don't stay in the bath too much longer, and after we dry off, Hayley suggests a movie night since it's only just gotten dark. And that works for me because I'm not ready for her to leave. I want to soak up these moments as much as I can because before too long, they'll be gone.

She picks a comedy I've never seen and I try to get into it, but I can't concentrate, my mind whirring while Hayley's amused giggles echo beside me, completely oblivious to my inner turmoil. Or perhaps, pretending she has no idea just like I suspect Bria always did.

Either way, she's content, and while I love that for her, I'm going crazy.

As though her body clock aligns with the movie, Hayley yawns as soon as the end credits roll and we hit that awkward part of the night. "You're welcome to stay here..." I begin but quickly add, "or I can drive you home." I want her to stay, always. But the choice is hers.

"You don't need to drive me. I can Uber or—"

"Or what?" I cut her off. "Hitchhike? I'll drive you."

"Fine. Then I'll stay." She quirks her lips as she playfully rolls her eyes.

"Good. You take the bed; I'll sleep on the couch."

"What? You slept on the couch last time I stayed over. Don't you have a spare room...or two?"

"I do. I actually have three. But it's been a while since I had guests over and I can't be bothered—"

"Looks like you're sleeping next to me then," she cuts in, her grin playful. "You'd refuse to screw me even if I was naked and begging, so it's safe to say I can trust you." I cringe and she laughs. "What? It's true."

She stares me down in challenge and I relent, nodding. "I'll sleep on the bed."

"Good, it's settled. I like the left side." She grabs my hand and drags me toward my bedroom while I swallow a lump in my throat, obediently following her.

"Good thing I prefer the right."

My phone vibrates across the floor, bringing me out of a dream to see that I'm wrapped around Hayley, my palm dangerously close to her breasts. I draw in a shallow breath and hold it, then carefully extract myself, refusing to enjoy it, even for a second.

Grabbing my phone, I sit up to check the time, my eyes widening to find that it's ten.

I never sleep that late.

Hayley softly moans as she seeks me out in her sleep and I still my body, careful not to wake her. She settles again and I relax, checking the notification that woke me.

> LUKE: You sure put on a show yesterday, Reed, my man. Amelia wants to know if it's real?

> REED: Still fake

In theory. In reality, it's way beyond that on my end. No matter how hard I try to fight it.

> REED: I did all that for the cameras

Sort of. Maybe. At least, most of it was.

> LUKE: Well it worked. Check out the gossip guru in The Hollywood Blaze

Without responding, I do a search on Hayley's name, assuming the article is about her, and immediately find what I'm looking for.

Has Hayley Jackman found her Prince Charming? Maybe she is the right choice for the role of Cynthia in the new Tristan Klines romantic drama. Only time will tell but this reporter is on her side.

Thank fuck.

It's all working out the way we planned. Hayley's going to get the part and all will be good in the world.

So why does my chest ache? And does that mean it's almost over?

Because, hell, I don't want to let her go.

CHAPTER FORTY-TWO

HAYLEY

"And cut."

I pull away from Aiden—the actor playing Cynthia's love interest in *Reckless Desire*—and hold his gaze before I smile. That was intense. I've had chemistry readings before—hell, my chemistry session with my *Jaded Beginnings* co-star was one for the record books—and yet, I have no idea how this one went.

For the first time in a while, my confidence is shot.

Reed has spent the past week calming my nerves after the images from the beach hit the media. But while the headlines have been mostly positive, I haven't allowed myself to hope. Not after so many failed auditions.

Jaded Beginnings was amazing for my career. It was released over a month ago and it's still making waves. Yet, I can't get another role. It's not like I expected my agent's phone to be ringing off the hook, or for me to be getting roles without auditioning, but I didn't expect the level of negativity I received because of the role. Or the personal attacks.

I've had directors politely, or not so politely, remind me it was *one* hit, suggesting I remain grounded. I've had fellow actresses whispering in the waiting room, thinking I can't hear what they're saying.

"Wait until she falls from grace."

"I don't see the appeal."

"One movie and she thinks she's a star."

And while I know it's just talk—or tall poppy syndrome at its finest—it still bloody hurts. I wonder if they even know what tall poppy syndrome is. Or even know that they're doing it—cutting people down that they perceive to be achieving more than them, trying to make them feel smaller.

Why can't we all build each other up? Support each other. Congratulate each other on the wins, sympathise on the losses.

I've been a mess these past few weeks—travelling back and forth to LA hoping to increase my chances of securing a role, without any luck—but with me through it all was Reed, keeping me smiling, making sure I value my worth.

And now...it all comes down to this.

"Wow." Aiden's the first to speak and my eyes dart to his. "I'm torn between wanting to kiss the fuck out of you and tear the world down to find the man who broke your heart. That was intense."

"Thank you?" *I think.*

"Aiden's right." The director smiles, drawing my attention to find him watching me in awe. "I felt everything you were feeling in that moment. And if I didn't know any better, I'd believe this was real life."

I rush out another thank you and the director laughs. This can't be real life. Because that would mean I might finally be getting another break.

"As we said when you first arrived, it's down to you and two other actresses." More *experienced* actresses was the term he actually used, but I let that slide. "We're seeing them both this afternoon and we'll make a decision after that."

"Thank you. I appreciate you taking the time to meet with me again. I look forward to hearing from you."

I look forward to hearing from you? My God, who am I? I'm usually so bubbly in auditions. I'm usually *myself.*

I turn to leave, but Aiden calls out before I've taken a step. "I'll walk with you. I'm taking a break." He loops his arm through mine and waves over his shoulder, turning as the door clicks shut. "For the record, I want you for the part. And I told them that *before* you came in and blew us all away."

"What?" My eyes widen.

"Mate. What do you mean, what?" His smooth American accent makes way for an Aussie twang and my jaw drops.

"You're Australian?"

"Fuckin' oath, I am. I'm an Aussie through and through. And I've been a fan of yours since I first saw you guest star on *Wilde Country.*"

"Jesus. That was years ago."

"It sure was. But you being an Aussie isn't why I want you for the role."

"Why then?"

"Because when they showed me your first audition, you *were* Cynthia. I saw *Hayley* when you said hello, and then she was gone and I will never unsee that. You embodied her, and in my opinion, the other two actresses failed at that."

"Wow. Thank you."

"Stop saying thank you. At the end of the day, I don't get any say in the final decision, but know that I'm rooting for you."

"Rooting?" I question and he nods.

"What can I say, I've been here a while. Just wait...you'll be talking like an American soon enough."

When we reach the street, Aiden says goodbye and heads left while I walk right to meet Reed, our conversation running on repeat in my mind. *I embodied her. I am Cynthia.*

The park where Reed's waiting comes into view, and he immediately steps into my line of sight, his gorgeous smile hitting me in the chest.

No matter what happens, I owe it to Reed. If I am Cynthia, it's his support that got me here.

I got the part. *I got the freaking part!* I can see the headline now.

***Hayley Jackman to play Cynthia Rose in* Reckless Desire.**

Releasing a squeal, I jump onto my bed and bounce in celebration, shaking my ass. I got it. I got it. I got it.

It *worked*. Reed and I *did* it.

Our fake relationship is coming to an end.

My stomach twists but I ignore it. Just like I've been ignoring the chest flutters and the warmth. We're friends. And when it's all said and done, I can't lose that. I need him too much.

Falling onto my mattress, I push my feelings aside and grab my phone to text him but hover over his number, calling instead.

"Hey Baby," he answers smoothly, his voice holding all the warmth I've come to treasure, and my traitorous heart jolts.

"Hey to you too." I smile, working hard to focus on my excitement instead of my future with Reed. "Are you busy?"

"It's the offseason." He chuckles and I picture his soft eyes as he smiles. "I have all the time in the world. I was actually on my way over."

"You were?" My brows furrow but a giddiness runs through me.

"Yep. I wanted to talk to you about something."

"About what? Tell me now. You know I hate surprises."

"It'll be easier in person. Are you home?"

"*Reed*," I warn, knowing it's useless.

"Please, Hayls."

"Okay, fine. My best offer... Two truths and a lie, but it has to be related to whatever it is you want to talk about."

Reed chuckles again and I thank my lucky stars he's good with my crazy. "Okay..." He trails off, probably giving it some thought. "Alright. I'm ready. One... I'm thinking about getting a dog. Two... My parents watched your movie. And three... I have a feeling you're going to get the part."

I squeal at number three, no longer able to keep it to myself.

"I got the part."

"You did?"

"I did."

"Hell fucking yes. Hayley! I'm so happy for you. And proud. I'm almost to your place. We have to celebrate."

"Wait," I call out before he hangs up. "You're not getting a dog, are you?"

"Nope. Not at this stage of my life."

"Oh my God." I cringe, covering my face as I audibly sigh. "Your parents watched *Jaded Beginnings*?"

"They sure did." He chuckles softly. "They saw the trailer and I couldn't stop them. They wanted to support you."

My chest fills with nervous energy. "I appreciate that. But I'm not sure I'm happy about it."

"Why? You were fucking phenomenal. And you're going to be just as amazing in *Reckless Desire*."

My heart races as the nerves make way for a smile. "Thank you. Now get your ass over here so you can tell me what you wanted to say."

"And celebrate."

"And celebrate. See you soon." I giggle before hanging up, but when Reed's parents drift back to my mind, my smile fades. If his parents watched my film, does that mean they know about me? I mean, of course they do. It's been all over the media—and Reed said they wanted to meet me—but do they *know* know about me? Or have they been fed the same lies? I can't imagine Reed lying to his parents, but I have no idea how he's playing this.

I spiral a little as I wait for Reed to arrive. I've hit my limit on random emotions today and I'm ready to escape.

With the world believing Reed and I have been dating for a few months now, the concierge sends him up without question, and when I open the door, he pulls me into his arms, spinning me around in the hallway.

"Reed," I squeal as my grip tightens. "I'm going to fall."

"Not possible. I'd never let that happen."

He comes to a stop and gently lowers me to my feet, holding me until I'm settled. "You did it, Hayls. You got the part."

"We did it," I correct him. "You deserve some of the credit."

"Okay, fine. I'll accept it. I never saw myself as an actor, but with you, it comes naturally."

"I think it's because we're only *half* acting." The words leave my mouth and I freeze, backtracking. "You know, since we're good friends."

Reed smiles genuinely and it takes my breath away. "Definitely. But either way, I'm excited for you."

"Me too. And we can celebrate in a minute. First, what did you want to talk about?"

"You really can't wait, can you?"

"Nope. Come on. I've already guessed it's about your parents."

"Yep." Reed sighs, his demeanor suddenly changing. "It's been over a month now and I still can't convince them to take the vacation I paid for. Even after telling them about the money Jace willingly accepted. When they asked him about it, he said it was a loan and that he plans to pay me back. Then proceeded to make them feel guilty about that too, saying it's because *they* never loan him anything. And as much as it pains me...I can't let my mother fall back into another state of depression. I refuse to do that to her."

My heart breaks for him but I'm also a little enraged. "God, I wish we could do something about him. He deserves a wake-up call from someone not connected to your family. From me. A hard shake should do it, maybe even a strong knee to the balls." Reed chuckles and though I know what he's going to say, I'm glad I at least made him happy for a beat. "In all seriousness, Reed, what the fuck is his problem?"

"I wish I knew."

"I mean this with all due respect, but has he ever seen anyone? A psychiatrist maybe? You mentioned he's narcissistic, but I'm wondering if he's a sadist too."

"He's both those things, Hayls. But he's her son. Mom will never cut him out of her life. No matter what."

"I hate that for her." And Reed. I hate that for Reed. "How can I help?"

"Help?"

"Yeah. I'm here to help in any way I can. Isn't that what you wanted to talk to me about? Please tell me you want me to hurt him?"

"Actually,"—Reed shakes his head, gripping the back of his neck—"I wanted to ask if you'd come with me."

"On vacation?" A vacation would be nice. I saw the resort he booked and—

"Home."

"Home?" I gasp as a laugh rushes from my lungs. "To your parents' place?"

"Yeah. Their birthdays are coming up and I think it will make them— Mom—happy to see you."

And everything he does, he does to make her happy.

"What do they know about us?"

"That we're dating."

"You didn't tell them it was fake?"

Reed's face contorts as he grimaces. "I couldn't. She'd mention it to my brother and he'd broadcast it to the media."

"Shit."

"Yep."

"He really deserves an ass kicking."

"Believe me, I know."

"When are their birthdays?" I hide my concern. While I want to be able to support Reed, I don't know my schedule for the foreseeable future; I don't know when *Reckless Desire* is filming. And on top of that, I think this is out of my depth. Jokingly threatening his brother is one thing, but meeting the parents and trying to help is another thing entirely.

"Their birthdays aren't until early July. I'm only asking now because if I mention it to Mom, it might lift her spirits for a while."

Jesus. "You know I'd love to, but by then, you'll hopefully have sorted things out with Bria. Shouldn't she go with you? I'll bet she's been before and—"

Reed frowns, cutting me off, making me feel awkward enough to glance away.

"Even if Bria and I *were* best friends again, I want *you* to come. *Our* friendship has nothing to do with mine and Bria's."

"Reed, it has *everything* to do with that. I think you should talk to her. I think you both need to get everything off your chests, including telling her how you feel." I have no idea why I'm bringing this up now, but the word vomit is happening and I can't seem to stop.

"I've tried calling her back. Just like you asked. But she's no longer answering."

"Because you ignored her. Try *harder*."

"Why are you pushing this?"

Good freaking question. "It's a big deal, Reed. She was your best friend for *years*."

"Even so, I don't think talking is going to help. I doubt our friendship will ever be the same."

Reed runs a hand through his hair with a sigh, and my stomach swirls with guilt. "I'm sorry."

"It's not your fault, Hayls. It was changing *long* before I got myself a girlfriend."

I smile but he's wrong. "What about before we were friends? It was good before that, right?"

"Was it?" Reed's forehead creases and he frowns again. "Was it good for me to have feelings for her and keep it to myself, essentially lying about our friendship?"

"She had to know and—"

"If she *did* know, was it good for her to act like she *didn't*?"

I cringe as a tightness settles in my chest, my heart breaking for him. Or maybe for me. I don't know what I feel, but I know what to say. "No. That's not good. I just wish you could work it all out. I hate seeing you sad."

"I'm not sad, Hayls. I truly believe it came to a natural end. And maybe that would have happened sooner if we'd both just admitted our feelings, or lack of feelings in her case. We'll always be friends, but the closeness isn't there. And I don't think we'll get it back. I don't even think I want to."

"*Reed?*"

"Nope. I'm happy, Hayls. I've got *you*." He smiles but there's something about it that doesn't quite reach his eyes, only before I can question it, he moves on.

"Anyway, we can talk about the details later. How are we going to celebrate?"

CHAPTER FORTY-THREE

HAYLEY

For the next few weeks, Reed and I act as though nothing has changed, neither of us bringing up our approaching end date. And with my stalker, or overzealous fan, seemingly giving up since we went to the police, life is good.

With my days spent at the studio and my nights with Reed, you'd think I had it all. But I don't. It feels like it's all about to slip away.

Script in hand for our final readthrough, I find my place at the reading table and sit down, taking in the nervous energy filling the room.

The *Reckless Desire* filming schedule comes out today, and while that should be an exciting time, it signifies the beginning of the end of our relationship, and I'm not ready to *fake* a breakup with Reed yet.

I need more time.

"I know we've been keeping you all in suspense," our production manager says as we quieten down. "But I'm excited to announce that we have our William."

About time.

My co-star, Brooklyn, subtly glances my way, her smile trapped between her teeth. *Reckless Desire* is an emotional romance that follows the relationship between Cynthia and Matteo across a decade of time. William is the antagonist, and they've been struggling to find the right actor for the job. He needs brotherly chemistry with the character Matteo, and while I personally love my Aussie co-star, Aiden can be difficult to work with if you don't meet his vibe. And apparently, everyone before now has failed, almost delaying production.

"Can you please extend a warm welcome to Cameron Walker."

Cameron walks in and I let out a squeal, jumping up to rush over, throwing my hands around his neck. He played an angel in *Jaded Beginnings*, and while he was only a minor role and didn't join us on the promotional tour, we got along well during filming.

"Congratulations." I smile wide as I step out of the hug. "I'm so relieved that it's you."

"Oh, yeah?"

"Yeah. It's always nice to see a familiar face."

Cameron smiles before introducing himself around, shooting me a wink as he sits down.

Our readthrough goes smoothly, and the next thing you know, they're handing us the filming schedule before it's time to leave. The room stills as everyone falls silent, and when I read page two, my stomach knots.

"Six weeks in Texas?" Brooklyn rushes out, her eyes wide, expressing the shock that I feel. "I thought it was only two?"

Our production manager frowns, his nose scrunching as he delivers the news. "The studio decided it would be more authentic if we filmed the bulk of the movie in Texas." *Well, obviously, since it's set there, but still...* "You'll all be accommodated and receive great bonuses."

"Can they do that?" Brooklyn whispers to herself.

"I think they just did."

I call my agent on the way home, and she reluctantly admits that she knew the extended travel was in the cards. One of the producers mentioned it when they negotiated my contract, but she didn't think it would worry me. I've always said I'd travel. And she got me more money because of it.

And in turn, more money for *her*.

I can't really blame her. She's not wrong. I *did* say I'd be happy to travel, but that was then. Now, I feel differently.

Now I've got Reed.

When I get off the phone, I redirect my Uber to Reed's place, hoping he's home, and when I find his truck in the drive, I breathe a sigh of relief.

"Hey, you. Come in." He smiles, welcoming me inside, not even questioning my appearance when I open the door without knocking.

Without giving a response, I beeline for his living room, falling onto the couch with a dramatic huff, only then telling him my problems. "I'm filming in Texas." I groan as he sits down opposite me, making him chuckle.

"Hey, Baby. How was your day? I missed you."

"I missed you too." I roll my eyes, ignoring the way my heart flutters when he plays pretend and we're not in public. "That's why I'm pouting." Since it's still the offseason, we've been seeing each other most days. It's going to feel strange not spending time with him.

"What are you worried about? You knew you were filming in Texas. What's changed?"

"The timing. I'll be gone for at least a month and a half now."

Reed's eyes widen but he quickly schools his features before assessing my reaction, seemingly working out what I'm trying to say. "You're going to miss me?" He plays down my feelings, a smile lighting up his face.

"I am." I pout again. "I've kind of gotten used to having you around."

"Yeah. It sucks to be you."

"Shut up." I throw a cushion at his face. "You're going to miss me too."

"When do you leave?" he asks, and while he doesn't respond to my remark, I don't miss the way the light dims in his eyes.

"Mid-June." I cringe. "I'll be gone for your parents' birthdays."

"That's alright. They'll understand. And that timing isn't so bad." He surprises me by smiling wide, his lips comically stilted. "I'll be busy with preseason by then. I won't even remember your name." He laughs at his joke but I call him out on the lie.

"Preseason starts in July."

"Officially, yes, but we start training together in June."

"Okay, good. So what you're saying is that I wouldn't get to see you that often anyway."

"Exactly."

I'm not sure which one of us needs more reassurance, but an emptiness overwhelms me, and I panic at how little time I have left before everything changes. Again. "We should probably break up soon then, right? We could blame my upcoming travel, the long distance, and—"

"No." Reed's quick to cut me off.

"No?"

"No. Our relationship is too strong for that. We'd definitely try and make it work."

He folds his arms over his chest and I bite back a smile, loving the seriousness in his expression. But when he winks, I grin. "You're right. We would do that. Should we also stage a big dramatic airport scene? I've always wanted to do that."

"Definitely. Can there be tears?"

"From you?" My eyes widen before he scoffs.

"Hell, no. From *you*. I'd be disappointed if there weren't any, considering you're constantly bragging about your ability to cry on cue."

"I told you that *once*."

"Me, yes. But I've heard you tell plenty of others."

Dammit. He's right. I do brag about that often. It's my party trick. But still, how dare he call me out?

"You know what? No tears for you." I waggle my finger. "You don't deserve it."

"We'll see." He bounces his eyebrows and I smile wide, keeping things light while inside I'm struggling. But of course, Reed, being the intuitive and caring guy that he is, notices.

"What are you really worried about?" he asks, leaning forward to grab my hand, running his thumb back and forth across my skin. "You're not yourself at the moment."

"I wasn't lying." My smile softens as I stare into his eyes. "I'm really going to miss you."

And I'm a little terrified about what the future will bring.

I n the lead-up to my filming in Texas, Reed and I keep up the happy couple charade, parading ourselves around whenever we can, showing the world how solid we are, smiling for photographers, signing autographs, waving while out on romantic adventures. Presenting ourselves as the golden couple they want us to be. And the media love it. Just like Reed said...they're eating it up.

Hollywood's newest IT couple, Reed Coombs and Hayley

Jackman, spotted on a romantic night out in the Marina District.

Are wedding bells in the cards for NFL star Reed Coombs and Hollywood starlet Hayley Jackman? Sources say Coombs was seen holding a distinct turquoise blue bag. And you know what that means.

Leading lady Hayley Jackman shines in her first photo as Cynthia Rose, looking every bit the part of America's sweetheart.

It's all going to plan except for one teeny-tiny minute change in our relationship—Reed hasn't touched me since I got the part. Since the *bath* incident. Since the moment he romantically washed me while his obvious erection pressed into my back. It's as though an unspoken agreement took place to keep things platonic between us after taking it too far. So while in public we are still very much a couple, behind the scenes, it's all about the friendship.

And I've got to say, he may be on to something because it's never been better.

Which I'm sure is why as he stands before me, staging our dramatic airport goodbye, the tears in my eyes are real.

"I don't want to go," I say honestly, dropping my forehead to his chest, as emotion overwhelms me. "I'm excited for the experience, but God, I'm going to miss you."

Reed chuckles as though I'm joking, grabbing my face in his hands, lifting my head until our eyes meet. "We'll talk every day. And you'll be so busy, you'll barely notice we're apart. As will I."

I bite my lip as I nod, standing tall, while inside I'm barely keeping my emotions in check. "You're right. Filming in the studio will be nothing compared to my Texas schedule. I have night shoots, early mornings, and multiple locations. We wouldn't have time to see each other anyway."

"Exactly, and before you know it, you'll be back."

"And we'll be breaking up." I whisper the last part and Reed frowns.

"That's the plan, but let's take it one step at a time."

Someone rushes past us, lightly bumping my shoulder, and it pulls my attention. I check my phone, cursing when I see that it's almost time for me to leave.

Reed must have noticed the same because the mood shifts between us, a somber energy replacing the fun. "This is it. Our big moment."

He pulls me into his hold, wrapping his arms around me while I snuggle into him, reluctant to let go. And the second I breathe him in, the tears fall.

"Hey, now." He pulls back and gently brushes his thumb under my eyes, catching the drops. "You really can cry on cue?"

I nod by way of answer, because if I told him that's what I'm doing, I'd be lying. There's nothing fake about it.

Movement catches my eye, but when I glance in that direction there's nobody there. Seems like my brain will conjure anything to focus on something other than the heartache I'm feeling

Reed blows out a breath, his gaze flashing toward security. "I better let you go though."

I nod again, unable to speak.

"Call me when you land?"

Another nod.

Grabbing my bag, I squeeze his hand and study his features, committing them to memory, and when I finally turn away, I internally curse myself. *What am I doing?* I left my friends and family back in Australia with no immediate plans to see them again, and not a single tear fell. I'll be seeing Reed again in a month and a half—this isn't a big deal.

I'm acting crazy.

"See ya, Hayls," Reed calls out. "Talk soon."

I wave over my shoulder as more tears prick my eyes, taking a deep breath to calm them. *I can do this. I can do this. I can—*

"Hayls, wait."

I spin to find Reed jogging toward me, but before I can question him, he's cupping my face in his hands and slamming his mouth to mine.

My lips part as I startle, but when my brain catches up, I curl my fingers into his shirt, pulling him close and holding on for dear life, meeting his fervor.

With his thumbs under my chin, Reed tilts my head to deepen the kiss, and my heart pounds as his name escapes my lips.

"Reed."

He groans in the back of his throat, his hands sinking into my hair, his tongue seeking entry. And for the first time, I pour everything I have into the kiss, molding my mouth with his, tasting him, savoring it all as though this is the last time our lips are ever going to touch.

And maybe it is.

Reed's hand falls to my back, and he pulls me in closer, bending slightly until we're flush. My knees go weak and my pulse spikes, but it's not until my entire body heats that I realize I'm screwed.

I'm not feeling this way because we're friends. I'm falling in love with him.

In fact, I'd say I've been falling for a while now.

All while he's in denial about loving somebody else.

Chapter Forty-Four

REED

It's been three weeks since Hayley left, and I still can't get our goodbye kiss out of my head. I think about it every time we speak. I think about it when I'm alone. Hell, I still think about it when I'm training with the guys.

Which is not at all convenient.

I'm consumed by her. She's ingrained in my mind. Some might say I'm obsessed. And it's driving me crazy.

This is supposed to be fake. We're supposed to be friends. But there's nothing fake or platonic about the way I feel.

Only how the hell can I tell if it's real? I've once again fallen for my best friend, like it's my fucking MO. *What the hell is wrong with me?*

Now I get to spend the entire weekend with my family while they undoubtedly ask me a million questions about Hayley and I work hard to pretend I'm okay.

My problems are small compared to what they're going through—the least I can do is keep the smiles on their faces—but they're still fucking problems.

After a long drive from the airport, I pull up in front of my parents' modest property and stare at the yellow front door, willing it to morph into something else. Somewhere else.

I wouldn't say I had a rough childhood. For the most part I was loved, and my parents were there cheering me on, supporting me, nurturing my potential. But it came in waves. And I haven't completely moved on. Not that I'd ever tell them that.

Out of the corner of my eye, the old lace privacy curtain shifts and I know I have about ten seconds before my mother walks out. Nothing happens around here without her knowing about it.

Right on cue, the door swings open, and she rushes toward me, her arms wide as I jump out of my rental.

"What are you hiding away for?" she asks as I bend down, letting her wrap me in her hold, rocking me tightly until she's gotten her fill. "I've missed you. It's been months."

"I know. I thought it was best to give you some time and—"

"He's at a music festival out of state," Mom cuts me off, smiling as though this is news to me.

But it's not.

Dad mentioned the festival was this weekend, so rather than coming for their birthdays last week, I held off and wired him the money to buy Jace tickets, under the guise that he won them. Dad even told him I wasn't coming home this year. But I have no doubt that Mom will tell him when he gets home.

Either way, for now, it's easier. If Hayley wasn't going to be here, there was no way I was going to face him alone.

"I already know," I admit. "It's a shame I won't see him," I lie and Mom laughs to herself, flashing me a knowing grin.

"Your father?"

"Yep." I nod, smiling to hide the pain. Mom's happy now, grinning from ear to ear, but according to Dad, the moments of happiness have been few and far between, especially in the last few weeks.

I've always wished I could do more, but since Mom's in denial about how awful Jace is, and my dad would do anything to keep her happy, this is the best I've got. *Being here* is the best I can do. Making her happy. Making *them* happy. Being their golden boy. The kid they never had to worry about. The son that made them proud. Did his chores. Passed his tests. Brought laughter into the home. *Helped.*

Whenever someone would speak about my brother in a negative light, Mom would change the subject to me, talking about a trophy I'd won, or the little old lady I'd walked across the street.

When I was younger, I faked all that, but as I grew, that version of me became real, much in the same way my feelings for Hayley have.

Which is why I can't trust them. Not yet.

"I'm so happy you're here, Reed." Mom interrupts my thoughts as she steps back, her motherly gaze running over me, assessing my well-being, as if she can tell how I am simply by looking at me.

"Shall we go inside?" she says after a beat, presumably deciding I'm good, even though I'm not. "Martha's over and she'd love to see you. The town's always talking about how incredible you are and fawning over your new relationship. Do you know some of the ladies had no idea Hayley was an actress? Can you imagine? She's a *huge* star. How could they not?"

"Wow. That blows my mind." I chuckle, not mentioning the fact that I had to show Mom who she was when I first started talking about her.

"I think she's the one, Reed. I have a feeling."

"Oh, yeah?" I laugh it off, while my heart slams in my chest. "You haven't even met her."

"I don't have to. I can hear it in your voice when you talk about her, and I see it in your eyes now. Call it mother's intuition."

What? My smile drops as a wave of emotion takes over me. "What did you think about Bria?"

"Bria?" Her nose scrunches. "What do you mean?"

"When I talked about her, what did you think?"

Her brows furrow as confusion mars her features. "You mean you don't know?"

"No, that's why I'm asking."

"We thought she was nice enough and knew you were a little infatuated, but she was never right for you. It was obvious by the way you always held back. As though something deep within you here"—she holds her palm above my heart—"was convinced there was someone else out there. And I think that someone was Hayley."

What. The. Fuck.

Mom links her arm through mine and begins walking me to the door, but I pull her to a stop, turning her to face me. "You really thought that?" Like me, Mom sees the good in everyone, but unlike me, she's a terrible judge of character and doesn't tend to look much past the surface. It surprises me that she noticed all that. If it's true.

"Yes, I really thought that. Why would I lie? You're a good guy, Reed. The best person I know. Better than anyone in this town. You're intuitive, thoughtful, observant. And you know you could have anyone you want." I open my mouth to protest but she cuts me off. "Don't pretend otherwise. You know it. Yet, you never made a move on Bria. Even in the early days when your crush began. And, on that note, can you remind me which of your tattoos belongs to her?"

"What?" I shake my head at the sudden change in direction.

"All of your tattoos belong to someone or something, right? You told me that the day I first noticed you'd gotten one. Only to find out you already had six."

Fuck. I did say that.

"The eagle belongs to your high school football team," she continues. "The guys that got you through the days when your brother was at his worst. The three hearts on the left of your rib cage belong to me, my mom, and your father's mother, while the fish on the right belong to the men in your life—you father and grandfathers."

Holy shit. She's a lot more observant than I realized.

"Tell me, Reed. Which piece of beautiful art belongs to Bria? I'm curious."

She's questioning me like she already knows the answer, but that's impossible. How could she? I have close to fifty tattoos. She doesn't know the meaning behind them all. Hell, she doesn't even know that some of them exist. I may have told her about a few, and others are easy to guess, but apart from that...

"I'm waiting..." She taps her foot impatiently.

"None," I blurt out honestly. "She's got none."

Mom nods before a small smirk pulls at her lips. "And Hayley?"

Fuck. Digging my palms into my eyes, I let out a groan before slowly lifting my tee, pointing to the paw print on my left pec muscle, close to my heart. A cat's paw to be precise. *My wildcat.*

Mom's eyes light up as she smiles. "That's what I thought. Mothers always know."

Linking my arm again, she walks toward the front door without waiting for me to respond, perhaps giving me the respite I so desperately need. *How the hell didn't I make that connection?*

I got that tattoo after our wakeboard park adventure, when we became close, but I didn't have feelings for her then, and yet, I never got one for Bria. *Never. What the fuck does that mean?*

The second I'm inside, Mom's friend pounces on me, asking me a million questions about my famous girlfriend—as though I'm not famous myself—and it pulls me out of my head, forcing me to move on and not think too deeply about my new revelation.

But when I'm in bed that night, and a vision of Hayley takes over my mind, I have no choice but to face it head-on.

And the truth becomes clear. I've definitely fallen for my best friend. *Again.* Only now I'm wondering... *Did I* really *do that the first time around?*

"**T**hen you pulled your pants down and proceeded to dance around the yard because you thought it would bring on the rain." Mom has tears in her eyes as she regales us with stories, reminding me of the many things I did as a kid in the name of making her happy.

"That's what TJ said would work." I shrug. "His parents always had the greenest grass. I had no reason to doubt him."

"Except that TJ's parents had fake turf." Dad gets his two cents in, glancing up with a smirk from behind his newspaper.

"I know that *now*." I fake an eye roll, letting them continue their laughter at my expense. After all, that's why I'm here. To lift my mom's mood. Even if it's fleeting.

"What was the story you were telling me the other day?" Mom asks my dad, drawing my attention. "It was a good one." She turns my way with a giddy smile and my stomach sinks. "He reminded me about the time you tried to wash your own sheets when you were sick, because you didn't want us to have to worry. Only you flooded the laundry room."

"All the bottles of liquid look similar. I didn't know I was putting in the wrong soap. To me soap was soap."

I laugh at myself while inside I'm crumbling. Did Dad mention that story to cheer her up? Is that what he does when I'm not around?

Mom brings up another couple of stories before moving the topic on to their night in the city. And the energy shifts in the room, the joy obvious in her expression. Imagine how happy they'd be if they'd gone on the full vacation I gave them.

I'd do anything to convince them to take off and enjoy themselves. But for now, I'll settle for this weekend.

It's safe to say Mom hasn't stopped smiling since I arrived. I even got a few rare smiles out of Dad.

Mission accomplished.

But come Sunday night when it's time to leave, the mood changes, and it breaks my heart to think about what's next.

"I wish you'd visit more often," Dad says as he pats my back, his tired eyes flashing toward my mom. I force a smile and tell him I'll try, though we both know it's not that easy.

Guilt gnaws away at me, destroying me from the inside out, but I push through it. Succumbing to their sadness helps no one, and I promised to always be their light. I can't give up now.

"Maybe next time we'll see Hayley with you? We'd love to meet her. I don't think I've ever met an Australian."

For a short glimpse, Mom's happiness returns until her gaze drops to my bag and she frowns. "I'm going to miss you, Reed. It's not enough to only see you a handful of times each year."

"I know. And the offer still stands for you to move to San Francisco. We can find you a house near the beach. You always said you wanted that."

Dad straightens. "I've been trying to convince her but—"

"What if you get traded, or retire and move to Australia to raise babies? Your father and I will be alone in another state. We'd miss our friends. Dad won't have any work there."

"I know, Mom. It's a lot. But I can promise you I am *not* moving to Australia. America will always be my home."

"Well, I guess that's something. You'll be back for your birthday, right?" Mom asks with an expectant smile.

A lump forms in the back of my throat but I force it down, nodding. "Always."

When I moved away, I promised I'd be back for all our birthdays, as close to the date as possible. Mom lets me off the hook for missing my brother's special day, but because of that, he always makes sure he's around when I come home for mine.

"I'll make sure to bring Hayley next time," I lie. Who knows where our lives will be by then. But if I can leave Mom with a small piece of hope, her happiness might last a little longer than usual.

She pulls me into a tight hug and Dad shoots me a pointed stare, tapping his watch. If I don't leave now, my presence is going to cause an entirely new set of issues, and I can't do that to them.

"I better get going, Mom. I have a flight to catch. I'll see you very soon."

"Love you, Reed."

"Love you too."

I throw my bag in the back of my rental and wave, and as I drive away, my usual guilt kicks in. I should be doing more. But if I knew what, I'd already be doing it.

Chapter Forty-Five

HAYLEY

My shoulders sag after another emotional day on set, but I smile through the pain, accepting the praise from my fellow actors and offering the same in return.

With my movements slow, I get out of my costume and take my time walking back to my trailer, finding Cameron waiting for me on the step, his arms wide for a hug.

"Bring it in." He stands as I approach. "After that effort, you need some comfort."

He's right, I do, but he's not the one I want it from. My mind drifts to Reed as I smile. "You're not wrong. And even though I've read the book and knew the emotion behind the role, God, is it taxing."

Cam nods in understanding. "For what it's worth, you're doing an amazing job."

"Thank you. And thanks for waiting. But I have a call to make."

Cam's eyes bulge but he shakes it off and seems to force a smile. "Of course. I'll see you later, yeah?"

"Not tonight. I'm going to have a quiet one. I'll see you on set tomorrow afternoon."

Cameron nods a few times before widening his grin. It would be easy to believe he was happy, if I hadn't missed the way said smile morphs into a frown as he turns away. He's been there for me since day one of filming, always smiling, always offering to make me feel better, and I've barely given him anything in return.

Guilt hits me as he walks away, but I don't let it linger. I need Reed. It's a need, not a want, this time for emotional reasons.

I need to hear his voice.

When I'm settled in my trailer, I bring up his number but pause before calling. At first we were speaking daily, and then every other day, but for the last week, we've only spoken once, and that's on me. The last time he called, I kept getting interrupted and offered to call back at a better time, but a better time never came.

Until now.

We've texted, but it's not the same.

And I'm praying he answers.

Taking a deep breath, I click on his name and wait.

"Are you magic?" he asks as he answers, an awe in his tone that has me giggling. Only Reed could completely calm me with barely any words.

"I don't think so. Why?"

"Because you called the *exact* second I needed you."

My smile fades and I sit up, curling my knees beneath me. *His parents' birthdays.* Goddammit. I forgot.

"What happened? Was it awful?" I can't believe I never called him to check in. "I should have called yesterday."

"Why? You're calling now. And it actually went well. It was wonderful seeing them again. Laughing with them. My mom's smile never left her face."

"That's great, but..." *There has to be a but.*

"But I had to leave. And you'd swear I was taking their happiness with me. Robbing them of everything they had."

"Oh, Reed."

"I'm okay, I promise. That's not why I wanted to talk. At least, not the only reason."

"God, what else was I *not* there for?" *Why am I in Texas?*

Reed chuckles and the sound of it runs through me. I never imagined I'd miss that sound, but God, I love his laugh.

"You're where you should be, Hayls. Exactly where you should be. I just miss you."

"Oh, yeah?"

"Yeah. But it's not long now—"

"I wish you were here," I cut in, the words flying out of my mouth. "I wish you were here, right now, sitting next to me instead of on the other end of the line. And not just today. I've imagined opening my door to you so many times..." I trail off and when silence fills the air, I panic. Did I say the wrong thing? Too much? "Reed, I—"

"Fuck, I want that too." He sighs and...thank God.

I release a breath and smile. "Like you said. Not long now. I—"

"Wait." He cuts me off before pausing for a second, and I swear he says "fuck it" under his breath. "I'm coming to Texas."

"*What*?" My eyes widen in disbelief. "Don't you have preseason training and practice?"

"It's not official yet. Training camp doesn't start for another couple of weeks. I can spare the weekend. I've been killing it in the gym. Working my ass off. My girlfriend's away, so I've had plenty of time to dedicate to football. What else am I supposed to do with myself?"

I snort when his voice comes out a little *woe is me*. "Oh, poor Reedy boy. You should be used to this. You haven't had a girlfriend during *any* other season of your career, right?"

"Well aware, Hayley Baby. But I had Bria. And just like you, she took up most of my spare time."

My smile fades upon hearing her name, but I don't let it get to me, keeping the conversation on us. "You love it when I do that."

"I do. I'm not ashamed to admit it."

My heart jumps as my chest tightens. "Don't tease me about Texas. Please."

"I'm not."

"Really?"

"I'm booking my flights as we speak. Can you hear me typing?" He must put the phone down near a keyboard because sure enough, I hear the keys. Only no one can type that quickly, so he's undoubtedly pressing a bunch of random buttons. He's not booking anything.

"Done," he lies, unconvincingly. "I'll send you the details in a little bit."

"You're hilarious. What you really mean is that you'll send me the details when you've actually booked your flights?"

"Busted. Yes. I'll do it when we get off the phone."

"You're really coming?"

"I am. I'm going to book my flights now. I promise. I'll message you when I'm done."

"Wait," I call out before he hangs up. "Thank you. You've made my day."

"Anytime, Hayls. That's what friends are for."

I'm on edge for the next few days, counting down the seconds until Reed arrives. I knew I missed him, but now that he's coming, I'm both nervous and excited about it.

Reed's flight lands at the same time I finish filming for the day, so the second we're done, I rush back to my hotel to shower and change, quickly tidying up.

I've just finished drying my hair when he texts.

> REED: I'm here

My heart jolts as my entire body tingles, and there's no denying my feelings anymore. Only I'm still not sure what to do about it. All I know is that I'm desperate to see him and I can't wait any longer.

Racing out the door, I lock it behind me and jump in the lift—elevator, bouncing on my toes when it stops on multiple floors, slowing my journey.

I smile at my travel companions, faking a patience I don't have, but the second the doors open, I push through the crowd congregating in the busy lobby, calling out his name when I see him in the distance, his back to me.

Reed turns and his smile makes my world slow.

Throwing caution to the wind, I run forward and launch myself into his arms, crashing my lips to his, smothering him in a bruising kiss.

And despite catching him off guard, he meets my fervour, his lips parting to welcome my tongue, his arms curling around me, *almost* convincing me it's real.

We stay like that for God knows how long until someone wolf whistles and he smiles against my lips.

"Wow. You really *did* miss me." He chuckles when we finally part, his eyes locked on mine as he continues to hold me in his arms.

"I really did." I laugh, sensing eyes on us from around the room and leaning in to whisper, "The question is, how much did you miss me? We've got an audience. Is it safe for me to move?" I glance between us and Reed chuckles, rolling his eyes.

"I'm good. There was no inappropriate rubbing this time."

"Would you like me to change that?"

Squeezing his eyes shut, he groans and I light up inside. We may not have had any kind of physical relationship in months, but I still love to tease him.

"Maybe it's best we go to your room," he jokes, teasing me right back.

"I like the way you're thinking." I wink, grabbing his hand to lead the way, a thought hitting me when we reach the elevator. "Oh and by the way, I have plans for us tonight."

Reed's eyes widen before he smirks, his mind going exactly where I thought it would, not that I think he'd actually make a move. "Are you going to fill me in?" he asks, his gaze full of questions.

"Dancing, Reed. We're in Texas. We're going dancing."

Chapter Forty-Six

REED

Hayley closes the door to her suite and my chest tightens with the soft click. She smiles as she turns, and when our eyes lock...I'm a goner.

I mean, I've kind of known that for a while now, but with the way my heart's flipping out, it's so much worse than I thought.

I'm in love with her.

And it turns out, I've never been in love before.

"Now that we're alone, I'm so glad you're here." She squeals as she takes off in another run, launching herself at me for a second time. "God, you smell good."

I chuckle as she breathes me in, and I have to admit, she smells amazing herself. Like fancy hotel soap mixed with the floral perfume she always wears, and...home. She smells like home.

"So dancing, huh?" I change the subject, needing to get out of my head.

"Yep." She bounces her eyebrows. "A few of us found a genuine cowboy bar and we're going boot scootin'."

"Please tell me you didn't call it a 'genuine cowboy bar' or say that you were boot scootin' when you were there."

"Of course not. I said I was ready to line dance at the boot scootin' bar."

"Oh, Hayls." I huff out a laugh and she grins proudly. "Life is never boring with you."

"I'm glad you think that, because we're meeting everyone in an hour."

"In an hour?" Disappointment fills me but I smile through it. I wanted alone time, though I shouldn't be surprised. When she gets an idea... "Only my wildcat." I shake my head and she laughs. "I'm ready. Bring it on."

An hour and twenty minutes later, we're in the "cowboy bar" and Hayley's dancing with her co-stars, lighting up the room as she tries to master the moves from the people around her.

Like always, I watch from the sidelines, keeping my secret for a little while longer, holding back before I dance.

Hiding a smile behind my beer, I stare in amusement as one of the girls spins the wrong way and she and Hayley collide, bringing each other down as they burst out laughing.

My smile breaks free and I feel a sense of something new, finally at peace now that Hayley's close to me again. And when she finally stops laughing, she winks my way, not so subtly beckoning me over.

Not yet, Hayley Baby.

Raising a finger, I wave my beer, letting her know I'll be there soon. Then I continue to watch her, the smile never once leaving my face, my heart full and happy.

"Can I buy you a drink?" a stranger asks as she sidles up next to me, her southern accent reminding me of home. "You've been sitting here alone for a while now. I figured it was time you had some fun." Her eyes light up as my gaze flits to hers before settling back on the dance floor.

"I appreciate the offer, but I'm here with friends."

"Friends? Then where are they?"

I raise my beer, gesturing toward the dancers, and the stranger scoffs.

"Shouldn't you be out there?"

"I will. I'm just waiting for my moment." The corners of my lips quirk but it's not for the girl beside me. I'm thinking of Hayley's reaction when I show her I can "boot scoot" as well as the rest of them. I've been doing it for years.

"Which ones are your friends?" the woman asks, drawing my attention as her eyes scan the crowd.

I follow her gaze, watching as Hayley spins to face the man behind her, my body tensing when he grabs her waist. Her co-star—Cameron, I think his name is—mouths off to the guy and I stand up, ready to go over, even though I'm acutely aware that Hayley can hold her own.

They argue for a second before Cameron shifts his attention to Hayley, and something about his move has my hackles rising, seconds before he pulls her in close, pressing a kiss to her lips.

"The fuck." I jolt, slamming my glass down on the counter. "Excuse me."

Abandoning the stranger mid-chat, I push through the crowd just as the first guy storms away. But I no longer care about him. I've got my sights set on Hayley's co-star, and when she sees me, she realizes, rushing forward to stop me.

"Reed." She waves a hand in front of my face, vying for attention. "He was joking around, trying to get the other guy to back off."

"He kissed you, Hayls. Knowing you have a boyfriend."

Her gaze softens and she steps closer. "Technically—"

"Stop. *You have a boyfriend.* And if he touches you again, even an accidental brush of the hand, he's going to know about it. Same goes for anyone else."

Hayley nibbles her lip while she nods, a fire in her eyes I haven't seen before.

Stepping closer, she curls her fingers through the loops of my jeans, dragging me forward until our bodies touch.

I release a slow sigh, wrapping my arms around her neck while she snakes hers around to my ass, her palms settling inside my back pockets. She glances up at me, peeking through her long, thick lashes. "You're the one I want, Reed. Not—"

My phone rings, cutting her off as it vibrates against her hand, and she laughs, pulling it from my pocket. "Here."

Both our gazes dart to the screen to find Bria's name staring back at us.

"Bria?" Hayley asks, her eyes narrowed as she steps back. "I didn't think you were talking."

"We're not. We haven't."

"You better get it then." She shuffles farther away, her smile fading, and I audibly groan as she turns.

My phone stops ringing and I've just reached for Hayley when it incessantly starts up again. "Dammit," I curse under my breath, my eyes locking with Hayley's, imploring her to smile.

She nods reassuringly and motions for me to answer, maintaining her gaze as I hesitate.

I'm torn, but when Hayley nods again, I finally answer, seconds before it's likely to stop. "Hang on. I'm finding somewhere quiet." If she'd only called once, I would have left it, but calling right back is not something Bria does, unless it's important.

"Reed?" she responds, an urgency in her tone.

"Yeah, it's me. One sec."

I've just stepped into the hallway near the restrooms when I register her tears. "Bria? What's wrong?"

"My dad. He..." She sniffs as she trails off and my heart seizes, thinking the worst. "He had a stroke, Reed. He's alive but we almost lost him. And I didn't know who else to call."

"Christ, Bria. I'm so fucking sorry. How's your mom? Are you with them?"

"Yeah. I'm at the hospital in LA. Mom's staying strong but I know she's about to crumble. Thankfully they've brought in a recliner so she can stay tonight."

I breathe a sigh of relief as Bria fills me in on his condition, letting me know he's awake and able to communicate, and when she's finished, she sighs much the same as I did. "Can you come here? I know I'm asking a lot but..." She trails off and... *Fuck*.

My chest tightens and I hate that I have to let her down. "I'm not home, Bria. I'm in Texas. I—"

"Texas?"

"Yeah. I'm with Hayley."

"Oh, God. I'm sorry. I shouldn't have called. I'll let you—"

"*Wait*. It's okay. I'm here for you. Things may be different between us, but I'll always be here if you need me. Just in a different capacity." She falls silent, her quiet sniffs the only clue that she's still there. "Bria, I—"

"I knew, you know." She pauses and I stiffen. "I'm so sorry, but I knew how you felt, and I pretended not to. I couldn't stand the thought of losing you. I still can't stand it. But then I did in the end, so my silence was wasted."

Her words sting even though deep down, I always suspected that. "Thanks for letting me know. I never meant for our friendship to turn out the way it did. I didn't want to lose you either."

"But you did. You lost me and you never tried to get me back."

I massage my temples as my mind whirs. "Is that why you disappeared? So I'd fight for you?"

"A little," she admits. "I'm not proud of it, but I wanted to find out if you cared for her more than you loved me."

"And..." I pause, holding back on saying anything else, because if I do, I'm likely to snap at her. I thought she was hurting, not trying to manipulate me.

"And..." She sighs again. "I got my answer."

"*Bria.*" I run a hand down my face, trying to remember that she's hurting right now and yet... "Can you hear yourself?"

"I know. I'm sorry. But Reed, what if I told you I felt the same? Would that have changed anything?"

"Do you?" I don't know why I ask, since it doesn't matter anymore, but when she answers, I'm floored.

"I think I do. I can't stop thinking about you. I miss you. I..." She trails off and I wait for the spark in my chest, for happiness at finally getting what I always thought I wanted. But it doesn't come. Instead, my heart beats for Hayley, for the knowledge that I love her completely, with no doubt in my mind.

"I'm really sorry about your dad, Bria. I'll see if I can change my flight on Monday to include a layover in LA. That way I can stop past the hospital before heading home. In the meantime, let me know if I can help from afar."

I purposely don't respond to her admission, and the shock in her voice is obvious. "Oh. Ah. Thanks... Thank you. I will."

Everything is screaming at me to do more, but her dad's okay, and for once, I need to put myself first. "Please pass on my well wishes to your dad. I'm sorry again."

"I will. Thank you, Reed."

She hangs up and I sink my face into my hands, letting out an obnoxious grunt. *Fuck.* I did *not* see any of that coming.

Taking a deep breath, I groan again, letting out my frustration before composing myself and heading back to the main room, searching for Hayley.

When I find her, she's hugging her friend, instantly making me panic.

"What happened?" I rush over, grabbing her hand when they part.

"What happened with you?" she asks, her gaze dropping to my phone.

"Bria's dad had a stroke. She needed to talk to someone that knew him, I guess. Actually, no... She needed to talk to me."

"Oh, fuck." Hayley's shoulders drop as she frowns. "Is she okay? Is he?"

"They'll both be okay. It's just going to take time. He'll need rehab and may not be able to work anymore."

"*Jesus*. Do you need to go home? To San Francisco?"

"No, Hayls. There's nothing I can do. And I don't think that's a good idea right now. They're in LA, but I'll visit the hospital on Monday, before I go home."

"Okay. Let me know if I can help in any way." She smiles sympathetically, squeezing my hand, and my heart swells. She's been wary of Bria from the very beginning, but when Bria's hurting, she cares.

"Thank you, Hayls. But you just did. Now what happened here?"

Hayley sighs and the same sympathetic gaze shifts to her co-star. "Brooklyn just found out her boyfriend cheated on her, and Cameron's drunk ass decided to say something insensitive."

"He clearly wants an ass kicking." My gaze flits over to where he's dancing a few feet behind Hayley, never too far away. "We should go," I announce. *Before I give him one.*

"Ignore him." Hayley waves off my concern. "Brooklyn's fine now. I promised her we'd dance. And I haven't seen your moves yet."

"*Hayley.*"

"Please," she begs, her gaze boring into mine. "You're only here for two days. Dance with me?"

My eyes shift to find Cameron again, my fists clenching when I catch him watching us.

"Unless, of course, you can't?" Hayley taunts, drawing my gaze back to hers.

"Did you just challenge me, Jackman?"

"Depends. Do you accept?"

I hesitate, but deep down I know I'm going to give in. I once made a promise, and I never break promises.

Hayley frowns, her expression comparable to a sad little puppy dog. "Shame." She jokingly turns to walk away but I grab her wrist, pulling her into me, my palm gliding around her waist.

I lean in, brushing the hair away from her eyes, my lips meeting her ear. "I'll dance but I want you to promise me something."

"Yeah?" Her voice comes out breathy and I almost pull back to look at her.

"Promise me you'll come to me if you ever need to talk about anything. And if that dick makes you uncomfortable…" I trail off and Hayley shakes her head, standing on her toes so I can hear her.

"He's harmless. I promise."

"Either way, I'm here for you. Okay?"

Slipping a hand between us, Hayley pushes me back, her gaze locked on mine, her eyes full of emotion—a mix between vulnerability and acceptance. She blinks a few times before a soft laugh escapes her. "I think I understand Bria a little bit better now."

"Bria?" My brows furrow in confusion, noting the sadness in her eyes. "How?"

"I'm not sure I'll ever be ready to lose you. And yet, when all this is over and we're no longer playing pretend, I will."

"Hayley, I—"

She lightly slaps my chest, cutting off my words before she's playful again, her confidence back in full force. Or maybe veil is a better choice of word. She's hiding behind something.

"Let's go, big guy." She tugs my hand as she moves back toward the dance floor. "Show me what you've got."

CHAPTER FORTY-SEVEN

HAYLEY

I drag Reed into the thick of it, waving a hand at the dancers. "Are you ready for this?"

He releases a breathy laugh, biting back a smirk as he nods. "I am."

"These routines aren't easy." I raise a brow, teasing. "I've been practising for half the night."

"Are you doubting me?" He raises an eyebrow to match my own and I can't help but giggle, the humor between us almost enough to make me forget that Bria's back in his life.

"Never." I shake off my thoughts, smiling. "Let's go."

We join a line and it takes a little under thirty seconds for Reed to blow my mind. Not only can that man dance, but he's freaking phenomenal.

Thumbs in his pockets, he moves his hips in ways that should be illegal, keeping in time with the music, his feet working like magic. Reed's not an overly cocky guy, but the way he's smirking right now has my knees weak and my heart pounding in my chest. He's in his element. And I've only ever seen him that sure of himself on the field.

A few people recognise him and cheer before joining in on the fun, and I couldn't keep the smile from my face, even if I tried.

We dance for a few songs, with Reed perfecting every toe tap, every sway, while I do my best just to keep up, laughing through my mistakes.

When I start to slow down, Reed's eyes lock with mine, his expression full of warmth, and it gut punches me, making me pause. *This might be the most fun I've ever had with a guy. The most comfortable I've ever felt.* Reed loves my crazy. Whether he's watching from the sidelines or blowing me away with a hidden talent, like now, *he's with me*. And I've never had that before. No one has ever been that present in my life.

Catching my breath, I glance away for barely a moment, and when I look back, I snort, finding Reed now wearing a cowboy hat. As though it appeared by magic, with the cowboy gods selecting their new line-dancing leader.

I shake my head and he winks back at me, bouncing his eyebrows as he reaches for my hand.

A new song comes on just as our fingers touch, and the mood shifts, the rhythm slowing as the lines dissolve into free flow. Reed pulls me into him, his hands landing on my hips making it easy for me to curl mine around his neck.

And we dance.

Bodies molding as one, hips grinding, eyes locked on one another.

When the music turns sultry, he bends his knees, lowering himself until his face lines up with my stomach, rolling my hips. With his bottom lip trapped between his teeth, he glances up at me and I swear my panties melt.

I stifle a moan as he rises again and just when I think he's done with his theatrics, he dips me back, lowering me until my hands brush the floor. My heart pounds. I'm losing my mind to the euphoric feelings running through me, completely transfixed by the moment. By him.

We dance for another few minutes, our sweat-covered bodies moving in sync, my pulse pumping, the hypnotic beats coursing through me. And I can honestly say it's the best night of my life.

Everything's easy with Reed.

While my heart may be racing a million miles per minute, and I've never been more horny in my life, I know there's no pressure for how this night will end. Whatever I want, it's mine. *Unless I want it all.*

When the heat becomes too much, I fan my face and Reed nods, motioning to the edge of the dance floor.

With a lopsided grin, I follow his lead, conceding defeat, and my awe returns.

"I stand corrected," I rush out, still catching my breath. "You *can* dance. I am not worthy." I bow my head and Reed rolls his eyes as he chuckles.

"I can't believe you doubted me."

"Honestly, I didn't. I could tell those hips were made for moving. Only I never knew how well they could move." I tilt my head to the side, my eyes locked on his waist, imagining his hips moving again. "Trust me when I say, I've been giving it a lot of thought."

"I bet you have." Reed laughs, bouncing his eyebrows as he thins his lips. His flirtatious grin has my body heating, wishing his mouth was on mine.

"Stop." I playfully push him away, needing some space. "I can't believe I've never seen you dance like that before. Or that you're a cowboy." I nod to his hat and he chuckles again, swapping it to my head. My pulse races as I smile up at him, and when he uses the hat to bring my face closer to his, only stopping when there's barely a breath between us, I swear my heart stops.

With his hand still curled around the back of my head, his intense stare bores into mine, burning a path to my now pounding heart as he pulls me into a kiss. His warm lips caress mine, sending a spark of electricity straight to my core, and for the first time, I'm not convinced it's for show.

The kiss is gentle and explorative, but full of so much passion it sends my mind spinning. With a breath caught in my throat, I mewl in contentment. I can't remember a time I've ever been kissed like this.

I'm so caught up in the moment that when someone bumps me from behind, I jolt forward, falling into Reed's arms, snapping me out of whatever spell I was under. Snapping us *both* out of our stupor until we're laughing out loud.

"I need a drink." I fan my face again as Brooklyn waves at me from the other side of the dance floor, bouncing around to get my attention.

Reed squeezes my hips. "I'll get the drinks. You go and see what she wants."

He turns toward the bar, but I grab his arm, pulling him to a stop. "Your hat?" I grab the brim, ready to give it back until he shakes his head. "I mean, whoever's hat this is." I grimace but he waves me off, smiling.

"Keep it for now. It looks good on you and it matches your boots." He points down at the cowboy boots I borrowed from the costume department. I was waiting to see if he'd comment on them. "We'll give it back in a bit." He winks again and I'm so freaking giddy I'm embarrassed for myself.

He disappears to get me another water—with me still keeping up my America's sweetheart charade—and my mind races as I smile after him.

It's official—I am crazy about that man.

Shaking off my thoughts, I turn to search for Brooklyn just as Cameron waltzes over, his lips pulled into a goofy grin, his body swaying uncontrollably. He shakes his hips and I almost grin until a thought hits me... I don't think I've ever seen him this drunk. Hell, with the way he's struggling to make eye contact, he may even be on something.

"Cam, are you—"

"He doesn't like me, does he?" Cam cuts me off, nodding toward the bar where Reed's staring our way.

"He's my boyfriend, Cam. And you kissed me. Do you blame him?"

Cam grabs my waist and I casually laugh it off, pushing him away until his grip tightens. "I know you liked it," he whispers, the heat of his breath making me squirm. "I felt the way your body melted into mine."

"I love Reed," I snap, saying the three little words just to shut him up. Only, as they leave my lips, my heart swells. "He's my—"

"Tell me something," Cam cuts me off, releasing his hold. "Did he send you flowers for your premiere?"

"What?" My eyes flash to his as my mind drifts back to that night.

"What about chocolate?" he adds, smirking. "Does he know your favorite type? Does he send you letters?"

Letters?

Oh, God.

I fake another laugh, grabbing his arm, flirting to buy myself time.

Cam sent me flowers. Cam wrote me letters. Cam put my favorite chocolates in my trailer. It's been Cam, the whole time.

"You can do better than him, Hayls," he continues, unaware of my internal freakout. "I've always been here for you."

"You're drunk, Cam." I fake a coy smile, brushing off his comments. "You don't want me."

My gaze flits to Brooklyn and she smiles back at me until I flash her a hint of my panic and her face drops.

"I've wanted you for over a year, Hayley," Cam continues. "We'd be—"

"Hayley, where have you been?" Brooklyn interrupts, curling her arm through mine. "I've been looking for you."

I smile, holding back a relieved sigh. "I've been lighting it up on the dance floor, line dancing with my man."

"Oh, I saw him and *damn*."

"Right?" I smile again but a nervous energy still runs through me. The last thing I want to do is piss Cameron off. I told Reed he was harmless and I thought I meant it, but now I don't know what he's capable of.

He's been following me. Stalking me. And all this time I thought we were friends.

"Speaking of, here he comes now." Brooklyn's eyes bounce to somewhere behind me and I turn to greet Reed, unsure how to play this.

I'm about to say something flirty when his jaw clenches, his assessing gaze roaming my face. For all the times I've teased him about being a bad liar, truth be known, I can never get anything past him.

I subtly shake my head and he schools his features, handing me my water as he leans in, whispering in my ear. "Are you okay?"

I shake my head again, squeezing his waist as I step back. "Reed wants to introduce me to someone," I lie to Cam, my eyes flashing to Brooklyn. "We'll be back." I don't want to leave them alone, but there are plenty of people around. I don't think he'll do anything here.

And it's me he wants.

God, I don't even know if he's dangerous. He's never hurt me before, but I obviously don't know him as well as I thought.

Reed squeezes my hand as we walk away, and the second we're out of earshot, he spins my way, concern clear in his features. "What's wrong, Hayley? You're scaring me."

"I... Shit. Please don't overreact."

"Hayls," he growls and I grimace. *What a shitty thing to say.*

"Sorry. I—"

"Did he touch you again?"

I jerk my head in disagreement, and before I can think it through, I blurt, "I think he's my stalker."

"What?"

"I think—"

Reed slams his glass down on the table beside us and storms across the room, his hands curling into fists. *Fuck.*

"Reed, wait." I drop my glass beside his, ignoring the water that sloshes to the table, chasing after him as I swerve through the foray.

I manage to catch up as he reaches Cam, grabbing his shoulder to still him. "Reed—"

Without a word, Reed snakes his arm behind him, securing me out of harm's way. Then he rears his free hand back, ready to strike. "Stay the fuck away from her."

"Reed." I grab his elbow this time, using both hands to hold him back. "I might be wrong and—"

"*Hayls.*" He turns to face me, his wild gaze pleading with mine, but I can't let him do this. I can't let him fight over me.

"He's not worth it. He—"

"What's the matter, Golden Boy?" Cameron taunts just when I think I've got him. "Scared I'm going to steal your girl?"

Dammit.

Reed shakes out of my grasp, spinning to face Cam with his fist still clenched, but before he's had a chance to swing, Cam's jamming a left hook into his stomach.

And there's no going back after that.

Reed slams his fist into Cam's face, over and over, connecting with his jaw, his cheek, his nose while taking every hit Cam delivers.

I panic, begging them to stop, but when neither of them hear me, I try another approach.

"Reed," I scream, putting myself in his line of sight. "Stop, please."

He stills, his expression stoic as his eyes flash to mine, the brief distraction allowing Cameron to deliver another blow. This time to the ribs.

Without flinching, Reed lowers his fists just as Brooklyn rushes over with a guy from our film crew, both of them jumping in to break up the fight. The bouncers arrive next and Reed's pulled in one direction with Cameron dragged toward the exit, his drunken ass yelling abuse as he leaves.

"Fuck." Reed tugs against the bouncer's grip, though it's obvious he's not really trying. He could easily break free if he wanted to. "You can't let him go."

"Come on." The bouncer spins, pointing Reed in the opposite direction. "You're coming with me. You can wait in the back office until your *friend's* gone." He drags Reed toward a discreet door behind the bar, and Reed doesn't bother fighting as I rush to keep up.

"I—"

"I know who you are, Coombs," the bouncer says when we reach the door, his eyes darting between Reed's and my own. "I know who *both* of you are. And I have no doubt that guy must have deserved what he got, because that's *not* you. At least it's not the guy the media claims you to be. Cool off in here, and we'll let you go."

"Thanks, man." Reed forces a smile as they both walk inside, his eyes drifting back to mine. "I appreciate it. Can my girlfriend come in?" He points to where I'm hovering, but I don't bother listening to the response, pushing my way inside, grabbing his hand to check for bleeding.

"I'm fine," he growls, and I roll my eyes.

"You're not fine. You—"

"Mr. Coombs?" Reed and I glance up to find another bouncer standing with an officer on duty, his apologetic gaze boring into ours. "The police were on-site for another issue and—"

"I'll take over," the officer says, stepping closer as my grip on Reed tightens. "Are you Reed Coombs?"

"I am."

"We're going to have to ask you to come down to the station."

"I—"

"What the hell?" I cut in before Reed can speak. "Did that asshole report him? He threw the first punch. Did he tell you that?"

"We'll be speaking with *both* parties, ma'am. But we need Mr. Coombs at the station."

I shake my head but Reed squeezes my hand in reassurance. "It's okay, Hayls. I'll go. We have to speak to them anyway. To tell them what we know."

He presses a kiss to my temple as my body trembles. "I'm coming with you." I glance up at the officer, standing tall. "I need to give evidence. I'm the reason they're fighting."

With a defiant gaze, I stare into his eyes and refuse to back down, my body tense, willing to plead my case if I have to.

He holds my gaze for a beat before shaking his head, seemingly giving in. "Come on, then," he snaps, and... *Thank God.*

Sighing in relief, I curl my fingers through Reed's as we exit, ignoring the stares aimed our way—aimed Reed's way—as guilt takes over me.

What the hell did I do?

Chapter Forty-Eight

REED

I flinch as Hayley runs my hand under the cold water, a forced laugh escaping her. And while it's devoid of her usual lightness, I offer her a tight-lipped smile, at least grateful to finally be back at the hotel.

"I can't believe you did that," Hayley curses me for the tenth time, her voice reflective. "I have every reason to end this charade right now," she jokes but there's a little bite to her tone. "I only *just* turned my reputation around, and—"

Ouch. "Let's not play pretend, Hayley," I cut her off. "You're not annoyed because I hurt *your* reputation. You're annoyed I damaged *mine*."

She stares at me for a beat before stamping her foot like a child, and fuck, it's adorable. "Damn straight. That's exactly what I'm pissed about. You're the league's golden boy. Squeaky clean. The sweetest guy in football. And I'll be damned before I ruin that image of you."

She's trying to be cute, but I'm still in a mood, my mind whirring from our useless police interview. Of course, the fucker denied it all. Now we have to wait for them to speak with the San Francisco police in the morning. But that's not the issue right now. Right now, I need to settle this argument with Hayley.

"I don't give a shit about my image, Hayls," I tell her honestly. "This is who I am. I'm not trying to be someone the media paints me to be. They've created that narrative because I *am* that guy. But another thing about me is that I won't stand for people hurting my friends. You more than anyone else. If you hadn't screamed, I would have done more. I—"

"Why do you think I screamed?"

My shoulders drop and I suck in a breath. *What a fucking night.* I need to calm the fuck down. "Do you want me to thank you?" I deadpan and her brows furrow until I lighten the mood with a smile.

"Ha. You're so funny."

"I know. Believe it or not, I'm more than just the sweet guy you think I am."

"Reed." She frowns, stepping forward to brush her finger under the cut next to my eye. "I'm currently debating whether or not I need to take you to the hospital for stitches. Trust me, I *believe* you."

"Told you, I can be—"

"But," she cuts me off, wagging her finger in my face, "your intentions were sweet. You were protecting me."

"Damn. Can't catch a break, can I?"

"Nope." She shakes her head, releasing a soft laugh. "You'll always be golden to me."

"Is that another challenge? I bet I can prove that I'm not."

"What? What aren't you telling me?"

"Nothing at all, Hayley Baby. Nothing at all."

"Two truths and a lie." She folds her arms over her chest, her brow raised in challenge.

"Me or you?"

"You."

"Okay. Easy. One, I think my face is broken. Two, I've been to that bar before. And three..." I pause knowing this has the power to change *everything*. "I want to fuck your brains out."

Hayley's wide eyes make me smile until her breath hitches and she shakes off her thoughts, grinning when she seemingly realizes I was paraphrasing her first ever response to me. "Very funny."

"Who's joking?"

"You're drunk."

"I only had three beers and that was hours ago."

"Delirious from being punched in the face?"

"This isn't a conclusion I just came to, Hayls. I've wanted to fuck you since you first wrapped your pretty little mouth around my throbbing cock, sucking me dry. It's throbbing now, just thinking about it."

"Jesus Christ, Reed. I want that too. But we can't."

"Why?" I'm quick to respond. I realized how much I loved her tonight and I'm done holding back. "We kiss, we hold hands, we whisper sweet nothings into each other's ear. We do everything else. So why not take it all the way?"

"Because it's fake."

"Is it?" I ask as my heart pounds in my chest.

"Reed." She huffs out a laugh. "What's gotten into you?"

Fucked if I know but I'm going for it. "Say for argument's sake that it *is* fake. Have you never fucked someone after a first date just for the fun of it?"

"You know I have."

"And so have I. Hell, we weren't even dating. So, think of it that way. Only you've been a tease and made me wait months while I fawn over you whenever I get the chance."

"Reed, you're being ridiculous." Hayley bursts out laughing, likely thinking I'm joking, but it's either this or I tell her I love her, and she's not ready for that.

I need to show her first.

"Okay, Wildcat." I shrug, getting up to shower. "Your loss."

I move to undo the buttons on my shirt, but a sharp pain shoots through my knuckles and I almost double over. Here I was trying to make Hayley want me, and now I'm in crippling pain. Which, of course, she notices, rushing to my aid.

"Let me do that so you don't open your wound."

"I'm fine." They patched me up at the police station, only there wasn't much care given. Not that I'm complaining; they could have held me overnight.

"You're not fine," Hayley snaps. "Let me help." She doesn't wait for me to respond before working her way down my buttons, her movements fast until she gets to the last one and my shirt falls open. "Jesus, Reed," she hisses, her eyes on the bruise I felt forming below my abs, where that asshole got me multiple times.

"You should see the other guy," I joke, and she tries to fight it but after a few seconds she bursts out laughing, making me laugh along with her, and... "Fuck, that hurts."

"Stop joking then."

"What else do you want me to do? Cry?"

"Do you want to cry?"

"Fuck, no. I'm fine. I've had worse bruises playing football."

"But you wear protection."

"Not when my fake girlfriend decides I should give Aussie Rules a try, all in the name of charity. That sport is brutal. Why the fuck don't they wear anything under their jerseys?"

"Under their guernsey, you mean?"

"Whatever."

"Well, they're not pussies," she jokes. At least, I hope she's joking or— She giggles again and I fake a smile. "Oh, your face. It's a completely different sport. You threw yourself into it a lot harder than they do considering it was some fun on the beach."

"So you're saying I was better?"

"God, no. I would use the word 'different.'"

"Okay, Jesus. Can you finish undressing me already? Let's get the rest of my humiliation over with before I shower." I deliver my request with a gruff voice and straight face, until Hayley's eyes widen and she bites back a smile.

"Okay, tough guy, let's get you cleaned up."

A visual of Hayley on her knees springs to mind, and I imagine her sucking my cock as water cascades down her back. I wasn't kidding when I said I wanted to fuck her, but we've moved way beyond *want* and straight through to *need*. Either that, or I'm going to have to suffer through the pain while jerking myself off.

Dammit, now I'm getting hard.

Working to replace the naked visuals with something else like kittens or broken fingers, I feel a warmth against my chest and flinch, my eyes flashing to Hayley as she gently kisses my bruise.

"Sorry." She lightly shakes her head, staring at me bewildered. "I have no idea why I did that."

Thinking quickly, I reach for her hand and pull her in close. "It helped," I say, my voice raspy as my chest swirls with some fucked-up anticipation.

Hayley's eyes briefly widen before she tugs at her bottom lip and nods. "Yeah?" she whispers breathlessly, my heart racing as I nod back.

Without a word, she leans forward and lowers her head again, pressing another kiss to my abs, only this time she lingers, brushing her lips across my skin, pausing on each individual tattoo. When she makes her way up to my pecs and stops on the paw print, I shiver.

"We should get you in the shower." She smiles up at me, misunderstanding my reaction.

"Hayls, I—"

"Let me help. No more joking. I promise."

I nod as her hands drop to the waistband of my jeans, her fingers working the button before she undoes the zipper. After rolling the denim down my legs, she ignores the obvious bulge in my briefs as she waits for me to step out. "Do you need help with your jocks too?" she asks, her voice soft, a complete contrast to the girl she was before.

I let out a half laugh, half groan. On one hand her Aussie term is funny, but on the other hand, I hate needing so much help. But since I've already balanced on the tightrope of our boundaries tonight, what's a little bit more. "Please."

Hayley gets to work confidently, but when my cock springs free, her throat bobs as she innocently glances up at me. I move to speak, but she shakes her head and stands. "I'll leave you to it."

I only allow her to take one step before I react without thought, moving on pure instinct as my arm shoots out to stop her, curling her into me as I walk us the two short steps toward the bedroom. When we're both inside, I lower her onto the mattress and slowly remove her boots one at a time, my heart racing as she silently stares up at me, her eyes hooded as her lashes flutter.

When I'm done, I hover above her, leaning in until there's barely a breath between us. "Tell me you don't want this." My voice cracks until I clear it and try again. "Tell me you don't want this and I'll walk away."

My cock throbs and I try hard to keep it away from her. I'm not going to take this any further unless I hear those words. But God, I don't want to stop.

Hayley's chest heaves as her eyes bounce between mine, and fuck is she beautiful. With her long, blonde hair fanning out beside her flushed cheeks and her doe eyes staring up at me, I've never seen her more perfect.

She opens her mouth and closes it again, releasing a soft sigh. "I shouldn't want this," she whispers and I'm hooked on her every word. "We shouldn't want this. But if you don't fuck me right now, I think I might explode."

And there she is. My Hayley. My wildcat.

Standing up, I leave her to rummage through my bag, finding the protection I brought on the off chance that something happened between us. And thank God that I did.

Hayley sits up and studies me with a smile, undoing the button of her jeans, lifting her ass to lower them quickly, removing her panties at the same time.

She follows me with her eyes, watching me move around the room, sighing when I'm settled in front of her.

Dropping the condom on the mattress, I lower to my knees and spread her legs, gliding my palms slowly along her thighs until the tips of my thumbs brush against her center. My right hand stings from the movement, and I reluctantly accept that if I want to please her, I'm going to have to use my left.

Shifting my balance, I press my left thumb against her clit, but she grabs my hand to stop me. "Wait. I'm already worked up." She reaches for the condom and waves it in front of me. "Please." The desperation in her voice almost convinces me to give in, but while I want nothing more than to sink inside her, we have time.

"I remember our conversation about the importance of foreplay." I smirk when she giggles. "Lie back, Hayls. Let me worship this beautiful pussy before you take my cock."

Without waiting, I lick a path from her hole to her clit, flattening my tongue against the bud, finally tasting her again. And God, she tastes amazing. It's been too long. And if I'm being honest, I wasn't sure we'd ever get here again.

After teasing her clit, I stare up at her, my fingers dancing against her entrance, loving the way she clenches for me as I glide easily though her heat.

She wriggles impatiently beneath me until I sink two fingers inside her, scissor them to stretch her before adding a third and fourth, getting her ready, knowing she can take it. She arches her back and rolls her hips, riding my fingers, her pussy squeezing around me. "Fuck, Baby. You're so ready for me. Ready for my cock. Ready for me to take this pussy and make it mine."

With a gasp, Hayley's eyes widen before her head lolls back, her hips continuing to grind as my fingers work her pussy, my tongue lavishing her clit. Her breathing picks up and she grabs the sheets, curling them beneath her fingers, grounding herself as her hips buck.

I massage her walls, working her harder until she convulses around me, crying out as her arousal coats my fingers, forcing me to bite back a groan.

"That's it, Baby. Give me what you've got. I want it all."

Her back arches as her body jolts, and it's only when she begs me to stop that I remove my fingers, licking them clean, one by one as she watches in silence, her blue eyes dark with desire.

Her breath shakes, and when I'm done, her gaze lifts to mine as she licks her lips seductively. Raising a finger to her mouth, she bites the tip before sucking it between her freshly wet lips. "I could die happily with your face between my legs."

"Please don't." I chuckle. "I'm not done with you yet."

She reaches up to grab my hand but I gently brush her away, standing with a smile. "Not yet," I scold.

"God, I need to touch you. Please."

"I told you, I'm going to worship you first. Let me have my moment or you get nothing."

"Jesus. You've already given me an orgasm."

"I'm aiming for five."

"Five. Holy shit, Reed. You—"

Crawling onto the bed, I cut off her words as I flatten my palm on the mattress near her face.

Moving her hand away from her mouth, I replace it with my own, brushing a finger across her lips. "God, you're beautiful."

"Reed—"

"You know what? I'm too impatient for five. We've got forever to do that. For tonight, I want two more." I raise an eyebrow as she smiles, waiting for me to continue. "I want one now and the final while I'm pounding into you. You're going to take me until your pussy's squirting for me, soaking my length as you scream out my name."

Hayley cries out as her ass lifts off the bed, her pussy brushing against my length. "God, yes. I want that too. Take me, Reed. I want it all."

CHAPTER FORTY-NINE

REED

"Oh. My *God*." Hayley screams through her second release and I lick my lips as she comes back down to earth. When her breathing slows, her eyes lock with mine and the energy shifts between us.

Trying not to draw attention to my pain, I stand up and grab the condom packet from the bed, ripping it open as she watches me.

But when I try to roll it on, I flinch.

"Jesus. We shouldn't be doing this." Hayley sits up, her concerned gaze appraising my hand.

"Nothing is going to stop me, Hayls. *Nothing*." To prove a false point, I flex my fingers and smile through clenched teeth until Hayley rolls her eyes and gets up.

"Let me help." With a half laugh, she snatches the condom from my grasp and waves it in front of me.

"Well, this is romantic," I mumble under my breath, making her smile before her gaze travels to my cock and her expression turns serious again.

I open my mouth to thank her, but before I get the chance, she wraps her fingers around my girth, cutting off my train of thought, pumping me once...twice...three times before lowering herself to the carpet. "The condom can wait."

"Fuck." A deep growl releases from the back of my throat, but I catch her under the arms and force her to stand. "As much as I'd love to see you on your knees again, opening your throat to take my cock like the good girl you are, right now, I'm fucking this pussy." I cup her heat and gently brush a finger through her arousal, making her squirm. "I *need* it."

Hayley nods as a soft sigh escapes her, but when her gaze drops to my ribs, she flinches.

She opens her mouth to undoubtedly argue, but I reach out and grab her waist, silencing her protest, pulling her flush against me.

"I promise," I whisper. "I'm fine."

Her breath hitches but she steps back, her lip trapped between her teeth. And after a slight exhale, she rolls the latex over my length, letting her fingers drag across my skin, her movements painstakingly slow.

I try not to react and when she's done, she glances up at me, her gaze wary as she slips a hand between us, gently brushing her fingers across my wound. This time I can't hold back my wince as my body heats from her touch. "It only looks bad because of the dry blood."

"*Reed*." She glances away.

"Nope. I'm fine. Just think of it as another tattoo. And if you can't do that, then how about you fuck the pain away."

The heat in her gaze returns when her eyes flash my way, but I don't miss the concern in her expression. "Come on." I grab her hand to distract her. "I've got an idea."

Without another word, I lead her into the bathroom to the oversized shower, and turn on the water, my fingers still curled around hers.

Releasing my hand, she reaches for the buttons of her shirt, but I stop her, stepping forward to take the lead. I pop the first button, and the second, ignoring the pain, my heart trapped in my throat as my breathing picks up speed. I've seen Hayley naked before, but knowing I'm about to sink inside her has my pulse running wild.

Her shirt falls open, revealing her flushed skin and pale pink bra, and because it's too tempting not to, I run a finger through the gap between her breasts, imagining my cock in its place, loving when her chest heaves as I groan.

"God, you're perfect. I want to worship every damn part of you, and one day, I'm going to fuck these too." Pushing the shirt off her shoulders, I release her tits from the cups of her bra and roll my thumbs over her nipples, squeezing the mounds under my palms. "One day," I repeat, my voice gruff.

"God, Reed. Your mouth." Her eyes close as she mewls. "I want more."

I quirk my lips and lean forward, reaching behind her to unclip her bra, watching as it falls to the floor. "You want more?" I kiss her neck, sucking the flesh into my mouth—marking her—smiling against her skin, imagining the looks she'll get from her makeup team come Monday. "Are you willing to beg for it?"

Hayley's head falls back and she moans through her words. "Yes. Please. Don't stop."

"Patience, Baby. But first..." Reaching my hand back, I check the temperature of the shower and release my hold on her, leaving her naked and waiting. I step under the water, letting the heat soothe my aching muscles as each drop washes away the blood.

Hayley watches, her lips parted, and it takes everything in my power not to beckon her over before I'm done.

When the water runs clear, she steps forward and reaches out to caress the skin beneath my wound, releasing a slow breath. "You will always be my golden boy, Reed. But God, did I love this new side of you. The dirty talk, the demands, the way you defended me... Jesus, that was hot."

"Oh, yeah?"

"Yeah." Her eyes fill with want until she snaps herself out of it, her expression severe. "But don't *ever* do it again. I've had my bad boy fill of you." She laughs, gently touching the cut next to my eye. "I'm good for a while."

With a smile, I hold back another flinch. "That's a shame," I rasp, my eyes raking over her. "I really wanted to slap your pussy with my other hand wrapped around your throat. Only that doesn't seem like something a golden boy would do."

"Fuck, Reed." Hayley melts into me as I smirk. "I'll allow that. You can do anything to me. Just no more fights."

"Hmm." I suck my lips into my mouth as I glance away in thought. "I'll think about it."

"Tease." She grins. "You—"

Cutting her off, I pull her under the water and spin us both around, my lips hovering at her ear. "I want to do all the things, Hayley. *All* of them. But first, I'm going to fuck you until you forget every guy that's been here before me. Until I'm the only one you see."

"Reed. I—"

Grabbing her face in my hands, I push her against the wall and press my lips to hers, stealing her breath as the water cascades around us. She claws at my waist as she melts into me, yielding all control, her mouth vibrating against mine as she moans.

My chest aches but I ignore it, releasing her face to grab under her ass, lifting her into my arms as she curls her legs around me. When she's balanced against the wall, I reach between us, gripping my cock, pumping it once before lining it up with her entrance.

"Take a deep breath, Baby. I'm about to fill you like never before."

Hayley gasps, but before she can speak, I sink into her, groaning as her walls squeeze me, feeding her pussy inch by inch until I'm buried to the hilt. Her head drops back as she moans my name, clenching her legs to unbearable levels.

"Fuck, Hayls. I've imagined this moment every time I've fucked my hand, but I could never do it justice."

"God, Reed. This... You... I want you to take everything from me. Destroy me. I *need* this."

"Consider it done." Grabbing her waist with my free hand, I lift her up and slam her back down, bucking my hips at the same time. She cries out, her hands sinking into my hair, tugging at the strands as she meets my fervor. With a roll of her hips, she matches me thrust for thrust, and I've never been more in sync with a woman.

The room spins while I curl my hands under her ass, pumping into her as she bounces on top of me, studying our connection as I make her mine.

Her walls tighten and I glance up to speak, but when our eyes lock, I freeze, floored by the emotion staring back at me.

No one has ever looked at me like that. She's at my mercy and vulnerable, but there's a softness there that wasn't there before. Dare I say love?

In this moment, there's no doubt in my mind that she wants more—that she wants me—and my chest swells.

Slowing my movements, I hold her gaze, my eyes boring into her soul, my heart pounding, knowing this moment has moved beyond sex. I'm making love to my girl.

Make no mistake, Hayley's *mine*. And I'm going to make sure she knows that. Make sure she *feels* it.

Balancing her in one hand, I continue our slow rhythm as I grab her face, staring into her eyes, begging her to see through what she believes us to be, to realize what we are.

Nothing about this is fake, and for me, it's been real for longer than I've even been willing to admit.

Emotion clogs my throat as she holds my gaze, but when her body shivers, I break our trance, releasing her face to slide my hand between us, pressing my thumb to her clit.

She cries out as her pussy pulses and her walls clench around me. "Reed," she gasps, and my name from her lips has never sounded sweeter.

"That's it, Hayley Baby. Take what you need. Use me."

Her body jolts and when she screams out my name, her pussy strangles my cock, her embrace so tight my release shoots out of me, filling the condom as my body spasms.

"Fuck, Hayls. Yes."

Slamming my lips to hers, I steal her breath and consume her, pouring everything I have into the kiss, making sure she knows that nothing will ever compare to our connection. That she was meant for me and I was fucking made to complete her.

I may not have realized it at first, but it's always been her. I've just been waiting for her to arrive.

I continue to kiss her until our breathing slows, and when she pulls back, I smile.

"Wow," she whispers with a giggle, making me chuckle. "That was..."

"The best sex of your life."

"Of my life?" She laughs breathlessly, her eyes lighting up, confirming I'm right. "It was pretty bloody spectacular." She shakes her head in disbelief as I lower her to the tiles, holding her close until she supports her own weight, pushing me back. "My fake boyfriend is a sex god," she announces and I groan at her words, grabbing her hand, lifting it between us.

"Feel this." I hold her palm over my heart and press down, allowing her to feel the way it pounds for her. "Feel what you do to me." My eyes lock with hers, emotion pouring from my gaze. "Nothing about this is *fake* anymore."

Hayley's eyes snap to mine before she springs back as though I hurt her, shaking her head again, this time in a panic. "I can't. I can't. You don't. This is all wrong."

"Wrong? What the fuck, Hayls. Tell me you didn't *feel* something just now or ever. Tell me and I'll back off."

"We can't do this. We're supposed to stage a breakup and—"

"What? Are you serious right now?"

"Yes. We can't. This isn't supposed to happen."

I frown, confused, my heart breaking. "So, what... You want me to keep pretending? To shower you with affection in public. To kiss you. To hold your hand. To *fuck* you. And then break your heart, all while pretending I'm not in—"

"Don't. Please." She throws her hand out to stop me and my heart cracks.

"Don't what?"

"Don't say it. Not now."

Fuck. Not now or not ever? Did I get this all wrong? I was sure she felt the same, but... "I guess that gives me my answer."

"No, it doesn't. Not at all. Look at this from my perspective." She stalks out of the shower and grabs the towel off the rail, wrapping it around her. "Not too long ago you were in love with someone else. What happened to that? Have those feelings just gone?"

Jesus. She's hurting? "Other than today, Bria and I haven't spoken in months. We've talked about this. I don't feel the same about her anymore. Those feelings aren't there. And the more time I spend with you, the more I realize that they never really were."

"Come on, Reed. This whole thing started so you could get over her."

"No, Hayley. This whole thing started for *you*. I was always doing it for you."

"You wanted to move on. You wanted to get over her."

"So now you're attacking me because I did?"

Hayley's shoulders drop as she briefly closes her eyes. "I'm not attacking you. I just don't think it's that easy. And I don't want to..." She trails off but it's not hard to fill in the blanks. *She doesn't want to get hurt.*

"Hayley—"

"No. Wait." She raises a hand between us. "I think you should kiss her."

"The fuck." I fumble to remove the condom and grab the second towel, securing it around my waist before running a hand through my wet hair. This is not a conversation we should be having while naked. "What the—"

"I think you should kiss her and see how you feel."

"That's insane, Hayls. It's—"

"Is it? What if I fall in love with you and your feelings come back? What if you go to LA on Monday and when you see her at the hospital, she's begging you to love her?"

"That's not going to happen, Hayls. That—"

"Wrong answer. Because if you're moving forward only because you think that way, then your feelings haven't changed. You're just really good at telling yourself they have."

Hayley turns to walk away and my chest aches. "Fuck," I groan. "Hayley. *Wait*. You're wrong."

"I need to be alone." She can't even look at me as she collects my clothes from the floor and heads to the bedroom door, motioning for me to walk through it. "Let's talk tomorrow, when we both have a clear head."

"No, Hayls."

"No?" She pauses, her shoulders dropping before she spins to face me. "Why—"

"I'm not kissing Bria. Not now, not ever. But it's not because I'm scared to face my feelings. Or deluding myself in saying I've moved on. I'm not kissing her because I don't want to. She told me on the phone tonight that she feels the same way I did. I *did*. Past tense. And do you know what I felt?" I pause, letting that all sink in before repeating my question. "Do you?"

"No."

"*Nothing*, Hayls. I felt *nothing* for her. Except maybe sadness, knowing our friendship will never recover from this."

"Reed." Hayley's eyes soften as she steps forward, but it's my turn to hold up my hand.

"No. Wait. I have *never* felt for anyone the way I feel for you. Deny it all you want, but I know you feel it too. This thing between us has been real for a long time. You don't want me to kiss Bria for *me*. You want me to kiss her because you're scared. And that's the exact reason why I won't. Because I would never do that to you. This is real. We *are* together, and I'm no cheater. I liked her once, sure. Hell, I more than liked her. But it's nothing compared to how I feel about you."

"You can't know that unless you—"

"Fuck that, Hayley. I'm nothing like the guys you used to date, so don't try and turn me into that. It won't work. You said so yourself. I'm your golden boy. *Your* golden boy. And you're *mine*. You can fight this all you want, but I lo—"

"No. Please. Don't."

"Hayls?"

"Don't say it." She shakes her head and I audibly sigh. "Please."

Dropping my face into my hands, I let out a guttural groan before I stand tall and nod, giving in. "Okay." I sigh in resignation. I'm not going to win this argument tonight, but I refuse to give up.

Doing as she requested, I move toward the bedroom door, grabbing my clothes from her outstretched hand. But I've barely taken a step when she intertwines our fingers, attempting to stop me. "I'm not ready," she rushes out, her fingers squeezing mine. "I'm not ready," she repeats and I close my eyes, letting out a relieved breath as my head falls back.

"Reed?" she questions before I've turned to face her, and when I do, her sad expression breaks me. "Please don't give up on me. Not yet." Her voice shakes and I drop my clothes, pulling her into my arms, my chest tightening along with my hold, my body deflating as all the frustration and hurt seeps from my pores.

"*Hayls.*" She's so strong all the time but it's these moments that mean the most. When she lets me in.

Wriggling out of my grip, she steps away and a nervous smile tugs at her lips.

Without a word, I pull her back into me, pressing my lips to her forehead, breathing her in. I'm not giving up. I don't have it in me to leave her. Not yet. "I'll wait, Hayls. Of course I'll fucking wait."

"Thank God." She curls her hands around my arms and holds on for dear life. "I can't lose you. I don't know what I'd do if that ever happened. And that's what scares me the most."

"You're not going to lose me, Hayley. But I can't kiss her. I won't."

"I understand. I'm sorry. It doesn't matter. I just need time. Please just wait." Resting her chin on my chest, she glances up at me, hitting me with another rare moment of vulnerability, her expression uncertain as she pleads.

"I promise. I'll wait. But you have nothing to worry about... I don't love you anyway," I lie, speaking into her hair, smiling when her body shakes in amusement.

She doesn't respond, but she doesn't have to. We've already established I'm a bad liar.

And now she knows the truth.

I love her. And I'm never letting her go.

CHAPTER FIFTY

HAYLEY

Being the gentleman that he is, Reed offers to sleep on the couch, wanting to give me a moment to myself—his words, not mine—proceeding to tell me to take all the time I need.

I smile in understanding, but the second the bedroom door clicks shut, I fall in a heap, sliding down beside the bed, my knees tucked up to my chest.

I'm not sure how much time passes with me staring at the wall, but when a siren blares just outside the window, I finally snap out of it.

What am I doing? I'm pushing away the only man I've ever come close to loving, because of what? Because I'm scared he'll break me beyond repair? That's not me. I'm not the girl that thinks about the long-term consequences. I make choices on a whim, I throw caution to the wind, and yet, suddenly I'm running away.

Getting up, I pace the room quietly so I don't wake Reed, giving myself a pep talk. If I screw this up because I refuse to take a chance on us, I'm only going to hurt myself that much more.

That man out there—that beautiful soul with a dirty mouth—somehow became my world, and I can't bear the thought of being without him.

He's the calm to my tornado. The peace to my crazy. The golden retriever to my wildcat. The— *Wait.*

Wildcat? Reed's tattoo. He has a new paw print on his chest. With claws... I remember seeing that weeks ago. Months even. But it wasn't there the first time I saw his bare chest. It wasn't there at the wake park.

What am I doing?

I rush to open the door but pause when I find Reed's large frame sprawled out on the couch, one arm covering his eyes. From the outside, you'd think he was peacefully sleeping, but I know him well enough to say that's not the case. Especially considering his fist is clenched and he still has the towel wrapped around his waist.

He's awake.

With a soft smile, I tiptoe to the couch and lift his arm, curling myself into his body.

Balancing in the small space beside him, I wrap his arm around me, locking myself against his hard chest.

With my head close to his heart, I both feel and hear his relieved sigh, the warmth of his palm settling on my back, holding me tightly.

"Fuck, Hayls," he whispers, his raspy voice penetrating my thick skin. "I missed you."

He presses a kiss to my head and I giggle. "I don't think it's been that long."

"Even so. I'm not sure you understand the crazy that goes through my mind whenever you're around. All I see is *you*, Hayls. And it's been like that for a while now."

My eyes focus on his wildcat tattoo and I smile. "How long?"

"What?"

"How long have you wanted me?"

"I think I've wanted you since the day we first met."

I draw in a breath and hate that my mind goes where it shouldn't. "But Bria—"

"That's the thing, Hayls." He wriggles around, effortlessly repositioning me until he can look me in the eyes. "Bria's the reason I think that way. From the moment you walked into my life, I felt Bria pull back. As though she was threatened, or couldn't stand sharing the attention. But I'm only now realizing how stupid I've been, because it wasn't Bria at all. It was *me*. I pulled back. *I* changed."

My breath hitches and I want to believe him but... "You loved her once," I say, glancing away, my heart pounding as the words fall from my lips. We've joked about this and he always denied it, always said it was merely attraction. But how can he be so sure?

Reed's forefinger and thumb curl around my chin before he lifts my head to face him, forcing me to see the emotion in his eyes. "I don't think I *ever* loved her. I can't have. Not considering how much I care for you. But even if I did, I don't feel that way anymore."

"I'm sorry." My voice comes out raspy until I clear my throat. "I'm just so freaking scared."

"I know, Baby."

My hands flatten against his chest as he pulls me into his arms, pressing another kiss to my head. "I know," he repeats against my hair. "But you're only scared because you're making our story about someone else. And it shouldn't be. It's just you and me, Hayls." He lifts me as he sits up, perching me on his lap, his hands cupping my face. "It's always been you and me. It just took us both far too long to see it."

I let his words sink in and wrap around my heart, feeling them down to the very depths of my soul. "Okay," I whisper, unable to form the right words.

"Okay?" He raises a brow in question.

"Yes, I came out here because I realized something... I may not be ready to say those three little words, but that doesn't mean I can't *show* you how I feel, or listen when you bare your heart. As I opened that door, I had a question on my lips." My eyes drop to his tattoo again and a fresh wave of emotion overwhelms me. "But the second I saw you, it didn't matter. Because I know the answer. You can say it now. I think I'm ready to hear it."

Reed's eyes widen before his hands sink into my hair, his hold possessive as his gaze bores into mine. "You think? How about I soften it a little... Hayley, I have never *not* loved someone the way I *don't* love you." His lips pull into a soft grin and I match it, my heart jolting in my chest.

"You're the worst liar," I whisper as his love warms me from inside. "I—"

"Wait." Reed presses his lips to mine, cutting me off, and when we part again, I gasp at the intensity of his gaze. "I want to tell you the truth. Please."

"Okay," I whisper. "I'm ready."

"Are you sure? It's going to be deep and probably corny."

I snort as I laugh. Only Reed would know exactly what to say to calm me. "Hit me with it."

"You, Hayley Marie Jackman, are the bane of my existence." My eyes narrow as he laughs, but before I can say anything, he presses a finger to my lips. "Before you, I thought I knew who I was and what I wanted. I was happy to coast through life, smiling and doing the right thing. But you changed all that. You changed *me*. I went from being someone that looked for the good in every situation to wanting to burn the world down to protect you, desperate to shield you from anyone that might want to cause you harm. And I've never felt more like myself. I know you're strong. I know you can look after yourself. Probably better than I can. But I want to be the man that stands by your side. I want to be your person. The guy you come home to after a tough day. The guy you trust to watch you break, while you're holding it together for the rest of the world. The guy you laugh with, cry with, the guy you choose to take on all your crazy adventures. I want to be that man. And I'm willing to wait a lifetime to get there. You're my rock, my heart, my oxygen. And I plan to spend all my days showing you *exactly* how you deserve to be loved."

I sniff as my eyes fill with tears and the world around us ceases to exist. "I want all of that too, Reed. But I'm scared. Our fake relationship is the deepest connection I've ever felt to another human, and I *know* I'm falling in love with you. I am. I'm just terrified that I'll mess it all up. Or *you* will. That you'll realize I'll never compare to Br—"

"Hayley—"

"No, wait. I promise after this I'll never worry about her again. But I need to get it off my chest. I told you about my family. And I wasn't lying. They loved and supported me, but that love never felt anywhere near as strong as yours does. And that raises the stakes. If they hurt me, my heart would crack, but if *this* ends, if I lose you, it'll obliterate my soul, my very being. Because I have never felt more vulnerable than I do with you. I've never allowed myself to feel that. Somewhere along the way, my heart became yours. *I* became yours, and if I lose you, I lose a piece of myself. I'll never be the same again."

Reed shakes as his throat bobs. "I would never let that happen, Hayley." His voice cracks with the weight of emotion. "You have *all* of me. I surrender it all to you. Let me show you that I'm worth taking a risk on. Let me prove to you that I'm not going anywhere." He places his hand on the paw print above his heart and my chest swells. "Because you're here," he whispers, his eyes locked with mine. "Forever etched onto my soul."

"That tattoo's for me, isn't it?"

"It is." Reed smiles and a moment of pride takes over him. It could be the fact that I figured it out, or it could be something more.

"And the rest?" I grimace as I voice the question I should have kept to myself, and from his frown, he knows what I'm really asking. "It doesn't matter," I add before he can respond. "I promised I wouldn't worry and—"

"There are none, Hayls. Not a single one."

Though it probably shouldn't, my heart soars as I'm overcome with emotion, and when it all gets too much, his words from earlier float through my mind. "It's always been you and me. It's just you and me."

And God, I hope it always will be.

After spending the weekend together, as a *real* couple, Reed takes a piece of me with him when he leaves early Monday morning, though it eases my mind knowing I'll be home before long.

I'm not needed on set Monday, but when I'm due on location Tuesday, I feel confident turning up, safe in the knowledge that the production team has my back.

After speaking to the police, Reed held my hand as I filled in my agent and the *Reckless Desire* production manager. And while I know it's hard for them to completely side with me when Cam's pleading his innocence—claiming that all he did was send flowers and chocolates to a friend—it was nice to have their support.

It may be because I filed a restraining order, but they're taking my suspicion seriously. So, now it's a waiting game until the damn thing gets implemented.

"I can't believe he was stalking you," Brooklyn says as she links her arm through mine, walking with me to set.

Despite the fact that security has been advised not to let Cameron on the premises, I've had an unofficial bodyguard with me all day. And right now, it's Brook.

"Honestly, I can't believe it either."

"Wait." Brooklyn shakes her head. "I didn't mean it like that. The truth is, I *can* believe it. I'm just shocked."

"What do you mean?"

"He was always looking at you. Watching. I stupidly thought he was staying in character, but I should have said something." She grimaces while I rush to reassure her.

"This isn't on you, Brooklyn. I didn't see it either. No one did."

"Well, I'm glad your hot football-star boyfriend was there when it all came out."

"Me too," I half lie. I wish he'd never been caught up in it, but I'm thankful he was with me.

Our first day without Cam runs relatively smoothly, and for the next two weeks, life moves at a snail's pace, my days dragging, my nights lonely, an anxious feeling settling in my chest right until the moment our chartered flight touches down at San Fran International.

Then I'm happy again. I'm home.

CHAPTER FIFTY-ONE

REED

I bite back a groan as I walk through the locker room the Wednesday after my Texas trip, my smile bright as all eyes flash my way. I look like I've gone a few rounds with Mike Tyson. Actually, no...it looks like Mike Tyson beat the shit out of me and I never even got a punch in.

I thought it was going to be okay, since I only caught a couple of fists to the face, but it's day five now and the bruising looks worse. But it's not even the bruising that has me wanting to groan; it's my goddamn rib cage. For a guy half my size, that fucker could throw a punch. And his aim was on point, hitting me in the same spot every single time.

With that being said, I'd do it all again. In fact, I wish I'd done more after what he was doing to Hayley.

While my teammates have definitely noticed my face, I somehow make it to my locker without question and breathe a sigh of relief, until...

"Am I seeing things or is our golden boy not so golden anymore?" *Dammit.*

I turn to find Luke and my groan finally releases. "What can I say? Keeping up with Hayley is a full-time job."

"Damn." He bounces his eyebrows before stepping closer and leaning in. "If it's like this when it's fake, imagine what it would be like if shit got real." His head falls back and he laughs at his own joke while I stare at him deadpan, laughing on the inside. *That's no joke, my friend. It is as real as it gets. Just you wait.*

Luke walks away, still chuckling to himself and I can't help but smile. I'll always be golden where it counts, but you better believe I'm going to fight for my girl, especially with fuckers who think it's okay to follow her around.

The team's lucky I'm here because right now, the only thing keeping me sane is that Cameron's been sent back to California and she's safe in Texas. But until Hayley's restraining order gets signed off, I'm going to be on edge.

The next two weeks fly by, and when it's time to meet Hayley at the airport, I'm not at all ashamed to admit I'm fucking giddy about it. We've spoken often, but having her back, and finally in my arms, will put my mind at ease.

We agreed to meet near the baggage carousels, but I can't wait that long, jogging through the terminal to catch her when she exits the secure area, my heart pounding in my chest.

I arrive just as she moves through the doors, pausing at the threshold when our eyes lock, knowing with certainty that when she smiles, this is real.

Just like she did the last time we'd been apart, she takes off in a run and throws herself into my arms, but this time instead of doing it for the cameras, I wish we were alone.

Catching her easily, I slam my lips to hers, my tongue immediately seeking entry, and we kiss like nobody's watching until I realize they probably are.

Hayley's grinning when I pull back. "Oops. I'm not sure if that was PG, but God, I missed you." She presses her lips back to mine before kissing my cheeks and nose. "It should be illegal to be separated from your boyfriend for that long."

I chuckle as I lower her to the carpet but keep her close in my hold. "We were apart for longer before my visit."

"Yes, but it wasn't rea—"

I growl low in my throat, cutting her off. "We're not playing pretend anymore, Hayls. You know it's been real for longer than that."

"I know." Her lips curl into a smirk and I roll my eyes. "But I love it when you growl."

"I don't growl."

"Yeah, you do. And it makes me want to ride you like a horse."

"I thought I was the cowboy?"

"So you want to be the one to ride me?"

"You bet your ass I do. But we're in the middle of the arrivals lounge surrounded by hundreds of people that think they know us." I step closer and brush the hair away from her ear, making her shiver. "I'd appreciate it if you didn't give me a boner this time."

She bursts out laughing as I step back, shaking my head. "Does that mean you're not open to a public romp?"

"I don't share. *Ever*. No one gets to see your pleasure but me. Now let's go." I point toward the exit before glancing back her way. And when I note her flustered expression, I smile, offering to take her bag.

"I think I'm going to enjoy being your girl, Reed," she says with a bounce in her step. "I really should have done this sooner. But there's no time like the present." She smiles wide before my phone buzzes at the same time hers does.

"I bet it's the Bennetts," she says with a grin, pulling her phone from her bag. "Yep. It's Amelia."

"Then this will be Luke." I slide my phone from my pocket, reading my message while Hayley reads hers.

> LUKE: BACK TO SCHOOL PARTY PEOPLE!! BE THERE OR BE SQUARE

> LUKE: It's tomorrow by the way and I'm not taking no for an answer

Hayley laughs, drawing my gaze, but with her eyes locked on her phone, I keep reading my messages.

> EASTON LEFT THE GROUP

> LUKE ADDED EASTON TO THE GROUP

> LUKE: I forgot to mention... Amelia already texted the girls. East... future wifey rsvp'd. See you soon.

I chuckle when the messages stop and lift my gaze to find Hayley staring back at me.

"Let me guess. Party tomorrow?" She shows me her screen and I smile.

> AMELIA: Back to school party at our place tomorrow

> AMELIA: And yes... that's what Luke's calling it. This didn't come from me

> PAIGE: We'll be there. I'll drag Easton by the ear if I have to

I show Hayley my screen next and she laughs out loud, and while I smile at her happiness, a thought hits me.

"Are you ready to make our official debut?" I ask, a mischievous joy taking over me.

"I sure am. But let's have some fun with it." Hayley winks, linking her arm through mine.

"Anything for you, Baby. Anytime."

Hayley's on the pool deck when I arrive at Luke's, her long, blonde hair pulled away from her flawless cheeks, her smile radiant as she chats with Amelia. And just like always, my heart jolts. It's safe to say she gets more beautiful every time I see her, and right now, in her see-through dress over her scarlet bikini, I've never loved her more.

It doesn't matter that she hasn't said it back. She doesn't need to. If keeping those three little words close to her chest helps her feel protected, she can keep them to herself for the rest of her life. Because I don't need her to say it. I can feel it.

She loves me just like I love her.

And I've never been happier.

I watch her for a moment, her face alight with excitement, and it's not until she glances up, her gaze locking with mine, that I finally make my way over.

"You're here!" Hayley lights up in excitement and, in a move we've mastered, throws herself into my arms before pressing her lips to mine, molding our mouths in a deep kiss reminiscent of our moment in the airport. And just like then, we have an audience, only this time, our audience makes themselves known.

"Get a room," Luke whines behind me. "My daughter does *not* need to see that."

"She's napping inside, Luke," Lainey scolds. "Leave them alone."

I chuckle against Hayley's lips before pulling back with a smile. "Hey, Baby. I missed you." I wink, loving it when she giggles. "It's been *too* long," I tell her, even though it hasn't—she woke up in my arms this morning— but I can't get enough of her.

"What's going on here?" Amelia interrupts, her eyes bouncing between mine and Hayley's, her expression suspicious. "Something's different."

"Nope. Just kissing my girlfriend." I shrug like it's no big deal while Hayley bites back a grin.

"Your girlfriend or your *girlfriend*?"

"Aren't they the same?" I tease.

"No, they're very different and... Oh my God," Amelia squeals and I never pictured her as a squealer. "You're together. You're *together* together."

"Well, that didn't take long." I jokingly check my watch. "It's barely been five minutes."

"Amelia's very perceptive," Hayley notes, reaching forward to squeeze Amelia's hand.

"That and the fact that Reed just mauled you as though you're the air that he breathes."

That makes sense, because she is. "What can I say? We're a cliché. Just like the movies. The fake became real."

"Oh. My. God." Amelia squeals again before dragging Hayley as close as she can and whispering in her ear.

I let them have their girl time, while I head off to talk to the guys, ignoring Luke when he bounces his eyebrows.

"So it's official?" he asks, pulling his phone from his pocket. "I think that means Dylan wins fifty bucks."

"What?" My eyes flash to Dylan's and he grins proudly.

"I saw it coming a mile away." He gloats while I fake a groan.

"Why are you even here?" I joke. "You're retired."

"Can't help myself; I miss being a part of the action. Plus, I'm still on the group chat."

"A group chat *I* don't really need anymore," I say as Easton appears out of nowhere, as if that talk of the group chat summoned him.

"Guess there's no point in having it now," he's quick to say. "May as well shut it down."

"No chance, Wilder." Luke grins, clapping him on the back. "You're with us until you die."

"Or you do?" Easton raises an eyebrow conspiratorially, and I chuckle.

"East,"—Luke steps forward, cupping Easton on the shoulder—"I can promise that you'll never escape me. I'll take pride in haunting you for the rest of your days."

"So, no different to now?" Easton chuckles as he jokingly massages his temples, his out of character behavior drawing attention.

"Did Easton just laugh?" Keeley calls out and Luke smirks gloatingly.

"Of course he did." Luke waves her off. "I'm a funny man." Amelia snorts at the same time Hayley erupts with giggles, both of them choosing that moment to join us.

"He's got a good laugh, right?" Luke adds, clearly a little tipsy. "Maybe if we all told him that, he'd laugh more." He nudges Easton in the stomach, and Easton's smile fades.

"Way to ruin the moment, Luke," Amelia teases, making Easton bite back a grin as Paige wanders over. I'd say his newfound happiness has less to do with seeking compliments and more to do with his relationship with Paige. He's definitely more open because of it. Like her sunshine rubbed off on him.

And I get it. I thought I was happy before Hayley but now...it's tenfold.

For the next couple of hours, Hayley and I spend some time together, but most of it is spent apart, and an ease settles in my chest. I hate comparing things with Bria, but we were friends for years and she never got to know my teammates and friends, while Hayley fits right in like she's always belonged here. And I truly believe that she did. That she does.

It feels right. Meant to be. *Forever.*

As though reading my mind, Hayley glances up from where she's talking to Dylan and Summer, and her beaming happiness steals my breath, distracting me from my conversation. *Not that I was listening.*

"Reed?" Thomas waves a hand in front of my face before he laughs. "And another one's down."

"You won't hear me arguing. I'm happy to admit, I'm a goner."

Thomas chuckles just as Isaac rushes past, chasing after Luke's dog. He dodges a chair and bumps into Hayley, sending her flying toward the pool. My stomach sinks until Landon catches her at the last second, pulling her away from the edge.

"Thank fuck," Thomas says from beside me while my heart returns to normal. "That was a close one. But the panic on your face... You *are* a goner."

"No doubt about it."

Hayley's still smiling when I wander over to where she and Landon are standing by the edge, her eyes locked with mine. And when I reach her, she grins.

"You said you wanted a dog, right?" she asks, confusing me until I make the connection with what just happened. "You know, we never talked about kids," she adds. "And I'm thinking...one or the other."

Her infectious laughter always draws me in, but I'm too caught up in her words to respond. All I can do is stare in awe as she continues to talk. "Luckily, Landon was there to help. *Again.*" She wraps an arm around his shoulders and his face reddens. *Poor innocent fucker.* "I feel much safer now that he's joined the group."

Landon laughs awkwardly while I roll my eyes, snapping out of my moment. "Thanks for saving my girl, Landon. I appreciate it."

Before he can respond, Hayley grabs my hand and drags me away. "I need a drink," she announces, beelining for the makeshift bar.

When we reach the fridge, she turns my way and smiles brightly, taking my mind back to what she said before talking to Landon. *She's bringing up kids?*

My awe returns and she giggles. "Reed? Did—"

Grabbing her face in my hands, I silence her with my mouth, wordlessly showing her what she means to me. She may not have told me she loves me, but after that, I don't need her words. She gave me the future. And now I'm going to do everything I can to protect that.

"What was that for?" she asks, her cheeks flushed, when I pull away.

"Get used to it, Hayls. I love you. I'm going to kiss you whenever I damn well want." I wink and she lets out another laugh.

"Fine by me. Are we going for round two? Or are you ready to drink?"

Without answering, I wrap my arms around her waist and kiss her again, bending her backward until she squeals—as if I'd ever drop her. After lifting her to standing, I turn away and open the fridge. "I'm ready for a drink."

Hayley giggles behind me but doesn't say a word until I've handed her a cider. "You amaze me, boyfriend. Never a dull moment."

"Like almost falling in the pool?" I smirk.

"Exactly."

A splash draws our attention, finding Luke in the water, his phone raised above his head as Thomas laughs from the edge. "We've got a game in a week, Bennett. You need to work on your balance."

"You pushed me, asshole," Luke retorts.

"You were arguing with my wife."

"She's my sister."

"Either way, it shouldn't have been that easy to push you in. You need to be better. It's my last season and I've got another Super Bowl to win."

"What?" All eyes turn to Thomas while mine flash to Lainey, catching her surprised expression.

"I thought you weren't going to announce it yet," she says, her head shaking as she rolls her eyes.

"I changed my mind." Thomas shrugs like it's no big deal.

Luke pushes up out of the pool, and as the shock wears off, the questions start firing from around the yard. I listen to Thomas's answers, but when Hayley giggles, my attention shifts to her.

"Now I wish I'd gone in," she says, her eyes on the pool. "It looks nice in there."

I smile in response, my gaze locked on her lips as they quirk into a grin. God, I love her.

"Stop staring. It's creepy," she says without looking my way, her smile turning coy. "I've already got a stalker."

"Hayls." I groan, tugging her hand until she faces me. "That's nothing to joke about."

"I have to joke or I'll never stop thinking about it. I still get the feeling I'm being watched."

Fuck, I hate this for her. Despite the fact that she finally got a restraining order, I'm still pissed off that asshole denied almost everything.

The police department has tried to make a connection, but unless we find more evidence, they've got nothing to go on. And it has me on edge. "It's going to feel like that until that fucker is charged, but I promise you, I will always be there to protect you. And if I'm not, one of our friends will."

Hayley releases a slow breath as she smiles. "You're right. I shouldn't have joked about it." She pouts and it's so fucking adorable my lips twitch.

"It's fine." I wave her off. "But let me promise you this. If he ever breaks the rules of that restraining order, I'll kill him."

I don't even think I'm kidding. Just because her job is in the public eye doesn't give people the right to try and forcefully enter her life, or make her feel scared to be out in the world.

Hayley's eyes widen but before she can comment, Amelia drags her away to help with Juliet.

I move to join the rest of the group when my phone buzzes with a text, and I curse when I see that it's Dad.

> DAD: Any chance you can come back before your birthday and bring your girl? Things are not great around here

My heart seizes as I put on a smile, pretending I'm okay, and as the day turns to night and the drinking kicks up a notch, I ignore my family for the first time in forever, letting myself off the hook.

Drinking my troubles away.

Living in the moment. I'm surrounded by friends, the season's about to start, and I've got the girl. *It's about time I focused on my happiness instead of everyone else's.*

Hayley throws her hands over her head as she dances with Paige, her hair illuminated by the glow of the moon, reminding me of our night on the beach.

And I know exactly what I want—or need—right now. It's her.

As if sensing my thoughts, she raises a brow before twisting her fingers, summoning me over. And like the good boy I am, I go, pulling her into my arms when I reach her.

"Has anyone ever told you how perfect you are when you dance?"

"I've heard it once or twice." She winks and my eyes widen as she laughs out loud. "But none of them matter except you."

"Good answer." I bite my lip before leaning forward, sucking the skin beneath her ear. "Want to get out of here?" I whisper, making her shiver.

"Now?" she questions, her eyes bouncing around the room.

"Yes, now. We've been here all day and I've barely had time to talk to you."

"So you want to talk?" Her gaze drops to my chest before she tilts her head in contemplation.

"No, I don't want to talk." I lean in close again, this time nibbling on her lobe. "I want to fuck." I want to live in the moment for once.

"Shit, Reed. I want the same." She grabs my hand and shamelessly leads me to the back gate, ignoring the questions from our friends.

"You're not going to say goodbye?" I ask.

"I think they got the picture."

"Trust me, they didn't. I'm the golden boy, remember? I guarantee no one is picturing the dirty things I want to do to you."

"Jesus. Add tipsy Reed to the list of Reeds I like. This just keeps getting better and better."

Chapter Fifty-Two

REED

A week later, I read Hayley's good morning text twice and smile before the anxiety kicks in.

After leaving Luke and Amelia's, we'd shared an amazing night together, and when I woke up with her in my arms, I told her about my dad's text, relaxing when she didn't hesitate to offer to come with me.

For the next week, we spent every spare moment together, around her additional days of studio filming and my practice.

But now we're apart.

I'm in Florida for our first preseason game of the year, while she's back at home, staying at my place because it's closer to set.

I finally understand why some of my teammates leave our celebrations early. I get it. I already miss her and it's barely been a day. The strangest part —or maybe it's not so strange now that I know my true feelings—is that I never really missed Bria like this. For years I thought I was on the way being in love with her, but it turns out, I had no idea what love really was.

And God, I wish Hayley and I had gotten our shit together sooner. We could have spent more of the offseason as a couple.

After stretching my body, I lie in bed for a few extra minutes before getting up, trying hard not to think about leaving Hayley alone in the same city as her stalker, while also worrying about my mom.

I should be thinking about my pregame rituals, like I have for the past fifteen or so years of my life.

But that life is different now, and it's time to adjust.

When I'm up, I bounce my shoulders and head toward the en suite in my room, determined to get in the zone, until the hotel phone rings, making me jump. *Am I late?* I check the time as I answer, and relief fills me when the clock reads six fifteen.

I'm early. I still have plenty of time.

Why am I up? And why did Hayley text me in the middle of the night, her time, to say good morning?

Shaking off my thoughts, I rush to grab the phone and hesitatingly answer. "Hello?"

"Mr. Coombs," one of the concierges says in his sharp professional voice. "I have Miss Jackman here for you. It's our policy to—"

"Miss Jackman?" My brows crease. How is that possible? "Can I speak to her?" I'd never usually question it, but considering all that Hayley's been through, I want to make sure I'm not about to find a stranger at my door.

Hayley and I may have only recently become a couple, but according to the public, it's been months. It wouldn't be hard for someone to pretend to be her.

The phone goes quiet before Hayley whines, "Let me up, Reed. It's early and I'm freaking exhausted."

The phone crackles and then a man's voice comes back on the line. "Would you like me to—"

"Please send her up," I cut in, desperate to see her. "Thank you."

"Of course."

He hangs up and I abandon my shower, throwing a towel around my waist before tossing the covers over the bed and meeting Hayley at the door.

"Didn't believe it was me, huh?" She sashays toward me and my heart races. She's here. In Florida. For me.

"The surprise was too good to be true. What are you doing here?" I pull her into my arms and press my lips to her head but it's not enough. Grabbing her face, I steal her breath with a kiss and she surrenders easily, moaning against my mouth.

With our lips connected, I walk backward, pulling Hayley over the threshold, kicking the door shut when we're both inside. She mewls, her fingers grazing my body, and I groan right back. I could spend a lifetime kissing this woman and never tire of it, but when my phone buzzes, she breaks away, making me pout.

"Oh, stop." She smiles brightly. "I didn't come here to monopolize your time. I came to watch my boyfriend play football."

She sucks her lips into her mouth, hiding her smile, while I grin excitedly. "I like the way that sounds."

"How much?"

"More than you can imagine. How about I show you?" I don't give her a chance to respond before I bend down and grab her around the waist, throwing her over my shoulder. She squeals as she smacks my ass, trying to remove my towel, but I'm too quick, dropping her on the bed with a thud, pinning her beneath me.

"What about your phone call?"

"Shhh." I press a finger to her lips and smile. "You're going to get me in trouble."

"Why?"

"Because I have a girl in my room." I raise an eyebrow and her eyes bulge.

"I thought that was a college thing."

It is a college thing, but from the fire that just ignited in her eyes, I almost wish it wasn't. "You love the idea of this being forbidden, don't you?"

"A little bit." She bites her finger while I stifle a groan. "What time are you due at the stadium?"

"Very soon," I lie. "If I'm late, one of our coaches will come looking."

Hayley's eyes narrow before she laughs. "I know you're messing with me, but I'm going to play along. Are we talking minutes?"

I lean forward until I'm so close my breath warms her skin. "Want to find out?"

"God, *yes*."

My cock twitches in anticipation. But I have to say something first. Grabbing her chin, I guide her face to mine, letting my hand fall to her heart, staring into her wide eyes.

"I'm about to fuck you hard, Hayls. So before I do, I want to remind you that I love you, and I'm grateful that you're here." She gasps and her chest rises, her heart pounding beneath my palm. "You're my girl, Hayls. I love being your man."

With her lips trapped between her teeth, she takes a deep breath, her gaze boring into mine. "And I love being your girl."

"Good." *Close enough.* I'll take it. "Now where were we?"

Curling my fingers around her wrists, I lift them above her head, holding both securely with one hand. "I don't think you understand how good it feels to have you here. In my arms." I slide my hand beneath her tiny shorts and cup her pussy, feeling her soaked panties beneath my palm. "Someone's ready." I massage her core, my eyes locked on mouth.

"I am and I think I have an idea," she gasps, bucking into my hard cock. Her breath quickens and I smirk until she whispers, "You promised me a hard fuck and I'm waiting."

"The sass," I growl, squeezing her wrists tighter as I slide my knee between her legs, settling my hand around her neck. "Ride my knee, baby. You'll get my hands and mouth when I'm ready."

She lets out a breathy mewl as her hips buck, and when I roll my knee, she groans. Tightening the grip on her neck, I lean forward and capture her bottom lip between mine, nibbling on the flesh.

Her mouth opens in a silent gasp and I take advantage, swirling my tongue with hers, rocking my leg in time with her thrusts.

Her perfectly flushed body shakes as I kiss a path down her neck, stopping when I reach her button-up shirt. Smiling, I let go of her wrists and neck and release the top button. "This is convenient, since I have you on your back."

"What can I say? I find it sexy to watch a man work for it."

"Is that right? Well, I hope you're not in love with this shirt, because I don't plan on working too hard." Sitting up, I grip the material with both hands and rip it apart, watching the buttons pop to reveal her see-through lace bra. "Fuck, you're gorgeous. Look at these perfect nipples begging for attention. I can see them through the lace."

Licking my lips, I kiss my way from her navel to her breasts and bite down on each nipple, sucking the bud into my mouth as she cries out.

"Do you think it's time I fucked these?" I ask as I straighten, not giving her a chance to answer before I crawl on top of her, careful not to crush her under my weight. "What do you think? Would you like my cock between your tits, or..." I trail off and she bites her lips.. "Would you prefer my cock filling your pussy while my finger plays with your ass? I remember you liked that."

"Oh, God. I want you inside me, Reed. I need it. Now."

Removing my towel, I release my cock and we both watch as it bounces between us, a bead of cum pooling at the tip.

Hayley lifts to her elbows for a better look and I groan when one of her breasts brushes my tip. "Fuck, you're glorious. Maybe I'll do both."

Pushing her back down with my palm, I shift up the bed and hover above her, struggling to maintain control when she licks her lips and grabs her breasts, squeezing them together. "I want you, Reed. But be quick. I need you between my legs."

Fuck. My cock twitches as I lower myself, sliding my length between her tits, riding her as she rocks against me, her tongue peeking out to lick me every time my tip gets close. She lifts her feet to the bed and I glance back, catching her rolling her hips, fucking the air behind me as I move on top of her, my knees shaking from holding my weight.

"Reed, I—" She circles her nipples with her thumbs and groans, her eyes closing, her expression pinched in ecstasy.

"Are you ready for my cock, Baby? Ready for me to sink inside you?"

"Yes. Please." Her eyes flash open and she stares up at me, her gaze thick with desire.

"I'm going to need your help first."

"Anything," she rasps, her voice breathy as she lifts to her elbows again. And fuck, I love this version of her. The hint of submission as she takes what she needs. Just the thought of her begging has my cock pulsing so hard it aches.

Needing a release, I move up her body and brush my tip against her lips, biting back a groan. "Get it wet for me, Baby." I pump my cock against her mouth, brushing the tip across her lips. "I need to feel you bare. Just for a second."

Hayley moans as she wraps her perfect lips around my girth, flattening her tongue against the tip. My cock throbs in her mouth and I groan as my head falls back. "That's it, Baby. Take it all."

A shaky moan escapes her as she sucks, and the sound of it vibrates against my skin, sending a spark straight to my balls. "Fuck, yes."

Curling her fingers around my thigh, Hayley drags me into her until my tip hits the back of her throat. "Jesus." I jolt, a deep growl releasing from my chest. "That's enough or I'm going to come before I've had a chance to fuck you."

With one last roll of her tongue against my length, Hayley releases me with a pop, licking her lips while I groan again.

Desperate for more, I'm quick to climb off the bed, repositioning myself between her legs, reaching for the waistband of her shorts. She lifts her ass so I can drag them down her legs before curling my fingers through the string of her thong.

"I'm on the pill," she says suddenly, her hand gently stopping me. "And we've already had the other chat."

She stares at me pointedly and my cock throbs, imagining the feel of her wrapped around me. "Are you sure?" I slow my pace in a moment of panic, my gaze bouncing between her eyes.

"Yes. God. Yes. Please. I need to feel you too."

"Thank fuck." Ripping her panties from her body, I toss them across the room before grabbing her arms and pulling her to stand. "Turn around and crawl onto the bed," I demand, until her brows rise and I jokingly roll my eyes. "Sass me and I'll fuck my hand."

"I call bullshit. But I'm not going to sass you. I'm so ready for this I'm dripping for you."

Spinning around, she does as I asked and crawls on the bed, only stopping when she's in the middle. Then with a quick glance over her shoulder, she hits me with a smile before spreading her knees and burying her face in the sheets, angling her pussy toward me.

And holy fuck. My balls tighten as I take in the beautiful sight, running a finger through her slick heat, spreading her arousal over her, my own pre-cum pooling at my tip.

"I think you like being told what to do, Hayls." She whimpers yes. "And God knows I like telling you."

Grabbing her hips, I drag her to the edge of the bed and line myself up with her hole, pushing inside her slowly, feeling her warmth as she coats my cock.

"Fuuuuck, this feels so good. You feel so good. Jesus."

When I'm buried as deep as I can go, I freeze, needing a second to adjust to this new sensation, being bare for the very first time.

"Can you feel that?" I ask, my voice raspy. "Feel the way your pussy sucks me in, the way it swallows me whole." Hayley cries as she bucks against me, and I grunt when my cock jolts. "Jesus Christ, Hayls. Warn a guy."

"I'm going to do it again, Reed. Now." She rocks into me again, but this time I'm ready for her, meeting her thrust, slamming into her with force.

She rears back as her face lifts off the bed. "Oh, God. Yes, Reed."

With my fingers biting into her skin, I rock her hips, working her hard as I slam into her, taking my fill, my release building.

Her walls tighten and I reach for her clit, flicking the bud before coating my fingers in her arousal and moving my hand to her ass. "Are you ready for me to fill both holes?"

"God, yes, please."

"Good girl."

Slowing my movements, I gently apply pressure, rocking into her as the tip of my thumb seeks entry.

Her hole puckers as her body shakes, but she pushes against me, seeking more.

I try again, pushing into her ass at the same time I pound into her pussy. And when she cries out, her body jolts and she covers her mouth with her hand, biting down on her thumb.

"Again," she mumbles, rolling her hips as her breaths turn ragged. "I need more, Reed. *Please.*"

Biting my lip, I release a guttural groan and push farther inside her, filling her with my thumb as my movements quicken.

She meets my fervor, pushing against me, her pussy squeezing me as my body quivers.

"Oh, God. Oh, God."

"That's it, Baby. You take me so well. So perfect."

"God, Reed. It feels so good. I've never done this and oh, Godddd."

Christ. Removing my thumb, I lean forward and brush her hair away from her ear, my weight almost bearing down on her. "Are you ready to come?" I don't wait for her to answer just yet, snaking one hand to her front, rolling a finger across her clit. "Tell me you're ready so I can fill you up."

"God, Reed. Yes." Her body jolts as her walls tighten uncomfortably. "Fill me. Please."

"Fuck, baby." I explode into her as she screams my name, burying her face into the bedding, drowning out her cries as we both fall over the edge.

Her body convulses as I continue to move inside her, and I shake from the intensity of the orgasm.

Our rhythm in sync, we both naturally slow until Hayley drops to the bed and I fall into place beside her.

Naked and sated, I drag her into my arms, running my fingers up and down her back, my touch light as a contented sigh leaves my lips. I'm just about to kiss her when my alarm sounds and I curse. "Dammit. I have to go." I'd give anything to sink inside her for round two, but I can't be late. "I wouldn't want the coach to come knocking," I joke before lifting Hayley and repositioning her on the pillow, resting on my elbow to stare down at her. "We've got a meeting before our warmup today. The *text* earlier was Thomas reminding me. They're giving us tips on how to address the media when asked about the General Manager situation. It's come back up in the news."

"God, that sucks." She frowns up at me, her flushed cheeks and messy just-fucked hair making it difficult for me to leave. "Hopefully this one sticks," she continues, pulling me out of my head.

"Wes? I have no doubt. According to Thomas and Dylan, he's a good guy, and from what I've seen during preseason, they're right."

"Good, because he's hot." She fans her face with a grin. "I saw a photo and—"

"He's married with kids," I deadpan.

"Shame."

"Are you going to be trouble all our lives?" I bite back a smile as she nods.

"For as long as you'll have me."

"So, that's a yes?"

"Yes. But you know, you're my main man."

That I do. "It's obvious in the way you ogle me. You can't keep your eyes off my body. It's been that way since we first met."

"What? No way."

"Yes way."

"Fine. What can I say? I'm attracted to the bad boy types and I assumed, when I first saw you, that you were one of them."

She waves her hands at my tattoos as though that proves her point, and I bark out a laugh. "I sure had you fooled. Never judge a book by its cover."

"I'm glad I was wrong. Because you, Reed Antony Coombs, are perfect exactly as you are."

My heart jolts and I hate that I have to leave, but we have a lifetime of these moments ahead of us. With my palms on the bed, I lean forward and press a chaste kiss to her lips before jumping up. "I love you and I wish I could stay—"

"No, you have to go. That's why I'm here."

A thought hits me and I panic, not wanting her to be alone. "Are you here with someone? I don't have a ticket for you and—"

"I'm here with Keeley and Lainey. Keeley has a pass waiting for me."

"Good." I rush out a relieved sigh. "I better get ready."

"And you better win. Otherwise, I wasted my time."

"Hayls, I just gave you the best orgasm of your life. No time was wasted."

"Valid point. But I still want you to win."

Chapter Fifty-Three

HAYLEY

Lainey jumps into the air as Thomas launches the ball to Zane. With seconds to go, we've already won the game, but if we secure a touchdown before the whistle, I'm told it'll be a record win. At least where the Storm is concerned.

I hold my breath as Zane runs toward the end zone, dodging a strike from the opposition's defense, his eyes on the prize as Luke takes the competition down.

Time ticks by, and just when I think their tackle is going to get him, Zane leaps into the air, slamming the ball down over the line, his body crashing to the ground.

And the Storm fans go wild. What a way to start the season.

"They did it, Hayley," Lainey screams, her eyes a little watery. "They did it."

"You're thinking about Thomas's retirement, aren't you?"

"Yeah. It's all he's ever known. I'm scared he'll be lost without it."

"He's got you."

"That's true, and we're getting our new puppy this month, so that'll keep us busy."

"Definitely. Just watching Shadow and Isaac last week made me tired." Lainey smiles knowingly and I laugh. "Nope." I shake my head, anticipating her question. "I'm not thinking about kids...or pets. Yet. But for the first time, I have someone that I might want to explore that with."

"And have fun practicing in the meantime." She winks and I giggle, remembering the way Reed blew my mind this morning. I don't even recognize the woman I become when he speaks dirty to me.

"*Exactly*," I agree with a smile.

After the guys leave the field, I wait around with Lainey and Keeley while they finish with their media commitments, and the second I see Reed, I greet him with my usual response, jumping into his arms.

"I am definitely getting used to this," Reed says as he catches me. "You know I'm going to expect this after every game." He chuckles to himself before his smile fades. "Not that you have to come to all of my games. I know you've got other stuff going on and—"

"Whoa. Hold up. I'll be coming to as many games as I can. I just got your name on my back." I wriggle out of his arms and spin, gathering my hair in my hands, glancing over my shoulder. Reed's eyes fall to his name and he groans.

"Fuck, I'm glad I didn't know that until *after* the game." He steps forward until he's close enough for only me to hear. "I would have been distracted thinking about what I'm going to do to you in this jersey."

My eyes widen until his sad face flits back to my mind. "We have time for that later. For now, I'm here to support you, Reed. I'll be here as often as I can."

"Thank you, Hayls. It's nice to know I have someone in the stands."

"Do your parents ever go when they're visiting you or when you play near your hometown?" The question leaves my mouth and his nose immediately scrunches.

"They've been to a couple, but..." He trails off and I get it.

"How come Bria never went? If she knew you didn't have anyone, you'd think she'd go for you."

"She wasn't...isn't a huge football fan. And she worked so hard during the week that she said she needed her Sundays to herself."

"God, you were so pussy-whipped and you never had any pussy." I fold my arms over my chest and huff, pissed off on his behalf. But it has the opposite effect, making Reed burst out laughing.

"I let her get away with a lot for sure, but the only person that could ever pussy-whip me...is you."

"Good to know, Reedy boy. Good to know."

"It's time to par-tay!" Luke calls out, his hands in the air, waving around as though he's already listening to music.

"You wanna head out?" Reed asks, but after the pussy-whipped comment, I have other ideas.

"I do. But I left my purse at the hotel and—"

"Believe it or not, I've got money."

"But you don't have my ID."

"Damn. Okay." He grabs my hand as he turns to Luke. "We'll be there. We just have to go back to the hotel first."

"I bet you do." Luke bounces his eyebrows and I grin while Reed's quick to clarify.

"Hayls needs her ID."

"Poor excuse." Luke shakes his head. "Everyone knows who she is."

"We'll meet you there." Reed stays firm, no room for arguments, not that Luke cares.

"You better."

As we're about to leave, Reed gets caught up in a conversation with Landon, while I hover, only partially listening in.

"Hayley?" Reed says my name, confusion in his expression.

"Sorry, what? I was in my own world."

"Landon asked how you're doing after your pool incident."

"Oh." I laugh out loud. "I'm a little more wary of kids chasing dogs, but otherwise I'm fine. I'm lucky you were there. My hero." I laugh again as my eyes flash to Reed. I'm trying to include Landon as much as I can. Reed said he needed a confidence boost and I'm doing my bit.

"Right place, right time." Landon shrugs, brushing it off.

"Even so, I'm grateful. This one didn't even bat an eyelid." I point to Reed and he fakes a gasp.

"I was on the other side of the pool."

"Exactly. What's that about? Shouldn't you be obsessed with me and always by my side?"

"I apologize, my love. I'll be better. Wait until you see how obsessed I can be. You'll be begging me to stay away."

Landon chuckles awkwardly and I feel for him. "Don't mind Reed. I promise he's still the team's golden boy. I haven't corrupted him too much."

Reed shakes his head, curling his arm around my waist before pulling me into him. "I wouldn't let her if she tried. She thinks she's in control, but she's not."

"*Reed*," I playfully scold. "What's gotten into you? Let's go."

I push him away from me and direct him down the hall, smiling when he waves over his shoulder. But when I turn back, Landon's frowning. "I don't think Landon's going to want you as his mentor anymore. You've gone mad."

"Nope. I'm just a little excited. We won our first game. My girl is here. By my side. I'm living the dream."

"Well, put that dream away in front of the rookies. They need your serious golden boy persona."

Reed glances back and I follow his gaze to see that Landon's gone. "Fine. Next time I'll behave."

Before we've made it to the door, Thomas grabs Reed for a quick chat and I once again wait—not so patiently this time.

Finally, forty-five minutes after first announcing we were leaving, we set off, and we've barely been walking when I groan. "I swear the hotel didn't seem this far away when I walked with Lainey."

Reed chuckles and the sound echoes, sending a message to my core. "What's the rush?"

"Wouldn't you like to know?"

"That's why I asked."

I shrug my shoulders as we round the corner, letting out an exaggerated sigh when we finally see the hotel. But when a lone figure comes into view, I pause, taking in his hunched demeanor. "Is that—"

"Zane. *Shit*." Reed jogs ahead to check on him while I power walk to keep up.

Zane was amazing today. I don't think I've ever seen him play that well. And with his cockiness usually on full display, this is a stark contrast.

"Are you okay?" Reed asks when he reaches the steps of the hotel, sitting down beside Zane.

Zane's eyes flash to Reed's and he stands up, clearly forcing a smile. "Fuck, yeah, I'm good. Just tired. I killed it today and—"

"Cut the crap, Zane," I cut in when I get closer, making Reed snort as he stands. "We weren't born yesterday."

Zane sighs in resignation, running his hand through his already mussed hair. "I grew up about an hour from here and..." he trails off but Reed answers for him.

"You haven't been back until now?"

"That's right. We haven't played here before. At least not while I've been with the team. I was relieved when I got drafted to the Storm. We're a different conference. The only time I'd ever have to come back here was if we..."

He waves his hand and shrugs as though that's an answer, but I'm confused until Reed adds, "Met them in the playoffs or preseason."

"Exactly."

"Fuck."

"Yep. Anyway." He bounces his shoulders and huffs out a laugh. "I've had my moment. Now I'm good. The guys heading to Bar 80?"

"They sure are, but Zane—"

"I'm good. Are you that pussy-whipped that you're calling it a night?" I bite back a smile at his comment, while Reed shakes his head. "Here I was convinced that the two of you were faking it for the media."

This time I can't help but smile, despite knowing his sudden attitude is a front for his feelings.

Reed, however, ignores his comment completely. "We'll be back in a minute," he says. "So, if you wai—"

"*Nope,*" I cut in before Reed offers anything to Zane. I feel bad for him, but at the same time, he doesn't want Reed's help and Reed has enough going on right now. I want to take his mind off things. "We'll be longer than a minute. We'll be down *after* I give Reed a celebratory blow job."

Reed chokes on nothing while Zane barks out a laugh. "Good for you. Guess I was wrong. I'll see you there, looking more satisfied than you are now."

Zane walks away and Reed turns to face me, his expression awed. "A blow job, huh?"

"Do you really think I'd make you walk all the way back here because I forgot my ID? Everyone knows who I am."

"I honestly did. But I'm more than happy for the alternative. Only I hate leaving Zane alone and—"

"He wanted to be alone, Reed. That's why I said what I said."

Reed's eyes flash toward the corner Zane disappeared around and he sighs. "You're right. Thank you. Why are we still here? My cock needs attention." Curling his fingers through mine, he tugs me toward the steps before an older lady garners his attention, struggling with her bags near the front door. "Shit. I'll meet you up there." He presses a kiss to my head before racing up the steps and helping her inside.

That's my Reed. I giggle to myself watching him until someone calls my name from behind me. "Hayley. Hayley, wait."

I spin to find Landon and wave, stopping on the bottom step. "Landon, hi. You're not out celebrating?"

"Nah, I'm still trying to prove myself and wanted to make a good impression, get an early night."

"That's not a bad idea. I like your dedication and I know Reed will too. Are you coming in?" I point to the hotel doors and smile as Landon comes to a stop beside me.

Assuming he is, I turn to head up the steps but stop when Landon speaks.

"Actually..." He grabs my arm as he trails off, frowning to himself before he stands tall. "Actually," he repeats, "I wanted to talk to you first."

"To me?" My eyes flash to his fingers curled around me before I glance toward the door, but Reed's nowhere in sight. Knowing him, he's probably walking the woman to her room.

"Yeah. You." Landon draws my attention back. "If that's okay."

"Of course." I'm confused, but I smile to reassure him. "What's up?"

"I overheard something about you and Reed, and it got me thinking."

"What kind of something?"

"It's fake, right?"

A laugh bursts out of me while Landon stands frozen, his gaze boring into mine, apparently not seeing the humor.

"It's a little more complicated than that, but I can assure you, it's *very real* now."

"Now?"

"Yes. We're together."

"Why?" His tone changes and I'm taken aback, though I try not to read too much into it.

"Why, what?"

"Why are you together?" he asks, his expression genuinely confused. "It doesn't make sense."

"You're right, it doesn't." My chest tightens as I think back to our last conversation and self-doubt enters my mind. He thinks I've changed Reed. I saw it in his eyes. "You know...sometimes great things don't make sense." I smile again, hoping that's enough to stop him from telling me I'm not good for Reed, but he shocks me when he finally speaks after a moment of silence.

"You deserve better." *What*? I stare at him blankly. "Everyone says he's in love with his best friend."

Oh. "That was a while ago and—"

"Can we go somewhere and talk?" He cuts me off, his voice quivering before he nods confidently, and an unexplained panic runs through me.

"What?"

"Can we go somewhere to talk? I just want to make sure you've thought this through. You know Reed's been mentoring me, right? Well, we've gotten close. I've seen and heard things that I think you should know."

"Oh. Ah. I appreciate you wanting to help. Always a hero." I force a smile. "But I'm okay. I've thought about this a lot and—"

"*Now*, Hayley." He shakes as he speaks and while my panic rises, I contemplate reasoning with him. That is until he taps his pocket and I freeze. *What the hell is he insinuating? Does he have a weapon?* He just played football. *What the hell is going on?*

"Landon, I—" He grabs my wrist this time, his hold painful as he shifts onto the step above me, towering over me in a power move.

"I've been watching you both," he admits and my skin crawls. "You're not right for each other. And you need to see that."

With panic and confusion coursing through me, I stare up at him as his words register. *I've been watching you both.*

"Did you know I was coming today?" I ask, wondering how closely he's been watching, unable to hide the shiver that runs through me.

"Nope." He shakes his head. "It was a nice surprise." His voice turns light and his demeanor instantly changes. But while he seems calmer, it doesn't make me any less nervous. *Where the fuck is Reed?*

"Okay, but you do *know* things, right?" I want to glance toward the hotel doors, but that will only draw attention to the possibility of Reed coming back.

"I do know things. Like I said, I want to talk. Come on. I'll fill you in over a drink." He points behind him and I shake my head.

"I don't think that's a good id—"

"You're coming. *Now*," he snaps again, shaking his head, until his anger makes way for a smile, his expression morphing in front of me. "I just want to talk," he adds calmly, and it hits me that he might be a lot more dangerous than I realized.

"Okay. Sure." I change tack. "Let's talk. I just have to tell Reed where I'm—"

"*No*. He's not here. You can text him when we get there."

"He'll be back any second."

"Let's go, Hayley." He tugs on my arm, but I pull him back.

"Okay. But please let go of my arm. I promise, I'll come with you. Happily. I'll listen to what you have to say. But if you're holding my hand and Reed sees you, he's not going to like it."

"That just proves my point. He used to be a good guy. And now..." He trails off and I cringe.

"Please." I tug against his hold, hoping to delay our walk. But when I remember his pocket, I change my mind. "Actually, it doesn't matter. Let's go."

Landon eyes me suspiciously, but he drops my arm seconds before Reed walks out the door. "What are you doing out— Landon, hey." Reed smiles as he moves toward the steps. "Sorry that took forever; that woman can talk."

I fake a smile as Landon stiffens beside me. "You're too nice," I say before my gaze shifts to Landon, catching his bitter expression when Reed looks away.

And I'm at a loss as to what to do.

"Do you still need your ID?" Reed grins as his eyes flash to the door, and I take that as my out.

"I do. Let's go." I move in Reed's direction but Landon grabs my hand, linking our fingers.

"Not yet." His fingers crush mine and I fight not to cry out. "We were going to talk."

What is he doing? I just told him—

"What the fuck, Landon?"

"Hayley wanted to talk and we're going to talk. Right, *Hayls*?"

Is he crazy? His nails bite into the palm of my hand and my eyes water, but I smile wide to stave off the tears, turning to Reed. "Reed, baby. I won't be long. I—"

My words cut off as Reed's face drops and my panic makes way for full-blown hysteria, desperately needing Reed to stay calm, hoping he'll understand. I mouth "call the police" and his eyes widen. But instead of stopping, he pulls his phone from his pocket, pressing the buttons as he jogs down the stairs.

"Please," I beg out loud this time, and Landon releases his hold, raising his hands in the air.

If he's pleading his innocence, it's too late.

The second he reaches us, Reed grabs Landon by the shirt, curling his fists into the material while Landon laughs, shaking his head.

"You've got it all wrong, *Reedy boy*." He uses my occasional nickname for Reed and I feel nauseous. How often has he been watching us? "I'm trying to help you both," Landon continues. "Like Hayley said, I'm her hero. And to do that, I have to tell you, this isn't right. You're not meant to be together."

"What the hell? What's going on?"

Landon's smile drops before he scoffs. "You've changed, Reed. Even you can admit that. And Hayley deserves better."

Reed's grip tightens as he growls. "Who the fuck do you—"

"I'm just trying to help you. Like you've helped me."

"The fuck." Reed walks him backward, putting some distance between us, and I watch on in horror. I'm struck silent, but when Landon slides his hand into his pocket, I scream.

"Help!" I call out as Reed throws Landon against a wall, shoving his arm into his neck. "Reed, please. Let him go. I'm okay. Let's—"

"Can't you see it?" Landon croaks out, his wild eyes not really focused on anything. "Exhibit A. The golden boy wouldn't do this. Are you jealous?"

"You think this is jealousy, asshole?" Reed tightens his hold on

Landon's neck, and I reach out to grab his waist, trying but failing to drag him away. "I'm doing this to protect my girl."

"That may be so *now*, but what happens when she does something you don't like? I think you've been holding on to a lot of anger and you're ready to unleash it. Just look at what you did to her stalker." He laughs again and my eyes widen. *It was never Cam.* He was telling the truth. "What happens if you do something to her?" Venom coats Landon's voice, and I frantically shake my head.

"Reed, no. You—"

"Stay the fuck away from her," Reed yells, his anger rising just like Landon said it would. "I don't know what the fuck you think you're doing, but it's not going to work." Reed clenches his fist at the same time I catch movement somewhere down the road. And I'm about to call out when Landon lunges forward, his hand no longer in his pocket.

"*Reed!*" I rush ahead, slipping between them as Landon reveals a knife, the blade stopping inches from my face. "Don't do this, Landon." I try to stay calm but my voice trembles with fear. "Please. I'll come with you. I'll—"

Landon stabs the knife toward me, and my eyes slam shut as I'm pulled backward. I wait for the sting, but I'm thrown to the side, opening my eyes when I slam into a hard chest, turning in time to see Reed double over, clutching his side before he falls to the ground. Landon raises his knife again, but before I can react, I'm forcefully shoved away and Zane runs past me, tackling him to the ground.

"*No!*" I cry out, but I'm not sure what I'm yelling about because it's too late.

Dropping to the ground, I crawl to Reed, my knees scraping against the rough concrete as I reach for his hand, pulling it away to find it covered in blood.

"My phone," he rasps, handing me his bloodied phone, his voice barely audible. I check the screen to find it connected to 911 and glance up to catch Zane slamming Landon's head into the pavement.

"Hello," I call out into the phone as nausea consumes me. "I need help."

Chapter Fifty-Four

HAYLEY

Someone touches my hand and I startle awake, my gaze bouncing around the space.

For the few seconds before my mind registers the hospital room and Keeley's broken expression, I let myself believe it was a dream.

"I'm sorry," Keeley rushes out, squatting down until we're eye level, grabbing my hand. "I didn't mean to startle you."

"That's okay, I—" My voice cracks until I clear my throat and try again. "I'm okay. Just a little jumpy."

"Understandably." Her eyes flash to Reed lying unconscious on the bed, and my chest tightens as emotion wells in my throat.

Why won't he wake up?

He's been back from surgery for hours and he's still out of it. He still needs to be intubated to help him breathe.

"Have the doctors been in?" Keeley asks, pulling my gaze back to hers as I bite my cheek to stave off the tears.

"They have. A few times but all they keep saying is that he needs time to heal. And that he's lucky to be alive. As if that's not something I already *freaking* know."

A nurse walks in and my face reddens. I know the doctors are helping and can't tell me much. I should be grateful he's okay. But I need more.

I need him to be awake.

"Sorry to interrupt." The nurse smiles warmly and I force a grin. "I'm Blair. I'll be Reed's nurse today and tomorrow. I just wanted to pop in and say hi." She wanders over to his machines and checks his charts, assessing God knows what, and when she's done, she heads back to the door.

"Do those machines tell you when he's going to wake up?" I ask, all my hope riding on her answer.

"I'm afraid not." She smiles sympathetically and my hope fades. "But his vitals are good. I'll be back to check in again soon."

"Thank you."

She walks away and I release a slow breath, glancing back at Keeley.

"Do you know what happened?" she asks, her eyes still on Reed.

I nod even though she's not looking my way, my eyes filling with tears once more, and it's barely a second before the first one falls.

"He went into shock from a stab wound to his spleen. They were able to repair the damage, but his body is still recovering. Of course they used more technical terms than that—hypo-something. But you get the gist."

"Hypovolemic shock. *Jesus.*"

"Yep. That's it. All that muscle and it didn't help." It sounds like I'm joking but I've run that fact through my mind over and over. If Reed hadn't lunged for Landon at the same time Landon raised the knife, it never would have happened.

"At least you know he's in good hands," Keeley tries to reassure me, but it doesn't work. "He's had surgery. The doctors have helped him. We just have to wait."

"I know. But I'm done waiting. I waited too long to let myself *feel* and now—"

"Don't finish that sentence. Reed's going to wake up and you're going to have a great life together."

Keeley and I are friends, but I've never really spoken to her about my past. Only Amelia and Reed know the true depth of my hesitancy toward putting my heart on the line, and yet something about the look in Keeley's eyes suggests that she understands. And if that's because she feels the same, I hate that for her. But I can't think about that now.

"What if—"

"No what-ifs," she cuts me off. "I've never seen either of you as happy as when you're together, and I have no doubt in my mind that there's more to your story."

I force a smile and it actually helps. "Thanks, Keeley. I needed that. I appreciate you coming in. Did you miss your flight home?"

"I did but it doesn't matter. I'm here. For as long as you need me."

"I appreciate that too, but I'll be okay. I promise. I'm sure you're busy and—"

Keeley laughs quietly but there's a sadness to it. "I'm staying. You're my friend, and Reed and Zane are part of the team so that makes them like family. I'm exactly where I need to be."

Zane? *Shit.* I hadn't even thought about him.

"Do you want to talk about it?" Keeley questions before I can ask about Zane.

"Ah... Oh... I don't know. A little part of me wishes I was in denial."

"That's not healthy for either of you, but I'll go along with anything you want. Take your time."

"No, you're right. It might be better to talk. I think I'm still processing what happened."

"I'm happy to wait. I'm here to listen whenever you're ready."

My mind drifts back to last night, and a shiver runs through me.

W*ith a racing heart, I rush to tell the operator what happened, giving her all the information I can while trying not to panic.*

"I've dispatched the police and an ambulance," she reassures me. "The ambulance is a couple of minutes away and—"

I stop listening and turn to Reed, grabbing his hand to fill him in. "An ambulance is coming. Just—" He flops forward and my heart stops as I drop the phone, a whimper escaping as I catch him in my arms, his dead weight forcing me to lower him to the ground.

A sharp pain registers in my arm but I push through it.

"Reed." I shake him, but he doesn't move. "Reed," I cry out, louder this time, and my voice quivers. "Reed, baby. Wake up. Help is coming. You have to wake up. Reed!" I scream his name and grab his face, all rational thoughts leaving my mind. "Please. Please."

Searching his body, I'm careful not to move him, when I notice the sheer amount of blood he's lost and my body convulses as I sob uncontrollably. "Reed. I need you. You have to wake up."

I'm not sure how much time passes before someone pulls me away, and I try to fight but the grip is too strong. "Let go of me," I scream. "He needs me. Let go."

The grip on me tightens as I thrash against my captor, and on a deeper level, I know I should be scared, but I can't bring myself to care. I just need to know Reed's okay.

"The ambulance is here, Hayley. We need to move." I vaguely recognize the voice and stop moving, my body going rigid. "I've got you. I'm here."

"What did I do? He has to be okay. I can't lose him."

"You didn't do *anything. This isn't your fault. He's in good hands." I register the voice and my movements still.*

Zane holds me as tears cascade down my cheeks, pooling in my mouth and I watch on in silence. But when the EMTs cut through Reed's shirt, I cry out again. "Nooo. Please, Reed. Wake up."

The world slows as they lift Reed onto a gurney with all sounds ceasing to exist other than the faint words of comfort coming from Zane. "Shhh. It's okay. Shhh."

One of the EMTs walks over but I don't register what he's saying, my mind still on Reed. Where it should be. You have to wake up. Please. You have to.

I lightly pat the bandage on my arm where the knife struck me, and when I focus on Keeley again, she's wiping tears from her eyes. "Have you seen Zane?" I ask, needing to get out of my head.

"Not yet. The nurse that came in before said he was sleeping. He lost a lot of blood himself and—"

"He what?" I sit up straighter, my eyes flashing to the door. *How did I not know that?* "Is he okay?"

"He's okay, Hayley. Are you?"

"I'm fine. Never better." I fake a smile and Keeley frowns. Physically, I'm fine. My wound is barely a scratch. I was so focused on Reed that I didn't even feel it at the time.

And I hate that.

How is that fair when the two people that came to my rescue are lucky to be alive?

"You're far from fine." Keeley cuts into my thoughts, grabbing my hand again for attention. "I'm going to let that one slide," she says with a frown. "But you're allowed to be hurting, Hayley. You—" I yawn and when

Keeley sees it she cuts herself off. "You need to sleep. You've been through so much and you need to look after yourself."

"I know. But I don't want to miss Reed if he wakes. I already fell asleep before."

"I'm sure he'll wake you."

"It's Reed, not Luke. Reed's too nice for that."

"Very true." Keeley's eyes flash to the door. "How about I stay here? I'll wake you if Reed doesn't."

"Thanks, but I can't let you do that. I'll be fine. I promise."

"Okay. Well, I'm not going anywhere just yet. If you need to, take a nap."

While I try hard to fight it, I must fall asleep because when I wake up some time later, Keeley's no longer next to me and Reed's still asleep.

If you removed the tube from his throat, he'd actually look peaceful. Though he's far from it. And I'm terrified of how he'll feel when he wakes up. But God, I hope it's soon.

Soft voices drift in from the hall and a door creaks. "You're awake?" Keeley gasps, pulling my gaze away from Reed. "Of course you'd wake the moment I leave the room."

I smile, though it doesn't reach my eyes. "It's fine. I didn't expect you to stay."

A flash of dark hair appears in the doorway and I pause.

"I know I didn't have to stay. But I wanted to and—"

"Is Luke here?" I cut Keeley off, my gaze over her shoulder.

"What?" She tries to look confused and this time I genuinely laugh.

"He is, isn't he?"

"He's in the hall. Probably listening in on our conversation."

"I am not." Luke pops his head in and I laugh again until guilt works its way into my chest. Reed's unconscious. I shouldn't be happy.

"How'd you know I was here?"

"Because I thought I saw you peeking, and it made me think that if Amelia couldn't be here she'd make you stay."

"No one left." His lips pull into a soft smile as he steps forward. "At least none of Reed's friends."

"What?"

"D'Angelo put us up in a fancy hotel close by."

"Wow. Um. What about..." I trail off, struggling to say his name.

"Landon?" Luke fills in the blank. "He's here somewhere. But luckily he's on police guard because if any of us saw him, we'd—"

"He's on life support," Keeley cuts in, her voice soft, and I gasp. "He hit his head pretty hard and—"

"What?" Luke and I speak in unison, both of us wide-eyed as we stare at Keeley.

"I quickly went to check on Zane and he told me. He was informed by the police. They stopped by here, too, but since you were sleeping, they said they'd be back."

"I—" I swallow a lump in my throat. I don't know what to say. He's on life support? *How?* It wasn't Reed and I didn't... Oh, God. "Is Zane okay?"

"Not really. I mean, physically, yes. But mentally, I don't know. His spark was gone, if you know what I mean."

For the first time ever, Luke falls quiet. As do I. But while the guilt inside me thickens, I can't bring myself to care. Reed's unconscious and lucky to be alive. Zane's lying in a hospital bed facing God knows what because he stepped in to protect me. And my world as I know it has shattered.

So yes, I may feel guilty, but I can't allow myself to feel anything else. Landon did this. He brought this on himself. And if I saw him right now, I couldn't be held responsible for what I'd do.

He hurt the one man that brings light into my world and extinguished his flame in the process. He deserves...

God, what if he dies?

No... what's worse...

"What if Reed doesn't wake up?" I sob uncontrollably just like I did when Reed first collapsed in my arms, the memory still raw. And it's only when Luke rushes to my side that I realise I spoke the words out loud. "What if I lose him? What if he dies?"

Wake up, Reed. You have to wake up.

CHAPTER FIFTY-FIVE

HAYLEY

P *lease wake up. Please, Reed. I need you.*

I wake with a start, again, my eyes instantly flashing to Reed's lifeless-looking body. After letting out a shaky breath and getting my bearings, I try to ignore my stomach when it growls. But when a throat clears behind me, I know I've been busted.

"You need to eat, Hayley." Luke takes his brotherly love one step further, drawing my attention to where he stands by the door. "When was the last time you left the room?"

I haven't, but I'm not about to admit that. "I'm fine. But if you want to get me some food, I won't say no."

"Not going to happen, Jackman. But I'll happily go with you."

"Luke," I groan out his name but he stands firm, folding his arms over his chest. "Ugh, fine. But we're walking quickly."

"Of course. Let's go."

I swear I'm only gone fifteen minutes but when I get back, Reed's breathing tubes are missing. With a gasp, I frantically rush to his side, cursing Luke for taking me away. "Reed, baby," I whisper, my heart picking up speed. "Are you awake?"

"Not yet." A voice comes from behind me and I freeze before spinning around.

I'm not alone.

"God, I'm sorry," the woman says as she clings to a man beside her.

"Who—" I begin to question them but pause when recognition hits me. "Mr. and Mrs. Coombs?"

"That's us." Reed's mum smiles softly but it doesn't quite reach her eyes. Understandably. Her son's currently lying in the hospital with a stab wound to his side. "We've been here about ten minutes or so," she continues. "I thought you saw us when you walked in."

Nope. I did not. "God. *I'm* sorry. I'm in my own world. I didn't mean to interrupt your time with Reed. I'll leave you alone." I hurry over to the chair and grab my bag from the floor, smiling awkwardly. "I'll be out—"

"Wait, Hayley." She reaches her hand out but stays by her husband's side. "You don't have to go. Reed would want you here."

I frown at her use of my name until I remember they've seen my movie and have likely seen photos of the two of us doing the rounds. They know who I am. Just like everyone else. I'm the reason Reed's here to begin with. "Thank you, but—"

"Please," she cuts me off again, her eyes pleading with me to stay. And since I'd like nothing more than to never leave his side again, I drop my bag and nod.

"Thank you." Mrs. Coombs sighs in relief and I force a grin, my gaze drifting back to Reed.

"Do you know how long ago they took the tubes out?" I ask, studying his features.

When I glance back at her, Mrs. Coombs frowns. "We weren't here but the doctor said he started breathing on his own just before we arrived."

"Did he wake up?"

"Not fully."

"Not fully? But he's okay? Right? That means he's okay?"

"It does." She smiles and for the first time, Reed's dad speaks.

"He had us worried. I don't know what we'd do without him."

I offer him a warm smile until I think about his home life and an unsolicited anger wells up inside me. I bite my tongue, holding back from saying something I shouldn't. Reed wouldn't want me to get involved. Everything he does is to make their lives easier. What I want to say would have the opposite effect.

"What was he thinking?" he continues on, and I wish he'd never opened his mouth. "The doctors didn't say much except that he got in a fight and the other guy stabbed him in between his ribs, damaging his spleen. But Reed doesn't fight."

His gaze meets mine, and for the briefest of seconds I register the blame in his eyes until he schools his features. "Were you there?"

"I was."

"What happened?"

"Exactly what you said. Reed was stabbed during a fight."

"Why was he fighting?" There's accusation in his tone and I don't like it. "He's always been so..."

He trails off but I answer for him. "Good? Is that what you were going to say?" I don't wait for him to respond before continuing on, ready to give them a piece of my mind. "Reed *is* good. He's inherently good. And that will never change. But he's so much more than that."

I pause for a beat, sensing Reed's mom wanting to speak, but now that I've opened the gates, I can't hold back the flood of words ready to be released. Words they should have heard years ago. "There is so much to Reed that you *don't* see. But I see it. All of it. And while God knows I should be trying to impress you, I can't bring myself to care because I'm so *mad* at you both. *You don't know what you'd do without him?* Well, join the club. But how about you treat him right while you *do* have him. You should know...I'm in love with your son, so bloody in love with him that I can't see straight. But I never told him that and I could have missed my chance." My voice cracks but I keep going, needing to get it all off my chest.

"You're here now, sure. But you've been missing out on a fulfilling life with your amazing son, all over an asshole that treats you like the dirt he kicks in your faces. I don't want to hurt you—I know you're both hurting enough—but Reed deserves better than that. Hell, he deserves better than all of us. He wouldn't be here if it wasn't for me. And I will never forgive myself for that. But I love him and I'm trying to be good enough. I will always be trying. Which is why I will never understand *you.*"

I walk over to Reed's bedside and take in his peaceful expression now that the breathing tubes have gone. "I can't deny you've raised an incredible human, but he's so much more than just the guy you use to make yourselves *feel* better when your other son fucks up. Excuse my language. But it's true. You should be cheering him on at his games and witnessing how talented he is. You should be visiting him at his home, and basking in his warmth when he welcomes you into his sanctuary. You should want to spend time with him because he's hilarious and kind and sexy...sorry—ignore that one. You should want to spend time with him because he's a light in this otherwise dark world. But he's not a light for our benefit. He's a light because he has one of the most beautiful souls that has ever existed and he chooses to be that way. Every day, he wakes up and chooses to be a decent human being. Better than you or I could ever be. And despite being in the hospital, he's going to do the same today. I know it. You should be grateful he's touched your lives in any shape or form, not taking him for granted."

I squeeze Reed's hand before walking over to the table, needing water. "We could have lost him," I whisper to myself as much as to them. "We almost did. It's time to be better."

Silence fills the room and my heart aches. *God, what am I doing?* Taking a deep breath, I turn to Reed's parents and grimace. "I—"

"Wow," Reed croaks from behind me and I freeze, my words trapped in my throat. "That was some speech. I want to meet that guy."

My eyes fill with tears and I spin around to find Reed's smiling face staring back at me, his happy expression falling when our eyes lock. "Hayley, Baby." He lifts a hand in my direction. "Why the tears? I'm okay."

"You're—" I snap out of my shock and race toward him, grabbing his outstretched hand, immediately intertwining our fingers. "You're awake." I let the tears fall, not even trying to stop them. "Thank God, you're awake."

Reed's mom lets out a wail, and Reed turns her way as he pulls me closer, his eyes widening in shock. "How long have I been out for?"

"Almost thirty-seven hours."

"That's specific." He chuckles, his smiling eyes meeting mine again.

"What can I say; I've been counting." I finally smile and Reed's laughter deepens until his face scrunches and he groans.

"Damn. That hurts. But anyway... I guess that explains it." He tugs at my hand, pulling it toward his face, pressing a kiss to my knuckles.

"Explains what?" I ask curiously. "Are you okay?"

"I'm fine. It explains why I miss you so much."

"Shut up." I shake my head with a grin. "You were asleep the whole time, *and* your parents are here. Less of the corny, please."

Reed smirks and the sight of it hits me in the chest. "I can see that." He winks my way before turning his gaze to his parents. "Hi, Mom. Hi, Dad. So...that big speech was for you, huh?"

I cringe and lean over the bed, burying my face in the pillow beside his head, mumbling that I'm sorry. *How much did he hear?* "I—"

"Don't be sorry," Reed's mom responds and I straighten, my eyes anxiously wide as I glance her way. "You clearly needed to get that off your chest."

My thoughts exactly, but I can't tell if she's pissed off or processing what I said. "Reed, honey." She walks slowly to the other side of the bed, cautiously reaching for his other hand as though suddenly looking at him in a new light. "I'm sorry. We'll be better. We—"

"It's okay, I—"

"No, Hayley's right. We almost lost you, and I never would have forgiven myself if we had. We'll be better."

Reed's dad joins his wife's side, and I feel awkward hanging around. "I'm going to let the others know you're awake." I pull my hand from Reed's grasp, but he's faster than I am and grabs me again, holding me tightly.

"Don't go. Not yet."

"I promise I'll be right back." I shake myself free before excusing myself and darting to the door, hearing Reed's mom cry as I softly pull it shut behind me.

Instead of heading to find the others like I said I would, the second I'm in the hallway, I catch a glimpse of Zane's room down the hall, and I'm overcome with emotion, collapsing to the floor as my chest heaves. Reed's okay. He's okay. But I almost lost him and—

The door opens to Zane's room, drawing my attention as one of Reed's nurses walks out, her hand covering her mouth, visibly upset. My heart seizes before the first tear falls. I'm not equipped for this. I fake emotion. I can't handle the real deal.

"Hayley. Fuck." Luke's voice enters my consciousness and I glance up to see him running toward me. "I just left you. What happened?" He drops to the ground beside me, pulling me into his arms. "Is—"

"Reed's awake." I wipe under my eyes. "He's okay."

"Jesus, fuck. You gave me a heart attack."

I cringe as the nurse passes by. "Sorry. I guess I'm not used to these heavy emotions."

Luke nods because he gets me, but at the same time, I can tell he's not entirely sure what to say. "If he's okay, why are you out here?"

"He's with his parents."

"And they kicked you out?" He balks and the look of disgust makes me snort.

"No, I left to give them space, and to find you, to tell you that he's good."

"Well, you did a great job at that." He bumps his shoulder to mine teasingly and I actually laugh.

"Thanks, Luke. I needed that. No offense, but I wish Amelia was here."

"You and me both, Hayls. You and me both."

We fall silent, and I sigh as my mind drifts to the events that brought us all here.

"Have you seen Zane?" I ask, my gaze shifting to his room again. "I tried to visit yesterday but he was asleep."

Luke nods. "They cleared him to leave last night."

"He's gone?" I'm not sure why but panic runs through me.

"Nah, he's around." Luke eases my mind. "He's been waiting for Reed to wake up. Just like the rest of us." My heart jolts as Zane's words come rushing back to me. *Shh. It's okay. Shh.*

"He's a better guy than we all realised, huh?"

"Yep. It turns out, he's not so bad. He just made some bad decisions."

"And some good ones."

I fall silent again, and after another deep breath, I shake off my sadness and jump up, dragging Luke with me. "Should we go and see Zane and the others?"

His mind elsewhere, Luke frowns at something over my shoulder, grabbing my hand. "The police are coming this way. Do you want me to stay?"

I glance behind me to see two officers walking in my direction and suck in a breath. "No, that's okay. You tell the others. I've got this."

"Are you sure?"

"I'm sure."

"Hayley Jackman?" one of the officers asks, even though he knows the answer. I can see the recognition in his gaze.

"Yes." I nod, taking a second to breathe before I straighten. "How can I help?"

"Mind if we ask you a few questions?"

"Sure." I nod again, swallowing a lump in my throat. "I'm ready to tell you everything."

Ready as I'll ever be.

CHAPTER FIFTY-SIX

REED

After a visit from my doctor—telling me I'm lucky to be alive and freaking the fuck out of my parents—Mom delivers her own emotionally charged speech before she and Dad leave with the promise to come back later today.

And to be better.

When I was younger, I used to beg Mom to listen, and so did Dad, but it was always futile. Hayley calls them out once and she's changed? As much as I love Hayley and think the world of her and her incredible speech, I'll believe it when I see it.

The second I'm alone, I watch the door expectantly, waiting for my beautiful girl to waltz back in so I can finally tell her I love her again.

Only she's nowhere to be seen.

And the next time the door opens, the smile drops from my face.

"Reed Coombs?" a police officer asks, his expression somber as his eyes bounce around the room.

"That's me."

"How are you feeling?"

"I'm alive, so that's something." I force a smile but get nothing in return.

"Yes, you're lucky on that front. Do you mind if we ask you a few questions?"

"Of course. Go ahead." I try to sit up, but when a sharp pain shoots through my side, I think better of it. "Hope you don't mind me lying down." I cringe awkwardly and the younger officer smiles.

"We won't be long."

The officers run through the standard questions I was expecting, and I answer as best I can, but for the life of me, I can't think of *any* reason as to why Landon would have had a knife. Or why he'd pull it on Hayls. Or me. I'm not even sure who his anger was aimed at.

"I wish I knew. I wish I'd seen something. Did he mention I was mentoring him? He was kind of shy, but other than that, he was like any other player on the team. I just wanted him to break out of his shell. I never once saw him display any anger; I never even saw him upset. He's a good guy. I never would have expected this."

"Hayley mentioned you charged him after she told you to call the police."

"She said charged?" I raise a brow in question. I highly doubt that. "I dialed the police and raced to her aid, pinning him against a wall so he couldn't hurt her. She thought she was hiding it, but I could see the fear in her eyes when he was dragging her away."

"Okay. And the knife?"

"He pulled that out seconds before Hayley stepped between us. I'm ashamed to say, I hadn't even noticed his hand in his pocket."

"Thank you. Do you remember where you were when Zane arrived?"

"Zane?"

"Yes. He heard Hayley scream and came back to help. He's the one that stopped Landon from attacking Hayley after you fell."

"Fuuck. *Shit.* Sorry. I had no idea." I rack my brain for any moments that feature Zane, but I can't recall any. "Honestly, I can't recall much after getting stabbed. The last thing I remember is Hayley dropping down beside me. Is Zane okay?"

"So you don't remember him tackling Landon?" the older officer asks without answering my question.

"No." I glance away, my face scrunched as I try to focus, but I can't remember. Hayley stepped in front of me, I saw the knife and pushed her out of the way, and in the next second I was shaking and my head started to spin. But... "Did you catch him? Landon, I mean?"

The officers' eyes meet and a silent exchange takes place.

"Landon suffered a head injury when he hit the concrete. He was brought into the hospital with a suspected concussion but has since been put on life support."

"He what?" I stare at the officers as a thick fog overwhelms me. "That... I... Are you sure?"

They both nod.

"Jesus." I struggle to take in air as my chest tightens. I wanted to hurt him for scaring Hayley, but life support? A thought hits me and I panic, sending my machines into a melodic chaos. "Is Zane okay?" I repeat my earlier question, only this time, I'm wondering why I'm really being questioned. If Landon dies...from Zane's tackle. God, I can't imagine what he's going through right now.

A nurse comes rushing into the room to check on me before anyone can answer, but after seeing I'm okay, he disappears quickly. "Well?" I ask again, needing answers.

"He's been released from the hospital."

That doesn't answer my question. "Are you charging him?"

The officers glance at each other again before finally filling me in. "Not at this stage."

"Thank God." I release a long, drawn-out breath and cover my face with my hand.

Or is that only because Landon's still alive?

Before I can ask, the officer continues. "We may need to ask you a few more questions once we get further into our investigation, but it looks like Landon was stalking both you and Hayley. We found images of the two of you on his phone and notes regarding your whereabouts. We're working with the San Francisco PD to run a search of his home and will speak to his family and friends. We'll have to wait and see what happens with Landon before closing the case. But with both Zane and Hayley's statements matching up, and the camera footage from the hotel, we've got a fair idea of what went on."

"Thank you," I say as my pulse finally starts to slow.

"Thank you for your time. Next time you're here we'd appreciate it if—"

"I stay out of trouble?"

"No, you lose the game."

The younger officer smirks and I laugh. "Not a chance." But fuck, I hope I'll be playing next time.

After they leave, I stare at the wall while racking my brain to remember more. And I'm still staring when Hayley returns, bringing a smile to my face the second I see her.

"Hey you." She grins from the threshold, her stunning blue eyes easing my gut-wrenching pain. "Want some company?" Her face scrunches and I roll my eyes.

"Get your ass in here, Hayls. I don't *want* you. I *need* you."

She shuts the door behind her and skips to the end of my bed but doesn't come any closer, confusing me until she pouts. "I should be mad at you," she scolds, her cute little button nose scrunching again.

"Oh, yeah? And why is that?"

"Because you were supposed to stay away. I begged you and you ignored me." Her expression turns serious, but I can't be serious right now. I need to keep things light or I'm likely to fall apart.

"That I did." I nod. "And I stand by that decision."

"You could have died, Reed."

"Better me than you, Hayls. And that will always be the case."

"But I can't live in a world you don't exist in."

"Luckily, you don't have to." My mind drifts to Landon but I shake off my thoughts. I was protecting Hayley, and Zane was protecting us both. There's nothing more to it. "Come here." I beckon Hayley over but she shakes her head no.

"Hayls," I scold jokingly but when her eyes water, my heart aches for her. "Now, Hayls." I try the tough love approach, knowing she loves that. "I can't come to you and I need you in my arms."

She takes a couple of steps closer but stops just out of reach. "Two truths and a lie?" she rasps and I huff out a laugh, sitting up until a pain shoots through me. *Why do I keep doing that?*

"Okay, Hayls." I bite back a groan. "Two truths and a lie. Me or you?"

"Me," she responds quickly and I nod as she takes a deep breath. "One... I've never been more terrified of anything in my life than when you bled out all over me." The tension in my chest tightens and I suck in a breath, quietly staving off tears. "Two... I'm sorry I told your parents off; I was out of line." A laugh bursts out of me and I cringe from the pain. I can't tell if I'm laughing because it's funny or because of how fucked up this entire situation is.

"And three?" I croak out.

"Three... I have something important to tell you." She sucks in a breath just like I did and I put on a grin.

"The second one's a lie. You're not sorry. And if you are, you shouldn't be."

The smallest of smiles pulls at Hayley's lips before she releases a breathy laugh. "You're right. I'm not sorry."

I chuckle softly so I don't hurt myself again, but when I think of her truths, the laughter fades. "I'm sorry I scared you, Hayls. I'm not sorry I pushed you away and ended up in the hospital, but I'm sorry for what you had to go through."

"Oh, Reed." She finally takes the last few steps to settle at my side, intertwining our fingers. "You *saved* me. You have nothing to be sorry about. *I'm* sorry. Sorry I didn't see the signs sooner. Sorry I never recognised Landon when he was following me around. The police said it was him, you know? He was the stalker. He had photos on his phone. But not just me. Of both of us."

I frown even though it's not news to me. "None of this is your fault, Hayls. And while I'm still coming to terms with Landon's condition, I'm thankful we're okay."

"Thankful? Reed, you're not okay. You—"

"I am okay, Hayls. I survived."

"You survived, yes, but you were unconscious. I've been here for almost two days, desperate for you to wake up." Her eyes water again, and I wish more than anything that I could stand up and hug her.

"I know," I whisper. "And if I could change that part of it, so you didn't have to worry, I would." I squeeze her hand before gently tugging her toward me, thankful when she lets me get her close enough that I can cup her face. "I'm sorry, Hayls. I am. But I'm okay because it was me and not you."

"Here's the thing. I love that you want to take care of everyone and be the guy people can count on, but who's taking care of *you*? Who's out there protecting you when you don't look after yourself?"

"You don't know?"

"*No.*"

"*You,* Hayls. I never asked you to and I never would have agreed to it if you'd suggested being my protector, but you've been looking out for me for months, maybe even years. And it turns out I have Zane too. And Luke and Thomas and Dylan. Hell, probably even East."

"*Reed*." She pulls her hand away and when it takes me a second to let go, she subtly flinches.

"Are you hurt?" My pulse spikes as I assess her. "Did you get hurt?"

"It's just a cut, I promise. I'm fine."

"Show me."

She lifts her sleeve to show me a small dressing on her upper arm. "See, just a cut."

I hate that he hurt her, but I'm certain the emotional pain is worse.

"Are you sure it's not more than you're telling me?"

"I promise."

"Thank God. Good. Can we talk about your next truth now? I'm particularly interested in that one." And I need to hear something positive.

"You are?" Hayley's brows furrow as she glances away, but when she rests her hand back in mine, I relax a little.

"I am." I nod. I have a memory of her saying she's in love with me, but I know that's never happened. It makes me wonder if she said it while I was unconscious.

Hayley nods back at me but doesn't continue for a beat, clearly nervous. "You don't have to tell me if you don't want to. I know the last couple of days have been hard on you and—"

"I love you, Reed," she blurts out, and my heart races as my entire body heats. I always knew I'd like it when I heard those three little words, but nothing could prepare me for the euphoric happiness consuming me.

I knew how she felt. I *knew*. But this is everything.

"Actually... That's not enough for how I'm feeling. I'm in love with you. And it turns out that I've been in love with you for a while." She laughs to herself and my smile widens, but I work hard not to let it turn cocky. "You can gloat." She playfully rolls her eyes. "You knew, didn't you?"

"I had a feeling." I glance away to hide said gloating, but she sees it.

"Of course you had a feeling. I'm not mad about it. I love the way you can read me and the way you see me better than anyone ever has. I love the way you deal with my crazy, never making me feel like I'm hard work. And I love the way you make me laugh. I just love *you*. Period."

"Fuuck. I may have known, but God, I love hearing that. Say it again."

"I love you."

"Again."

"I love you."

"Aga—"

"Now you're making it less meaningful."

I want to laugh but think better of it, squeezing her hand before lifting myself up the bed, forcing myself to sit up. The pain's excruciating but I endure it. I have to, because... "I love you too, Hayls, and I'm gonna need you to kiss me. Since I can't fucking do it for myself."

And I've never needed to kiss her more than I do right now.

CHAPTER FIFTY-SEVEN

REED

Two by two, our friends and my teammates pop in to say hello ahead of their chartered flight home, and I spend the entire time in awe of how amazing they are. I'm the guy that always checks in on the people I care about, and I've never held anyone else to that standard.

So to find out that they're still here—for me—has me floored.

Keeley's the last to visit and when she's gone, I draw in a breath and smile. "We really do have incredible friends," I say, my heart full as I turn back to Hayley.

"That we do. On top of everyone here, I've had Amelia and Paige blowing up my phone. And I texted Bria. She—"

"What?" I do a double take as Hayley cringes. "How?"

"Did you know face recognition works when your eyes are closed?" She cringes again while I frown. "Are you mad?"

"Mad? No. I'm in awe of you."

Bria and I haven't spoken since I visited her dad in the hospital, waiting until she was gone so we didn't cross paths. After Hayley asked me to kiss her, I decided to distance myself a little. Not that I told Hayley that. She would have felt guilty when she shouldn't have. But still, letting Bria know I was in the hospital and unconscious was the right thing to do.

"Thank you. We may not speak anymore, but I would have wanted to know if roles were reversed."

"Oh, good. We've texted a few times but I can't see us being the best of friends anytime soon."

"Good. Because you're *my* best friend, Hayls. Don't make me get jealous."

"God, you're corny sometimes."

"You love it."

"Anyway...moving on." She bites back a smile and I laugh, holding my ribs so it doesn't hurt. "Lots of people care. Even my parents have called checking in on you. I thought I should fill them in, especially considering it was only a matter of time before the media got ahold of the story."

"Let me guess; it's already out there?"

Hayley's nose scrunches and I have my answer. Another scandal for the San Francisco Storm. As if Zane doesn't have enough to think about.

"Knock, knock." As though I conjured him, Zane's voice echoes through the room as he raps his knuckles on the open door. "Mind if I come in?"

"Of course." I try to sit up but Hayley gently pushes me back down wearing a loving smile. I'm about to argue, but when I don't feel any pain, I quietly thank her.

"How are you?" she asks, turning to give Zane her full attention.

"I'm fine. I don't know why they even kept me here overnight, to be honest. It was barely a scratch." He lifts his tee to show off his wound dressing, and when I try to sit up again, I cringe, making him chuckle. "I should be asking how *you* are," he says to me.

"I'm fine." I answer the same way he did. "But I don't think Hayley was referring to the physical pain."

"Right. I knew that, but..." he trails off and both Hayley and I frown.

"I'm sorry, Zane." Hayley walks forward and lightly grips his arm, her expression broken. "I'm grateful but sorry."

"Don't be sorry." Zane pats Hayley's hand before stepping out of her reach as though he doesn't deserve the comfort. "I did what anyone would have done in my situation."

"That may be true for some of it. But I don't think I would have coped if not for you."

"Nah. I don't believe that. You would have stayed strong for Reed. You didn't even notice you'd been cut until the medic asked you about it. You only had eyes for Reed. Speaking of, it's good to see you awake, man. You had us all worried."

"Believe me, I would have woken sooner if I'd known. Thank you for waiting around. I appreciate it."

"Ah, no worries. I had to take a few days off practice anyway, so where else was I going to go?" He laughs off my thanks but fails to hide the vulnerability in his eyes. And it's at that moment that Thomas's words come back to me. *I think he's self-destructing.* If Thomas is right, then what if Landon's accident is the thing that breaks him?

We're all going to need to be there for him, ready for if that happens.

Zane tells us he's hoping to be cleared to play next week, and I try hard to conceal the jealousy I feel with a few more tests needed before I'll know my own future.

Barely a few minutes pass before his eyes flash to the door, clearly uncomfortable. But I can't let him go without mentioning Landon.

"Zane, wait. I know you're going to brush me off, but I need to say this. You are not to blame for what happened. I'm not sure how much you've been told, but he was stalking Hayley, following her around and taking pictures. He knew where she lived, he..." I trail off when our beach day comes to mind. *Jesus.* Landon acted shocked to see us but he was there. At the exact time we were. Nowhere near his apartment. "He knew a lot about her."

"About us," Hayley adds.

"I have no idea what he wanted that night, but he hurt Hayley and he had a knife. Please don't let his current situation weigh on your mind."

Zane curses under his breath. "I swear I knew something was off with him. But I couldn't figure it out. I'm sorry you went through all that. Don't worry about me. Just look after yourselves."

Not possible, Zane. Especially after that response.

A nurse pops her head in, and Zane's eyes flash her way before he frowns and uses her arrival as his excuse to head off.

"You're going to worry, right?" Hayley asks after the nurse finishes her checkup, and we're alone again, bringing a smile to my face.

"God, I love you, Hayls. I don't even think you realize how amazing you are."

Her gaze softens and she hits me with the most beautiful grin. "I've always been confident, but you make me see a different side of myself, and I like the person I am in your eyes."

"Good. But I love every side of you. And I always will."

I t's another few days before the doctors clear me to fly home but only after delivering another blow.

"I'll send your files over to your doctor in San Francisco, but you should be prepared for a long recovery. You were lucky; the rupture could have been much worse, but it's still going to take time. Most people return to fitness training within 6-12 weeks after surgery, but to get back to your level of performance, it could be longer."

My initial thought was that at least they didn't rule out football altogether, but when I walk through my door at home, dumping my bag near the entry, my reality sinks in. Twelve weeks is almost the entire season.

"Fuuuck. What am I going to do with myself? You're going to regret loving me."

A twinge of guilt settles in my chest for being worried about this when we still don't have news about Landon, but I push it from my mind when Hayley bites back a grin. *She's safe.* And that's what matters right now.

"I'll admit, you being home all the time does raise concerns. I bet you're insufferable when you're not playing football. We need to get you a hobby."

I huff out a laugh, pulling her into my arms.

She's safe.

"What hobby would you suggest?"

"Solitaire? Reading? Worshipping your girlfriend?"

"Hmmm." I tap my chin as I peer away, lost in thought. "All great options but one of them stands out... I think I was born to play solitaire."

Hayley lightly shoves me away as her beautiful laugh sweetens the air. "That's too bad," she sasses. "I was really looking forward to you becoming a reader. Especially if you need glasses. I could get used to coming home and finding you shirtless and curled up with a book."

"Why would I be shirtless?"

"Why wouldn't you be?"

I chuckle at her crazy but my mind drifts back to something else she said. "If you're coming home—here—I'll be waiting however you want me to wait."

"Are you asking me to move in?" She raises an eyebrow but otherwise keeps the emotion off her face.

"Would you say yes?"

"I'm not sure. Ask and find out."

"Hayley Jackman, baby, will you move in with me?"

She scrunches her nose and glances away in thought just like I did. And after the longest thirty seconds of my life, she responds with a smile. "No, thanks."

"You're cute." I bop her nose. "Looks like I'm moving in with you."

"What?"

"I almost died, Hayley. But worse than that...someone I thought I knew, someone I brought into your life, tried to hurt you."

"So, why not get me a bodyguard?"

"No need. I'm never letting you out of my sight."

"You know that sounds a little bit stalkerish."

"Fuck, Hayls."

"Too soon?"

"That will always be too soon. So what will it be...your place or mine?"

Hayley's eyes bounce around the kitchen before she walks into the hallway and surveys from one end of my house to the other, staring longingly out my back door. "Fine. I guess I'll choose yours. If I have to."

Without a word, I stride her way, cupping her face in my hands when I reach her, capturing her lips in a bruising kiss. She moans against my mouth, her hands gently curling around my waist before she grips on for dear life. We've barely begun when my phone buzzes incessantly.

I try to ignore it, but Hayley pulls back. "Group chat?"

"Most likely, but they can wait." I grab her face again but she shoves me away, careful not to hurt me.

"They're probably checking in now that you're home. They deserve a response."

"Fine. But we are only pausing this. Be ready to pick up where we left off."

"Don't expect more than a kiss. You heard the doctor; you need to take it easy."

I groan. Loudly. Another reason to curse this damn injury.

Hayley slips out of my hold and grabs my phone, passing it over. Like she said, I expect to find welcome home messages, but when I open the chat, I'm floored by what I see.

EASTON ADDED ZANE TO THE GROUP

Wow. *What did I miss?* I'm glad Zane's been added since I want the chance to support him. But for Easton to add him... *I didn't see that coming.*

Unless...

I pause, waiting for Easton to leave the group, but he surprises me for a second time.

> EASTON: Welcome to the group, Zane

My jaw drops, but I can't help but chuckle when he adds...

> EASTON: Or what I like to call... Hell

My amusement draws Hayley's attention and she looks up from her phone. "What's so funny?" Her interest is piqued and I love the way her eyes light up.

"Easton called the group chat 'Hell.'"

"That sounds like him." She grins wide.

"And he added Zane to the group."

"What?" She freezes, her gaze darting to mine. "That does *not* sound like Easton at all."

"That's what I was thinking."

"Actually, I guess it makes sense. Zane was discharged from the hospital but stayed with the group to make sure you were okay. And from what Luke said, he was really worried about you."

Another message comes through, and Hayley tucks herself into my good side, reading it with me.

> ZANE: With that introduction, I'm not sure I want to be here

> LUKE: You're going to love it

> ZANE: I thought you hated me

> LUKE: People change. Feelings change

EASTON: That's funny coming from you, Luke

"And he's chatty. What is going on?" While I know this is a good thing, my brows still crease in confusion.

"They bonded over your unfortunate mishap." Hayley shrugs and I scoff.

"Mishap?"

"You know what I mean."

"Sure." I let out a soft chuckle before finally joining the chat.

REED: It's great to have you in the group, Zane. I always knew this day would come

ZANE: Thanks

LUKE: You better get ready for Reed. You'll never escape him now

ZANE: I don't think this group is for me. I'm out

Hayley snorts so hard, it makes me chuckle.

"Wow." I shake my head.

"What? That was funny."

LUKE: You know, Zane... If you hadn't slept with his GF, you and East could have been great friends. You're more alike than you realize

"Huh. I always thought Zane was more like Luke, but maybe he's a mix," Hayley points out.

"Or maybe he's his own person?" I wink and Hayley laughs again.

"Yeah, yeah. You always had faith in him, didn't you?"

"Not always. But I wish I had, and I wish he wasn't caught up in our mess."

Hayley ponders that for a second before shaking her head. "I don't. Things might have ended differently if he hadn't come back."

"Maybe so, but I can't get his defeated look out of my mind. When we first saw him sitting on the steps. I'm guessing he already has a lot going on in his life, and now he has Landon's uncertainty to deal with."

"It was an accident."

"I know. But it doesn't stop *me* from feeling guilty. I can't imagine what he's thinking."

Hayley frowns again before grabbing my phone and tossing it onto my bag. Linking our fingers, she drags me into the living room and directs me to sit on the couch. "I feel guilty too, but we can't let it get to us. And neither can Zane. I'm glad he's been added to your group chat, but even if he wasn't, I know you'll be there for him."

"I'll certainly try. And so will the guys. All in their own ways."

"Are you going to change the group chat name?" Hayley raises her eyebrow with the hint of a smile.

"Nah. Not yet. But Easton adding him to the group was pretty much the same thing. It's Zane's support group now."

"I really hope he's okay." Hayley curls into me, a soft sigh passing through her lips.

"Me too. Just like I hope *you're* okay." I readjust my position so I can wrap an arm around her.

"Me?" She glances up at me. "I was the only one *not* hospitalised."

"I don't mean physically."

"I'm good." She stares at me pointedly. "I promise. And I've got you."

"You do have me. Always."

"Always." She bites back a grin. "That's a big commitment."

"I'm a big commitment kind of guy. None of this half-assed bullshit."

"Then I'd say it's lucky for you that I'm no quitter. You're stuck with me now." She places her hand on my heart and burrows herself into my chest, once again careful of my wound.

"I wouldn't want it any other way."

"Then it's meant to be."

I sigh in contentment, and just when I think we're going to rest here for a while, Hayley shifts out of my hold, positioning herself on her knees beside me, her eyes ablaze with excitement. "So...what should we do now?"

I know that look. Something just came to mind.

"We plan an adventure?" I wager a guess.

"I don't plan." She waves me off. "But I've got an idea."

And just like that, we begin our new life together. I'll follow her anywhere.

Even if I do just sit back and watch her shine.

Epilogue One

REED

SIX MONTHS LATER

I finish a chapter of my latest read and mark the page with a ripped piece of paper, instantly searching for Hayley.

"Hayley Baby, are you done?"

After months of me telling her to make my place her own, she finally started redecorating two weeks ago, the week before the Super Bowl, claiming the timing felt right. refusing to admit she needed something to distract her from the upcoming game.

Just like the doctor said, my recovery was slow, and I wasn't cleared for a full training schedule until a few weeks before the playoffs, making Hayley anxious that I was putting too much pressure on myself.

But she didn't have to worry.

Football may have been my priority for the past fifteen years, but that changed when I met her. I wasn't going to do anything that put me back in the hospital. I knew my body. I'd worked with my doctors and physical therapists. I was ready.

And I fucking killed it in the Super Bowl game.

We won, securing the trophy for a second time and giving Thomas the send-off he deserved while also acknowledging that it was another strange season for the team.

After a few months on life support, we lost Landon to his head injury. And if I'm being honest, it broke me a little. I wanted to hurt him for what he'd done to Hayley, but I never would have wished him dead. Hayley says she's okay about it now, but at the time, it shocked her just as much. And Zane. He went through hell because of it. Not that he'd ever admit that.

When the media caught wind of what happened, and for the months after, Zane went through a lot of public scrutiny, and even Hayley and I copped a bit of flak. *God, look at me talking like Hayley now.* The point is that we were in the headlines. A lot. With not all of it positive.

Despite the fact that it was discovered that Hayley and I weren't the first victims of Landon's stalking, people still voiced their opinions, telling anyone who'd listen that we could have handled it better.

But I truly believe there's nothing more we could have done.

And the knowledge that he'd done this before put my mind a little more at ease. Landon had been stalking another girl during his freshman year of college, but since she never pressed charges, it wasn't on the record. If she had, our lives may have been very different. Even Landon's.

Hayley and I may have recovered, and Zane may be telling us all he's okay, but none of us will ever get over what happened that night.

Though we are moving on.

It's a new year. The season's over. We finally have an amazing general manager with Wes. And Cam admitted to inappropriate behavior after finding out about Landon, taking responsibility for making Hayley uncomfortable. Which we considered the best we were going to get.

With things settling down for both of us, I'm ready to spend some quality time with my girl.

She's just finished filming a challenging support role on a mini-series in LA and is now waiting for the publicity tour for *Reckless Desire*. The timing couldn't be more perfect.

"Hayls?" I call out again before jumping up and going in search of her. She wanted today's redecorating project to be a surprise, but she knows I don't like going too long without seeing her, and it's been hours. She'd better hurry.

"Ready or not, here I come."

I check the kitchen first because redecorating is hungry work, but when I find it empty, I frown. Though it turns out reading is hungry work too because I'm in need of a snack.

"I've bought you some time," I call out. "I'm making a sandwich."

With a chuckle to myself, I've just grabbed the bread when our community gate alarm sounds, alerting me to a visitor, and I remember our builder was coming over today.

I quickly let him in and get back to my food until my phone buzzes with a message.

> HAYLEY: Come find me

> REED: I'm in the kitchen, come find me

I smile, giving her the sass I know she'd give me.

> HAYLEY: My boobs are out

Dammit. I love it when her boobs are out.

> REED: You're always in some form of undress. Give me a better reason

I'm teasing now, but let's face it; it's not going to last long before I rush to find her. I'm obsessed.

> HAYLEY: Two truths and a lie

> REED: Hit me

> HAYLEY: I have a new toy, I'm as naked as the day I was born, and I'm surrounded by water

Fuck. I take off running in case the water part is true. If she's naked in our pool, our builder is about to get a huge shock since he's on his way there.

On top of the redecorating, Hayley suggested we build an extension on the house to enclose part of the pool, making it usable all year round. And I couldn't say no. It made perfect sense. She'll get more use out of it, and when we have kids, it'll protect them from the sun with their pale half-Aussie skin tone. Plus, I do love to fuck her in there, and it will be nice to have a little more privacy.

If circumstances were different, I'd be up for that right now. But they're not.

"Hayley," I call out as I rush out the back door, scanning the water.

"Wrong again." She laughs from behind me, standing at the threshold, buck naked with a bright pink vibrator in her hand. "I knew that would get you here quickly."

The sound of the builder's truck permeates the air and I jog back to Hayley, covering her with my body, pushing her through the door before he comes into sight.

She giggles as she wraps her hands around my neck and jumps up, securing her legs around my waist. "Such a shame you don't like public fornication. I could use a bit of vitamin D."

"You know I love your crazy, Baby. But nobody gets to see this body except me. Your fans may get a lot of you." I push her against a wall and slip my hand between us, cupping her pussy before slowly running a finger through her already wet folds. "But this is mine."

"Forever."

"Damn straight."

Her toy hits me in the back as she laughs and I drop her lightly to her feet, locking her with my questioning gaze.

"Do I not do it for you anymore?" I joke, because we both know that she's more than satisfied in the bedroom.

Hayley throws her head back with a giggle, making her breasts lift to greet me, drawing my attention away from her face.

"Reed?"

"Huh?" I ask, momentarily forgetting we were talking. I will never tire of her goddess-like features.

"I said...you always do it for me, but I have an idea for our next adventure."

I raise an eyebrow and smirk. "Enlighten me." An adventure in the bedroom? I'm up for that.

"How about I show you?"

She spins on her heels and sashays toward our room, walking past the furniture stacked in the hallway.

I notice three new mirrors and my eyes widen. It looks like we're definitely going to have a few new bedroom adventures, and I'm not at all mad about it.

When Hayley reaches the bed, it's my turn to take over. It's what she likes best.

"Get on the bed with your legs spread. You're going to fill me in while I fill you."

She visibly melts as I grin. "Yes, sir." She nods, crawling onto the bed and spinning to face me.

"Before we start?" She scrunches her nose, biting down on the tip of her finger. "How long have we got before your parents get here?"

Goddammit. My parents. I'd forgotten about that.

"Remind me why I wanted them to move to San Francisco?"

"So you could protect them from your brother, and so they'd be around when we decide to raise a family."

"Fuck. Both good answers. But did they have to come today?"

After her life-changing speech, Hayley assumed my parents would actually sit down and talk to my brother, and that he'd miraculously show up at the hospital a changed man.

Bless her heart.

And we thought I was the optimistic one.

In my brother's case, I am convinced that some people never change, or more to the point, some people don't want to. And that is Jace.

But while Jace might still be an asshole, he no longer has the same control over my mom, and that's made all the difference. For everyone involved.

Hayley holds the pink vibrator up in front of me and smoothly raises her perfectly manicured brow. "This beauty isn't on loan, Reed." She waves the vibrator through the air. "We've got plenty of time." She's quick to stifle her grin but it's too late; she's already sassed me. Checking the time, I note we have an hour before my parents arrive, and that's plenty of time. But I don't want to rush it.

"Spread your legs." I remind her of my earlier demand. "I want to fuck that dripping pussy before I take your phenomenal ass. And we've only got fifty-eight minutes."

"Fifty-eight?" Hayley sucks in a breath, her eyes wide with wonder. "That's plenty of time."

"Not with what I have planned. You're not the only one with ideas."

Her lips part but she recovers quickly and smiles. "I knew there was a reason I loved you."

"That and my charm." I laugh before diving on the bed and pulling her into me, crashing my lips to hers.

Epilogue Two

HAYLEY

TWO YEARS LATER

Reed's mom, Molly, fawns over the new piece of jewelry adorning my finger, and I smile with pride. I never would have guessed that when I met the NFL's golden boy almost four years ago that I'd be standing here today, engaged and planning a ridiculously over-the-top wedding.

"He did good," she says with a quiver in her voice. "I'm so happy you're joining the family."

"Hey now," Reed interjects as he walks into the kitchen where his mom and I are baking, something we started doing together to bond. "Hayls has been a part of the family for a long time."

After my grand speech in the hospital room all those years ago, Molly told Reed instantly that he'd made the right decision, but it took some time for her to actually forgive me for shattering her heart when it was already so close to breaking.

And I completely understood her feelings.

My timing could have been better, but I will never regret what I said. It was the push she needed to finally look into therapy, and after a few months, she took the biggest step of her life, distancing herself from Reed's asshole brother.

The subsequent weight that lifted from Reed's shoulders is something I will always cherish.

He's still my golden boy, and he's still the first to take on other people's problems and offer to help. But he's significantly lighter and more open to sharing the load than ever before.

He's even spoken to Bria about it. The two of them will never share a friendship like they once did, but we catch up occasionally. I say "we" because Reed always drags me along, even though I trust him completely.

Reed's mom pouts, brushing him off. "I know that, *Reed*. But I'm excited the two of you are making it official."

"Me too. And I'm excited to go dress shopping. Will you come with me?"

Reed shakes his head violently and raises his hands in the air. "Been there, done that. I'm out."

"I wasn't talking to you, jackass." I grab his hands and pull him into me. "You're not allowed to see the dress until the day."

"Is that so?" He curls his arm around my waist and smirks. "I never took you for one to follow traditions."

"Reedy boy, I'm always going to keep you guessing."

"That you are." He presses a kiss to my head before a sniff silences our teasing, both of us spinning to find Reed's mom in tears.

"Shit, Mom. What happened?"

"You want me to go dress shopping with you?" she asks and a smile tugs at my lips, my heart jolting.

"Of course I do. I'm going to need your help with *everything*. If you want to."

"What about your mom?"

"My mum? My parents are flying over for the wedding, but not before. They said they'd take the opportunity to travel around the US after our nuptials. And yep, that's exactly how she said it. Nuptials." I shake my head but continue. "My dad can only take so much time off work."

Reed frowns but I wave off his concern. For a while I was sad to be missing out on time with my parents, but now I have Reed, and soon, we'll have our own family.

"So what do you say, Mom?" I try really hard to say Mom instead of Mum, and while Reed chuckles when I butcher the simple pronunciation, his mom cries.

"Yes, Hayley. You just made me the happiest mother on earth. I'd love to. I'd bloody love it."

I burst out laughing as Reed's chuckle turns to a groan. "Not you too, Mom?"

"Yes!" I fist pump in happiness. "I'll turn you all into Aussies before I'm through."

"You'll never get Dad." Reed folds his arms over his chest and raises his brows in defiance.

"Oh, yeah?"

"Yep."

Reed's dad chooses that moment to walk past the kitchen and I call out. "Don, what are you making for dinner tonight?" I ask, already knowing the answer.

"I'm cooking a barbie, Hayls. You know that."

"Right. I forgot. Thank you."

He keeps walking and I turn back to Reed, punctuating my words with a satisfied smirk. "You were saying?"

"Motherfuck—"

"Reed!" Molly scolds and I burst out laughing again.

"Sorry, Mom, but this entire family's gone mad."

"Mad for your girl?" I challenge and he finally smiles.

"I guess that's not such a bad thing. She is pretty spectacular." He curls his arm around my shoulder this time and pulls me flush against him, capturing my lips in a kiss.

"And that's my cue to leave," his mom announces from behind us, making me smile against his mouth.

I always wanted a more traditional family, and now that I've got one, I couldn't be happier.

The second the room falls quiet, signaling Molly's departure, Reed breaks the kiss and grabs my face in his hands, his eyes boring into mine. "What do you say we head home right after dinner? It's time for us to celebrate. Alone."

I roll my eyes as his brows bounce in anticipation. "You proposed last week, Reed. We've been celebrating every night. Sometimes more than once."

"Yes, but now we're celebrating that you made my mom cry."

"Reed! What an awful thing to celebrate."

"Not when you know that it's the happiest anyone's ever made her." He smiles while I laugh.

"And you want to celebrate that by fucking like rabbits?"

"What?" His face drops. "Fuck. Not when you put it that way. I've changed my mind. No sex for you."

"We'll see." I waggle my eyebrows just like he did and sashay out of the room, giggling when he groans behind me.

Despite joking about it, my stomach throws our sex plans out the window when I feel nauseous during dinner. Don went out of his way to put on some of my Aussie BBQ favorites, and even the smell made me ill.

Reed flashes me a concerned look as we drive home, but I ignore him until a thought hits me and I freeze. We shouldn't even be able to have sex this weekend. I should have my period. "Stop the car!" I yell, and without looking behind him, Reed slams on his brakes.

"What happened?" he asks, finally checking for other cars before putting his truck into park.

"We need to go back to the twenty-four-hour pharmacy."

"Shit." He cringes in sympathy. "Is it that bad?"

"No. Well, yes. But it's not that."

"Not what?"

I bite my lip before grabbing his hand. "I think we should get a pregnancy test."

Reed's jaw drops.

"Is that a good jaw drop or a bad one?"

Without a response, he throws his truck into drive and U-turns right there in the narrow back street, heading to the closest strip mall. The one he knows will be open. "It's a bloody good jaw drop, Hayls. I'm fucking stoked."

I laugh at his Aussieism, before my hand falls to my stomach, praying I'm right now that I've seen Reed's excitement.

My eyes water as I read the pee-covered stick, the positive markings staring back at me. "Reed?" I glance up as the first tear cascades down his cheek, and the most beautiful smile lights up his face.

"We're having a baby?" he asks, his voice full of wonder.

"We are."

"We're having a baby!" he yells as though announcing it to a room full of people before lifting me into his arms and spinning me around, wincing once he's set me down. "Sorry. I hope I didn't hurt you or the baby."

"I'm fine and I'm sure the baby is too. That's gentle compared to the way you were pounding into—"

"Fuuuck." He runs a hand down his face and I snort.

"This is going to be fun. I can assure you, that didn't harm the baby."

"Are you sure?"

"Yes."

"Good." His relief-filled sigh makes me laugh louder until a panic takes over me.

"God, we have so much to do now. We've got a wedding to plan, and a baby on the way. We'll need to time it right so that I'm not huge for our big day. I don't mind showing, but I don't want to be so uncomfortable I can't enjoy myself. We'll also need to figure out which room works best for a nursery, and oh my God, I can't be pregnant in my next movie. I'm playing—"

"Easy there." Reed grabs my shoulder to still me, his expression warm. "I thought you weren't a planner?"

"I'm not, but this feels like something we should plan for. Right?"

"Wrong."

"Wrong?" My eyes widen in shock.

"Not right now anyway. We'll figure out the wedding and the nursery in time, and as for your next movie...you've had success after success. *Reckless Desire* is still talked about to this day. They'll make it work to keep you. Right now, we need to live in the moment."

He walks out of our en suite and grabs his phone, pressing buttons until "Tennessee Whiskey" by Chris Stapleton comes on over our house speakers.

"Okay... What's that about?"

He drops the phone on the bed and stalks my way, resting his elbow on the door frame as he takes me in, the pregnancy test still in my hand. "I'm living in the moment."

"I don't think now's the time to listen—"

"Dance with me, Hayls."

"What?"

Reed takes the stick from my hand and gently places it on the counter before curling his fingers through mine, walking me through the house, only stopping when we reach the living room.

"So *now* you want to dance?" I ask, faking a pout. "How many times have I asked you?"

Without answering, Reed rolls his eyes and bites back a grin, pulling me into him, securing his free hand on my waist.

"What—"

He spins me around, forcing me to dance while I protest.

"Reed, we need to talk. We—"

"Shh." He presses a finger to my lips, his smiling eyes meeting mine. And I've got to admit, it's infectious.

My heart pounds as I think, but when the next words leave his mouth, I laugh, finally giving in.

"Shut up and dance with me, Hayls," he says, twirling me under his arm. "I love you, and I love our growing baby, but right now, it's time to shut up and dance."

THE END

Thank you for reading Reckless Storm, I hope you enjoyed Reed and Hayley's story.

If you want more from the Storm men, Zane's book - Careless Storm is now available on Amazon. Keep reading for a sneak peek.

Also By Katherine Jay

SAN FRANCISCO END GAME SERIES
Beautiful Storm (Luke and Amelia)

Delicate Storm (Easton and Paige)

Reckless Storm (Reed and Hayley)

Careless Storm (Zane and Blair)

Fierce Storm (Salvatore and Keeley)

HOLIDAY ROMANCE
Mistletoe Mail (Mason and Jenna)

SYMPHONY OF SOUND DUET
The Sound Of Silence (Jesse and Willow)

The Sound Of Forever (Jesse and Willow)

HEARTSTRINGS SERIES
When Nothing Else Matters (Summer and Dylan)

Still Here Without You (Joel and Delilah)

It Had To Be Us (Logan and Dani)

Truly Madly Deeply Mine (Wes and Lucy)

A Sky Full Of Stars (Thomas and Lainey)

Ain't No Sunshine (Nate and Cory) – novella

ALL KATHERINE'S BOOKS ARE AVAILABLE ON AMAZON AND
KINDLE UNLIMITED

CARELESS STORM
SNEAK PEEK

C ade beats me in the sigh department, letting out the mother of all sighs, and I'm about to tell him he's being dramatic when an angel walks into my line of sight. A drunk angel who's using her friend to support her weight. *Shit.*

"I've got to go."

"What? Why?"

"Because I'm out celebrating my win and my teammates are staring at me through the window," I lie. "They're wondering why I'm being such an antisocial asshole."

"I can appreciate that. Can we talk tomorrow?"

My head falls back and I clench my fist before I answer. Why? Why am I letting myself be pulled back into that world? I left for a reason and I should have stayed gone.

"Zane?" he asks, his tone pleading.

"Yep. Sure. Let's talk tomorrow. Bye."

I hang up before he can say anything else and take off across the road, not bothering to look for traffic until some fucker honks at me. "You're fine. You had plenty of room," I yell back, rolling my eyes as I reach the sidewalk, coming face-to-face with Blair.

Actually, face to foot is a better description—her face to my foot—as she vomits all over my shoes.

Jesus. She's blind drunk.

Blair groans without looking and my stomach knots. "Please tell me he's *not* hot," she asks her friend, and as her friend giggles, I allow myself to relax. A little.

"I hate to say it, babe, but he's fucking gorgeous." Her friend eyes me slowly as her grip on Blair loosens and I chuckle softly, securing my hands on Blair's waist, helping her straighten.

"You okay there, B?"

Blair's eyes snap to mine and her face scrunches. "Motherfucker."

"Told you." Her friend laughs, misunderstanding Blair's reaction.

Being the nice guy that I am, I bite back my amusement, hitting her with an innocent smile. "What would it matter if I was hot, B? You have a boyfriend."

"Wait." Her friend's eyes widen as she completely lets go of Blair, forcing me to tighten my hold. "You two know each other?"

I readjust my grip until I have Blair tucked into my side. "We do," I admit, surprised Blair's letting me hold her.

"How?"

Blair groans again and a little of my joy shines through.

"Want me to fill her in? Or..." I trail off, squeezing her waist as she huffs, stepping out of my grasp—or rather stumbling out of my grasp. I move to grab her again, but she waves me off, holding a light pole for support.

"This is Zane. The guy—"

"Noooo." Her friend's eyes flash to Blair before settling back on me. "Are you kidding me with this?" Her lips part, and she shakes her head. "We were just—"

"Leaving," Blair finishes for her. "We were just leaving."

That's not what her friend was about to say, but I let it slide. "Leaving so you could puke?"

"No," Blair denies at the same time her friend says, "Pretty much."

Holding back my amusement, I glance around the busy street and frown. "How are you planning to get home?" Fuck, *home*? The thought of her going back to a place she shares with Nathan makes a shiver run down my spine.

"Don't worry, we don't need your help. You don't have to look so disgusted."

"Disgusted? What—" Oh. *Yep, I'm disgusted, but not for the reason she thinks.* "I'm not *worried*, but I am going to help. Where is home? And speaking of home... Where's your goddamn *boyfriend*?"

Careless Storm is available on Amazon and Kindle Unlimited.

CARELESS STORM
A right person / wrong time sports romance

Blair Stevens' thought she had it all — until one devastating moment shattered her world.

Seven years ago, Blair shared a secret love and a future with her brother's best friend, Zane Fitzpatrick. But fate sent them spiraling in opposite directions.

Now she's drifting through life, dating Zane's biggest rival, while he's the NFL's infamous bad boy, making headlines for all the wrong reasons.

Just when she begins questioning everything, Zane reappears, looking at her like no time has passed. And despite her efforts to keep her distance, Zane's unwavering support begins to reignite the strength she thought she'd lost forever.

As the undeniable pull brings them closer together, they're forced to face something bigger.

Because it turns out, Blair's not the only one who's broken. And the only way forward is to face the past... together.

FIERCE STORM
A forbidden, age gap sports romance

He's her boss, her brother's future father-in-law and her best friends dad. She's twenty years younger than him and the one woman he can't get out of his head.

What happens when they give in to temptation?

Find out when the final Storm book releases in June 2026

AVAILABLE NOW ON AMAZON, KINDLE UNLIMITED AND AUDIBLE

ABOUT THE AUTHOR

Katherine writes angsty and emotional, character-driven romance full of banter, steam and the kind of love that's always worth fighting for.
When she's not lost in a fictional world (writing or reading), she's travelling, falling down a binge-worthy television rabbit hole, or letting the perfect song absolutely wreck her.
Katherine lives in Australia with her husband and two boys, which means she's constantly outnumbered, but wouldn't have it any other way.

For more information, visit
https://www.katherinejayauthor.com

If you want to stay up to date with all things Katherine Jay, come and join her Facebook Reader Group – The Angsty Lovers Playlist — for fun, exclusive content and sneak peeks. Or sign up to her newsletter via her website.

Are you following Katherine on social media? If not, you can find her on Instagram, Facebook and TikTok.